LIFE SENTENCES

LIFE SENTENCES

Laura Lippman

WINDSOR
PARAGON

First published 2009
by Avon
This Large Print edition published 2009
by BBC Audiobooks Ltd
by arrangement with
HarperCollinsPublishers Ltd

Hardcover ISBN: 978 1 408 43113 9
Softcover   ISBN: 978 1 408 43114 6

British Library Cataloguing in Publication Data available

Printed and bound in Great Britain by
CPI Antony Rowe, Chippenham and Eastbourne

In loving memory of James Crumley, 1939–2008.
Take my word. It was fun.

I detest the man who hides one thing in the depths of his heart, and speaks for another.

—THE ILIAD

Chapter One

'Well,' the bookstore manager said, 'it is Valentine's Day.'

It's not that bad, Cassandra wanted to say in her own defense. But she never wanted to sound peevish or disappointed. She must smile, be gracious and self-deprecating. She would emphasize how wonderfully intimate the audience was, providing her with an opportunity to talk, have a real exchange, not merely prate about herself. Besides, it wasn't *tragic,* drawing thirty people on a February night in the suburbs of San Francisco. On Valentine's Day. Most of the writers she knew would kill for thirty people under these circumstances, under any circumstances.

And there was no gain in reminding the bookseller—Beth, Betsy, Bitsy, oh dear, the name had vanished, her memory was increasingly buggy—that Cassandra had drawn almost two hundred people to this same store on this precise date four years earlier. Because that might imply she thought someone was to blame for tonight's turnout, and Cassandra Fallows didn't believe in blame. She was famous for it. Or had been.

She also was famous for rallying, and she did just that as she took five minutes to freshen up in the manager's office, brushing her hair and reapplying lipstick. Her hair, her worst feature as a child, was now her best, sleek and silver, but her lips seemed thinner. She adjusted her earrings, smoothed her skirt, reminding herself of her general good fortune. She had a job she loved; she was healthy.

1

Lucky, I am lucky. She could quit now, never write a word again, and live quite comfortably. Her first two books were annuities, more reliable than any investment.

Her third book—ah, well, that was the unloved, misshapen child she was here to exalt.

At the lectern, she launched into a talk that was already honed and automatic ten days into the tour. *There was a pediatric hospital across the road from where I grew up.* The audience was mostly female, over forty. She used to get more men, but then her memoirs, especially the second one, had included unsparing detail about her promiscuity, a healthy appetite that had briefly gotten out of control in her early forties. *It was a long-term-care facility, where children with extremely challenging diagnoses were treated for months, for years in some cases.* Was that true? She hadn't done that much research about Kernan. The hospital had been skittish, dubious that a writer known for memoir was capable of creating fiction. Cassandra had decided to go whole hog, abandon herself to the libertine ways of a novelist. Forgo the fact-checking, the weeks in libraries, the conversations with family and friends, trying to make her memories gibe with hard, cold certainty. For the first time in her life—despite what her second husband had claimed—she made stuff up out of whole cloth. *The book is an homage to* The Secret Garden—*in case the title doesn't make that clear enough—and it's set in the 1980s because that was a time when finding biological parents was still formidably difficult, almost taboo, a notion that began to lose favor in the 1990s and is increasingly out of fashion as biological parents gain more rights.*

It had never occurred to Cassandra that the world at large, much like the hospital, would be reluctant to accept her in this new role. *The story is wholly fictional, although it's set in a real place.*

She read her favorite passage. People laughed in some odd spots.

Question time. Cassandra never minded the predictability of the Q-and-A sessions, never resented being asked the same thing over and over. It didn't even bother her when people spoke of her father and mother and stepmother and ex-husbands as if they were characters in a novel, fictional constructs they were free to judge and psychoanalyze. But it disturbed her now when audience members wanted to pin down the 'real' people in her third book. Was she Hannah, the watchful child who unwittingly sets a tragedy in motion? Or was she the boy in the body cast, Woodrow? Were the parents modeled on her own? They seemed so different, based on the historical record she had created. Was there a fire? An accident in the abandoned swimming pool that the family could never afford to repair?

'Did your father really drive a retired Marathon cab, painted purple?' asked one of the few men in the audience, who looked to be at least sixty. Retired, killing time at his wife's side. 'I ask only because my father had an old DeSoto and . . .'

Of course, she thought, even as she smiled and nodded. *You care about the details that you can relate back to yourself. I've told my story, committed over a quarter of a million words to paper so far. It's your turn.* Again, she was not irked. Her audience's need to share was to be expected. If a writer was fortunate enough to excite people's

3

imaginations, this was part of the bargain, especially for the memoir writer she had been and apparently would continue to be in the public's mind, at least for now. She had told her story, and that was the cue for them to tell theirs. Given what confession had done for her soul, how could she deny it to anyone else?

'Time for one last question,' the store manager said, and pointed to a woman in the back. She wore a red raincoat, shiny with moisture, and a shapeless khaki hat that tied under her chin with a leather cord.

'Why do you get to write the story?'

Cassandra was at a loss for words.

'I'm not sure I understand,' she began. 'You mean, how do I write a novel about people who aren't me? Or are you asking how one gets published?'

'No, with the other books. Did you get permission to write them?'

'Permission to write about my own life?'

'But it's not just your life. It's your parents, your stepmother, friends. Did you let them read it first?'

'No. They knew what I was doing, though. And I fact-checked as much as I could, admitted the fallibility of my memory throughout. In fact that's a recurring theme in my work.'

The woman was clearly unsatisfied with the answer. As others lined up to have their books signed, she stalked to the cash registers at the front of the store. Cassandra would have loved to dismiss her as a philistine, a troublemaker irritable because she had nothing better to do on Valentine's Day. But she carried an armful of

4

impressive-looking books, although Cassandra didn't see her own spine among them. The woman was like the bad fairy at a christening. *Why do I get to write the story? Because I'm a writer.*

Toward the end of the line—really, thirty people on a wet, windy Valentine's Day was downright impressive—a woman produced a battered paperback copy of Cassandra's first book.

'In-store purchases only,' the manager said, and Cassandra couldn't blame her. It was hard enough to be a bookseller these days without people bringing in their secondhand books to be signed.

'Just one can't hurt,' said Cassandra, forever a child of divorce, instinctively the peacemaker.

'I can't afford many hardcovers,' the woman apologized. She was one of the few young ones in the crowd and pretty, although she dressed and stood in a way that suggested she was not yet in possession of that information. Cassandra knew the type. Cassandra had been the type. *Do you sleep with a lot of men?* she wanted to ask her. *Overeat? Drink, take drugs? Daddy issues?*

'To . . . ?' Fountain pen poised over the title page. God, how had this ill-designed book found so many readers? It had been a relief when the publisher repackaged it, with the now de rigueur book club questions in the back and a new essay on how she had come to write the book at all, along with updated information on the principals. It had been surprisingly painful, recounting Annie's death in that revised epilogue. She was caught off guard by how much she missed her stepmother.

'Oh, you don't have to write anything special.'

'I want to write whatever you want me to write.'

The young woman seemed overwhelmed by this

5

generosity. Her eyes misted and she began to stammer: 'Oh—no—well, Cathleen. With a *C.* I— this book meant so much to me. It was as if it was my story.'

This was always hard to hear, even though Cassandra understood the sentiment was a compliment, the very secret of her success. She could argue, insist on the individuality of her autobiography, deny the universality that had made it appealing to so many—or she could cash the checks and tell herself with a blithe shrug, 'Fuck you, Tolstoy. Apparently, even the unhappy families are all alike.'

To Cathleen, she wrote in the space between the title, *My Father's Daughter,* and her own name. *Find your story and tell it.*

'Your signature is so pretty,' Cathleen said. 'Like you. You're actually very pretty in person.'

The girl blushed, realizing what she had implied. Yet she was far from the first person to say this. Cassandra's author photo was severe, a little cold. Men often complained about it.

'You're pretty in person, too,' she told the girl, saving her with her own words. 'And I wouldn't be surprised if you found there was a book in your story. You should consider telling it.'

'Well, I'm trying,' Cathleen admitted.

Of course you are. 'Good luck.'

When the line dispersed, Cassandra asked the bookstore manager, 'Do you want me to sign stock?'

'Oh,' the manager said with great surprise, as if no one had ever sought to do this before, as if it were an innovation that Cassandra had just introduced to bookselling. 'Sure. Although I wouldn't expect you to do all of them. That would be too much to ask. Perhaps that stack?'

Betsy/Beth/Bitsy knew and Cassandra knew that even that stack, perhaps a fifth of the store's order, could be returned once signed. *So many things unspoken, so many unpleasant truths to be tiptoed around. Just like my childhood all over again.* The book was number 23 on the *Times*'s extended list and it was gaining some momentum over the course of the tour. *The Painted Garden* was, by almost any standard, a successful literary novel. Except by the standard of the reviews, which had been uniformly sorrowful, as if a team of surgeons had gathered at Cassandra's bedside to deliver a terminal verdict: *Writing two celebrated memoirs does not mean you can write a good novel.* Gleefully cruel or hostile reviews would have been easier to bear.

Still, *The Painted Garden* was selling, although not with the velocity expected by her new publisher, which had paid Cassandra a shocking amount of money to lure her away from the old one. Her editor was already hinting that—much as they loved, loved, loved her novel—it would be, well, *fun* if she wanted to return to nonfiction. Wouldn't that be *FUN*? Surely, approaching fifty— *not that you look your age!*—she had another decade or so of life to exploit, another vital passage? She had written about being someone's daughter and then about being someone's wife. Two someones, in fact. Wasn't there a book in being her?

Not that she could see. This novel had been cobbled together with a few leftovers from her life, the unused scraps, then padded by her

7

imagination, not to mention her affectionate memories of *The Secret Garden.* (A girl exploring a forbidden space, a boy in a bed—why did she have to explain these allusions over and over?) On some level, she was flattered that readers wanted her, not her ideas. The problem was, she had run out of life.

*   *   *

Back in her hotel room, she over-ordered from room service, incapable of deciding what she wanted. The restaurant in the hotel was quite good, but she was keen to avoid it on this night set aside for lovers. Even under optimal circumstances, she had never cared for the holiday. It had defeated every man she had known, beginning with her father. When she was a little girl, she would have given anything to get a box of chocolates, even the four-candy Whitman's Sampler, or a single rose. Instead, she could count on a generic card from the Windsor Hills Pharmacy, while her mother usually received one of those perfume-and-bath-oil sets, a dusty Christmas markdown. Her father's excuse was that her mother's birthday, which fell on Washington's, came so hard on the heels of Valentine's Day that he couldn't possibly do both. But he executed the birthday just as poorly. Her mother's birthday cakes, more often than not, were store-bought affairs with cherries and hatchets picked up on her father's way home from campus. It was hard to believe, as her mother insisted, that this was a man who had wooed her with sonnets and moonlight drives through his hometown of DC, showing her monuments and relics unknown to most. Who recited Poe's 'Lenore'—*And, Guy de Vere, hast thou no tear?*—in honor of her name.

One year, though, the year Cassandra turned ten, her father had made a big show of Valentine's Day, buying mother and daughter department store cologne, Chanel No. 5 and lily of the valley, respectively, and taking them to Tio Pepe's for dinner, where he allowed Cassandra a sip of sangria, her first taste of alcohol. Not even five months later, as millions of readers now knew, he left his wife. Left *them,* although, in the time-honored tradition of all decamping parents, he always denied abandoning Cassandra.

Give her father this: He had been an awfully good sport about the first book. He had read it in galleys and requested only one small change—and that was to safeguard her mother's feelings. (He had claimed once, in a moment of self-justification, that he had *never* loved her mother, that he had married because he felt that a scholar, such as he aspired to be, couldn't afford to dissipate his energies. Cassandra agreed to delete this, although she suspected it to be truer than most things her father said.) He had praised the book when it was a modest critical success, then hung on for the ride when it became a runaway bestseller in paperback. He had been enthusiastic about the forever-stalled movie version: Whenever another middle-aged actor got into trouble with the law, he would send along the mug shot as an e-mail attachment, noting cheerfully, 'Almost desiccated enough to play me.' He had consented to interviews when she was profiled, yet never pulled focus, never sought to impress upon anyone that he was someone more than Cassandra Fallows's father.

Lenore, by contrast, was often thin lipped with unexpressed disapproval, no matter how many times Cassandra tried to remind people of her mother's good qualities. Everyone loves the bad boy. Come April, her father would be center stage again, and there was nothing Cassandra could do about that.

She sighed, thinking about the unavoidable trip back to Baltimore once her tour was over, the complications of dividing her time between two households, the special care and attention her mother would need to make up for her father being lionized. Did she dare stay in a hotel? No, she would have to return to the house on Hillhouse Road. Perhaps she could finally persuade her mother to put it up for sale. Physically, her mother was still more than capable of caring for the house, but that could change quickly. Cassandra had watched other friends dealing with parents in their seventies and eighties, and the declines were at once gradual and abrupt. She shouldn't have moved away. But if she hadn't left, she never would have started writing. The past had been on top of her in Baltimore, suffocating and omnipresent. She had needed distance, literal distance, to begin to see her life clearly enough to write about it.

She turned on the television, settling on CNN. As was her habit on the road, she would leave the television on all night, although it disrupted her sleep. But she required the noise when she traveled, like a puppy who needs an alarm clock to be reminded of its mother's beating heart. Strange, because her town house back in Brooklyn was a quiet, hushed place and the noises one could hear—footsteps, running water—were no different from hotel sounds. But hotels scared her, perhaps for no reason greater than that she'd seen the movie *Psycho* in second grade. (More great parenting from Cedric Fallows: exposure to *Psycho* at age seven, *Bonnie and Clyde* when she was nine, *The Godfather* at age fourteen.) If the television was on, perhaps it would be presumed she was awake and therefore not the best choice for an attack.

Her room service tray banished to the hall, she slid into bed, drifting in and out of sleep against the background buzz of the headlines. She dreamed of her hometown, of the quirky house on the hill, but it was 4 A.M. before she realized that it was the news anchor who kept intoning *Baltimore* every twenty minutes or so, as the same set of stories spun around and around.

'. . . The New Orleans case is reminiscent of one in Baltimore, more than twenty years ago, when a woman named Calliope Jenkins repeatedly took the Fifth, refusing to tell prosecutors and police the whereabouts of her missing son. She remained in jail seven years but never wavered in her statements, a very unique legal strategy now being used again. . . .'

Unique *doesn't take a modifier,* Cassandra thought, drifting away again. *And if something is being used again, it's clearly not unique.* Then, almost as an afterthought, *Besides, it's not Kuh-lie-o-pee, like the instrument or the Muse—it's Callie-ope, almost like* Alley Oop, *which is why Tisha shortened her name to Callie.*

11

A second later, her eyes were wide open, but the story had already flashed by, along with whatever images had been provided. She had to wait through another cycle and even then, the twenty-year-old photograph—a grim-faced woman being escorted by two bailiffs—was too fleeting for Cassandra to be sure. Still, how many Baltimore women could there be with that name, about that age? *Could it—was she—it must be.* She knew this woman. Well, had known the girl who became this woman. A woman who clearly had done something unspeakable. Literally, to take another word that news anchors loved but seldom used correctly. To hold one's tongue for seven years, to offer no explanation, not even the courtesy of a lie—what an unfathomable act. Yet one in character for the silent girl Cassandra had known, a girl who was desperate to deflect all attention.

'This is Calliope Jenkins, a midyear transfer,' the teacher had told her fourth-graders.

'Callie-ope.' The girl had corrected her in a soft, hesitant voice, as if she didn't have the right to have her name pronounced correctly. Tall and rawboned, she had a pretty face, but the boys were too young to notice, and the girls were not impressed. She would have to be tested, auditioned, fitted for her role within Mrs Bryson's class, where the prime parts—best dressed; best dancer; best personality; best student, which happened to be Cassandra—had been filled back in third grade, when the school had opened. These were not cruel girls. But if Calliope came on too fast or tried to seize a role that they did not feel she deserved, there would be trouble. She was the new girl and the girls would decide her fate. The

12

boys would attempt to brand her, assign a nickname—Alley Oop would be tried, in fact, but the comic strip was too old even then to have resonance. Cassandra would explain to Calliope that she was named for a Muse, as Cassandra herself had almost been, that her name was really quite elegant. But it was Tisha who essentially saved Calliope's young life by dubbing her Callie.

That was where Cassandra's memories of Callie started—and stopped. How could that be? For the first time, Cassandra had some empathy for the neighbors of serial killers, the people who provided the banalities about quiet men who kept to themselves. Someone she knew, someone who had probably come to her birthday parties, had grown up to commit a horrible crime, and all Cassandra could remember was that . . . she was a quiet girl. Who kept to herself.

Fatima had known her well, though, because she had once lived in the same neighborhood. And Cassandra remembered a photograph from the last-day-of-school picnic in fourth grade, the girls lined up with arms slung around one another's necks, Callie at the edge. That photo had appeared, in fact, along with several others on the frontispiece of her first book, but only as testimony to the obliviousness of youth, Cassandra's untroubled, happy face captured mere weeks before her father tore their family apart. Had she even mentioned Calliope in passing? Doubtful. Callie simply didn't matter enough; she was neither goat nor golden girl. Tisha, Fatima, Donna—they had been integral to Cassandra's first book. Quiet Callie hadn't rated.

Yet she was the one who grew up to have the

most dramatic story. A dead child. Seven years in jail, refusing to speak. Who was that person? How did you go from being Quiet Callie to a modern-day Medea?

Cassandra glanced at the clock. Almost five here, not yet eight in New York, too early to call her agent, much less her editor. She pulled on the hotel robe and went over to the desk, where her computer waited in sleep mode. She started an e-mail. The next book would be true, about her, but about something larger. It would include her trademark memories but also a new story, a counterpoint to the past. She wouldn't track down just Callie but everyone she could remember from that era—Tisha, Donna, Fatima.

Cassandra was struck, typing, by how relatively normal their names had been, or at least uniform in spelling. Only Tisha's name stuck out and it was short for Leticia, which might explain why she had been so quick to save Calliope with a nickname. Names today were demographic signifiers and one could infer much from them—age, class, race. Back then, names hadn't revealed as much. Cassandra threw that idea in there, too, her fingers racing toward the future and the book she would create, even as her mind retreated, hopscotching through the past, to fourth grade, then ninth grade, back to sixth grade—her breath caught at a memory she had banished years ago, one described in the first book. What had Tisha thought about *that*? Had she even read *My Father's Daughter*?

Yet Callie would be the central figure of this next book. She must have done what she was accused of doing. Had it been a crime of impulse? An

14

accident? How had she hidden the body, then managed not to incriminate herself, sitting all those years in jail? Was there even a plausible alternative in which Callie's son was *not* dead? Was she protecting someone?

Cassandra glanced back at the television screen, watched Callie come around again. Cassandra understood the media cycle well enough to know that Callie would disappear within a day or two, that she was a place-marker in the current story, the kind of footnote dredged up in the absence of new developments. Callie had been forgotten and would be forgotten again. Her *child* had been forgotten, left in this permanent limbo—not officially dead, not even officially missing, just unaccounted for, like an item on a manifest. A baby, an African-American boy, had vanished, with no explanation and yet no real urgency. His mother, almost certainly the person responsible, had defeated the authorities with silence.

That's good, Cassandra told herself. She put that in the memo, too.

First Words

I didn't speak until I was almost three years old. And then it was only because my mother almost killed me. Almost killed both of us, but she had the luxury of making the decision. I was literally just along for the ride.

My mother didn't worry about my silence, however. It was my father, a classics professor at Johns Hopkins University, who brooded

15

constantly. The possibility of a nonverbal child—and all the other intellectual limitations that this circumstance implied—terrified my father so much that he would not allow my mother to consult specialists. He knew himself well enough to understand that a diagnosis could change his love for me. My father believed in unconditional love, but only under certain conditions.

Besides, he was not irrational to hope that I might be keeping my own counsel for as yet undisclosed reasons. I had walked early and hit the other developmental milestones more or less on time. And I wasn't mute. I had a three-word vocabulary: *yes, no,* and *Ric,* which is how my father, Cedric, was known. I'm not sure why I had no term for my mother. Perhaps 'Lenore' was too subtle for my baby mouth. More likely, I didn't recognize that my mother was a separate entity but saw her as my larger self, capable of detaching from my side in order to meet my needs. With her, I didn't even use my three paltry words, instead pointing and grunting to indicate my desires. 'We should have named her Caliban instead of Cassandra,' my father said.

My refusal to speak continued until almost a month before my third birthday. It had snowed, an early-spring snowstorm that was uncommonly common in Baltimore. On this particular day—a Thursday, not that my three-year-old mind could distinguish days, but I have checked the family story against newspapers from that week—my mother set out to do the marketing, as she called it then, at the old Eddie's supermarket on Roland Avenue.

The snow had started before she set out, but the

radio forecaster was insisting it would not amount to much. In the brief half hour she shopped, the snow switched to rain, then changed over to sleet, and she came out to a truly treacherous world, with cars spinning out of control up and down Roland Avenue. She decided that the main roads would be safer and calculated a roundabout route back to our apartment. But she had forgotten that Northern Parkway, while wide and accommodating, was roller-coaster steep. The car slithered into its left turn onto the parkway, announcing how dangerous her choice was, but it was too late to turn back. The unsanded road lay before her, shining with ice, a traffic light at its foot. A traffic light at which she would never be able to stop. What to do?

My pragmatic, cautious mother killed the engine, took her foot off the brake and coasted down, turning our car, a turquoise-and-brown station wagon, into a toboggan. I bobbled among the sacks of groceries, unmoored and unperturbed. The car picked up speed, more speed than my mother ever anticipated, yet not enough to get her through the intersection before the light changed to red. She closed her eyes, locked her elbows, and prayed.

When she opened her eyes, we had come to rest in the tiny front yards of the houses that lined Northern Parkway, shearing off a hydrant, which sent a plume of water into the air, the droplets freezing as they came back to earth, hitting our car like so many pebbles. But the last might be a detail that my father added, as he was the one who told this story over and over. Careful Lenore, rigid Lenore, skating down a hill with her only child in the back of the car. My mother could barely stand

17

telling it even once.

That night, at dinner, decades later as far as my mother was concerned—after the police came, after the car was towed, after we were taken to our apartment in a fire truck, along with the groceries, not so much as an egg cracked—my father finished his characteristically long discourse on his day in the groves of academe, which my father inevitably called the groves of academe. Who had said what to whom, his warlike thrusts, as he called his responses, an allusion to Maryland's state song. His day finally dispatched, he asked, as he always did, 'Anything to report from the home front?'

To which, I am told, I answered, although not in a recognizable language. I babbled; I circled my pudgy baby arms wildly, trying to simulate the motion of the car. I patted my head, attempting to describe the headwear of the various blue-and-yellow-suited men who had come to our rescue. I even did a credible imitation of a siren. Within twenty-four hours, my words came in, like a full set of teeth.

'And from that day forward,' my father always says at the end—'From that day forward'—he is a great one for repeating phrases, for emphasis—'from that day forward, no one could ever shut you up.'

From *My Father's Daughter* by Cassandra Fallows, published in 1998 and now in its nineteenth printing.

BRIDGEVILLE

February 20–23

Chapter Two

'Cassandra Fallows? Who's she with?'

Gloria Bustamante peered at the old-fashioned pink phone memo the temp held out with a quavering hand. The girl had already been dressed down three times today and was now so jangly with nerves that she was caroming off doors and desks, dropping everything she touched, and squeaking reflexively when the phone rang. She wouldn't last the week, an unusually hectic one to be sure, given all the calls about the Harrington case. Too bad, because she was highly decorative, a type that Gloria favored, although not for the reasons suspected by most.

The girl examined her own handwriting. 'She's a writer?'

'Don't let your voice scale up at the end of a declarative sentence, dear,' Gloria said. 'No one will ever take you seriously. And I assume she's a writer—or a reporter—if she's calling about Buddy Harrington. I need to know which newspaper or television program she reps.'

Gloria's tone was utterly neutral to her ears, but the girl cowered as if she had been threatened. Ah, she had probably hoped for something far more genteel when she signed up at the agency, an assignment at one of those gleaming start-ups along the water. Arriving at Gloria's building, an old nineteenth-century town house, she would have adjusted her expectations to something old-fashioned but still grand, based on the gleaming front door and restored exterior, the leaded glass and vintage lighting on the first two floors.

Those lower floors, however, were rented to a more fastidious law firm. Gloria's own office was on the third story, up a sad little carpeted staircase where dust rose with every step and the door gave way to a warren of rooms so filled with boxes that visitors had to take it on faith that there was furniture beneath them. 'I want prospective clients to know that every one of the not insignificant pennies I charge goes to their defense, not my décor,' Gloria told the few friends she had in Baltimore's legal community. She knew that even those friends, such as they were, amended in their heads, *It's not going to your wardrobe or your upkeep, either.* For Gloria Bustamante was famously, riotously, deliberately seedy, although not as cheap with herself as she was with her office. The run-down heels she wore were Prada, her stained knit suits came from Saks Jandel in DC, her dirty rings and necklaces had been purchased on lavish trips abroad. Gloria wanted people to know that she had money, that she could afford the very best—and could afford to take crappy care of the very best.

The girl stammered, 'N-no, she's not a journalist. She wrote that book, the one about her, um, father? *Father.* I read it for book club? I mean, I did, I read it for book club.'

'Pretty young girls go to book clubs? I thought those were for ugly old broads such as me. Not that you'll catch me in a room full of women, drinking wine and talking about a *book*. Drinking, maybe.'

The girl's eyes skittered around the room, trying to find a safe place to land. Clearly, she was unsure if she was obliged to contradict the inescapable truth of Gloria's appearance or if she should pretend that she hadn't yet noticed that Gloria was old and ugly.

'It was a mother-daughter book club,' she said at last. 'I went with my mom.'

'Thanks for the clarification, dearie. Otherwise, I might think you went with your prepubescent daughter, conceived, in the great local tradition, when you were a mere middle schooler.'

The girl took a few steps backward. She had that breathtaking freshness seen only in girls under twenty-five when everything—hair, eyes, lips, even fingernails—gleamed without benefit of cosmetics. The whites of this girl's eyes were more startling to Gloria than the light-blue irises, the shell-pink ears as notable as the round, peachy cheeks. And she had the kind of boyish figure that was increasingly rare in this era of casual plastic surgery, when even the thinnest girls seemed to sprout ridiculously large breasts. Gloria remembered the tricks of her youth, not that she had ever bothered with them, the padded bras, the wads of Kleenex. They had been far more credible in their way than all these perky cantaloupes, which looked, in fact, as if they had been molded with very large melon ballers. Real breasts weren't so *round*. She hoped this girl wouldn't tamper with what nature had allotted her.

'I grew up in Ruxton?' the girl said, and it was clear that she intended the well-to-do suburb to establish that she was not the kind of girl who had a baby at age twelve. *Oh, you'd be surprised, dearie,* Gloria wanted to say. *You'd be shocked at the wealthy families who have sat in my office, trying to decide what to do when one of Daddy's friends—or*

23

Daddy himself—has helped himself to an underage daughter. It happens. Even in Ruxton. After all, Buddy Harrington happened in a suburb not that far from Ruxton.

'I'm sure you did,' Gloria said. 'So Cassandra Fallows wants to write a book about Buddy Harrington? She must be one of those true-crime types who specialize in whipping books out in four to six weeks. We'll give her a wide berth.'

Buddy Harrington was, as of this third full week in February, being held responsible for 80 percent of the murders in Baltimore County this year. Granted, the county had only five homicides so far, as compared to the city's thirty or so. Still, Harrington was charged with four of them—his mother, father, and twin sisters, all shot as they slept. The sixteen-year-old had called the police on a Thursday evening two weeks ago, claiming to have discovered the bodies after returning home from a chorale competition in Ocean City. He had been charged before the day was out, although he had yet to confess and was pressing Gloria to let him tell his story far and wide. She was holding him back precisely because of that eagerness, his keenness to perform. For Buddy Harrington was not the kind of boy who inspired the usual descriptions of those who snap—quiet, introverted. He was an outstanding student, a star athlete, and a gifted singer, well liked by classmates, admired by teachers. The community was stunned.

Gloria, who had spent several hours with Buddy since his arrest, was not. She also knew that all the things that Buddy considered his assets—his good looks, his normalcy—would undercut him. Nothing

24

terrified people more than an all-American sociopath. And until—unless—she got Buddy into the juvenile system, she had to keep him from tainting his future jury. Which would not, of course, be a jury of his peers, but a dozen middle-class mothers and fathers who would be undone by his poise, his composure. Especially—shades of O.J.!—if he stuck to this help-me-find-the-real-killer scenario.

'No, it's not about Buddy. She wants to ask you about an old case?' The girl squinted at her own handwriting. 'Something about a calley-ope?'

'A calley—do you mean Calliope?' Gloria could afford to keep her office in disarray and limit her exposure to computers because the entire history of her practice was always available to her. She had a prodigious memory. On those rare occasions when someone felt intimate enough to challenge her on her drinking, she maintained that it was the only way to level the playing field.

Not that she was likely to forget Callie Jenkins under any circumstances. She had tried.

'Yes, that's it. Calliope. Calliope Jenks.'

'Jenkins.'

'Right.'

'What, specifically, does she want to know?'

'She wouldn't say?'

'Did you ask?'

The girl's downward gaze answered the question more emphatically than any statement-question she might have offered in return. Gloria leaned across the desk and tried to take the paper, but the girl was out of reach. She moved forward tentatively, as if Gloria might bite her, jumping back as soon as Gloria had the phone memo in her

25

hand.

'It's an out-of-state number,' Gloria said. 'New York, I think, but not the city proper. Long Island, maybe Brooklyn. I can't keep all the new ones straight.' She had, in fact, once been able to recognize every area code at a glance. She knew state capitals, too, and was always the one person at a party who could complete any set of names— the seven dwarves, the nine Supreme Court justices, the thirteen original colonies.

'But she's in town,' the girl said, thrilled that she had gleaned an actual fact. 'For a while, she said. That's her cell. She said she plans to be in town for a while.'

Gloria crumpled the pink sheet and tossed it in the overflowing trash can by the desk, where it bounced out.

'But she's famous!' the girl said. 'I mean, for a writer. She's been on *Oprah.*'

'I don't talk to people unless they can help me. That case ended a long time ago, and it's better forgotten. Callie's a private citizen now, living her life. It's the least she deserves.'

Was it? Gloria wondered after dismissing the girl. Did Calliope have the least she deserved or far more? What about Gloria? Had she gotten more than she deserved, less, or exactly her due? Had Gloria done the best she could for Callie, given the circumstances, or let her down?

But Gloria didn't like the concept of guilt any more than she liked the word *guilty* coming from a jury foreman, not that she had a lot of experience hearing the latter. Guilt was a waste, misplaced energy. Guilt was a legal finding, a determination made by others. Gloria didn't have time for guilt,

26

and she was almost certain she didn't deserve to feel it, not in the case of Callie Jenkins. Almost.

She called the temp agency and told them she wouldn't be able to use the new girl past this week. 'Send me someone new. More capable, but equally pretty.'

'You're not allowed to say that,' the agency rep objected.

'Sue me,' Gloria said.

Chapter Three

'Why aren't you staying with me?' her mother asked, and not for the first time. 'That was the original plan.'

'Yes, when I was going to be in Baltimore a week. But for ten, twelve weeks? I would drive you crazy.' *And you me.*

'But a hotel room, for all that time—you won't be able to cook for yourself—'

'It's an apartment, the kind set up for short-term corporate renters.' Cassandra anticipated her mother's next protest: 'It's not that expensive.'

'Did you sublet your place back in New York?'

'No.'

'So you're carrying two rents for three months. And you'll need a car here.'

'Mom, I have my own car. I drove down. I drove here, it's parked in your driveway.'

'I don't know what the point is of having a car if you live in New York.'

'I like to be able to get away—visit friends upstate or at the . . . beach.' She used the generic,

27

beach, instead of the specific, *Hamptons,* out of fear that the latter would provoke another spasm of worry.

The reviews of the last book had been hard on her mother. Her mother's e-mails had been hard on Cassandra. Until this winter, she hadn't even known that her mother could initiate e-mail. She seemed to use the laptop that Cassandra had given her for nothing more than playing hearts and solitaire while depending on the reply-to function to answer Cassandra's sporadic notes. Even then, she was extremely terse. 'Thank you.' Or 'That's nice, dear.' Lennie Fallows seemed to think e-mail was the equivalent of a telegram or a long-distance call back in the seventies. It was a mode of communication to be limited to dire emergencies or special occasions, and even then brevity was required.

Then, back in January, the e-mails had started, with no 'RE:' in the subject headers, with no subject headers at all, which made them all the more terrifying, as Cassandra had no idea what conversation her mother was about to start.

'I wouldn't worry about the Kirkus.' 'The PW is good, if you omit the dependent clause.' 'Sorry about the New York Times.'

Except she hadn't written 'the *New York Times*' or even 'NYT', come to think of it, but the critic's surname, as if the woman were a neighbor, an intimate. This detail saddened Cassandra most of all. All she had ever wanted was to give her mother a sense of ownership in Cassandra's success. She had felt that way even as a teenager, back when Lennie was, in fact, a profound embarrassment, running around town in—oh, God, the memory

28

still grated—painter's pants or overalls, that horrible cap on her head, tools sticking out of her pockets. Yet Lennie insisted on crediting Cassandra's achievements to her ex-husband's side of the DNA ledger. Even the book that had forged Cassandra's reputation had been problematic for her mother, arriving with that title that slanted everything toward *him.*

But the life that book brought Cassandra—ah, that her mother had loved and gloried in, and not because of the small material benefits that came her way. She adored turning on the radio and hearing Cassandra's voice, basked in being in a store and having a neighbor comment on one of Cassandra's television appearances. Once, in the Giant, Cassandra had seen how it worked: Her mother furrowed her brow at the mention of Cassandra's most recent interview, as if it were impossible to keep track of her daughter's media profile. Was it *Today*? *Charlie Rose*? That weird show on cable where everyone shouted?

You must be very proud of her, the neighbor persisted.

And Lennie Fallows—it had never occurred to her to drop the surname of the man she detested—said with steely joy, 'I was *always* proud of her.' In her mother's coded lexicon, this was the rough equivalent of *Go fuck yourself.*

Cassandra opened the refrigerator to browse its contents, a daughter's prerogative. It was huge, the kind of double-wide Sub-Zero one might find in a small restaurant. The kitchen had been Lennie's latest project, and superficially, it looked great. But Cassandra knew where to find the corners her mother never stopped cutting, a legacy of the lean

29

years that had left her so fearful. The refrigerator and the stove would be scratch-and-dent specials, with tiny flaws that prevented them from being sold at full list. The new porcelain sink would have been purchased at Lennie's 'professional' discount—and, most likely, installed by her, along with the faucet and garbage disposal. She had kept the palette relatively plain. 'Better for resale,' she said, as if she had any intention of putting the house on the market. Like Penelope stalling her suitors, Lennie continually undid her own work. By Cassandra's reckoning, this was the kitchen's third renovation. Lennie was desperate not to leave the house, which had been big for a family of three, almost ruinous for a single mother and daughter, simply ridiculous for a woman now in her seventies.

But this conversation was already too fraught to take on the subject of the house, which her mother had come to love and defend against all comers. Instead, Cassandra asked her mother, 'Do you remember Calliope?'

'An organ? You mean at the Presbyterian church? And I think it's pronounced differently, dear.' Her father would have made the correction first.

'No, in my class. Callie Jenkins. At Dickey Hill, starting in fourth grade. She's in one of the photographs. She wore her hair in three fat braids, with those little pompon things on the ends.'

Cassandra bunched up a fistful of her own hair to jog her mother's memory.

'Three—oh, she must have been black.'

'Mother.'

'What? There's nothing bigoted in saying that.

30

Unless you're me, I guess. I'm not allowed to notice the color of anyone's skin.'

Cassandra had no desire to lecture her mother. Besides, she had a point.

'At any rate, I was watching CNN and there was a story about this case in New Orleans—a woman's child is missing and she took the Fifth, refused to say where the child is. Someone said it was similar to a case here years ago, involving Calliope Jenkins. It has to be the same person, don't you think? The age is about right, and how many Calliope Jenkinses could there be in Baltimore?'

'More than you might think.'

Cassandra couldn't tell if her mother was being literal or trying to make some larger point about infanticide or her hometown. 'Don't you think that would make a good book?'

Her mother pondered. That was the precise word—she puckered her forehead and considered the question at hand as if she were Cassandra's literary agent or editor, as if Cassandra could not go forward without her mother's blessing.

'True crime? That would be different for you.'

'Not exactly true crime. I'd weave the story of what happened to Callie as an adult with our lives as children, our time in school together. Remember, she was one of the few girls who went to junior high with me.'

'One of the few black girls,' her mother said with a look that dared Cassandra to correct her for referencing Callie's race.

'Well, yes. And race is a small part of the story, I guess. But it's really Callie's story. If I can find her.'

'Even if you do find her, can she speak to you? I

31

remember the case—'

'You do?'

'Anyone who lived here at the time would remember.' Was there an implicit rebuke in her mother's words, a reminder that Cassandra had disappointed her by moving away? 'I didn't recognize her name, but I remember when it happened. The whole point was that she wouldn't talk. But if she did kill her child, she can still be charged. If she didn't, why didn't she cooperate all those years ago?'

Cassandra was well aware of this particular problem; her editor had raised it first. They had agreed the book wouldn't be dependent on a confession, or even answering all the questions, but the reader would need to believe that Cassandra had reached some kind of conclusion about her old school friend. *Old school friend* was the editor's term, and while Cassandra had initially tried to correct the impression, using *classmate* and *acquaintance,* she soon gave up. What was a 'friend', after all, when you were ten or eleven? They had played together at school, gone to birthday parties together.

'I can't plan this book in advance. That's what makes it exciting. With the first two books, they were already constructed, in a sense. I had lived them, I just didn't know how I would write them. And they were very solitary enterprises. Solipsistic, even. But this time—I'm going to interview Callie, once I find her, but also other girls from the class. Tisha, Donna, Fatima. And Callie's lawyer, I guess, and the police detective who investigated her . . . heavens, I'm not sure three months here will be enough.'

'And, of course,' her mother said, staring into her tea, 'you'll be here for all the hoo-haw surrounding your father.'

'One event in a week of events,' Cassandra said. 'A simple onstage interview, and I'm doing it only because it will raise money for the Gordon School's library building fund. We do owe the school a great debt. Besides, it will be interesting, interviewing Daddy in front of a captive audience. He's the king of digressions.'

'Yes,' her mother said. 'Your father loved *digressing.*'

'It's not a big deal,' Cassandra said. She wished, as she often did, that they were a family comfortable with casual touches, that she could place her hand over her mother's now.

'I know,' her mother said. 'I just hate the way he . . . romanticizes what he did, to the point where he won't even talk about it. Or her.'

Cassandra respected her mother for holding on to that 'Or her' for all these years, refusing to say Annie's name unless forced. It might not be particularly healthy, but it was impressive. Cassandra shared her mother's talent for grudges—it was, she liked to say in speeches, a useful quality for the memoirist, the ability to remember every slight, no matter how small. They called it their Hungarian streak, a reference to her mother's mother, who had gone thirty years without speaking to her son and lived just long enough to see her granddaughter immortalize this fact in her first book. Nonnie hadn't minded, not in the least. It had given her a little bit of cachet in the retirement center where she lived, largely indifferent to her neighbors. On what would prove

33

to be Cassandra's last visit with her, Nonnie had insisted on going to the dining hall, parading her successful granddaughter past the other residents: 'My granddaughter, she's a writer, a real one, a bestseller.' Cassandra wasn't sure if her grandmother had even read the book in which she took such pride; the volumes—only one book then, but Nonnie had purchased the hardcover *and* paperback—stood on a table in her apartment. They were, in fact, the only books in the apartment, perhaps the only books her grandmother had ever owned. Nonnie had been mystified, but proud, when her daughter had married a learned man, as she called him. And, true to her own unfathomable principles about loyalty, she continued to like Cedric Fallows even after he betrayed her daughter.

'I've never understood,' Cassandra said at that last lunch, 'why you could forgive my father but not your own son. What did he do?'

Her grandmother waved the question away, as she had repeatedly while Cassandra was working on *My Father's Daughter*. 'Pfftt. I don't talk to him and I don't talk of him.'

'Okay, but what Daddy did was pretty bad. Does that mean Uncle Leon did something even worse?'

'Your father, Uncle Leon . . . who knows?'

'Someone must know.'

'It doesn't matter. The book is good.' Meaning: It sold a lot of copies. 'It doesn't have to be true. *War and Peace* isn't true.'

'My book is true, Nonnie. It's a memoir, I made a point to get everything right.'

'But you can only get things as right as people let you.'

34

'Are you mad that I told the story about Uncle Leon and you? I asked your side.'

Nonnie pointed a fork at her. 'I know how to be mad at people and if I were mad, you wouldn't be here.'

A month later, she was dead. Cassandra was surprised to see her father at the funeral, more surprised that he had the tact not to bring Annie. He seldom went anywhere without her. Still, when the rabbi invited people up to share their thoughts, Cedric simply couldn't resist getting up to say a few words, awkward as that was. Uncle Leon didn't get up, nor did Cassandra's mother, but the son-in-law who long ago ceased to be a son-in-law waxed eloquent about a woman he had never much liked.

Later, at a brunch in her mother's house, Cassandra ventured to her father, 'Nonnie said I didn't know the truth of the things I wrote, that I got them wrong.' They were alone, by the buffet table, and she was struck by the novelty of having him to herself.

'Nonnie was the queen of the mind-fuckers,' her father said, spearing cold cuts. 'Do you know why she was so angry at your uncle Leon?'

'No, she would never tell me.'

'That's because she couldn't remember. He did something thirty years ago that pissed her off, but she would never tell him what it was. Then she forgot. She forgot the precipitating incident, but she never forgot the grudge. Your uncle Leon was desperate to apologize, but he never knew what he did. Your mother used to go visit her and try to guess what Leon did, so he might make amends, and your grandmother would say, "No, that's not

35

it," like some Alzheimer's-addled Sphinx or a Hungarian Rumpelstiltskin, forcing the princess to guess his name when he didn't know it himself.'

Could it really be? Cassandra decided she believed him, although her father had never let the facts get in the way of a good story.

'Those are your mother's people, Cassandra,' her father said. 'Thank God you take after me.'

Now, more than a decade later, her mother was saying, 'Thank God you take after me, Cassandra. In your resilience. You'll come back from this, I'm sure of it.'

'From what?'

'Well—I just mean that I think you're right, this *next* book could be something special.'

Her mother did not mean to suggest Cassandra was a failure. Lennie simply couldn't escape the context of her own life, which she saw as a series of mistakes and disappointments. Yet she had actually enjoyed a brief burst of local celebrity when Cassandra was in high school, appearing on a chat show as 'Lennie the handywoman', demonstrating basic repairs. That was when she had started to wear overalls and painter's caps, much to her teenage daughter's chagrin.

A more ambitious woman might have parlayed this weekly segment into an empire; after all, the cohost of *People Are Talking* was a bubbly young woman named Oprah Winfrey. Years later, when Cassandra took her place on Oprah's sofa, she had asked during the commercial break if Oprah remembered the woman who had provided those home repair tips, the one with the short sandy hair. Oprah said she did, and Cassandra wanted to believe this was true. Her mother had always been easily overlooked, which was one reason she had been enthralled with vivid, attention-grabbing Cedric Fallows.

Cassandra had always thought her mother's transformation would be the focus of the second memoir. But sex had taken over the second book—her first two marriages, the affairs in and around them, a bad habit she had renounced on the page, if not quite in life. Her mother's cheerful solitude had seemed out of place. In fact, it had been embarrassing, having her mother in proximity to all that sex. But her mother's story, alone, was not enough to anchor a book. It was too straightforward, too predictable. 'It's a little thin,' her first editor had said. 'And awfully sad.' The second part had surprised Cassandra, who thought she had written about her mother with affection and pride.

'Does it bother you,' Cassandra asked Lennie now, 'that I never wrote about your life in the same way I wrote about Daddy's?'

'Oh no,' her mother said. 'It's the nicest thing you ever did for me.' Recovering quickly, she said, 'Not that it's bad, what you do. It's just not my style, to be all exposed like that. That's your father. And you.'

'You just said that I take after you.'

Lennie was at the sink, her back to Cassandra as she rinsed dishes. Lennie had a top-of-the-line Bosch now, but she hewed to the belief that dishes had to be washed before they could go in the dishwasher. 'You take after me in some ways, but you take after him in other ways. You're strong, like me. You bounce back. But you're . . . out there, letting the world know everything about you. That's your father's way.'

Cassandra carried her empty mug over to the sink and tried to quiet the suspicion that her own mother had, in her polite way, just called her a slut and an exhibitionist.

Chapter Four

Stove hot.

Baby bad.

Stove hot.

Baby bad.

Stove bad.

Baby hot.

Stove bad.

Baby cold.

Stovebabyhotcold. Stovebabyhotcold. Stovebaby hotcold. Cold stove. Cold baby. Hot stove. Hot baby. Bad stove. Bad baby. Babystove, babystove, babystove.

She awoke, drenched in sweat. Supposedly part of the change, but she didn't think that was the whole explanation in her case. After all, she had been having this dream for more than a decade now. Although it wasn't exactly a dream, because there was nothing to see, only words tumbling over each other, rattling like spare change in a dryer.

But even if the nondream dream caused tonight's bout of sweating, she knew menopause was coming for her. Up until a year ago, she had really believed there would be time to have one more child, to grab the ring that had been denied her repeatedly. First with Rennay, then Donntay.

38

She wanted so little. Sometimes, she thought that was the problem. She had wanted too little. The less you asked for, the less you got. The girls who had the confidence to demand the moon got the moon and a couple of stars. They never cut their price. A man bought what they were selling or moved on. As soon as you began to bargain, the moment you revealed you were ready to take less than what you wanted—no, not wanted, but needed, required—they took everything from you.

The flush had passed, but she couldn't go back to sleep. She changed into a dry nightgown, put on her robe, and went out to the glassed-in porch, which overlooked her neat backyard, her neighbors' yards beyond it. It was a house-proud street, not rich, but well tended. Pretty little house, pretty little town, pretty little life. Bridgeville, Delaware.

She would rather be in jail.

She was in jail, actually, only this time, there was nothing to sustain her, no hopes or dreams or promises. No, not jail. Hell. She was in hell. Which was not, as it turned out, a place of fire and brimstone, of physical discomfort and torture. Hell was a pretty little house in a pretty little town, with plenty of food in the refrigerator and enough money in the bank. Not a lot, but enough, more than she had ever known. Her mind free from workaday worries, she had all the time in the world to dwell on what had gone wrong and could never be made right. *What if she –? What if he –? What if they –?* Bridgeville, *Hell*-aware. Most people would think it was a better fate than she deserved.

They would be right.

Amo, Amas, Amat

I was five when my father decided that I should start studying Latin and Greek. No one found this odd. He was, after all, a professor of the classics. He had named me for Cassandra, the ignored prophetess. This was after my mother refused to consider Antigone, Aphrodite, Andromeda, Atalanta, Artemis, any of the nine Muses, or—his personal favorite—Athena. After all, Athena sprang, fully formed, from her father's head, while her mother, Metis, remained imprisoned inside. My father admired this arrangement.

My mother would have preferred to call me Diana, as Artemis is known in Roman mythology. But my father hated the Roman names and often railed at their primacy in our culture. When I had to learn the names of the planets, I couldn't rely on mnemonic devices—*My very elegant mother just served us nine pickles*—because I had to transpose them in my head: Hermes, Aphrodite, Earth ('Gaia!' my father would correct with a bark), Ares, Zeus, Cronus, Uranus ('The one Greek in a batch of Romans, that sly dog, and incestuous to boot,' my father liked to say), Poseidon, Hades.

Again, no one found this odd, least of all me. My father was a man of many emphatic opinions, which he announced with the same vehemence of callers to WBAL shouting about the Orioles and the Colts. The Greek gods were preferable to the Romans. Nixon was a criminal—my father's verdict long before Watergate. Mr Bubble was bad for the skin *and* the plumbing. Stovetop popcorn would give you cancer. Pornography was preferable to any ghostwritten syndicate novel, such as Nancy Drew or the Hardy Boys. Girls should not wear their hair short.

The last, at least, was mounted in my defense, when my exasperated mother wanted to chop mine off because I fought so during shampoos. 'You take over her hair,' she challenged my father, and he did, finding a gentle cream rinse and a wide-tooth comb that tamed my unruly mane. 'It's too much hair for a girl, but you'll be glad when you're a woman,' he often said. One of my happiest memories is of standing in the never-quite-finished bathroom off my parents' bedroom, my father pulling the comb through my hair, insistent but never cruel. My father—incapable of throwing a ball, bored by most sports—would have been lost with a son. The only man he understood was himself.

So, in the world according to Ric Fallows, insisting on language lessons for his only child was not at all strange. But everyone wondered why my father didn't tutor me himself. He could read both languages, although he was far more skilled in Latin. Instead, my father took me to the home of a faculty colleague, Joseph Lovejoy, whom I was instructed to call Mr Joe, in the Baltimore fashion.

Mr Joe and his sister, Miss Jill, lived in our neighborhood in a place I liked to call the upside-down house. It was built into a bluff above the Gwynns Falls, with the living room on the top floor, the next floor down housing the kitchen and dining room, and the bedrooms on the garden level. Mr Joe sat with me in the study on the top floor, while my father helped Miss Jill prepare

41

tea—not just the beverage but a proper tea of sandwiches and sweets. The Lovejoys were British, visiting Baltimore on some kind of academic exchange program. Miss Jill had what my father called that famous English skin, although it looked like anyone else's skin to me. Mr Joe was tall and gaunt, and he had skin that no country would claim.

One particularly warm Saturday afternoon in May, the teakettle whistled on the floor below us. It continued to sing for almost a minute and Mr Joe decided to investigate. I could hear him walking around the floor below, then continuing down the steps to the first floor. He returned a few minutes later and announced that would be all for today. My father arrived, but not Miss Jill with the sandwiches.

'What about tea?' I asked.

'There will be no tea today,' Mr Joe said.

'Did the kettle run dry?'

'Did the—yes, yes, it did.'

'And the sandwiches, the cakes?'

'Cassandra, your manners,' my father said.

I was almost fifteen before I figured it out. By then, I knew my father had lots of romances—'Not romances! Dalliances. The only *romance* I ever had was with Annie, and I married her.' But I didn't know about any of the others until he left my mother for Annie and I started piecing together my father's long history of infidelities. He rejects that word, too. 'I was never unfaithful or faithless where your mother was concerned. Sex meant nothing to me, it was a bodily function. That was the problem. I didn't know you could have both, sex and love, until I met Annie.'

42

We had this conversation a few days before I headed to college. My father had decided to lecture me on the double standard, persuade me that my own virginity was precious. He was a little late.

'And Miss Jill?'

'Miss Jill. Oh, the redheaded Brit. Yes, she was one. But not right away. It wasn't a plan. Well, maybe it was a little bit of a plan.'

'What did her brother think?'

'Her brother? Her brother?' My father was genuinely puzzled.

'Mr Joe.'

'Mr—oh, honey, he was her husband. Where did you get the idea that they were brother and sister?'

To this day, I comb my memory, certain I will find the moment of the lie. Perhaps it was my father's insistence on calling them Mr Joe and Miss Jill, a localism that my father normally belittled. But what would have been the point in deceiving me? A sibling relationship may have kept Mr Joe from being a cuckold, but it would not excuse what my married father did with Miss Jill while 'making tea'. A tea, I see now, that required no preparation—the cakes were store-bought, the sandwiches made well ahead of our visit, the crustless bread dry from the air yet damp from the cucumbers that had sweated on them.

Why did I think they were brother and sister? Because even my five-year-old self sensed something was off. My language lessons ended when the Lovejoys went back to England that summer. Miss Jill—*Mrs Lovejoy*—sent us Christmas cards for several years, but my mother never added them to our list. I spent my junior

43

year abroad in London and discovered I hated the social convention of tea. But I loved Englishmen, especially redheaded ones—gingers—and fucked as many of them as I could.

BANROCK STATION

February 25–28

Chapter Five

Cassandra had begun her last two projects by packing a laptop and retreating to a weekend resort, attempting to replicate the serendipitous origins of her first book. *My Father's Daughter* had started almost by itself, an accident of heartbreak and idleness: A romantic getaway, planned for West Virginia, had become a solitary one when her first husband left her, walking out after revealing a gambling addiction that had drained their various bank accounts, meager as they were, and saddled their Hoboken condo with a second and a third mortgage that made it practically worthless, despite the robust real estate market of the mid-nineties.

Disconsolate, terrified of the future, but also aware that the room was prepaid, she had driven hours in the wintry landscape—God help her, it was the weekend before Valentine's Day—thinking that she would spend the two nights and two days crying, drinking, and eating, but she ran out of wine and chocolate much faster than anticipated. The second night, a Saturday, she awoke at 2 A.M., her head strangely clear. At first, she chalked it up to the alcohol wearing off, but when she was still awake an hour later, she pulled on the fluffy robe provided by the bed-and-breakfast—one of *two* fluffy robes, she noticed, feeling the clutch and lurch of fresh heartbreak—and made her way, trancelike yet lucid, to the picturesque and therefore infuriating little desk not really intended for work.

She found a few sheets of stationery in the center drawer and began scratching out, with the crummy B and B pen, the first few pages of what would become *My Father's Daughter.* She had kept those pages, and while the book changed considerably over the next six months, as she wrote to blot out her pain and fear, those first few pages remained the same: *I didn't speak until I was almost three years old.* Later, when she began to query agents, a famous one had said he would represent her, but only if she consented to a rewrite in which she excised that opening.

He took her to lunch, where he explained his pet theory of literature, which boiled down to *The first five pages are always bullshit.*

'It's throat clearing,' he said over a disappointingly modest lunch of spinach salad and bottled water. Cassandra had hoped the lunch would be grander, more decadent, at one of the famous restaurants frequented by publishing types. But the agent was in one of his drying-out phases and had to avoid his usual haunts.

He continued: 'Tapping into a microphone. Is this thing on? Hullo? Hullo?' (He was British, although long removed from his native land.) 'It's overworked, too precious. As for prologues—don't get me started on prologues.'

But Cassandra believed she had written a book about a woman finding her own voice, her own story, despite a title that suggested otherwise. Her father was simply the charismatic Maypole at the center; she danced and wove around him, ribbons twisting. She found another agent, a Southern charmer almost as famous but sweet and effusive, unstinting in her praise, like the mother Cassandra

48

never had. Years later, at the National Book Awards—she had been a judge—she ran into the first agent, and he seemed to think they had never met before. She couldn't help wondering if he cultivated that confusion to save face.

She had started the sequel at a spa in the Berkshires, another shattered marriage behind her, but at least she was the one who had walked out this time. Paul, her second husband, had showed up in the final pages of her first book; she had believed, along with millions of readers, that he was her fairy-tale ending. Telling the truth of that disastrous relationship—along with all the others, before, after, and during the marriage—had felt risky, and some of her original readers didn't want to come along for the ride. But enough did, and the reviews for *The Eternal Wife* were even better. Of course, that was because *My Father's Daughter* had barely been reviewed upon release.

Then, just eighteen months ago—not enough time, she decided now, she hadn't allowed the novel to *steep* as the memoirs had—she had checked into the Greenbrier, again in West Virginia, but much removed, in miles and amenities, from that sadly would-be romantic place where the first memoir had begun. Perhaps that was the problem—she had been too self-conscious in trying to recapture and yet improve the circumstances of that first feverish episode. The woman who had started scratching out those pages in the West Virginia bed-and-breakfast had an innocence and a wonder that had been lost over the subsequent fifteen years.

Or perhaps the problem was more basic: She

wasn't a novelist. She was equipped not to make things up but to bring back things that were. She was a sorceress of the past, an oracle who looked backward to what had been. She was, as her father had decreed, Cassandra, incapable of speaking anything but the truth.

Only this time, the answers were not inside her, not most of them. Last night, in her sterile rental, she had started jotting down, stream of consciousness, what she could remember. Her list wasn't confined to Calliope but covered every detail of life at Dickey Hill Elementary, no matter how trivial, because she knew from experience that small details could unearth large ones. The memories of the latter had come readily: *foursquare, the Christmas pageant, Mrs Klein teaching us about Picasso and Chagall, the girl group*. The girl group—she hadn't thought about that in ages, although it had been key to a scene in the first book. Now and Later candies—did they even make those anymore?—the Dickeyville Fourth of July parade, her own brief television appearance, lumpy in a leotard, demonstrating how adolescent girls cannot do a full, touch-your-toes sit-up at a certain point during their development. She couldn't decide what was funnier—her desperation to be on television or the fact that people believed those sit-ups accomplished anything.

But where was Calliope in all of this? The girl-woman who was supposed to be at the center of Cassandra's story remained a cipher, quiet and self-contained. No matter how hard Cassandra tried to trigger memories of Callie, she was merely *there*. She didn't get in trouble, she didn't *not* get in

50

trouble. Was there a clue in that? Was she the kind of child who tortured animals? Did she steal? There had been a rash of lunchbox thefts one year, with all the girls' desserts taken. Was there something in Callie's home life that had taught her early on that it was better not to attract attention? Cassandra had a vague impression—it couldn't even be called a memory—of an angry, defensive woman, quick to suspect that she was being mocked or treated unfairly, the kind of woman given to yanking children by the meat of the upper arm, to hissing, *You are on my last nerve.* She had done that at the birthday party, upon coming to gather Callie. No, wait—Fatima's mother had picked the two up, and she would not have grabbed another woman's child that way. Still, Cassandra believed she had witnessed this scene with Callie, not Fatima.

Abuse—inevitable in such a story, but also a little, well, tiresome. She hoped it didn't turn out to be that simple, abused child grows up to be abusive mother. Hitting the wall of her own memory, but feeling too tentative to press forward in her search for the living, breathing Calliope, she decided to spend an afternoon at the library, researching what others had learned about the adult woman presumed to have murdered her own child.

* * *

The Enoch Pratt Central Library had been one of the places where her father brought her on Saturday afternoons, after the separation. That was the paradox of divorce in the sixties—fathers

51

who had never much bothered with their children were suddenly expected to *do* things with them every other weekend. It was especially awkward in the Fallows family because Ric wanted to involve Annie in their outings and Lennie had expressly prohibited Annie's participation. Ric defied his estranged wife, setting up fake chance encounters with his girlfriend. At the library, at the zoo, at Westview Cinemas, at the bowling alley on Route 40. *Why, look who it is!* You couldn't even say he feigned surprise; it was more as if he feigned feigning. Annie, at least, had the grace to look embarrassed by their transparency. And nervous, with good reason. People were not comfortable with interracial couples in 1968 and not at all shy about expressing their objections.

Cassandra liked Annie. Everyone liked Annie—except, of course, Cassandra's mother, and it was hard to blame her for that. In fact, the outings were more fun when Annie was along because Annie didn't give the impression that she felt debased by the things that a ten-year-old found pleasurable. Annie was only twenty-six, and a young twenty-six at that, but her interest in Cassandra was always maternal. She expected to be Cassandra's stepmother long before anyone else thought this might be possible, including Ric. In his mind, he was having a great romance, and romance was not possible within a marriage.

But Annie assumed she would be his wife. 'She set her cap for him,' Cassandra's mother said with great bitterness, and Cassandra had tried to imagine what such a cap looked like. A nurse's hat? Something coquettish, with a bow? (She was the kind of ten-year-old who knew words like

52

coquettish.) She imagined the hat that the cinematic Scarlett O'Hara lifted from Rhett Butler's box, the girl in *Hello, Dolly!* who wanted to wear ribbons down her back, the mother in *A Tree Grows in Brooklyn,* setting her jade green velvet hat at a jaunty angle. But Cassandra could not imagine round-faced Annie, who wore her hair in a close-cropped 'natural', in any kind of hat, much less see her as calculating.

Annie had been literally thrown into her father's arms, her dress torn, people ebbing and flowing around them. Then, even as Ric tried to help her out of the melee, he had been sucked in, with far more serious repercussions. 'A riot is . . . an odd thing,' Annie had told Cassandra years later, when she was trying to re-create that scene for the first memoir. 'Remember when Hurricane Agnes came through, and the stream flooded, and that man got out of his station wagon and saw it just float away, even as he stood there, holding on to a tree? It was like that, but the water was people, the wind was people. They didn't know they were people anymore. Does that make sense?'

Cassandra had thought it made perfect sense, and when the book was published, Annie's passages were often the ones cited in the reviews. Yet Annie was the one person who would never speak to the press, no matter how much she was pursued. 'I owed you my story,' she told her stepdaughter. 'But I don't owe it to anyone else.' Five years later—her words translated into twenty-eight languages, her likeness, in one of the frontispiece photos, having traveled to countries that Annie herself had never heard of—Annie was dead from ovarian cancer at the age of fifty-nine.

Cassandra had worried her father would be one of those men who begin ailing upon their wife's death, especially given that she was so much younger. But, while he had a thousand minor complaints, he remained robust. *Too* robust, according to the administration at the retirement community where he now lived. Cassandra was going to have to make nice with the director on her next visit there and she was dreading that visit. But for now, she had to go to the library.

*   *   *

Cassandra had to endure a tedious explanation of how things worked—where to find the reels, how to load them, how to print, where to return the reels when finished—before she was allowed to take a spin on the microfiche machines. Orientation done, she began yanking out the drawers of boxed reels, feeling as if she were at the beginning of a scavenger hunt. Calliope's life as a headline had coincided with the merger of the city's last two newspapers, the *Beacon* and the *Light,* which meant there was only one newspaper to study, but it was still more than she had anticipated. Various Internet searches had narrowed down the year for Cassandra, but not the month of the precipitating incident, and the newspaper's pay archive didn't go back that far. She would have to start at January and trudge through all of 1988. But the snippet of film she had seen on CNN had clearly been from a cold, wintry month—there had been a bare tree in the background.

It took her a while to establish an efficient yet

comprehensive way of searching—checking the front page, then zipping ahead to the local section, pushing the machine full speed to the gap between editions and starting over. The smell and the movement made her nauseous. Should she have hired someone for this dreary task? But she had never paid anyone to do her own work. Besides, she liked immersing herself in microfiche, which she had used to research parts of her first book. She just wished she could recapture the giddy ignorance of those days, the joy in writing without expectation, the smallness of her daydreams.

She found Calliope lurking at the end of March, which must have gone out like a lion that year. Yes, in fact, the weather was part of the story. February had been full of ice storms. At least, that was the excuse offered by a social worker, Marlee Dupont, charged with checking up on the child: Roads had been impassable, especially in Calliope's West Baltimore neighborhood, always last to be plowed. The social worker had called, but the phone had been shut off. That explained why one month had gone by without a visit; the second month was never really explained. When the social worker finally did arrive at the apartment on Lemmon Street, all she found was Calliope.

'Where's your baby?' she asked, according to the article.

'I can't tell you,' Calliope said.

It was, more or less, all she would say for the next seven years.

When had the legal defense, the Fifth Amendment, first been introduced? It was hard to tell because reporters had come to the story from a distance, too, after much had happened. It wasn't even clear why Callie was under the social worker's supervision. Cassandra jumped ahead to the resolution, finding more detail in the stories about Callie's release, almost seven years to the day later. She began jotting down a timeline in her Moleskine notebook. March 1988: Social worker discovers Calliope's three-month-old baby is missing. So, working backward, December 1987: Calliope's son Donntay is born. A previous child, also a boy, had been taken from Callie for neglect, but the department, citing her privacy rights, refused to say anything else, other than that this incident was not the reason a social worker had been assigned to Donntay upon his birth.

A previous child had been taken. That detail had been missing from the television report, and it was given only scant attention here. Calliope's parental rights had been terminated seven years earlier. That child would have to be—quick calculation— twenty-seven. How tantalizing. What had become of that child? Was that part of Callie's story? Should it be? Cassandra had researched 1980s adoption as part of *The Painted Garden* and knew that various groups began pushing for greater openness in adoption in the nineties. But that wouldn't affect Callie's first son. He would be able to find his mother only if they signed up for a mutual registry.

Images on microfiche tend to be grainy, especially when printed out, but Cassandra pressed the button anyway, capturing the 1988 photo of Callie when she was first jailed for contempt. Calliope's face was hard, her eyes hollow, and the cords in her neck looked almost painful. Yet, even in a shapeless winter coat, there was the suggestion of a striking figure, a model's figure. Drugs? Cassandra had heard somewhere that heroin users have killer bodies, that drug abuse gives them raging metabolisms that never stop, even if they clean up. Callie's eyes were downcast in the photo, but her lawyer, holding her by the arm, looked straight into the camera. That was the woman who had yet to return Cassandra's calls, an unanticipated development. These days, *everyone* returned Cassandra's calls. True, she hadn't been able to find anyone who would help her contact the retired police detective who had worked the case, but those people had at least had the courtesy and professionalism to pick up the phone.

Studying the younger version of the lawyer, she found herself projecting all sorts of qualities on her. Bulldoggish. *Homely.* Cruel, but accurate. What was it like to be an ugly woman? Cassandra, like every woman she knew, was full of self-doubt about her own appearance, had several moments every day when she was disappointed by the face she saw in the mirror. The older she got, the more she felt that way. Yet she also knew, on some level, that she would never be described as *ugly.* What would that be like? Obviously, she wouldn't enjoy it, although—this just occurred to her—physical attractiveness didn't seem to have much to do with whether women were paired or single. The plain women she knew seemed to do better relationship-wise. There had been some faux-economic explanation of this recently, an appalling bit of pop journalism that had boiled down to the usual advice: *You're not getting any younger, so you better*

57

take what you can get.

Cassandra, a two-time loser at matrimony, had no interest in getting back into the pool, especially after her second husband's attempt to break their prenup. That was pure blackmail, and it had worked: She had given him more than he deserved in the hope that he wouldn't gossip about her. She still liked men—she had a married lover, in fact, someone ideal, who required almost no attention—but she had no use for marriage. Her father was right: Marriage had nothing to do with romance. The end of her first marriage had been truly tragic—her college sweetheart, undone by demons he had hid all those years, destroying them both financially. The second one had been a mistake, plain and simple, and her account of it had been a cautionary tale that boiled down to this: *If, on the eve of your wedding, you wonder if you are making a terrible mistake—you are.*

She inserted the 1995 reel, the one that held the story of Callie's release, interested to see if the photo could reveal anything about the experience of seven years in jail. Funny, Callie was coming out of jail about the same time Cassandra started writing. In the second photograph, Callie actually looked better physically, but her expression was incredibly sad. To Cassandra's eyes, this was not a woman who felt vindicated. But then—why would she? Callie, upon her release, was still a woman believed to have killed her child and to have evaded justice on what many would call a technicality, a trick.

The homely lawyer was gone, replaced by a man. A strikingly handsome man. He seemed happy, at least—not out-and-out grinning, but allowing a tight smile that showed the hint of a dimple. Reginald Barr—the name was dimly familiar. Tisha had been Tisha Barr and she had a little brother, but he was known as Candy, in part because he was sweet, just a total charmer. But there was another, more peculiar reason for the name. The Reggie bar? No, that came much later. Candy's nickname was from his signature dance, the way he imitated an obscure singing group.

Cassandra's mind, when it raced toward a stray memory, was like a horse heading for a fence. She either slammed into the limits of her own mind or sailed over, finding what she needed. But she knew *this;* it had come up in her first book. The Astors, another quartet of Temptations wannabes. She had watched them on some dance show— *American Bandstand* or Baltimore's own Kirby Scott?—and her father couldn't shut up about the name. 'The Astors! The *Astors*! I wonder how much of the family fortune *they* inherited.'

But there was a part where the singers simulated bees buzzing around the sweet girl's head, and Candy Barr had turned that into a comic bit, slapping at the horde in mock terror. He also had a funny, hop-hop pelvis move, extremely precocious, a little nasty. Whenever he started doing that, Tisha chased him from the room. Gee-whiz . . . something, something.

So Tisha's brother had worked on Callie's defense. It was the kind of small-world touch that Baltimore was known for, all the more likely in the tight-knit black community of the Northwest Side. Plus, that was pure Tisha, looking out for an old classmate, trying to save Callie once again. Cassandra knew exactly how to play it: She would let Reg lead her to Tisha, then allow Tisha to take

59

her to—everyone. Because she was, after all, writing about them all, even if Callie was her focal point. She wouldn't be too up-front about her interest in Callie, not at first, although she would keep trying to find that police detective. *Gee-whiz,* as the Astors sang. *Have you seen our girl?*

Chapter Six

Where the hell is Banrock Station?

Teena Murphy put the box of chardonnay on the conveyor belt at Beltway Fine Wines, something she did—*damn*—every six days, on average, and it might have been a little more frequently, but she allowed herself vodka on the weekends. Yet this icy February day was the first time she had been moved to consider the name of her weeknight wine of choice. Box wine had many advantages—the price, the relative lightness of the carton, a key consideration for her—but Teena preferred it because she didn't have to confront how quickly the level was dropping.

'You having a party?' a voice behind her asked, a playful tenor. 'How come I wasn't invited?'

She turned, surprised that anyone at Beltway Fine Wines would joke with her that way. Teena had been a knockout in her prime, but her prime was a long time ago. She had also let her hair go gray, which made her look older still, as did her small, fragile-seeming frame. People didn't joke with slightly hunched, gray-haired ladies in the after-work rush at Beltway Fine Wines.

Unless they knew you once upon a time.

'Lenhardt,' she said. 'What are you doing in my home away from home?' If she made the joke, it couldn't be true. Right?

Her former colleague laughed. He had aged, too, but then—it had been fifteen years, easy, since they had seen each other last. Teena still got invited to the Christmas parties, the retirement parties, even the homicide squad reunions, but she never attended. Her invitations may have arrived on the same paper, in the same envelopes as everyone else's, but there was a whiff of pity about them. Pity and contempt.

'You look good, Teenie,' he lied. Even in his wilder days, between his two marriages, Lenhardt had been able to compliment a woman without making it sound like a pass.

'You, too,' she said, and it wasn't as much of a reach. He looked as good as he ever had. Lenhardt—now in his fifties—had always been a little stocky, and there was only a touch of gray in his sandy hair.

'Where you living these days?'

'On Chumleigh, off York Road.' Quickly, defensively, always aware of the gossip that she had cashed in on her misfortune. '*West* of York Road. And it wasn't so expensive when I bought in.'

'Chum*leigh*!' He laughed at her blank look. 'You don't remember the cartoon Tennessee Tuxedo? His walrus friend, Chumley? And Don Adams was the voice of the penguin? No? Ah well, as a Baltimore Countian, you're one of the citizens I'm charged with protecting and serving, not necessarily in that order. You working?'

'At Nordstrom.'

61

'Explains the fancy duds. But then—you always liked clothes, Teenie. I remember—'

'Yeah,' she said, not wanting him to finish the sentence: *How excited you were when you got to join CID, wear your own clothes.* She had dressed beautifully once she got out of uniform. It had been the eighties, not fashion's finest hour in hindsight, and she had gone into credit-card debt for that outlandish wardrobe. It had been the age of fluffy excess—oversize shirts, big jewelry, riotous prints. She remembered one skirt with enormous cabbage roses. Oh, and those big Adrienne Vittadini sweaters, which someone of Teena's height could practically wear as dresses.

Her colleagues had teased her, saying she looked like a punk, not getting that the look was, in fact, a romantic take on the downtown look. She had even been called in, told to tone it down, but her union rep had stepped in and said her clothes were within the guidelines for dress. The department was used to fashion plates, but the male version, peacocks strutting in expensive suits and ties. The other women in homicide, all two of them, went for that boring dress-for-success thing, suits and little bows. Teena would have rather gone back to wearing a uniform.

Now she wore dark, somber knits purchased at her employee discount. To sell other women expensive clothes, she had found it helped to have a neutral look, one that couldn't be pinned down in terms of label or cost. Because, of course, that was the paradox of waiting on wealthy women, the unspoken accusation hurled out when someone discovered she couldn't wear something new and trendy: *What do you know? You can't afford these things.* But Teena knew the clothes better than anyone. She lived among them, day in and day out. She thought of her life at Nordstrom as akin to a position in some strange animal orphanage, full of exotic beasts that needed new homes. She was careful about matching her charges to their future owners, determined that the rarest specimens go to customers who were worthy of them.

'It's funny, running into you,' Lenhardt said. His cart was filled with what Teena thought of as *reputable* purchases—three bottles of wine, a bottle of Scotch, a case of Foster's. She wondered how long those would last him, how often he shopped here, if he drank one beer with dinner, or two, or three. 'It was only a day or so ago that I got a call from someone looking for you. But that's how it goes. You go years without seeing an old friend, then, *boom,* the name's suddenly in the air. Ever notice that?'

The clerk loaded her box back into the shopping cart. Beltway Fine Wines had a distinctive smell that Teena could never quite pin down, a combination of wood, damp cardboard, and something spicy. She wondered if the various spirits under its roof slipped into the air. She always felt a little ... *altered* when she was here, but then, she came here after work, when she was in the middle of the transition from work Teena to home Teena. No one called her Teenie anymore, but she still couldn't carry her full name, Sistina.

'Someone called you, looking for me?'

'She was shut down by the public information officer in Baltimore City, I think, so she dug around, found some of your old compadres, those of us who jumped ship back in the early nineties. I guess she assumed we were disgruntled types, more likely to break rank. She was half-right.'

Lenhardt had left when a new chief tried to force a rotation system on the homicide squad. Teena might have joined the exodus, but she had her accident a few months later.

'*She?*'

'Some writer. Kinda famous, I think—I remember my wife reading one of her books for book club. She's working on a new book.' He swiped his credit card, took his bagged purchases from the clerk. Teena realized she was blocking other shoppers trying to make their way to the exit. She began rolling slowly forward, but Lenhardt caught up easily and fell into step beside her.

'Why does she want to talk to me?'

He gave her a look. 'Do you want to talk to her?'

'No.'

'That's what I thought. I didn't tell her anything. I didn't have anything to tell, but if I had—I wouldn't have, Teena. You know that.'

'But—why? Why now?'

'She just realized she knows—what was her name, the one who never talked?'

'Calliope Jenkins.' She felt like a child risking the candy man. Say the name three times and she'll appear. Not that Teena was scared of Callie Jenkins. Not exactly.

'Right. They went to school together.'

'And that's a book?' Her voice screeched a little on the last word, but the whoosh of the automatic doors provided cover. They were outside now, and the wind was cutting, carrying little pinpricks of rain that stabbed exposed skin. She had forgotten to put her gloves on and her hands ached. The

64

medical experts hired by the other side during the arbitration said Teena's Raynaud's was coincidental, that she couldn't prove it was a direct result of the accident. Small-framed women were prone to it, they said. Still, Teena never minded the cold before the accident.

'Her name is Cassandra Fallows,' Lenhardt said. 'This writer, I mean.' He had followed her to her car and she had a pang of embarrassment at its plainness. An out-and-out hooptie would have been less humiliating than this green, well-kept Mazda, which seemed to announce to the world how small and dull her life was. 'On caller ID, she comes up as a New York area code. Begins with a nine at any rate. In case she does find you. Although I admit I tried, out of curiosity, and your number is unlisted, although your address comes up readily enough through the Motor Vehicle Administration. Not that she can get that without driving down to headquarters in Glen Burnie. Still, you know, if she's even a half-assed researcher, she'll be able to find your address. Unless—you own or rent?'

'Own.'

He grimaced. 'Well, that's good—I mean, rent is just throwing money away—but that makes it easier to find a person. Sorry, now I sound like your father. I am a father now. A boy and a girl, Jason and Jessica.'

'Congratulations.' She meant it. Being a father, a parent, seemed miraculous to her. Anything normal did. But her mind wasn't really on Lenhardt's kids. A writer, doing a book. Every couple of years or so, back when the case was fresher, she would get a letter from a reporter,

65

usually someone new at the *Beacon-Light,* an eager kid who had just stumbled over the story. She should have expected this, with the New Orleans case kicking up Calliope's name, however briefly. She herself had started when she heard the news. But it had been so long since anyone had spoken of Callie to her. That was another reason not to attend cop parties. No back-in-the-day, no war stories.

'Bye, Lenhardt. It was nice seeing you.'

'Maybe our paths will cross again,' he said.

'Maybe,' she said. *Especially if you shop here regularly.*

She drove home and, as it often happened, was shocked to find herself there fifteen minutes later, panicky to realize that she had driven so mindlessly. She had always been prone to zone out that way. It was part of the reason she almost never drank outside the house—at her size and weight, a generous glass of wine could edge her over the legal limit. Oh, it couldn't make her drunk—based on her consumption of box wine, it took quite a lot to make her drunk—but who would believe that, should Teena Murphy be pulled over in her fancy clothes and plain car? They would expect her to be drunk. It would explain how she survived being her.

Pulling into her parking pad, she heard something—a branch cracking perhaps—and almost jumped out of her skin. The sound was the only memory she had, and she wasn't even sure if that was true or something her brain had manufactured after the fact. But any kind of snapping, cracking noise threw her into a panic. She couldn't be sure, but she believed that she

66

hadn't screamed until she heard the sound, all those breaking, snapping bones, like twigs under a giant's foot. In her ears, it sounded like scoffing laughter, someone taunting her. Not that Calliope Jenkins had even smiled, much less laughed, in all the time she had tried to talk to her over the years. Still, Teena always believed she was laughing on the inside, delighted by her ability to play them all.

The accident happened a couple of months after they announced Callie Jenkins's release. Now *that* was sheer coincidence. Teena had gone to pick up a woman, the mother of a kid who had just been charged in a homicide, and the woman freaked out. Teena had always prided herself on not making the mistake of going for her gun too early, something women police were faulted for. Small as she was, she could and would take a beat-down. But she was tired that morning—*not* drunk—and she had gone for her gun, and the woman had knocked it out of her hand, sent it skittering under the car. Teena had been groping, grasping for it when the car started to roll backward.

She let herself into the small, neat rowhouse she had purchased with her settlement from the car manufacturer, the deep pocket that had finally swallowed responsibility for her accident. Oh, they didn't admit the parking brake was faulty, and they had done enough research, her FOP lawyer said, to know they could pretty much destroy her credibility in court. They just decided it was cheaper to settle and what was nothing to a big car company was more than enough to buy this house, in cash, on Chumleigh Road. *Chumley!* Now she remembered. She had watched that cartoon. She just forgot. She forgot a lot. She was forty-six years old and she could barely believe that she was once a little girl who had watched cartoons, who had decided she wanted to apply to the police academy because of Angie Dickinson in *Police Woman.*

'She's part of the gimp lineup, you know,' her father would say, referring to the other popular television shows of the day. 'There's a guy in a wheelchair, a blind guy, and a fat guy. She's a woman, and that's handicap enough.' He wasn't being mean, and he certainly didn't know he was being prophetic, that his daughter would one day join the gimp lineup twice over. Her father simply never understood why a pretty girl—and, although he never said it, a *straight* girl—would choose a career in the Baltimore City police department. Teena didn't dare to say it out loud, but she believed she could be the first female chief in the department's history, the first woman in the nation to lead a big-city police department. In the seventies, it wasn't weird to believe that kind of shit. Strange, now that there really were women heading departments—in Des Moines; in Jackson, Mississippi—it seemed less probable to her. When she had joined homicide in 1986, she was the third female detective. Now, twenty-two years later, there were . . . two female detectives.

Teena lifted the box of wine from her trunk, favoring her right hand, and cradled it on the point of her hip, the way a woman might carry a baby. She would eat something—a frozen dinner from Trader Joe's, soup and a sandwich—forestall the first glass of wine just long enough to prove that she could. She would wash her dishes, tidy up the kitchen. Then, and only then, she would board the train for Banrock Station, chugging past all the

68

other little towns on the route, all the places she would never know or visit.

Chapter Seven

'The Elizabeth Perlstein Library will go here, and the old library will be converted into more classroom space, which we can definitely use.'

Cassandra studied the blueprints with pretend interest. She was not very good at conceptualization and could not envision the future building. But the headmaster—a new one, his name quite gone from her head—was clearly excited about the addition to what had always been, frankly, a grotty little campus, one of Baltimore's second-tier private schools, for those keeping score. Many were, as it turned out. Old-line Baltimoreans were geniuses at working a mention of Gilman, Friends, Bryn Mawr, Roland Park Country, Park School, even Boys' Latin into some not really relevant anecdote. Some expressed surprise that the Gordon School was still around, assuming it had collapsed into the ashes of its own hippy-dippy good intentions. The school, however, had never been the *Harrad Experiment*/free love fiasco that was enshrined in the public imagination. It had been intellectually rigorous, owing as much to English boarding schools and St John's College's classics-based curriculum as it did to the open-space experiment. The famed liberality had been confined to its lack of a dress code and its no-grades policy, which had included creating essentially fake records for colleges.

69

Gordon School had done extraordinarily well at placing its students before that latter practice was uncovered and outlawed. Luckily, Cassandra had already graduated from Princeton by then.

Whatever its flaws, the Gordon School had employed her uncredentialed mother as a lower-school math teacher. More crucially, it had offered Cassandra a scholarship for her last three years of high school. The combination of touchy-feely culture and exacting intellectual standards, but with no competition, had been perfect for a student of her temperament. She was genuinely thrilled for the chance to help the school now.

She was less happy about the ceaseless pressure to contribute more of her own money to the project. It was funny how wildly others misjudged her income. Most people thought she had much less than she did, because it was inconceivable to them that a writer could make money. But some, like the headmaster here at the Gordon School, had erred in the other direction, suggesting she might want to give at the 'Diamond' level, which started—*started*—at $100,000. God knows what kind of money was required to put one's name on a building; Elizabeth Perlstein, class of '88, was either one of those tech billionaires or married to one. Luckily, Cassandra had mastered the art of the graceful demurral, the ability to avoid the definitive no while never saying yes. Instead, she had waived her speaking fee, which was considerable, and persuaded her father to join her on the stage here for a fund-raiser, in which she would lead him, for the first time ever, through a public discussion of what had happened to him in the '68 riots. Tickets to the talk alone were $50 and

70

there was a private dinner for those willing to pay $250. The school stood to raise almost $50,000 from the event. Not Diamond level, but Platinum, and more than good enough by Cassandra's estimation.

'We feel so lucky to have you,' the headmaster said. 'We thought the University of Baltimore symposium would have snapped you up.'

'Oh, this is so much more meaningful to me,' Cassandra said. The fact was, the University of Baltimore had not even contacted her, nor had they asked her father to contribute an oral history to its extensive Web-based archive. She had been hurt by this omission, but not surprised, for there had been a small backlash against *My Father's Daughter* once it found commercial success. The critical talking point, first advanced by a so-so lesbian African-American novelist, was that Cassandra had usurped a major political event and turned it into—she knew the words by heart—a story about a white girl's birthday party, ruined by the assassination of Dr Martin Luther King, wah-wah-wah. The words had rankled, but Cassandra hadn't been foolish enough to respond. Still, in quiet moments, when that stinging criticism came back to her, she argued in her head with her nemesis, a one-book wonder rumored to owe at least three books to three different publishers. *Don't write me out of history. You, of all people, should know what it's like to be silenced, to be told that you have no role—because of race, because of gender, because of sexuality. My story is my story. And my father—complicated, less than admirable man that he was—saved a woman's life that day.* Yes, her pillow had received those words many

71

times over.

But this was only the fortieth anniversary. Perhaps by the fiftieth, they would be included. *Fifty, ten years from now.* Caught off guard by the realization that she was now at an age where, actuarially, she could not presume her father would be with her ten years in the future, Cassandra missed some point the headmaster was making. She smiled and nodded. Smiles and nods covered a multitude of oversights.

* * *

'Pedant,' Ric Fallows said a few hours later, after listening to her account of the meeting.

It was one of his favorite words, his all-purpose condemnation. *Pedant, pedantic, pedantry, pederast,* the last of which he seemed to use interchangeably with *pedant,* although he clearly knew better. The irony, of course, was that Cedric Fallows was far more pedantic, in the literal sense of the word, than those he labeled.

The pedant of the day was a neighbor here at Broadmead who had the temerity to complain about Mr Fallows sitting on his patio in his bathrobe. And nothing else. Given the retirement community's village-like aspect, with garden apartments built around shared courtyards, he could be glimpsed by his neighbors in deshabille.

'Only if they're looking,' he pointed out when Cassandra raised the issue.

'Well,' Cassandra said, 'apparently they are. And they can live with the bathrobe. Just not the lack of anything beneath.'

'That was last summer. Why bring it up now?'

'Because spring is *icumen* in,' she trilled. '*Lhude* sang the *cuccu* in his bathrobe.'

He smiled. 'It's *summer* that's *icumen* in. And your Middle English is deplorable.'

But she had played his game, used a learned reference to lighten a tense moment. She could let the subject drop, move on to a discussion of their upcoming appearance at the Gordon School.

'I'm not sure I want to go,' he said, surprising her. She thought her father would be dying for this bit of recognition. He had never had the academic career he envisioned, never published the big book in his head, the one he thought would change the way people read myths. 'Fuck Joseph Campbell,' he blurted out from time to time. Cassandra still wasn't sure if he saw Campbell as the usurper of his ideas or the antithesis of what he had hoped to say.

'We're committed,' she said nervously, thinking of those blueprints, the advance ticket sales. 'They've advertised—'

'Oh, I'll *be* there, if I must. But why can't you tell it, as you did in your book?'

'Because it's your story.'

'It was. Somehow it became yours.'

She weighed what he was saying. A complaint? An acknowledgment of a literal truth? Or something in between?

Yet her father had always seemed proud of her book. She remembered the first local signing, the one where no one had come, in a struggling independent in downtown Baltimore. Cassandra didn't have many friends left in the city. Her friends were from college, her years in New York. In New York, at her first-ever publication party, the bookstore had been full of friends and publishing types, and there had been a dinner afterward in a restaurant. In Baltimore, where the publicist had assumed she would be championed as a hometown girl made good, there were exactly five people: her father and Annie, her mother and her mother's best friend, and a woman who had clearly misunderstood the thrust of the book, believing it a history of the civil rights movement in Baltimore. The evening was notable, however, for it marked the first time since Cassandra's high school graduation that her parents and Annie had been in the same room. (A midyear graduate from college, she hadn't bothered to walk, just packed up her things and gone straight to a sublet on the Lower East Side, back when the Lower East Side was still the Lower East Side.)

She had been nervous that night, reading in front of her parents. And Annie. The section she had earmarked for bookstore appearances suddenly seemed inappropriate, centering as it did on her attempt to re-create the moment her father met Annie. Her parents had raised her to be direct and down-to-earth about sex, but did that apply to their own sex lives? Her mother had explained the biology of the matter to her when she was eight, while her father had spent his life instructing her in the more indefinable nature of desire. She had been six or seven when her father had pointed out a woman near the Konstant Kandy stand in Lexington Market. 'That woman,' he said, gesturing with the spoon from his ice cream, 'has a magnificent ass. In *Portnoy's Complaint,* Philip Roth compared such an ass to a peach, or maybe it was a nectarine, but that's a little flat-footed for

74

me. What do you think? A cello, perhaps, or an amaryllis bulb, with the backbone stretching up like the stem, the head the flower?' No, the timing was off, for Roth's book certainly wasn't around when she was six. In fact, she remembered seeing its yellow cover on her father's nightstand, in the apartment he shared with Annie, and thinking, *He says he's too strapped to get me new shoes, yet he buys himself hardcover books*. But her father considered books as essential as food. He would have been baffled if anyone suggested not buying the book he wanted the moment he wanted it. Besides, her father's library was a gold mine for a dirty-minded girl. Cassandra had read Roth and Updike and Mailer. She read *Candy,* although she didn't understand it until she read Voltaire in a college lit class. Her father's contemporary books, much more than his library of classics, prepared her well for the world she entered. The books didn't stop her from having a stupid affair with one of her college professors, but they armed her with the information that the professor didn't have as much power as a young woman might assume.

For all of Cassandra's hard-earned literary sophistication, she could not read the passage about her father and Annie in front of them. Or, for God's sake, her mother and her friend, starchy Lillian. She read from the prologue instead, but she wasn't prepared, and she tripped over words as if she had never seen them before. Later, her father and Annie took her to Tio Pepe's—had they won or lost the coin toss? Cassandra wondered wryly—and her father tried to suggest that Lillian was a repressed lesbian who had been in love with Lennie for years, but even Annie found that

75

ridiculous. 'Oh, Ric,' she said with a fluttering sigh, and he looked at her as if he could not believe she was his.

How sweet it had been, three years later, to return to Baltimore and speak in an auditorium at the Pratt library, the room brimming with people who had discovered the book in paperback. Women from reading clubs, in the main, but also some much younger girls, those who had their own problematic fathers, and even a few older men, the type who had studied her author photo a little too closely and thought they might help her with her daddy issues, whether they admitted that to themselves or not.

She wondered now if her father, despite all his years in classrooms, had a touch of stage fright.

'You're not nervous, are you?'

'When have I ever been nervous to face an audience?' he shot back. 'Besides, you do all the work, right? You're going to ask the questions, and I'm going to answer.'

'Well, they bill it as a conversation. It wouldn't be wrong if you had a few questions for me.' Her voice caught; she had stumbled into an old psychic tar pit, her father's incuriosity about her life. Cassandra knew the various ways her father might describe a woman's ass, but he wasn't sure what either of her husbands had done for a living. Ah, but if she had pressed him on it, he would have said, 'Well, neither one stuck around.'

'Sure, sure,' he said now. 'I'll lob you a few softballs.'

'And you'll talk about Annie?' Probing, careful.

'What do you mean?'

'About meeting her, the circumstances.'

76

'If need be. But, you know, it doesn't matter—'

'Of course it matters.'

'I didn't need a riot. I would have met her some way, somehow. Annie was my destiny.'

That had always been the rationalization, but there was no doubt that her father had come to believe it. He hadn't cheated on her mother; he had encountered his destiny and he knew enough not to defy the Oracle of Delphi. Yet her father didn't acknowledge destiny in any other aspect of his life.

It was hard, trying to come to terms with the fact that her father had such a huge and ruling passion, much larger than any Cassandra had ever known. Sure, she knew what it was like to be swept away in the early part of a love affair, but she was amazed by those people who never seemed to abandon that wildness, that craziness. Would it have been easier if her father's passion had been for her mother, or more difficult? In some ways, she was glad that her father's big love was for someone other than her mother, because she at least had her mother to keep her company. Around her father and Annie, she had been lonely, the odd girl out. Especially as a teenager, she couldn't help feeling that they spent their time with her wishing she would go away so they could have more sex. Of course, teenagers think the whole world is sex, all the time. But even now, as an adult with two marriages behind her, Cassandra still believed that her father's sexual passion with Annie had an unusually long life span. If Annie left a room for even a moment, her father looked lost. When she returned, the relief that swept over his face was almost painful to see. He was crazy about her.

That's the kind of line her father would have red-lined in an essay as vague, imprecise, and overwrought. Yet it was true in his case. And Cassandra didn't have a clue why.

Annie was beautiful, yes, the mild flaws of her face—the space between the front teeth, the apple roundness, the heavy brows that she never tended—balancing out the cartoonish perfection of her body. Sweet, too. Not unintelligent. But not sharp. This, more than anything, had bothered Cassandra, then and now. If her father, for all his snobbery, could choose a woman of ordinary intelligence, then what were the implications for his daughter? After an exceedingly awkward adolescence, Cassandra had grown into a reasonably attractive woman. Not necessarily pretty but sexy and appealing. Yet whenever she visited her father, she was reminded that the qualities that her father had taught her to value—intelligence, quickness—had nothing to do with the woman he declared the love of his life. The test of a first-rate mind, her father often said, quoting F. Scott Fitzgerald, was to hold two opposing thoughts simultaneously without going insane. Cassandra looked at herself, she looked at Annie, and she concluded that her father had a first-rate mind.

'Time for dinner,' her father said. Although his apartment had a kitchen, he took his meals in the community dining room, but he always insisted on a cocktail before dinner. He seemed a little shaky getting out of his chair, and Cassandra reached a hand out to him.

'I'm fine,' he snapped. 'Just a little light-headed from that expensive gin you insist on giving me. It has a much higher alcohol content.'

He had used his own gin and made his drink to his exacting specifications, but never mind.

'Come on, Dad,' Cassandra said. 'We'll climb the hill together.'

He smiled, pleased by the allusion to one of his favorite poems. 'But I'll beat you down.'

Tottering down

Dickey Hill Elementary, school number 201, new in the fall of 1966, opened in utter chaos. I stood in the hallway near the principal's office, willing myself not to reach for my father's hand. Just five minutes ago, I had shaken his hand off as he walked me to school, a rare treat. We had been climbing the hill past the Wakefield Apartments, prompting, inevitably, a recitation of 'John Anderson, My Jo'. In a Scottish accent, no less.

> *John Anderson, my jo, John,*
> *We clamb the hill thegither;*
> *And monie a canty day, John,*
> *We've had wi' ane anither:*
> *Now we maun totter down, John,*
> *But hand in hand we'll go,*
> *And sleep thegither at the foot,*
> *John Anderson, my jo.*

It was the first time I felt a twinge of embarrassment at my father's behavior. Fleeting, to be sure—I was still years away from the moment when everything about one's parents becomes unbearable, when the simple act of my mother speaking, in the car, with no one else there to hear, could make me cringe—but I remember speeding up a little so the students arriving by car and bus might not associate me with this odd man.

'Do you know what *brent* means, Cassandra?' my father quizzed me, referring to another line in the poem: *His bonny brow was brent.*

I pretended great interest in the Wakefield Apartments, and the pretense quickly became authentic. Apartments were glamorous to me, in general, and although these did not conform to my penthouse fantasies, the terraced units had that kind of compactness that often appeals to small children. I wanted to make friends with people who lived in those apartments, see what was behind their doors and windows. It was a frequent impulse, one that would later lead to my dismal attempt to support myself as a freelance journalist for shelter magazines. Wherever I went—the sidewalks of the Wakefield Apartments, the long avenues of rowhouses that led to various downtown destinations—I wanted to know the interiors of people's homes, their lives, their minds.

Because I was encouraged to tell my parents whatever passed through my quicksilver little brain, I told my father what I was thinking.

'I hope there are kids who live in those apartments and they're in my class and they become my friends and I get to go to their houses after school and play there.' It was lonely on Hillhouse Road, where I was the only child in the five houses. There were teenagers, but they had no use for me. We had so little in common that they

80

might as well have been bears or Martians or salamanders.

'Your mother won't like that,' my father said.

'Why?'

'Because your mother's a snob.'

I pondered that. A snob considered herself better than other people. This did not fit my sense of my mother, who seemed forever . . . *sorry* about things. She was always apologizing, mainly to my father. For dinner—its arrival time, its contents. For letting me sneak television shows like *Peyton Place* and, a few years hence, *Love, American Style*, which my father found so appalling that he couldn't stop watching it. Television, which my father despised, would become a regular feature of my weekend visits with him, a reliable way of 'entertaining' me. On Friday nights, I would sit rapt in front of the television, tuned unerringly to ABC, where I progressed from fantasy to fantasy—the blended world of *The Brady Bunch,* the domestic magic of *Nanny and the Professor,* the harmonious life of *The Partridge Family. That Girl* (my personal idol), *Love, American Style.* It was fun, or would have been if not for my father's running commentary. ('So this is what farce has become . . . forget Sheridan, forget Wilde . . . bug-eyed virgins, bugger them all.') By the time I was eleven, I knew about Sheridan and Mrs Malaprop, and Oscar Wilde, who said anyone could be good in the country, and even virgins, who were people who had yet to try to make babies. My father managed to avoid giving me *bugger,* however, and I was left to assume it was what happened to the bug-eyed. To be bug-eyed was to become a bug, and, therefore, buggered. I was twenty-one before

81

I knew what it actually meant.

On the first day of third grade, *bugger* was not part of my vocabulary yet, although I had other odd words. *Souse,* for example, my father's preferred term for drunks. *Delaine,* a fine fabric for which my mother pined as she decorated our house on the mingiest of budgets. *Antidisestablishmentarianism,* then reputed to be the longest word in the dictionary. I knew not only how to spell it, but—at my father's insistence— what it meant, vaguely. And, yes, I did know *brent,* if only from context—smooth, handsome. Entering third grade, it was my plan to use these words, super-casually, and establish myself as an intellect with which to be reckoned.

My classroom assignment unearthed, I said good-bye to my father, trying not to display any panic, and walked upstairs to Mrs Klein's room. Mrs Klein was young and pretty, the two best things a teacher could be. The class filled up quickly and I looked around, trying to decide who would be my best friend. I recognized a shy blond girl, someone I had seen around the neighborhood, but dismissed her. She had a strange look about the eyes, which were underscored with dark circles. I drifted toward the group that seemed the most confident, three girls in all. The desks had been arranged in configurations of four and they had seized a desirable quartet, alongside the windows, in the middle.

'May I sit here?' I asked the smallest of the three girls.

She cast a quick glance at the other two. One was tall and a little pudgy, but I could see in an instant

82

that no one would ever dare tease her about her weight. The other was pretty but too shy to make eye contact. All three were Negroes, the word I would have used then, and felt quite proud of using. The class was equally split between white and black children, a change from Thomas Jefferson, where there had been only two African-American girls. I did not choose the group for this fact, nor was I especially conscious of it at the time. Later, my parents would make me conscious, even self-conscious. My father would praise my friends far too much, and my mother would practically congratulate herself on how *nice* she found their mothers, how polite. Except Fatima's.

My father was particularly fond of Donna, whom he called doe-eyed Donna—always in those words, doe-eyed Donna—but he liked Tisha and Fatima, too. They would not be my only friends at Dickey Hill. I would, over time, find girls who lived in the Wakefield Apartments, go to their homes, and find it almost as interesting as I had hoped, the rooms so small and cunning, like something a mouse might build. But during the school day, this was my group. We were the smart girls, the leaders, each with a clearly defined role. I got good grades. (As did the others, but I got the best grades.) Donna was the artist. Fatima was the adventurer, destined to do everything first. And Tisha was the boss, looking out for all of us. We thought we were the future.

GLASS HOUSES

March 1–2

Chapter Eight

'Good morning, darling.'

Cassandra slept heavily and those who truly knew her well—her parents, two ex-husbands—understood that she was capable of answering the phone while still asleep and even managing several seemingly coherent sentences. She was particularly disoriented this morning, confused about her whereabouts—*Baltimore, right, the leased apartment*—confused about who might be calling her. She had been dreaming, and it had been pleasant, but that was all she could remember.

'Bernard,' she murmured after exchanging a few sleep-fogged sentences. Then: 'What day is it?'

He laughed, as if she were being droll, but it was a legitimate question. More than a decade into her life as a full-time writer, Cassandra had yet to become accustomed to how self-employment dulled the days, blurring all distinctions. Monday, Monday? She not only trusted that day, she rather liked it. As the workweek progressed, she could observe but not really share the rising tide of high spirits she saw in the people around her, at cafés and coffee shops. She especially missed the giddy high of Friday afternoons, the luxurious emptiness of Saturdays, but not so much that she would want to experience the lows of the working week. It was a bit like being on medication, she supposed, each day more or less the same as the one before.

Not that she had ever been on medication. Her father's daughter, indeed. Ric Fallows bragged about how he never took so much as an aspirin or an antihistamine, and while Cassandra knew her father's stance was a kind of bigotry, born of serendipitous good health, she couldn't help absorbing his views. It amused her, a little, when he had to start taking a cholesterol drug.

There was a period, just before her first marriage broke up, when she was given a prescription, but she never filled it, although she lied and told the doctor she did. He had gotten in touch with her after she revealed that detail in her second memoir, outraged. Outraged! By telling the world—well, about 800,000 readers, give or take—that she had ignored her psychiatrist's advice, he argued, she had branded him incompetent, unworthy. And never mind that she hadn't named him, his e-mail continued, anticipating her defense.

'As I will remind you,' his e-mail huffed, 'libel law requires only that a person be identifiable to some, not all. Your ex-husband, for example, would know that this passage refers to me, so it's inferences may, in fact, be libelous.'

She had written back, 'It's hard for my ex-husband to have a lower opinion of you than the one he has long harbored, given some of the "advice" you provided at the time. In the end, I am happy with how things worked out, so I don't really care that you were unethical and boneheaded and not a particularly good listener. But if you're worried about your professional rep, be advised that the possessive "its" takes no apostrophe and that only the listener may infer, so the word you want is "implications", not inferences. Cheers, your former patient, now quite sane, no thanks to you.'

She wouldn't write such an e-mail today, fearful that it would be posted on the Internet. But it felt good at the time. She had been wise, rejecting whatever drug the doctor had been pushing on her. *Not* feeling wasn't the secret to happiness.

Neither was Bernard.

'It's Saturday,' Bernard said, 'and Tilda decided to go up to Connecticut to visit her sister for the weekend. Can I come over?'

'You could, if I were in Brooklyn,' she said. 'But I'm in Baltimore, working on the new project. I told you.' She was awake now, hearing everything, even the things that weren't actually said.

'I thought you might come back, on weekends.'

'Some weekends. Although it never occurred to me that you would be free on a Saturday.'

'Me either,' he said. 'But you were the first person I thought of.'

'You're sweet,' she said, stifling a yawn. Bernard *was* sweet. And considerate—not only of her but of his wife. Granted, he was cheating on his wife, but he was conducting the affair in the kindest, most thoughtful way possible. Cassandra had been able to rationalize the relationship because it was truly about sex—sex and a little companionship. She had no interest in marrying again and the men she dated eventually found this intolerable. Bernard, who really did love his wife, had seemed the perfect solution, because he could be *scheduled,* usually weeks in advance.

But he had become clingy of late, demanding. He wasn't in love with Cassandra, but he couldn't bear the fact that she wasn't in love with him. They were on their last legs. She hoped the end wouldn't be ugly. In fact, she had calculated that he would fall out of the habit of her while she was in Baltimore, smoothing the way for a painless breakup.

'Maybe I could come down there,' he said. 'On a weekend, it's an easy drive.'

'I'm working,' she lied reflexively.

'On a Saturday?'

'I've scheduled some interviews.'

'How are things going?'

'Okay,' she said, hoping that was the truth. She really couldn't tell. But Bernard, whom she had met at a lecture a year ago, needed to believe she was never in doubt when it came to her work. He had read the novel, while it was still in manuscript, and pronounced it brilliant. Bernard worked on Wall Street, and his prognostications on money were much more sound than his opinions on literature. If only he had brought the same conservative, the-bubble-must-burst mentality to her last book. All commodities crash, Bernard had told her recently, speaking of oil, but Cassandra couldn't help wondering if it applied to her, too.

'I miss you,' he said in a tone that suggested he was trying to cram much meaning into those three words. At least it wasn't 'I love you.' That would be disastrous.

'I miss you, too,' she assured him. In some ways, she did. She would be happy to have him in bed with her right now. He was a thoughtful lover and excited by the fact of the affair, which he claimed was his first. Cassandra didn't quite believe him, but she understood that he had convinced himself of this fact. Her hunch was that Bernard was a serial monogamist on parallel tracks—he was faithful to Tilda, he was faithful to his lovers. Sort of like a subway line with an express track and a local track. On the local, he trod through life with Tilda, a sweet-faced blonde who sometimes got her picture in the Sunday Styles section of the *Times,* an old-fashioned New York wife with a conscience and lots of dutiful charity work. Then, on the express, he sped through affairs with women with whom he could never form a bond. Cassandra was his first creative type, and he probably would have tired of her by now if she had the good sense to pretend to be in love with him. She simply didn't have the energy.

'I—' he began, and she rushed to interrupt, to block the verb she could not afford to hear.

'I'll come back week after next, on Monday or Tuesday, to meet with my editor. You can usually get free in the evenings, right?'

'With notice, yes.'

'I'll give you plenty of notice.' *And cancel at the last minute.* Which, in the short run, would not achieve anything. If she continued to be this aloof, he might decide to leave Tilda. 'Good-bye, my love,' she added, hoping the use of the word as a noun would be sufficient.

Only now she was awake, on what looked to be a bright if chilly March day. It really was strange how much the weather affected mood. Gray sky or blue, her circumstances were the same day to day. Was she happy? She knew she should be. She had money and health and even health care. She lived as she wanted. She didn't have children or a husband, but those things were overrated. She had Bernard, although he represented a regression. Her second book had ended with the claim that she had moved beyond meaningless affairs, that

91

she was content on her own.

Was she happy? Was she even content? She had to think that a truly happy, content person wouldn't battle her aging body with such intensity, would let the gray hairs grow in, forgo facials, and, most of all, fuck the gym, that Sisyphean battle against gravity. But Cassandra also worried that her life was too soft, that small things became magnified in the midst of all this comfort, and the gym was the only place where she encountered active opposition. Or had been, until the publication of her novel.

Hadn't someone written a poem about how it was the small things, the fraying of a shoelace, that broke a man's spirit? She walked over to her laptop and typed *the fraying of a shoelace* into Google and got back nine entries, and half of those were about the Nicholson Baker book *The Mezzanine*. But there was some blog crediting it to Charles Bukowski, so she started over, with just *Bukowski* and *shoelace*. And here was the poem, called, in fact, 'The Shoelace'. Ah, it was *snapping*, not fraying, and it sends a man (or a woman, as Bukowski adds in a moment of preternatural political correctness) to the madhouse.

She read on, impressed by a poet she had never much considered. Her father, for all his progressiveness, hated the 'new' voices, as he called them—Bukowski, Ginsberg, Kerouac, Burroughs. Anyone who announced himself as a revolutionary could not be one, said Ric Fallows, and, in that way, managed to announce that *he* was a revolutionary because he was not announcing himself. Cassandra, a contrarian in so many ways, did not defy her father on this. She was too busy

92

reading Sidney Sheldon and Judith Krantz and this one really shocking book—*Laurel Canyon*?—in which a girl with a pronounced masochistic streak volunteered for a gang rape that another man witnessed for sexual pleasure. What teenage girl had time for Bukowski when there were books like that in the world?

But now she read on, interested in Bukowski's list of things that led to insanity. Car troubles, dental problems, a fifty-cent avocado. (*How quaint,* she thought.) These were, for the most part, the very things she had dreaded in her twenties and thirties. Car repairs, dental work—never adequately covered, no matter how good the health care plan. Add to the list Bulgarian wine, which she and her first husband had started drinking because it cost only five dollars a bottle; stealing toilet paper from the Burger King, which she had done several times while trying to survive as an assistant in publishing; chipping the new pedicure you couldn't actually afford or justify. Of course, Bukowski had his political litany, too, but she didn't really see world events driving anyone crazy. Not directly.

Which was the problem, she supposed. The burnt-out lightbulb in the hall might send you into screaming fits at the end of a long, frustrating day, but would your concern over global warming lead you to consider replacing it with a fluorescent bulb? She hated the coinage 'blank nation', but if she were to permit herself such a title, she would rant about how resigned people seemed, inured to their own powerlessness. Inert nation. Nowadays, your shoelace snapped, so you sat down at your computer and read about the latest insane

93

starlet, then zipped over to Zappos and ordered new shoes, because who had time to find *shoelaces.*

She clicked back to Google's rectangular robot mouth, always ready to be filled. So what if it was Saturday morning? She was in Baltimore, she had nothing to do and nowhere to go. She could work, after all, make the lie true. She started with *Leticia Barr.* Nothing. She tried *Tisha,* but that came up empty, too. *Donna Howard.* Too much came up; the name was shared by a Texas state representative and a psychic. Fatima, larger-than-life Fatima. Certainly she had made a mark on the world. Again, nothing. Had they all married, taken their husbands' names? Many women did, even good feminists, especially once there were children. Cassandra realized she knew one name that would kick back results: Reginald 'Candy' Barr, although without the nickname. Immediately, she had the official page for his law firm, Howard, Howard & Barr.

Wow—he was gorgeous. That hadn't been apparent in the newspaper photo. Perhaps this one had been sweetened in some way? Photoshop covered a multitude of sins, as her own author photo would attest.

She started to hit the contact button, but—no. E-mail was too businesslike. The form would be shunted off to some administrative assistant, and its very existence would indicate that she wanted something, would cement her status as a supplicant. Phone? Who would be in the office on a Saturday? She checked the address, a downtown tower with multiple offices, a place where a chance encounter would be credible. Yes, that's how she would begin.

Would he recognize her? People often did, claiming her face was remarkably like the one they remembered from ten, twenty, thirty, even forty years ago. Cassandra was never sure how to feel about that, if it was a compliment or a lie or an insult. A face *should* change over the years, and she thought hers somewhat improved from her childhood days of chipmunk roundness. More important—was it plausible that she would recognize him, was there any trace of the little Candy Barr she had known? Yes, the dimples still glinted, even in this professional portrait meant to convey seriousness, accomplishment, I-will-get-you-what-you-deserve.

Her plan was plausible, just. The only downside was that she would have to wait until Monday. Sighing, she checked the schedule for the movie theater in the neighborhood, wondered if there was something ambitious to cook, wished she had someone for whom to cook. If the fraying—snapping—of a shoelace led to the madhouse, what was the destination for those who never had to worry about shoelaces and fifty-cent avocados? Here, nine floors above a city that had once been her home, Cassandra felt wrapped in cotton, too far removed from everyday concerns. The gym could keep her body hard, but what would keep her *spirit* tough? She knew how she didn't want to define her life—through a man, or even by her work—but had no idea what else could define a person. She would never yearn to be twenty-three again, broke and scraping by. But she missed the adventure of unearthing Bulgarian wine from the bargain bins at the local liquor store, laughing

95

at its label, its price. Laughing at herself, a skill that was at risk of atrophying.

Chapter Nine

Unlike their counterparts in New York, most Baltimore buildings do not deny the existence of the thirteenth story. Gloria had always liked that lack of superstition in her hometown, its refusal to pretend that leaving a number off an elevator panel could make the number disappear. Calling the thirteenth floor the fourteenth doesn't accomplish anything—except for making a lie of every level from thirteen on.

Still, it was simple serendipity that had landed her on the thirteenth floor of the thirteen-story Highfield House. For years she had stalked the building, a Mies van der Rohe from the early 1960s, waiting for the right apartment to open up, then waiting another year while it was gutted and updated by a local architect. The building had little in common with its neighbors, redbrick high-rises that aspired to a more obvious grandeur. Made of glass and white bricks, rising on stilts, it sought to complement the landscape. Gloria had attempted to re-create the same feeling in her apartment, in order to showcase her collection of abstract art and mid-twentieth-century furniture. If Gloria ever entertained, her guests would have been amazed by the immaculate, modern apartment, so at odds with its owner's personal appearance.

But Gloria never entertained. She was

proprietary about her home, wanted it just for herself.

Today, she had awakened to the anemic winter light, allowing herself the Saturday luxury of easing slowly into the day. A pot of coffee, toasted cheese bread from Eddie's, the comforting tones of NPR's Scott Simon rumbling in the background. She didn't necessarily hear what he said, but she liked his voice, felt soothed by it. There was a page-one article on her Eagle Scout, Buddy Harrington, and Gloria was savvy enough about the press to realize this meant the *Beacon-Light* considered the story too weak to front the Sunday paper. It was what newspaper types called a thumb-sucker—it didn't have any real news. Instead, the reporter had placed the murders within a national context, using statistics to demonstrate how rare it was for children to kill their parents. Ah well, that should make everyone feel better, sitting down to Saturday breakfast with their families. Statistically, patricide and matricide were rare. Let's go to the mall and buy some stuff in celebration, then stop at McDonald's on the way home.

But what were children's odds of being killed by their parents? Much better. Gloria had been researching those cases in the event she had to defend her Eagle Scout à la Menendez. Parents were more likely to kill children than the other way around, although there were admittedly few cases of them turning on their teenagers. No, it was young children who died at their parents' hands. And when a child under a year old was murdered, the killer was almost always a mother, and the mother was almost certainly poor and probably

97

mentally ill.

Like Calliope Jenkins. Who, Gloria would be quick to remind a reporter—not that she ever spoke of Callie to anyone, much less reporters—officially was not a murderer. Nor was she officially insane. She had sat in jail for seven years, as much time as she might have been given for homicide, if not more, but she could not be called a murderer.

Gloria had been an associate at Howard & Howard when the case was brought to the firm. Pro bono, which the Howards did occasionally. But homicide wasn't the sort of thing that Andre Howard did and his brother, Julius, still thought he might be mayor or governor someday, although no one else did. So they had thrown this pro bono bone to a hungry associate.

And Gloria, ambitious late bloomer that she was, had been silly enough to think she was being rewarded, or at the very least tested.

She was already in her thirties, coming to the law after losing most of her twenties to Baltimore's public school system. She had been a high school English teacher, and even that had seemed an amazing achievement for the illegitimate daughter of a janitress. Baltimore gossip had long held that Gloria's father was a former mayor or city councilman, but that legend had been created in hindsight, an origin myth that sought to explain what had formed this tough-minded attorney. Gloria had no idea who her father was, but she knew this much: Her success as a lawyer wasn't in her blood, it wasn't something she was born to. It was something she had willed when she realized how much others doubted her.

She still remembered the first time she met Calliope. She hadn't been locked up, not yet, and although she had been stupid enough to agree to a police interview without a lawyer, she hadn't been stupid enough to say anything. As Gloria understood it, the police had requested a warrant to search her home, and the judge who had signed the warrant had apparently tipped off someone who brought the case to the Howard brothers. Gloria had accepted the assignment happily. Billing at the rate allowed pro bono cases, she would no longer be one of the top earners among associates, but this was clearly important to the Howards. Could she possibly be on the partner track? No white woman had made partner at the firm in those days; it was hard enough for white men.

She drove to the rowhouse on Lemmon Street, arriving long after the police had departed. Calliope's eyes had raked over her—not quite suspicious, but certainly not trusting. It was an unsettling gaze. Crazy? Possibly. Gloria always sensed that Calliope at once saw more and less than what was in front of her.

'I have nothing to say,' she said.

'I'm your lawyer,' Gloria said. 'I'm from Howard & Howard, and my firm will be representing you pro bono. Without cost.'

'I *know,*' Calliope said with a twisted smile, but it was unclear to Gloria if she knew the definition of *pro bono* or if she simply assumed her lawyer would be provided for free.

'As your lawyer, I want you to understand all the options in front of you. You have invoked the constitutional protection against self-incrimination'

99

—why was she being so wordy, so grandiose? There was something unnerving about Calliope Jenkins. Not necessarily evil, like the Eagle Scout she was representing, but some quality that made Gloria eager, almost desperate to please, impress. 'And that is a legitimate right. But a judge may hold you in contempt for this and could put you in jail to force you to reveal the whereabouts of your child. So if you can produce your son and demonstrate that he is safe, you should consider that option.'

'The courts took my first son away.' Calliope's words were flat and enervated. 'They would take Donntay away, too.'

'That's a reasonable fear,' Gloria said, trying not to show that the mention of the first child caught her off guard. She had known only that this child, the one reported missing by social services, had been monitored by the system since birth. Calliope had lost a previous child? Gloria wondered if they would be able to keep that quiet. But, no, DSS would leak it, through some back channel. Or would they? Their fat was in the fire, no doubt, for allowing a neglectful mother to go three months without a check. While the law was clear that previous instances of abuse and neglect could not be used to remove children preemptively, the public would be screaming for blood up the chain of command.

'I do not have to talk.' A mantra, a litany, parroted to remind herself, not to challenge Gloria.

'No, you don't. No one can make you speak. But, again, a judge will not take your silence lightly. The judge—the judge will be your son's representative, in a sense. And he will do whatever he thinks is in the best interest of your son—'

'My son.' Calliope's face crumpled; her voice was a low moan. She looked as if she had gone days without sleeping or eating. She definitely had not bathed. Calliope was rank. She smelled moldy, possibly piss soaked. Later, she would swear she wasn't a drug addict, but Gloria never quite believed that. She cleaned up, though. Seven years in jail, how could she not?

'If you can produce your son, if you can demonstrate that he is well'—being careful with her words, making sure to skirt anything that would invite a confession. Although it had not been made explicit, it was Gloria's sense that the case was only interesting to Howard & Howard on constitutional grounds. Andre Howard wanted her to press forward on this front, make the firm look good. 'If he is well, then you should prove it.'

'Well, well, well,' Calliope said. She seemed unhinged. How had she withstood five hours of interrogation without revealing anything? 'No, I will not *produce* him. I want to in—to in—'

'Invoke. But don't worry about the words. You can simply say you do not wish to speak. I'll be there with you, to explain the legal part. There will be a hearing. You may be put in jail at the end of that hearing, but I will be there with you.'

'You'll stand with me?' Hopeful, amazed.

'Yes.'

'For however long this takes?'

'For however long it takes.' She had never been more sincere. Or, as it turned out, more wrong. Calliope Jenkins was locked up for seven years, and Gloria served as her lawyer for only five of those seven years, leaving the firm of Howard & Howard to start her own practice, leaving Calliope to Reggie Barr, at one point Gloria's best friend in the firm, her confidant—and her rival for partnership. She betrayed Calliope, and the worst part was that Calliope wasn't angry or even surprised. Betrayal was the natural order of things in Calliope's world.

The only consolation was that Calliope turned out to be one of the few women on the planet who was cold to Reg's charm. 'I don't like his cologne,' she said to Gloria, who pressed to know why she was unhappy about her new attorney. 'Too sweet.'

Too sweet. Those were among the last words Gloria ever heard from Calliope Jenkins. *Too sweet*. In the years since then, Gloria had been reamed out by clients, accused of horrible things, asked to do horrible things, even been slapped on one memorable occasion. But nothing had hurt as much as Calliope Jenkins's emotionless resignation, her indifference to Gloria's broken promise. In the end, Calliope was being considerate of Gloria's feelings, trying to assure her that her new lawyer was fine. Except for his cologne.

A plane cut through the pale morning sky, southbound for the airport, a sight that always lifted her heart. Gloria, who traveled only for pleasure—and always in first or business class—could not imagine being unhappy on a plane. All trips were joyous, in her mind, and everyone on a jet was bound for a fabulous place or person. Yet Gloria, who had lived in Highfield House since the mid-nineties, had never noticed that the eastern sky was part of the local flight plan until the planes disappeared, for more than a week, in the wake of 9/11. Suddenly, the sky was empty and it took a while to register what was gone, what had changed. It was chilling, realizing that something could achieve presence only through absence.

In the year that Donntay Jenkins disappeared, the Department of Social Services in Maryland opened hundreds of investigations into complaints of possible abuse or neglect. But Donntay Jenkins, the child that no one ever saw—a child for whom there was not a single photographic likeness other than the hospital snapshot of him at birth, squinty, hairy, Martian-like—became the one child everyone cared about. Until the next child came along. A girl who had been starved to death, a toddler who had been fed methadone. Then another, and another. It happened every two years or so, and each new case replaced the old one in the public's mind, forcing the previous children down a notch. Until the New Orleans case had invoked his name, no one had thought about Donntay Jenkins for years. It turned out that even Donntay's alleged condition at birth, his status as a so-called crack baby, was a crock, a media invention. There were moments when Gloria almost doubted that Donntay had ever existed, wondered if all her efforts had been on behalf of some phantom child whose only life had been in the confused, cluttered mind of Calliope Jenkins.

Then she would hear that mournful wail again: 'My son . . . my son.' Whatever Calliope might be—junkie, crazy lady, cold-blooded killer—she had definitely been a mother. But everything else about her remained a mystery, thanks to the legal advice provided by one of the city's best law firms.

Chapter Ten

Although she was not forbidden to return to Baltimore—although, in fact, nothing about her arrangement had ever been spelled out—she knew it was expected that she would stay away, that she would never venture farther west than, say, the outlet shops on Route 50. They would probably prefer that she not enter Maryland at all but understood that she had to visit her mother, now in a nursing home in Denton. Certainly, she was not to cross the Bay Bridge under any circumstances. Why should she? Her mother was all the family she had. *All the family she had.* And whose fault was that? Hers, of course.

No, only a fool would risk venturing back into Baltimore. But then the others were fools if they didn't understand that she was exactly that, a fool, and she couldn't stop being one just because that would make it *nicer* for everyone else.

If only—but, no, she must not let her thoughts go all the way there, even as her car was hurtling toward a destination she should avoid. She understood now how fragile her mind was. In the absence of anyone else's love or care, she had learned to be solicitous of herself. She simply could not think about certain things or she might break down again, the way she had after her first son was born. She didn't want to go back to a hospital, even for a day. Yes, she knew that ideas had changed, that if she experienced another episode similar to those spells she had in her twenties, they would be more likely to try pills instead of talking so much and giving her those intelligence tests. Maybe, she thought fleetingly from time to time, pills could actually fix her. But to what purpose, what gain? And to what loss?

Growing up as she had, Callie knew there was always a catch. From the time she was three or four, her mother had walked her through their neighborhood, pointing out the junkies and the winos who were bringing the area down. 'They think they're happy,' she hissed at her daughter, yanking her arm, 'but they *smell*.' Odor was terrible, then, odor was the giveaway. Odor was the only thing that separated Callie and her mother from poor people. Don't ever smell, of anything. 'Is Myra Tippet going to have to show you how to clean?' her mother would say if Callie carried the smallest whiff of anything. Proper as Myra was, it had never occurred to her to claim the surname of Callie's father, to pretend that they had been married. Callie didn't mind that they had different names. It helped sometimes to think of her mother as 'Myra Tippet', as someone other than her mother. It was Myra Tippet, not her mother, who had scrubbed Callie raw every night, sniffed at her armpits when she turned twelve, later claimed that she could smell Callie's menstrual blood, and maybe she could. It was Myra Tippet who believed that appearances were all.

We do not need anything or anyone, Myra told Callie, beginning with your father. *What about his family?* Callie would have liked at least one grandparent, maybe an aunt, and Myra had no family. Ditto, Myra said. *Ditto* made Callie think of ditto sheets, the old mimeographs coming off

105

purple in her hand, the overwhelming smell. Confronted with that fragrance, she had been terrified to do her work, back at old school 88, lest she came home smelling and her mother took after her. Yet she would be just as angry if Callie got bad grades. Callie could never anticipate what might set her mother off. 'Does Myra Tippet have to teach a girl a lesson?' she would begin. As if Callie were forcing her, as if Myra had no desire in the world to hurt her daughter, but her daughter had forced her hand. Any grade less than a B? Stand in the corner for an hour. Left the milk out? Then you will drink it, spoiled though it may be. Too close to the stove? Then get closer, let me hold your hand to it, find out just how hot that hot can be, until the flesh made actual contact with the flame. *Does Myra Tippet have to teach a girl a lesson?*

It was strange to see her now, shriveled and needy, dependent on Callie in more ways than she would ever know or admit. Complaints were her only power. Just two days ago, listening to her mother's usual grievances, Callie had felt the tug of the west, the call of the bridge, and thought about continuing to Baltimore when she left the nursing home. After all, she had crossed the line into Maryland, if only by a bit. Why not keep going? She had managed to shout the voice down that afternoon. Now here she was at 4 A.M. on a Sunday, doing eighty above the Chesapeake Bay.

What had prompted this trip? Trouble sleeping, for one. Perhaps the way her name had surfaced in the news for a moment there last month, only to subside again. It was hard to see how quickly her image came and went, to be reminded that she was

106

a person of *no consequence,* as she had been repeatedly informed at the time, forever a footnote, capable of dragging others down but inadequate to the task of raising herself up. *Bad girl, sly girl, stupid girl.* The last, at least, was undeniably true.

But the trip also could have been motivated by nothing more than the hint of winter's end. Whenever the seasons changed, she felt a surge of restlessness. It was amazing to her how a journey of only eighty miles could carry her twenty, thirty years into the past. Once there, she never called anyone. There was no one to call. She was careful not to be seen, although she usually managed to see him from afar. His pull over her should have lessened with each passing year, but it didn't work that way. Every time she saw him, she wanted him anew.

But she had made a bargain, vague though some of the terms may have been. She had her little house, her little car, her little life. Her mother was cared for. All that could end if she angered the wrong people. Still, every now and then, she had to get in the little car and leave the little house. The little life? That went with her wherever she was.

It was comforting, in a way, to see that he had aged, too, although it did not dim his appeal. Still, it made her feel better about how unkind age had been to her. That was the cost of those seven years in jail. She had been sapped, tapped, trying to stay strong. The mind had fed off the body. When she came out of that jail, she was prematurely old at the age of thirty-six. Body thin, yet soft. Face hard, yet slack. Over on the Shore, in the pronounced salt air, one saw raggedy hoopties, lacy with rust,

107

engines running strong. That was her.

But, boy, she had been good looking once, the kind of good looking that comes out of nowhere at eighteen or nineteen, after the ugliest of teens— Brillo-pad hair, skinny and flat chested, growing up but not out, gangly as a preying mantis. Her sudden transformation made her bold. Too bold, some might say. She flew too high, she forgot where she came from, she believed all those pretty words. *Opportunity, future. Dreams.* When she fell, she crashed hard.

She still remembered the day the first social worker had come to her door, when Rennay was a baby. To the extent that she could think at the time, she had assumed they were trying to bust her for having a man on the premises. Welfare workers back then, they were always looking for evidence of a man—a pair of shoes, a shaving kit. She knew the drill from her mother, who had been investigated from time to time, ratted out by neighbors who believed she must have had extra income to live as she did. But Myra's extra money came from off-the-books cleaning jobs, not men.

'There's no man here,' Calliope told the social worker with a ragged laugh. 'That's the problem. No man's been here, no man's ever going to be here. I'm alone, this baby won't stop crying, and I'm going crazy.' She meant crazy in the everyday way, but they held that against her later.

Was she crazy? She honestly didn't realize that there were so many dirty dishes in the sink, couldn't smell the stink of the diaper, couldn't smell her own sour body odor. Still, she was caring for Rennay, best she could. To this day, she didn't believe that a roach walked out of her son's ear.

That was a lie. Perhaps it had been in the crib and come from behind his head, which wasn't good, she knew that much, but that was the landlord's fault, the bugs in the building. And, okay, she had not taken the trash out for days, and there was food sitting out. *But there were not roaches in her baby's ear.* That would probably kill a child. Yes, it had been days since she had eaten and, true, she probably appeared to be high as a kite, although she wasn't using then, just sick with grief. But Rennay was okay; she would never hurt him, even in her anguish and confusion.

And there were no roaches in her baby boy's ear.

Then and now, she could not help returning to that one fact, over and over. The public defender kept trying to tell her it didn't matter. 'Please focus, Callie. They want to terminate your parental rights. This is the least of your problems.' The lawyer wasn't much older than Callie and was, to use a favorite saying of Myra Tippet's, dumb as a box of rocks. Later, the second time, it was this memory that made Callie accept the private counsel, thinking she would be better served. She wondered about that choice. She wondered about all her choices. There were those who would say that she had done pretty well for herself. Her mother, for example, thought Callie had struck a brilliant bargain. Not that she would ever say as much, but the truth was there under all her criticisms. Complaining was a privilege of sorts. For years, Myra Tippet had no one but her daughter to complain to; now she had an entire staff to listen to her grievances. It was heaven to her, complaining about the detergent used to wash her sheets, the dryness of the cake at lunch, the lack of premium television stations on her little set. She was in paradise with so much blame to spread around.

Callie arrived in the city in darkness, with only an edge of light at the eastern sky. She felt as if she were racing the sun as she headed toward his neighborhood, racing time itself, years falling away with every block. She liked that he had never moved, and not just because that made him easier to find. She bet his wife nagged him to death over that decision.

It was tricky, spying on him without being seen. And it was a Sunday, too, a less-than-predictable day when it came to people's habits. But he was up early, as usual, and within an hour of her arrival, he came out for the paper. Oh so proper, in his robe and slippers, a real-life Dr Huxtable. Even scrunched down in her driver's seat, she could catalogue everything that was wrong or mockable in him. Years ago, she would list all his faults as she fell asleep, as if to cast a magic spell that would keep her from falling in love with him, but it hadn't worked then and it didn't work now. She noticed that the house itself looked a little worse for wear in the winter light. He was ridiculous, he was horrible, he had betrayed her, he was a monster.

She loved him.

She turned the key in the ignition a moment too soon and he seemed to start at the sound of the car engine on the quiet street. But he did not turn around, nor did he look back. He did not see her. Sometimes, she wondered if he had ever seen her, even as he described her to herself. Her eyes, her mouth, her skin, her body. He had sung her praises in great detail, as if she were blind, as if she had never glanced in a mirror. Back then, when cell phones seemed like something in a futuristic movie, such secret conversations were trickier, more fraught with discovery. He would call her from pay phones around town, or—more thrilling—from his office or an extension in his own home, rushing to squeeze in all the words, all the tributes, arguing his case for her. Back then, the mere sight of a phone could make her heart jump. Eventually, when people told her to move on, to find someone else, it was the memory of the *before* time, all those words, that made it impossible. There were two versions of him, and only she got to decide which one was true, authentic. She believed the man who said he loved her, not the one who betrayed her.

She sighed, wishing she had someplace else to visit, some other memory to poke and prod. Her hometown was a blank to her, a sketched-in background, as plain as a child's drawing. A stripe of green for grass, some scrawled blue strokes for sky, a yellow circle of a sun. Back in grade school, when all the girls had a passion for drawing, it was the people in those pictures on which she had lavished her attention, those fantasy families of four, so different from her sad little unit of two. A mommy, a daddy, a boy, and a girl. She spent the most time on the females, drawing their dresses and jewelry and hair in great detail, giving them purses and shoes, doting on every item. The men? Their faces were blank, empty circles above crude blue suits and red ties. It was like trying to draw God.

Thin Ice

My mother taught me how to skate. Nervous in so many things, she was the only mother in our neighborhood who didn't fret about the safety of skating on the pond above the dam. She also insisted that I learn on proper blades, not the twin, babyish ones that other children were permitted. Occasionally, she would break away from me, execute a dazzling spin, even a jump, but she spent most of her time instructing me. I realize now how selfless she was, putting aside her own fun, taking my mittened hands in her gloved ones and matching her movements to mine, hobbling herself. My father, hatless and gloveless like a teenage boy, watched from a broken ledge of concrete, calling out encouragement.

He was all of thirty-seven, younger than I am now as I write this. Of course, parents always seem ancient, finished, to their children, but my parents loomed larger still in my mind. I thought of them as Zeus and Hera and learned only years later that this was *too* apt. Like Zeus, my father tortured his wife with his infidelity. If only my mother could have summoned Hera's wrath, fought him tit for tat. Then again, it was always Zeus's conquests who were punished by Hera; he got away scot-free.

Yet for all my father's extravagant claims for his second marriage, it could not have occurred if he had not already fallen out of love with my mother several years earlier. How did *that* happen? With one failed marriage behind me, I need to understand this, or I'll end up having *two* failed

112

marriages behind me. When I consider Lenore Fallows as a woman, not my mother, I see how . . . *fetching* she was. No, not beautiful. Her face was round, her brows heavy. Her figure was always a little lumpy, even before I had my way with it, coming into the world via an old-fashioned Caesarean that left a scar and a permanent pooch. Still, she was smart, the quality that my father claimed to value above all others. My father would forgive anything if a person was smart—but then he also expected to be forgiven everything, because he was smart.

Lenore Baker Fallows was more than intelligent, although her most amazing capacities would not be revealed until after the divorce. Why would anyone stop loving her? He said he didn't, exactly, that he always loved her, but a day came when he wasn't in love with her, a simplistic bit of rhetoric that he would have red-lined in a student paper, damning it for the cliché that it is.

I may spend the rest of my life trying to come to terms with how and why my father stopped loving my mother. But I can pinpoint *when.* I mark the moment as the day he stopped calling her Lenore in favor of the more gender-ambiguous Lennie that everyone else used. My father had always despised the nickname, for both its casualness and masculinity. 'If you're Lennie, I suppose I'm George,' he would say. 'Do you want me to tell you about the rabbits, Lennie?' My mother laughed, delighted that my father believed she deserved her full, feminine name.

Then one day, seemingly out of the blue, he didn't.

'Lennie,' he said to my mother over the breakfast

table, 'did you see this piece in the *New York Review of Books*?' My mother, harried, as mothers often are in the morning, dropped my jellied toast on the floor. She cleaned it up and started breakfast again, eye on the clock. I was in first grade, still taking the bus to Thomas Jefferson, and she had to hustle me down the hill and wait with me at the bus stop, then head off to her teaching job at the Gordon School.

'No,' she said. 'I haven't had time.'

Even an oblivious six-year-old, pretending to read *Mr Tweedy* on the comics page, could catch the danger in my mother's voice. But my father either didn't, or didn't care.

'Don't let your mind go, Lennie, whatever else you might neglect.' Hitting the name hard, making sure she heard it.

The air in the kitchen turned dry and quiet, the lull that comes before a particularly severe thunderstorm, the kind of storm that sweeps across a city even as the sun continues to shine. (Here, too, I can imagine my father writing— cliché, cliché, cliché. *Don't be lazy, Cassandra. A storm to describe a marital spat? You can do better.* He actually did re-grade all my papers, often knocking the school's As down to Bs or even Cs.)

My mother stopped, considering her reply.

'Fuck the *New York Review of Books*,' she said. 'I don't have time for that bullshit.'

I could tell from my father's reaction that my mother's words stunned him. These were words that could rend the universe, a warning shot across his bow. (*Don't mix your metaphors, Cassandra,* he would write here.)

'Joan Didion—' he began, as if my mother had

not spoken.

'Fuck Joan Didion,' my mother said. 'And her little dog, too.'

Finally, something I understood. My mind dredged up the terrifying image of striped socks beneath the house in *The Wizard of Oz,* the way they curled and disappeared like cheap firecrackers.

It is only now, writing this, that I understand what happened in the kitchen the day that my father stopped calling my mother 'Lenore'. He was saying, *I see you as others see you now. Smart, yes. Capable, always. A good mother. Even a good companion. But I can't be romantic about you anymore, fixer of jelly toast, cleaner of kitchen floors. You are no longer sexual to me.*

My mother replied, *I see you, too. I see that you're rationalizing your infidelity, that you have slipped or are about to slip, and you need an excuse, flimsy as it is. You're probably sleeping with a woman who reads the* New York Review of Books, *but I don't have time to do that anymore because I am working, taking care of a child and this monstrosity of a house, this house that you wanted and insisted on, although it needs so much work and is so remote that I am virtually alone when I come home. Even when you're here, I'm alone.*

THE BRIER PATCH

March 3–5

Chapter Eleven

There was a coffee shop, an old-fashioned relic, in the otherwise glossy lobby of the building where Howard, Howard & Barr was housed. Cassandra nursed a scorched-tasting coffee at a table that afforded a view of the street and the lobby. She had a newspaper in front of her, but she wasn't really looking at it, just using it as a prop. She felt at once silly and adventurous, somewhere in between Nancy Drew and Mata Hari. Generally, she considered herself a forthright, honest person, not counting her occasional forays into infidelity, most of which had been retaliatory acts.

She had cheated on her second husband only because he cheated on her. Although she had seen her second marriage as a prime example of Hegelian synthesis, it ultimately made her see that her first marriage, for all its problems, was the one she should have fought to save. God, she and her first husband had been like children, throwing sand in each other's eyes. But they had loved each other as best they could. With the wisdom of hindsight, Cassandra had decided that getting married at twenty-two was going to be one of those things that turned out well or ended in disaster, no in-between. It was like running a marathon: You either finish, an achievement in itself no matter the pace, or you drop dead along the way. They had pulled up lame before the thirteen-mile mark.

Her second marriage? She could not think of a racing metaphor for that, unless it was an old-fashioned three-legged race, in which she and her husband were yoked to the people they really loved but couldn't be with. They hadn't even made much of a pretense, just kept testing each other to see who would get sick of whom first. The second time, it had been her turn to walk out, and she had discovered that it wasn't any more fun than being left. Had found, in fact, that the end of even the most beastly marriage was still more painful than anyone could guess.

Ah well, she could do *this*. She had been in public enough over the past decade to develop the social liar's smooth façade. It was more a defensive position than anything else; a certain amount of skilled feinting became essential once people decided that you had something they needed. She had learned quickly how to bob and weave—gracefully, she hoped—deflecting not only the endless requests for money and time, but also the more intrusive demands for friendship. She had made a point of writing about her life with as much candor as possible, and people thought they knew her.

They did—and they didn't. The life on display in her two memoirs had been presented through a scrim. A mainly transparent scrim, but a scrim nonetheless. She was truthful, but there was much she didn't reveal. Example: She would never write about her current lover, even if she could successfully shield his identity. Her readers forgave the mistakes from which she had *learned,* the errors of youth and even middle age. She had been forty when she made that absolute botch of a second marriage, but that had been a lesson in humility, the affairs a way of admitting that to herself. Her readers would not approve of

Bernard. Cassandra really didn't approve of Bernard. She would have to figure out a way to let him go with his pride intact, to make him feel it was his idea. After all, he thought the affair was his idea, and Cassandra had orchestrated the whole thing.

Still, was she disingenuous enough to pull off this fake coincidental encounter with Reggie Barr? If she nudged the conversation toward Calliope too quickly, wouldn't he suspect something was up? *So what?* she decided. He was a lawyer. He had his own tricks. He might be charmed by the sheer transparency of her actions.

Assuming he ever showed up. As her coffee cooled, she was beginning to feel ridiculous. Not to mention overheated and, by Baltimore's standards, overdressed in her fur coat, fake of course, and *Dr Zhivago*-style hat. Still, she looked pretty, and—she hoped—not just pretty-for-her-age. She wondered why she was thinking about her looks. Reginald Barr was still just Tisha's little brother, Candy, lurking at the edges, trying to crash the party, doing his silly dance.

And coming off the elevator, striding out in the bright, cold day, full of purpose.

She gathered her things and slid out the street entrance of the coffee shop, hoping—almost praying, in fact—that Candy would turn east, not west, as that would put them on a more credible collision course. He did. She caught his eye, and for one fleeting second, her resolve wavered. *What was she doing?* This was not how she worked. She was used to being alone, in a room, debating her own memory. But this hesitation, this falter, only made it more credible when she said, 'Candy Barr?

121

I'd know you anywhere.'

'I'm sorry,' he said, smiling. It was a public smile, warm yet generic. She had one, too.

'There's no reason you would remember me. I'm Cassandra Fallows. I went to school with your older sister, back in the day.'

'At Western High?'

'Yes.' No need to complicate things by admitting she was at Western only a year. 'But also at Dickey Hill Elementary, old number two oh one. Tisha and I started there in the third grade together, the year it opened. You would have been in the first grade that year, right?'

The mention of Dickey Hill did the trick. 'It's hard to believe,' he said with a much more genuine smile, 'that you were in school with my *older* sister.' The charm was automatic, effortless. 'But—yes, of course. The writer. I remember when your book came out, Tisha talking about it.'

She willed herself not to correct the singular, *book*. It was a common mistake. It happened to her friends with five, ten, fifteen books to their credit. Even they were asked about The Book, as if there were only one. How's The Book? What's going on with The Book? It was a social nicety, a slightly more specific version of *How are you*. We are what we do, so we ask mothers about The Kids and fathers about The Job or The Office, and writers are asked about The Book. But Cassandra found it particularly grating, this suggestion that she had written only one. Because, in a sense, she had.

'She's in there. But you are, too. At the graduation party. You danced for us. Remember? You had a special dance, very silly, that you would do to get attention.'

'Not to mention cake.' To her amazement and delight, Reggie 'Candy' Barr briefly slithered from side to side, his arms moving spastically. Cassandra burst out laughing. She couldn't help herself. The childish dance was even more incongruous when performed by a handsome man in a camel's hair coat, a briefcase in his hand.

'I'm running late,' he said, 'but I'll tell Tisha I saw you, that you want her to get in touch. Do you have a card?'

She had it at the ready. The meeting had gone eerily according to her plan, almost as if he were privy to her internal script. A chance encounter that he would never doubt, him offering to put her in touch with Tisha, the request for her card, getting his card in return.

What happened next, however, wasn't part of the plan.

'I'm in town for a few months, working on my next project.' She was taking time getting her card, letting him note the lushness of the things she carried—the Prada bag, the Chanel wallet, the leather gloves she had to remove to extract the simple but beautiful card she carried in a silver case, the heavy ring on her right hand, and the lack of any rings on the left. 'My cell is on the card, but let me write down my local phone, too.' She glanced at him through her lashes, the low-hanging fur of her hat. 'And why don't you take one, too? There's no law that says I can't have dinner with an old friend's little brother, is there? The fact is, you might be able to help me with what I'm working on.'

He took her card with his right hand, shifted it to

his left, watched her note his wedding ring, then meet his eyes. 'Really? A book, and I could help you? I'd be interested in hearing more about *that.*'

'Well, I hope I get a chance,' she said. 'Meanwhile, you tell Tisha to call me, hear? I really want to catch up with her.'

She strode away, cheeks burning. She should not have said the part about his ability to help her with a project. That had almost certainly tipped her hand. The idea had been to get him to offer up Tisha, then have Tisha disclose her brother's old connection to Calliope when Cassandra played whatever-happened-to with all their classmates. He would see through her, if he hadn't already. Why had she undermined herself this way?

Because when Candy Barr had danced for her on Baltimore Street, she had felt that solar plexus hit of chemistry, the kind of desire that she had assumed was over for her. Not out of any biological or chronological imperative, but simply because she knew too much now about how the brain worked. Head-over-heels love was for people who didn't know any better. Bernard—Bernard was simply another thing she did to keep herself youthful, not that much different from the spa or the gym, although she visited those places much more often than she saw her lover. But Bernard knew only her current self, not her history. Reggie Barr understood where she was from, in every sense, and there was something about knowing the little boy inside that handsome man that hit her *hard.*

Was he married? Yes, there had been a ring. Men like that were almost always married. It would be better if he were married, less

124

complicated. Better for The Book.

*   *   *

Reginald Barr walked east, toward the courthouse. The business card, tucked in his briefcase, seemed to beep every minute, like a smoke alarm alerting one to a dying battery. Only this was a warning that something was coming to life. He wasn't fooled by Cassandra's acting, such as it was. She had set up that little run-in. Why? True, Tisha lived and worked under her married name, which made her tricky to find. But if all Cassandra wanted was Tisha, why not call his office and explain the situation to a secretary? Had she set up that elaborate ruse to meet him? She wouldn't be the first woman to do that.

Reg, as he preferred to be known now, was vain and aware of this fact, although he considered his an earned vanity. Women approached him all the time. He was a good husband and a respectful one, which to his mind meant that the ruthless compartmentalization of his occasional affairs was done with great consideration for his wife, whom he adored beyond all reason. By the rules of that system, written and designed by him, no one could be more off-limits than a friend of his sister's. Because if she knew Tisha, she also knew Donna, his wife. Donna had read that book, too, although she had been bemused where Tisha had been pissed. He remembered the two of them drinking wine in the kitchen, Tisha's voice rising with agitation about errors and omissions, Donna saying it didn't matter, it would never matter. An old classmate of Tisha and Donna's. Forbidden

125

with a capital *F.*

The fact that she was white—worse still. And older. Who wanted older? He had a fifty-year-old wife at home, one who had kept herself up just as well as Cassandra Fallows, better actually, and he bought Donna things every bit as expensive as the ones that Cassandra had just flaunted in front of him. He had that. He didn't need to go looking for it.

Yet the fact that she could buy herself those things, the confidence that came with age—now that was interesting to him, novel. The young women whose companionship he sought out on occasion, they were not fully formed. They attached too much importance to sleeping with Reginald Barr and when it ended, they could be a little . . . volatile. Still, he had managed his affairs to date without too much fuss. He chose women of honor and when they threatened to squawk—to call his wife or the papers, not that the *Beacon-Light* would care about a private citizen's life, and he had no political aspirations—he reminded them that he had been honest from the first. He never promised love, only fun. Then he bought them something magnificent. A woman such as Cassandra Fallows was clearly more worldly, more relaxed. She wouldn't even begin to think she could snake him away from his wife. But she also wouldn't be susceptible to gifts when the end came.

What did she really want? Tisha, yes, but then she had mentioned he might be of help to her on a project. Bullshit? It was as good a line as any to get to someone you wanted to flirt with. He knew, he had used it himself. No, in this case, it seemed to

126

be a blurted truth, something that she didn't mean to say, the kind of thing on which he pounced in a deposition or interview. What did she do exactly? He thought she wrote books about her life, not that he had read them. Reg used his recreational reading for *real* history, not the narrow stories of individuals. Her notorious father, then something else? He remembered Tisha's central complaint: 'Cassandra thought everything was about her. She's incapable of telling a story where she's not at the center.' Donna had told Tisha that meant Cassandra was human.

She must be mining the past again, looking for another nugget that could be turned into something. How many pages could one fifty-year life produce if you weren't a head of state or a general? She had done her father, she had done— her husbands, that was it, which was an extension of the daddy thing, although maybe Reg was projecting there. The whole Oedipal drama. No, that was mothers and sons. They called the father-daughter drama something else, also Greek. Electra? He was pretty sure it was Electra, but maybe not.

Another Greek name of sorts went off like a steam whistle in his brain. *Calliope.* If Cassandra had gone to school with Tisha and Donna, she also knew Callie Jenkins. He couldn't imagine why anyone would want to speak to Calliope now, even with the New Orleans case in the news. But the real story was down there, another Katrina-related tragedy, a child lost in the system for almost four years. No one cared about Callie anymore.

He stopped and pulled out his cell phone. He didn't have Gloria Bustamante's number stored, but it came back to him readily, as if his brain had saved it all these years, knowing he would need it one day. He had to bully the dim-witted secretary to get through, but when Gloria finally picked up, he said without preamble, 'What do you know about Cassandra Fallows?'

'Enough to duck her,' Gloria said.

'Easy for you. But she's an old friend of my sister's, from back in the day, and she just buttonholed me outside my office. I can't avoid her.'

'Ask your father-in-law what to do. Or his brother. They always had all the answers.'

There was something dangerous in Gloria's voice, a challenge Reg decided to ignore.

'Andre retired last year. Julius is as good as.'

'Right, I saw that in the *Daily Record*. So you're the managing partner now, and Howard & Howard is Howard, Howard and Barr. *Well* done, Reggie.'

Hard to say who hung up first, him or Gloria. Had they really been best friends once upon a time? His office spouse, as his young associates said now, a curious term to Reg's ear. Who wanted another spouse? He had noticed two of the new crop, a boy and a girl, who were always laughing together, going to lunch, and he risked teasing the girl about her romance. 'Oh, he's just my office spouse,' she said dismissively. 'I have a fiancé, and Dwayne has a live-in girlfriend.' Office spouse. So that's what he and Gloria had been to each other, all those years ago. They had made a good team— plain, overachieving Gloria, dashing, just-getting-by Reggie. *I didn't backstab you over Callie Jenkins,* he wanted to say to her. *I didn't know, either, not for the longest time, and when I did put it together, it was just guesswork, same as you, Gloria. But then, you were always smarter than me.*

Chapter Twelve

Teena and her neighbors shared walls but little else. They were either remarkably quiet people or the rowhouses—wide and generous, by Baltimore standards, with individual touches that relieved them from cookie-cutter sameness—were exceptionally well insulated. Teena seldom heard any sound, from either side. No footsteps, no music, no raised voices. Five years ago, when the Morgans, the new family, as she still thought of them, moved in to the west of her, she had thought she heard a baby crying in the night. Weeks later, when she saw the family on the front porch, posing in Easter outfits for a snapshot, she had managed a rare sociable outburst and inquired after the littlest one's whereabouts.

'Doesn't the baby get to be in the picture?' she had asked.

'What baby?' the mother had asked, perplexed. 'It's just the twins.' Indicating, with a wave, the boy-and-girl pair, who were saddled with too-too cutesy names and, on this Easter Sunday, disastrous outfits in pale blue and egg-yolk yellow. Paul and Polly? Jack and Jill? Something like that.

'I thought—never mind.' Teena didn't want to consider, much less explain, how she had come to imagine a baby crying in the night. Yet after that day, she never heard those cries again.

The Morgan household, like most households with children these days, orbited around the twins and their activities, so there was little reason for their lives to overlap with that of an older, single woman such as Teena. Occasionally there was a pity invitation, as Teena thought of it—a Fourth of July barbecue, a holiday open house. It was hard to make excuses not to attend, as she would then have to figure out a way to leave her house for the duration of the event. Instead, she forced herself to put in an hour or two, but the effort must have been visible, and the invitations stopped. She wished there was a way to tell the Morgans that she liked them, or would have liked them, under normal circumstances. She might have even been intrusive, appointing herself Auntie Teena to Paul and Polly, Jack and Jill. Whoever.

She also wished there was a way to tell them that she wasn't an alcoholic, not exactly. She could never forget the look on the mother's face—more correctly, the *lack* of a look on the mother's face—when Teena's recycling bags had ripped one summer morning. That was before her discovery of box wine and before the county began the all-in-one recycling system, with no bags, no separation required, just discreet plastic monsters to swallow all your trash. *No worries!* She had caroled to the Morgan mom. *It looks like a lot more than it is.*

Her neighbor to the east was a male version of Teena—alone, self-contained, reserved. The only difference was that Mr Salvati was in his eighties, a widower of many years. In the summer, he liked to sit on a metal glider on his back porch and listen to the Orioles on WBAL. Teena found this charming. He no doubt had a television, and he definitely had air-conditioning, as she could see the compressor humming next to his concrete parking pad. Still, he sat outside on even the most sweltering nights, preserving a tradition started, most likely, in Little Italy or Pigtown, one of those places that people used to leave. No matter how hot it was, he wore trousers and a short-sleeved dress shirt over an undershirt, his snowy hair topped by a little straw hat. Teena had always heard—and seen, with her own father—that men were not as well equipped for widowhood as women, that they quickly followed their wives into the grave. But Mr Salvati's home almost glowed with his self-sufficiency, from the always clean car on the parking pad to the perfect yard to the back porch with vinyl covers that protected the furniture and old-fashioned charcoal grill. In winter, weeks went by without her glimpsing or hearing him, so Teena was glad for summer, his regular vigil by the radio. During the winter months, she worried about him. Not enough to do anything, of course, but she did worry.

Luckily, she caught a glimpse of him by the garbage cans Monday evening. Mr Salvati's garbage cans were pristine, of course, gleaming silver in an alley lined with utilitarian plastic. He and Teena exchanged their usual semiverbal hellos—a raised chin and a grunt of a syllable from him, a shrugged shoulder and a smile from her. Teena was halfway up her flagstone path when he called after her.

'That gal find you?'

She turned quickly, almost twisting an ankle. 'What *gal*?'

'A lady stopped by here today, said she was

looking for you, asked where you worked. I said I figured that your friends know where you work. Think she left something in your mailbox, though.'

The day was colder than forecast and Teena's hands were killing her. She needed to get inside.

'Did she say she was my friend?'

'No, she was clever that way. She wanted me to think she was your friend, but she wouldn't lie outright about it.'

'What did she look like?'

'About your age, big fur hat. When I saw her on your front porch, I thought for a minute she could be someone you know. She didn't look like she was selling anything. But she was trying to peek in, through your fanlight. That's when I came out and asked what she needed.'

'Was she—' But there was no polite way to ask the question, not that it would bother an old-timer like Mr Salvati. 'Was she white or black?'

'Oh, white, of course.' *Of course?* But Mr Salvati probably couldn't imagine white people having black friends. The bigotry was part of the package—the proper clothes, the hat, the tidiness of his surroundings. They were all qualities instilled in another generation, and it was a generation that was not particularly generous toward people unlike themselves. If Mr Salvati had seen a black woman on Teena's porch, he would have called the police. Fur hat or no fur hat.

But why did Teena feel disappointed? Why did she want to believe, for a second, that Calliope Jenkins sneaked over to her house during the day and tried to peer through her fanlight? Could it be because she wanted to believe that the haunting wasn't just one-way, that she remained as fixed in

132

Callie's mind as she was in hers? That she, too, heard crying babies that weren't there?

'Thanks for keeping close watch, Mr Salvati. I do appreciate it.'

'It's what neighbors do,' he said, easing into his spick-and-span Buick. Watching him back his car into the narrow alley was terrifying, a process that required five to six turns of the steering wheel, the car moving a few inches back, then forward. It was nothing short of a miracle when he ended up perpendicular to where he began, ready to head east to York Road. For the first time, Teena wondered where Mr Salvati might go at six o'clock on a Monday evening, if he had friends or family somewhere in the city. Where would she go, alone and retired—God, she hoped she was retired by the time she was his age. How long would it take her to back her car into the alley?

She was so distracted by these thoughts of her future self that it was twenty minutes or so before she remembered to check the mailbox. In addition to her mail—all junk tonight—there was a stampless letter addressed to Sistina Murphy. Rendered in green ink, her first name looked especially strange and unfamiliar. No one called her Sistina; she had never even met another Sistina. It had been her mother's invention, an attempt to impress her own heritage on her daughter. Her mother had been hurt when her daughter chose to be Teena instead, varying the spelling to create that much more distance from her given name.

The envelope opened, Teena's eye went almost immediately to another name, Calliope Jenkins, in the body of the letter, and jumped again to the signature, which also began with a 'Ca.' But, no, it had been signed by Cassandra Fallows. This was the woman who had called Lenhardt. He had tried to warn Teena that she was too easy to find.

She poured herself a brimming glass of wine—Banrock Station shiraz, because on a night as cold as this, she needed red—and sat down at her dining alcove, her laptop open in front of her. She didn't use her computer for much, although she had taken to paying her bills online. Everything with her hands was a negotiation, a compromise, a game of what-hurts-more. Bill-paying, with all those pen strokes, was more painful than the series of mouse clicks she had to make, but real-life solitaire was far more manageable than the computer version. Surfing the web, reading blogs? Her hands ached just thinking about those activities. She did shop online, using her insider knowledge to find bargains. Even then, she mainlined Advil beforehand.

A Google search on Cassandra Fallows yielded too much, and Teena couldn't figure out how to narrow it. How did someone produce so much *existence*? It was like watching her own recycling bags split again, her wine bottles clattering into the alley as Mrs Morgan tried not to register any reaction. Curious, Teena typed her own name, in full, and found only a website that helped people track down high school classmates. Then she tried Fallows's name with—it hurt just to type it—Calliope Jenkins's. Nothing, a goose egg, zilch. She paired herself with Calliope Jenkins, knowing it would yield nothing, given that her name alone had offered only one hit. How had Fallows found her?

The Public Information Officer had handled all the press inquiries in the Jenkins case. Besides, the focus had been less on the murder investigation than on the fact that a murder investigation had come to pass. The media had harped on the social worker's failure and while the DSS spokeswoman was one of the most magnificent stonewallers of all time, the social worker had decided to give a television interview, against all advice. A national interview, yet. It was like watching someone's skin being removed with a penknife, one inch at a time. The social worker believed that she had a side, that if she was heard, people would sympathize with her, understand it wasn't her fault that she had skipped those visits. She had failed to see that the story required a villain, a role that Calliope had ingeniously sidestepped through her silence.

The poor woman was dead. Drove her car into a tree off Route 140 in Carroll County. Clear day, sober as a judge, according to the tox screen. And, wouldn't you know, there it was in the news story of her death, a few paragraphs in, as if this one-car accident could be construed as a case of cause-and-effect, which Teena believed it was. Calliope Jenkins killed that poor social worker as surely as she killed her own son. And, again, she would never answer for it.

Her right arm throbbing, Teena reluctantly turned off the computer, reread Cassandra Fallows's letter. The woman used words prettily, but words on paper had little effect on Teena. She heard Mr Salvati pulling in, a much easier operation than leaving, but still one requiring several adjustments until the car was exactly in the middle of his parking pad. Then the night was

135

silent, as usual, the only sound the drone of her own television, tuned to a reality show where proper British nannies magically fixed dysfunctional families. Dysfunctional families that usually resided, Teena couldn't help noticing, in big suburban houses with plenty of land and few worries about money. Tonight, a child was throwing a tantrum and Supernanny held her by the shoulders, instructing her, kindly but firmly, to use her words.

Hey, Supernanny, Teena longed to say. *Come with me to a rowhouse in Southwest Baltimore, travel back in time. You can time-travel. You're Supernanny. The only thing you have to do is find the baby. Find the fuckin' baby, Supernanny, then have a go at fixing Calliope Jenkins. Make a job chart, shower her with rewards, tell her to use her big-girl words and give up the location of her baby. Use your words, Calliope, use your goddamn words.* Teena had, in fact, grabbed her by the shoulders once or twice, and not so kindly, but it never worked. *Use your words.*

Chapter Thirteen

Cassandra had to drive to the suburb of Columbia to meet Tisha for lunch, a location that surprised her. Tisha, as she recalled, had been quite specific about her desire to live in a big city, bigger than Baltimore. She had definite ideas about her apartment (a penthouse), her husband (an architect), and her children (three—girl, boy, girl).

Then again, Tisha had been no more than twelve

when she had outlined that. Cassandra would not want to be held accountable for the plans she had made in sixth grade. (Investigative journalist, married to a doctor, three children, a modern house in some unspecified New England wood.)

Still—*Columbia.* In 1967—Cassandra could date it precisely, because it was the year before her father left—Cassandra's parents had taken long drives to what had then felt like a faraway world. Her father was intrigued by the concept, this egalitarian 'new town' conceived by the developer, James Rouse. Her mother, trapped in the endless battle that was the renovation of her aging house, liked to fantasize about fresh starts, houses without history.

'Rouse is a good man, but he hasn't read his Toynbee,' her father said, even as her mother sighed over the compact kitchens with breakfast bars. 'Decadence will not be stopped.'

Her father, as was his infuriating wont, was right. The rural county that Cassandra remembered from those long-ago Sunday drives was a blobby suburb now; Rouse's dream of a heterogeneous town that was truly integrated, by race and income, had been overbuilt with McMansion monstrosities. Could Tisha really live here? At least the restaurant she had recommended looked promising. An old stone house, it had been converted into a wine bar and restaurant, and it had the good fortune to face one of the few undeveloped vistas on this two-lane highway.

Cassandra took a seat on the banquette, not too close to the door, but affording an unobstructed view. She didn't want to appear to be overeager.

The fact was, it had been anticlimactic,

137

connecting with Tisha. After her adventures in skullduggery—engineering her encounter with Reggie, finding Sistina Murphy's home in the online property records—it had seemed, well, *commonplace* to return someone's voice mail message, ask for a lunch date, and have the wish granted within twenty-four hours. Tisha hadn't seemed surprised that Cassandra wanted to see her, merely . . . skeptical. But then, that was a key facet of Tisha's nature, even when young. She had always been a little reserved, as if evaluating people. She thought before she spoke, too, and there had been an especially long pause when Cassandra proposed lunch.

'I'm self-employed,' Tisha said at last. 'An hour in the middle of the day—that's two hours of work time, when you include getting there and back.'

'I'm self-employed, too,' Cassandra had said.

'But you'll be working, right?' Tisha had always been direct, too. 'Reg said this was for a "project". By which, I guess, he means another *story.*'

She gave the last noun a lot of spin.

'A book, yes,' Cassandra said. 'But what I really want, more than picking your brain, is to catch up with you.'

'Huh,' Tisha said, then named the restaurant and the time in a way that did not allow for Cassandra to counter. If she wanted to see Tisha, it would be on her turf, at her convenience, on her terms.

She's beautiful, Cassandra thought when she saw her walk into the restaurant at the stroke of noon. Not that Tisha hadn't always been pretty. But the usual pattern, when seeing a long-ago friend, was to be dismayed by what age had done. In her fiftieth year, Tisha was more striking than she had

138

been at fifteen, with close-cropped hair and a strong sense of style. She was one of those women who used clothes as a canvas, relieving the black of her turtleneck and trousers with a spectacular necklace, twisted strands of silver hung with asymmetrical rectangles of semiprecious stones. She was smart enough not to pair dangly earrings with such an overwhelming piece, wearing small studs of tiger's-eye the same shade as her eyes. Her cheekbones were more prominent than ever, and her generous mouth showed no signs of thinning, an encroachment of age that Cassandra found especially dismaying in her own face.

'Tisha,' she said, rising, grateful for the table between them, as it meant she didn't have to puzzle through the physicality of the greeting. Hug, cheek kiss, handshake? Nothing seemed exactly right.

'Cassandra. It's still Cassandra, right?'

'Of course. What else might it be?'

'I always thought,' Tisha said, settling into her chair, 'that you'd give in, shorten it to Cassie, stop dragging that long thing around.'

'You remember, then, how my father was adamant that I never have a nickname.'

'I remember lots of things,' she said, her voice perfectly friendly. 'Not necessarily the way you do, but I remember them.'

Oh. So it was going to be one of *those* conversations. Tisha wouldn't be the first person to approach Cassandra with a chip on her shoulder, a determination to settle scores. Funny, the more marginal the person was to Cassandra's memoirs, the more adamant they were about what they always called *setting the record straight*. Her father, her mother, Annie—their lives had been laid bare, but they hadn't objected. Even her ex-husbands had been good sports, relatively. It was always someone at the edge of the story who wanted to quibble. Not that she considered Tisha marginal to her life. But she hadn't played that large a role in the two books.

She decided to treat Tisha's implied gauntlet as an excuse to get down to business. 'Do you remember Calliope Jenkins?'

Tisha smiled as if she had always known where this was headed. 'Somewhat. She was never really a friend. And she went to middle school with you, not us, and she didn't make it into the A course, so that was that.'

'But she came to Western in tenth grade, right?' Under the complicated system in place at the time, A-course students started high school in ninth grade, while the others arrived in tenth.

'Yeah, but we didn't mix much. We had been apart for three years by then. Friendly, sure. But not friends.'

'Yet your brother ended up working on her case.'

'My brother also ended up marrying my best friend. Baltimore's small that way. Especially *our* Baltimore.'

'Candy—Reggie—married Donna?' It bothered Cassandra that this information bothered her.

'He prefers to be called Reg these days. Donna prefers it, which means Reg prefers it. He's been in love with her since he was seven.' Tisha laughed. 'But he had to wait his turn, watch her marry her shit of a college sweetheart, make a botch of that. They celebrated their fifteenth anniversary last summer.'

It felt as if Tisha was taunting her, but that had to be in Cassandra's imagination. She had barely admitted to herself that little flame of attraction she felt for Reggie—*Reg*—Barr. There was no way his sister could have picked up on it. Maybe he had said something that indicated he found Cassandra attractive? She shouted the idea down as impossible, insane, even as her heart skipped in careless loops around her rib cage.

The waitress came to take their order, and Cassandra tried to set the tone, ordering an appetizer and entrée salad, asking for a three-ounce pour of the recommended wine pairing. Tisha got a chicken-salad sandwich and a glass of iced tea, looking pointedly at her watch.

'You said you were self-employed,' Cassandra said, 'but you didn't tell me what you do.'

'I'm a graphic artist.' She paused, seeming to expect some reaction. 'I wanted to be a painter, but, well, I knew that wasn't in the cards. I had to make a living. I took time out when the kids were born, started over when they got to school.'

'I remember your drawings,' Cassandra said. 'The future renderings of your family. Remember fifth grade, when we all drew pictures of girls getting ready for dates?'

'You said Donna was the artist,' Tisha said.

'What?'

'In your book. You said we all imitated *her*. But I was the one who started it.'

That was it? This was why Tisha was coiled with fury? The lack of credit for her childhood artistry? Cassandra had told eight hundred thousand readers that her second husband was impotent unless he paid for sex, and this was what Tisha felt

141

needed to be set straight? It was hard not to laugh.

'I did? I'm sorry, I didn't mean to imply anything by that. Donna's drawings stood out in my memory, for some reason. Remember, her girls were always slightly dog-faced in profile, more snout than nose?'

Tisha was not ready to be appeased. 'You were always giving my stuff to Donna,' she said, stirring sugar—and she used real sugar, not one of the pink-, blue-, or yellow-packeted substitutes—into the tea that had arrived. 'That whole story about the record party. That was mine, too. You got it confused with the graduation party, which was at Donna's.'

'Are you sure?' Cassandra had used her childhood diaries to help her reconstruct some sections of her life. She couldn't imagine being wrong about something as seminal as their first boy-girl party.

'You had Reg there, dancing. Why would Reggie be crashing a party at Donna's house? That party was at *my* house, and you didn't know half of what was going on.'

'Such as . . .'

'Such as Fatima going upstairs with Karl, the one who had a mustache in the sixth grade—probably because he had been left back three times—and going into one of the bedrooms, and he asked her for oral sex and she didn't know what it was, but she didn't want to seem ignorant, so she said sure—and used her teeth!'

Cassandra laughed. 'I wish I had known about that.'

'So you could put it in your book?'

'No—well, maybe. I wish I had known because

142

it's the essence of Fatima, game for anything.'

'Was, maybe. She's churchified now.' Tisha looked worried. 'Don't go putting that in a book. She would *die*.'

'I won't,' Cassandra promised, although she couldn't help feeling wistful. Not about the missed opportunity for using that anecdote, but for the reminder that there had always been a few things to which she was not privy, information limited to the inner circle of Tisha, Donna, and Fatima. *My best friend,* Tisha had said of Donna. Callie didn't go to junior high with *us*—Tisha, Donna, Fatima. Had Tisha always thought that way? Had she not seen the quartet as even, balanced? They had sat together for four years, their desks pushed together. Didn't that make them a foursome, at least when they were young?

'Do you keep in touch with Fatima? I assume Donna is part of your life if she's married to your brother.'

'Fatima doesn't keep in touch with us. She's not comfortable with anyone who knew her before she went to Spelman. My, she did put on airs about that.'

Tisha seemed amused by this, and Cassandra felt she was missing some subtle distinction. Spelman was a good college. Why shouldn't Fatima, who had grown up in a chaotic household, be proud of that?

'I mean, I went to Northwestern,' Tisha continued, 'and you don't hear me going on and on about that.'

'That is a good school.'

'Tell me about it. My oldest wants to go there and he doesn't begin to have the grades. Where

143

did you go?'

Cassandra would have given anything to avoid answering this question, but it had been put to her too bluntly to evade. 'Princeton.' *Sorry, Tisha, but you were the one who wanted to play this game.*

'Undergrad?'

'Yes, with an English major yet. No wonder I didn't have a real job—well, ever. I temped and freelanced through most of my twenties, worked briefly as an editorial assistant at a big publishing house, then began picking up adjunct teaching gigs and doing corporate writing, freelance. But until I started writing, in my late thirties, I was pretty lost.' She hoped that admission would balance things.

'I have an MBA. One of those kinds that you get on the weekends, but it's been good for my business, small as it is.'

'And you're married, with kids.'

'A boy and a girl.'

'I remember when you wanted three kids.'

'Oh, lord, two are enough.' There was a flash of something genuine, a feeling that the real Tisha had finally shown up, and Cassandra relaxed.

'Three kids, and your husband was going to be an architect.'

'Orthodontist,' Tisha said. 'Regular hours, not a lot of emergencies, and there's always a new crop of snaggle-toothed children coming up.'

'You like living out here?'

'Love it. It's a lot of driving—when the school day ends, I'm a full-time chauffeur—but it's been great for the kids. Besides, the oldest is a senior in high school, the youngest two years behind him. We might downscale, sizewise, but I think we'll

144

stay out here. It's where Michael's work is. Where do you live these days?'

'Brooklyn.' She added quickly, 'I bought in more than ten years ago, when it was still a relative bargain, and I borrowed against the equity to help my dad buy his place.'

'You're pretty rich, aren't you?'

Even by Tisha's standards, the question was direct.

'I don't have to worry too much about money, about small emergencies. I'm not sure I would describe myself as *rich*.'

'Your books are bestsellers.'

'You'd be surprised what that means on a balance sheet. And I'm all I've got, all I can count on. I may not worry about money in the present tense, but I do have to prepare for an illness that could wipe me out and think about retirement. I don't have near enough put away.'

Tisha nodded absently, using a fork to pick the pistachios out of her chicken salad. She wasn't so much eating her food as deconstructing it.

'Why did you write about my birthday party, anyway? I mean, even if you had gotten it right, what was the point?'

Whoosh, back to that. Why couldn't Tisha let it go? 'Well, it was our first boy-girl party. Remember? And I felt inadequate. When it came to that stuff, I was behind the curve. You and Donna and Fatima, you were ready for boys. I was still playing with toys. I gave you a toy, in fact, for that birthday, a stuffed cat. I could tell you thought you were beyond such things.'

'But—' Tisha seemed to be struggling, either with emotion or the attempt to find the right

145

words. 'It was *my* party. What was it doing in your book?'

Cassandra knew Tisha had not asked the question she wanted to ask, the underlying complaint: *Why did you get to write it?*

'I'm a writer, it's what I do.'

'But it was *my* life.'

'Lives overlap, intersect. If I wrote only about my life, I wouldn't write about anything.'

'Maybe that would be better,' Tisha muttered.

'Tisha, are you angry that I want to write about Calliope? As you said, she wasn't really our friend.'

'I just don't want to be in there, too. But I will be, won't I? We all will—Donna, Fatima, me. I thought you were done with us, at least.'

Tisha always had been quick.

'I don't know what I'm writing, but there's clearly a story there. She was one of us, once. Not part of our gang, but a classmate. I want to figure out how the path deviates, how we end up in middle age, safe and snug, and she flounders so horribly. Okay, you had a tight family and Donna's folks were practically Baltimore royalty. But Calliope wasn't that different from Fatima, and you say Fatima made something of herself. Callie's story will tell us something larger. About the accidents of fate, the choices and temptations we faced.'

'But I don't want to be a part of it. I just don't. Can't you leave us out of it?'

'You won't be the focus, Tisha, far from it. The real story is what happened to Calliope. Of course, I'll have to talk to your brother—'

'He can't help you, either.'

'He was her lawyer.'

146

'Gag order,' Tisha said.

'During the case, yes, I read that. But I don't think a gag order can be upheld in perpetuity.'

'He figured where this was going, told me that he can't talk to you. Nor can Calliope, even if you can find her, and Reg himself isn't sure where she is.'

'Can't talk to me,' Cassandra asked, 'or *won't*?'

Tisha sighed, checking her watch. 'Does it really matter, Cassandra? Maybe we're all just done being supporting players in the Cassandra Fallows show, starring Cassandra Fallows as Cassandra Fallows.'

'That's not fair, Tisha, not fair at all.'

'I've got to go.' She put down a twenty, far more than she owed, even with a generous tip. 'I have a teleconference at two.'

'It was nice to see you, Tisha.' Hurt as she was by that crack about the Cassandra show, she wasn't going to be sucked into picking a fight, closing any doors.

'It was good to see you, too, Cassandra. I'd love to talk to you, really talk—when you're not writing a book. I don't care what anyone says—I thought the novel was your best work to date. You should write more fiction. Not that you haven't written plenty already.'

Chapter Fourteen

Route 108 streamed past the windows of Tisha Barr-Holloway's 'mama car', an eight-year-old Dodge minivan that was fiendishly reliable, denying her any rational reason to trade it in. Even with her youngest approaching driving age, she still had to ferry a lot of kids around because of all the rules these days. Curfews, no more than two kids in a car at any time when there was a young driver behind the wheel. Lord, how the rules had changed since her sixteenth birthday, when she had gone down to Glen Burnie with her father and come back with a license three hours later, and the only real restriction was the fact that their family had only one car.

Tisha actually preferred the new way of doing things, even if it meant she was chained to the steering wheel for a few more years. Howard County had too many twisty country roads left over from its farming past. Route 108 was one, in fact, and Tisha was driving much too fast, given the light rain that had begun to fall. *I would kill Michael Jr. if I caught him driving like this,* she thought, continuing to drive ten, fifteen miles over the speed limit. She did not, in fact, have to be at home at any particular time, did not have a teleconference at two, but she had needed to get away from Cassandra. Ravenous, she mapped the area in her head, tried to remember where the nearest fast-food place was. A Jack in the Box, she thought, over by Wilde Lake. She'd backtrack and hit the drive-through.

148

That thing about the novel—why had she said that? She hadn't even read the novel, while she had read the two memoirs more attentively than she cared to admit. Tisha didn't have much use for lying, yet that one had just popped out, bold and unrepentant. She had read *about* the novel, after Reg told her to call Cassandra Fallows, but she hadn't even considered reading it. Yet if she had taken the time, she was certain she would have preferred it to the memoirs.

Tisha hadn't paid attention when *My Father's Daughter* was first published. She had two young children at home; she wasn't reading much of anything in those days. But the book, still in hardcover, had eventually crossed her path and she had noticed the name on its cover. Cassandra Fallows. Had to be the same girl she had known all those years ago, the one who had disappeared abruptly between freshman and sophomore year. Tisha picked it up, thinking only that it would fill in the gaps, tell her why Cassandra hadn't come back to Western High School after ninth grade.

Boy, did it ever. In Cassandra's version, her withdrawal from Western was because of an end-of-school beat-down administered by three East Baltimore crackers with whom Cassandra had been feuding all year. Only Cassandra had to make it some kind of karmic retribution, punishment for a slight she had administered to Tisha more than three years earlier, an incident that Tisha had all but forgotten.

'What *bullshit,*' Tisha had exploded the next time she saw Donna. 'Do you remember any of this?'

'I remember the beat-down. I mean, I remember hearing about it, after the fact. But I don't

149

remember that we were anywhere nearby. And if we were, so what? Can you imagine me wading into some fight? I don't *think* so.'

It was funny about Donna, how nothing shook her self-regard. She had made a disastrous first marriage, which was simply never discussed, then married Tisha's baby brother, yet it hadn't made her any less superior. She still considered herself above everything and everybody, Andre Howard's precious baby, the niece of state senator Julius Howard. Marriage to Reg had saved *her*, yet Donna managed to convey that her companionship was an enormous favor she had bestowed on him.

The Howards and the Barrs had grown up only five blocks apart, but they were big blocks. The Howards were serious shit, a family almost as storied as the Mitchells, for whom the downtown courthouse was named. The Howards were never quite the first at anything, but they had always been in the hunt. There had been a time when everyone thought Donna's uncle Julius would be Maryland's first black U.S. senator or governor, whatever he wanted. But those scenarios had assumed he would easily move from city council to city council president to mayor, and things hadn't progressed quite that smoothly. After a failed run for city council president, Julius Howard stalled out in the statehouse. A man of consequence, but not the one-of-a-kind, first-of-a-kind he thought was his due.

Still, the Howards *mattered* in a way that had always irked Tisha. She had befriended Donna when they were in kindergarten, instinctively adopting the old adage about keeping enemies close. Not that two five-year-olds could be enemies. But they would have been rivals, eventually, if they hadn't become friends. And she did adore Donna, just not as blindly as everyone else did, including Reg. Look at Cassandra, thinking Donna was the artist in the group when Tisha was the one that everyone was imitating. Tisha had started drawing those elaborate pictures of girls preparing for dates when they were in fifth grade, not fourth as Cassandra's book would have it. A small thing, but if Cassandra couldn't get the small things right, why should she be trusted on the big things?

She did have some of the details down: Donna's drawings had looked like dogs, Sweet Polly Purebreds, with those snoutlike noses and eyes on the sides of their head. Donna never did master dimension or perspective. Of course, Cassandra being Cassandra, she had to make a *thing* out of this whole drawing phase, place it against the backdrop of women's liberation. Why were they so fascinated with dating, images of girls caught in midtransformation? Wasn't it funny that it was the *preparation* for the dates that interested them, as opposed to the dates themselves? They loved the idea of dressing, of doing their hair, of applying lipstick. The dates would be anticlimaxes. 'Like the girls in the Comic Strip *Apartment 3-G,*' Cassandra had written, missing the point that the only variation in that comic strip was hair color. It never occurred to her that Tisha had been compelled to fill in the blanks, make up her own *Apartment 3-G,* where it wasn't about being a blonde, brunette, or redhead but about the texture of hair and how to combat it.

'That's the thing about white people,' Tisha had complained to Donna when she couldn't get her worked up about the way Cassandra had created bookends of two unrelated events. 'They never think anything is about race unless it affects them. Then it's *all* about race. Try to tell someone like Cassandra what it was like, looking for someone with a face like yours on the comics page of the Sunpapers or on television, and she'd think you were being so overwrought. But when she gets beat up—by three *white* girls, no less—that's all because she's, I don't know, Harriet Tubman, leading the little Negro girls to freedom.'

Donna had laughed. 'More Harriet Beecher Stowe. Although I'll grant that Cassandra's prose is a little smoother.'

God, why couldn't Tisha be like Donna, one of those people who skimmed the surface of life, never getting bogged down in anger or righteousness? 'I wouldn't show my face,' some people whispered when Donna came back to Baltimore after her first marriage collapsed. She had met her husband, who hailed from the Knoxville, Tennessee, version of the Howards, in college, persuaded him to work on her uncle Julius's campaign. The wedding ceremony was a year after Princess Diana's and almost as grand. The bridesmaid's gown had been among the most hideous Tisha had ever worn, and that was saying something.

Seven years later, the marriage was all ash, and no one really knew why, just that it must be something horrible for Donna to walk away without a red cent. Rumors circulated, shifted, inverted. *He beat her, she beat him, they beat each other. They lost all their money in a savings-and-loan scam, same as Old Court, only worse, and she didn't want to be with him if he was poor. He's gay, she's gay. He knows some dirt on her, that's why she's not getting any money, paying him off, if the truth be told.* Yet Donna refused to be cowed and declined to confide in anyone, even Tisha. 'It just didn't work out,' she said. 'We were too young, we grew apart.'

Meanwhile there was Reg, working for Donna's father. He may have been two years younger, but he wasn't silly little Candy anymore, trying to woo Donna with his antic dance. He was handsome, broad shouldered, and, after a rough start at the firm, in the starting blocks on the fast track. People gossiped about that, too, of course. Said Reg was made a partner because he was the boss's son-in-law. But Tisha had always believed it was the other way around: Andre Howard rewarded Reg with his only daughter because he had proven himself as a lawyer. He wasn't going to see his baby done wrong twice. Reg, dependent on his father-in-law for his livelihood, would never shame Donna.

It was strange how rich Reg was now. As Tisha's Michael liked to say, 'Doctors and dentists do okay, but the guy who *sues* the doctors and dentists does better.' Not that Reg did malpractice cases, but Tisha understood what her husband meant. She and Michael were comfortable. They didn't sweat the small stuff. A car repair, a big vacation, music lessons—they never had to ask themselves if they could afford it. But college—sweet Jesus, college! Their first house had cost less than the going rate for four years of tuition. She couldn't imagine those two years in the middle when the kids would both be in school, when they would be expected to put out almost $80,000 a year, but she also couldn't imagine saying no to anything they wanted. Tisha had been told she could attend any college where she got admitted and, by God, her kids were going to have the same deal. But there was no way, even adjusting for inflation, that her parents had paid anywhere near that much for Tisha and Reg, and they had helped Reg with his University of Baltimore law school costs, too. Her parents had been civil service workers, yet they hadn't seemed to have any problem paying for college. How could that be?

And Reg would be able to do the same for his daughter, born only eight years ago. Hell, Reg had paid a pretty penny just to bring Aubrey into the world, essentially renting some out-of-towner's womb, although the issue of surrogacy was taboo. The sky was the limit for that girl, and God help her if she didn't want to reach for it. Tisha had assumed Donna's conception problems were all age related, but Reg had said something once that suggested Donna had been damaged in some specific way and that it was part of the legacy of whatever awful things happened during that first marriage. 'Of course you know all about that,' he assured Tisha, and she said, 'Oh, of course.' It had been strange, realizing that Reg knew something about her best friend that she did not. She told herself it was natural, given that they were married. Still, she didn't like it much. She also hated going to their house, that *Architectural Digest* bougie palace in Bolton Hill, with the authentic this and the period that, an exhausting history behind almost every got-damn thing. *Whose*

154

history? she wanted to ask them. *Because when that mantelpiece was made, our people would have been dusting it. Even the Howards.*

She remembered the surge of superiority she had felt when she got into Northwestern and Donna, a less dedicated student, had settled for the University of Delaware. Then she remembered how casually Cassandra had topped her achievement at lunch. Princeton. Tisha probably could have gone to Princeton, in terms of grades and scores. But her imagination wouldn't let her. *Too white,* she had thought when the counselor suggested Ivy League schools.

Only Northwestern was just as white, inside and out, snow piling up to the windowsills until Tisha thought she would go mad. One day, she stood on her desk, peering out at the snow, and a rumor went around that the black girl—she was one of only two in her dorm—was trying to kill herself from sheer loneliness. There they went again, seeing race where all she was seeing was color, the endless white of the drifts, almost thirty inches that winter of 1979. *What was I thinking?* she had asked herself, staring down at the mounting snow. She should have gone to Tulane or Vanderbilt.

But she was generally happy at Northwestern, especially in the classroom of Sterling Stuckey, a teacher who had truly valued her mind. Thinking about Stuckey made her think about Br'er Rabbit, which brought her full circle to Cassandra and her habit of *just not getting it.*

It was fourth grade, spring. Tisha longed to believe that it was the week after Dr King was assassinated, but she knew that was simply too good to be true, that her memory was trying to

155

trick her into making the story better than it was. See, that's where she and Cassandra were different. Tisha *knew* what memory did, how it tried to fool you, how you fooled it. Because not even the Baltimore City school system could be clueless enough to screen *Song of the South* the week after Dr King was killed.

But something had happened, something disturbing that required herding the children together and putting them in the auditorium for a movie, a huge treat. Only—not in the case of *Song of the South,* especially when it was followed with lesson plans in which they read the Joel Chandler Harris versions of the Uncle Remus stories. Tisha had stared down at her book, embarrassed. The people she knew did not speak that way. Well—her father had a distant relative on the shore, and he wasn't exactly educated. There was Fatima's mother, with her Baltimore-isms such as 'There hit go', which actually indicated the location of something stationary, something that wasn't *going* anywhere. But even Fatima's mother didn't say 'Mawnin' or 'Nice wedder!'. Tisha had never heard anyone say, for example, that *so-and-so, he lay low,* the way Br'er Fox did while Br'er Rabbit chatted up the tar baby. Her mother was a demon when it came to grammar, especially lay-lie. No one in the Barr family was ever going to get away with saying, 'He lay low,' even if it was technically correct. It sounded wrong.

She had told her teacher as much. 'But this is dialect, Tisha. It's how people spoke once upon a time, in the South. Joel Chandler Harris wanted to preserve these oral traditions, lest these stories be lost to the ages.' Cassandra, always the suck-up,

156

had chimed in, 'It's not just a story. It's *history,* Tisha.'

Not mine, she wanted to say.

She found her way to the Jack in the Box, now a Burger King, and ordered a milk shake and some onion rings. Chicken salad with pistachios. She hated that kind of food. So why had she suggested the restaurant? Because—admit it—she wanted to impress Cassandra. Cassandra! Who had been a borderline geek in school, with that enormous mop of frowsy hair, her skinny, clumsy body. Time was Cassandra had sought Tisha's approval. It was a veritable chain of command: Tisha looked to Donna, Fatima and Cassandra looked to Tisha, and sad little Callie followed at Fatima's heels, asking for nothing but the right to stand on the sidelines. 'You playing kicksies?' she would say on the playground. 'You playing foursquare?' But she wouldn't play unless Donna or Tisha urged her to join. Fatima's invitation wasn't good enough, much less Cassandra's. Not that Cassandra ever thought to invite Callie, and now she had apparently forgotten how the girl tried to attach herself to them. Because if she did, that would be a chapter, maybe multiple chapters, maybe a book in itself.

Now how had Tisha gotten lost in this suburb where she had lived for seventeen years? Okay, so this wasn't her part of town, but she had gone wildly off track somehow. The trick to driving in Columbia, Tisha always believed, was not to think about it. She had gone right when she should have gone left or straight, turned into Faulkner Ridge, but then, she had Faulkner on the brain.

Tisha met Br'er Rabbit again in college, when she signed up for Sterling Stuckey's seminar on

157

what was then called black folklore. She was skeptical at first and confused that the assigned book of stories was credited to William Faulkner. Why was William Faulkner writing about Br'er Rabbit? But her professor had explained that this was William J. Faulkner, a former slave, telling the same stories as Harris, but in simple, direct language that granted the tales dignity and power. The professor had then drawn the parallels between Br'er Rabbit and the trickster rabbit of West African folklore, then linked this to the concept of Pan-Africanization, in which old ethnic divisions melted in the face of slavery. He returned Br'er Rabbit to Tisha, allowed her to see how plucky that little rabbit was, how smart. A trickster by necessity, because how else could a rabbit survive in this savage world?

A few weeks later in the semester, when they were reading a biography of Jelly Roll Morton, a white girl from Oklahoma said apropos of Morton's love of fine clothes, 'I always did wonder why black people all have fancy cars, even when they don't have much money.' There was a deep, almost frightening silence, a silence miles beyond awkward. Stuckey had gently led the class into a discussion of stereotypes and generalizations. But the girl had remained serene and unperturbed in her ignorance, believing herself validated. 'Right,' she said when the professor finished. 'It's very childish, buying fancy things when you can't put food on the table.'

Cassandra was never stupid that way, never quite that smug or insular. She had been a better sport about her stepmother than the woman's family had been, for sure. Annie Waters had been all but disowned by her family when she married Cedric Fallows. The gossip about *that* had been way, way above Tisha's young head, coded and obscure, but she had figured it out eventually. Everyone had, except Cassandra. Which was funny, because no one really cared except Cassandra. Until she wrote a book, and now millions of people had entered the time of King's death through this—*Sorry, Cassandra,* Tisha thought, pulling on her milk shake so angrily it grunted—*trivial* story. That had been the most infuriating part of the memoir, watching Cassandra blithely co-opt those three days to tell the story of her own personal tragedy. She hadn't known, couldn't know what had gone on in the living rooms and kitchens of black folks' homes that horrible weekend, the fear and grief and terror of it all. As Donna said, she meant no harm.

But Tisha knew that people who meant no harm were often the most dangerous people of all, the real tar babies from which one might never disentangle. Reg and Donna were crazy, thinking that Cassandra could be managed in any way, that they could let her a little way in and then dissuade her from dragging them into the process of picking the bones of Callie Jenkins's life. That poor sad woman, always on the sidelines, waiting to be invited. Whatever she had done—and everyone assumed she had killed her baby—leave her in peace now, Cassandra. Leave her be.

Reg and Donna could wrangle with Cassandra if they chose. Tisha—well, Tisha was going to lay low.

Bewitched

I was a television junkie as a child. Officially, I was allowed to watch television only an hour a day, but that was my father's rule and my mother seldom enforced it. When he moved out, television would become a passive way for us to be together, and the restrictions fell away. But while we still lived under one roof, my father cursed, reviled, and damned television. Which, of course, made it irresistible.

On school days, I rushed home practically shaking with anticipation. I started with *One Life to Live*, killing time until *Dark Shadows* came on, but the soap opera quickly eclipsed the supernatural in my imagination. Soap operas were the dirtiest thing going in the late 1960s, filled with illicit sex and unplanned pregnancies that trapped people into loveless marriages. I watched in a stupor until the news came on, then hurriedly did my homework, as my father expected it to be complete when he arrived home.

My favorite was *Bewitched*, a nighttime show and therefore not so easily hidden from my father. I claimed it as part of my allocated ration, but the show enraged him on principle. He seemed incensed that Darrin, whether played by Dick York or Dick Sargent, had snared Samantha, the beautiful witch. My father shared Samantha's mother's opinion that Darrin was unworthy—not because he was a mortal, but because he refused to let Samantha use her powers to enrich them. Even though my father's beloved myths repeatedly

160

demonstrated the dangers inherent in loving gods and goddesses, my father would not have shied away from pursuing an immortal. In fact, in less than forty-eight hours from this evening that I am describing, Annie would rise, Aphrodite-like, from a sea of writing bodies, and he would almost die for her.

But this was a Thursday. I turned on the television, thinking about how there's no in-between with witches, they were either ugly or gorgeous. I hoped to be gorgeous, but it didn't look promising. My mother said I was the prettiest girl in the world, but my father was conspicuously silent on the subject of my looks. He had stopped caring for my hair the summer between third and fourth grade, and it was now an unmanageable mass, as my mother had prophesied, and not at all flattering to my odd little face. Still, it was convenient to have hair to hide behind, in school and at home, where I could sense something was terribly wrong. Or about to be.

'We interrupt this program for a special bulletin'—remember those words? We don't seem to hear them as often now, since CNN came along, rushing information to us within seconds of it happening. Today, bulletins pass by on a *crawl,* humble and deferential, trying not to obscure the programming. Dr Martin Luther King Jr. was shot in Memphis at 6 P.M. central time, an hour before I settled myself at the television, and I was just learning about it. He was thirty-nine years old. Ancient to a girl who would turn ten in two days, but the same age as my father and five years older than my mother.

I called out to my mother, who was in the

161

kitchen. She didn't believe me at first: How can a little girl be the bearer of this news? Finally comprehending, she cried out—but no, that scream was later, I am conflating things. My mother will scream two months later, in the early-morning hours of June 5, when Robert F. Kennedy is shot. I will hear her scream and go to her bed, wonder at her wild grief over a man that we don't really know. It will be several minutes before I think to ask, 'Where's Daddy?' My mother will cry harder. So much happens in two months.

Within hours of the news of King's death, Washington, DC, and Detroit were engulfed by riots, but Baltimore was deceptively quiet. 'A city so behind the times that it can't riot in a timely fashion,' my father liked to say.

'But if people here had rioted right away, you never would have gone out Saturday,' I pointed out to him years later. 'And you wouldn't have met Annie. You met Annie because King was killed.'

'Don't be sloppy, Cassandra. Yes, you can say that I met Annie in circumstances that were a direct consequence of King's death. But it's fallacious to say I wouldn't have met her otherwise. After all, she worked over at that bakery in Westview Mall, not even three miles from here.'

'But would you have fallen in love with her in a less charged encounter?' I persisted. 'Would it have been love at first sight if you had met, say, buying pizza rolls at Silber's? Or riding the bus downtown?'

'Oh, yes,' my father always said. 'Annie Waters was my destiny.' Then, at the look on my face: 'Don't ask a question if you don't want to know the answer.'

162

COLLECTORS

March 11–12

Chapter Fifteen

The moment Teena spotted the shopper in the voluminous cape, she wanted to scream 'Mine!' like a hotdogging outfielder. It wasn't just that the woman was clearly someone who spent freely. She had money and taste and a relatively decent figure for her age—slender, not too hippy, although a little on the short side for true high fashion. She had the good sense not to dress younger than her age, which Teena put in the early to mid-forties. That meant she would avoid the trendiest clothes. But she would appreciate the best pieces in some of the new spring collections, be keen to find an item or two that allowed her to keep pace with fashion without being a slave to it.

'I'm Teena,' she told the woman, ignoring the glare from the other sales associate, Lavonne, who, by rights, should have snagged the customer. 'Let me know if you need anything.'

Lavonne wouldn't have meshed with this customer, Teena rationalized. Lavonne was too pushy, too insistent. She did better with the insecure ones. With a shopper like this, you offer help, then back away, making sure to gauge the exact moment when she wants assistance. Teena watched the woman flip through the high-end designers Nordstrom carried here. She had the air of a New Yorker, someone used to more and better offerings. A shopper of Bergdorf Goodman or the designer floors at Saks's flagship. Sometimes, on her day off, Teena bought a ticket on one of those up-and-back bus trips to New

York, the ones that charged only $35 and threw in a bagel. While her fellow travelers headed out to matinees and museums, she wandered the best department stores, drinking in the wares. She didn't try things on—professional courtesy, she wouldn't waste another sales associate's time that way—but she examined the clothes and studied the shoppers. The merchandise inspired envy, yet the customers left her grateful for her life in Baltimore. While many seemed nice, there was one type she could never suffer—loud and cawing, incapable of being pleased. Oh, she saw her share of bitches here, especially around prom time, but the Baltimore bitch was a different breed entirely, someone she could handle because she had known the type her entire life, even been one in her youth. She would have called it *confidence* then, or a *strong personality.* Same difference. In her twenties, pretty and ambitious, Teena had been careless with others' feelings. She had even secretly loathed unlucky people, believing they were responsible for their own fates. She had been ruthless about culling losers from her life, lest they prove contagious.

Then she had joined their ranks.

The woman was looking at a dress, a Tory Burch shift in pale green and pink. Teena had been selling the hell out of it—those two shades never went out of fashion in preppy Baltimore—but it wasn't right for this customer.

'It's pretty,' she ventured. 'And incredibly popular.' The woman winced. Good sign. 'I have a sense it's not to your taste.'

'I tend to be pretty somber,' the woman admitted with a laugh. 'Maybe I should change, though. It's

166

such a spring look and I'd like to believe that spring might finally make it here, although I know from experience that Baltimore won't get down to the business of spring until late April.'

'You're from here, then?'

'Originally.' She passed the Tory Burch by but picked the next dress on the rack, a fluffy Alice + Olivia. She was clearly in a romantic mood, drawn to pretty-pretty things quite different from the severe clothes she was wearing today. A woman in the mood for a change. Recent weight loss? But this woman did not move as if her body were new or surprising to her; quite the opposite. This was a woman who was used to being attractive, perhaps even overrated her looks a bit, lost track of how age chipped away at a woman. She had the languid aspect of someone who was dreaming, modeling these clothes for someone's appreciative gaze. Teena saw this quite a bit, across all age ranges. She wondered at it, the human capacity for silliness and love as the decades mounted up. That part of her was as dead as the nerves in her right hand.

'What about this? I think it suits your coloring.' She pulled out a jersey dress that was more rose than pink, and hue made all the difference. A Dolce & Gabbana, it also cost twice as much as anything else the woman had picked but was far more appropriate than the bubble dresses draped over her arm. Her figure was good enough, but someone who had made the decision to let her hair go silver—in contrast to Teena, who had just let her hair color *go,* period—couldn't carry those younger silhouettes. The shopper inspected the price tag, unfazed.

167

'Would you like a pair of pumps?' Teena asked, shooting a look at the suede boots. Gorgeous, with a high, stacked heel, but ill-suited to these clothes. It would be a shame to lose the sale simply because a pair of winter boots defeated the buyer's imagination. 'Size seven?'

'Eight,' the woman said with a knowing smile. She understood that Teena had been careful to underestimate her shoe size. Good for her. Teena had never understood this peculiar vanity. Granted, Teena wore a size six, but still. Your feet were your feet; no diet or exercise on the planet could change them. It was the one size that women should own with pride. Girly girl that she had always been with her love of clothes and makeup, Teena remained baffled by some other aspects of femininity. There had been moments, in the box with Calliope Jenkins, that she believed this was the root of her problem: She didn't understand women, much less mothers. Teena couldn't break Calliope because she wasn't female enough. Ironic, given that she had lobbied for the assignment—and been granted it—on the basis of gender. Calliope Jenkins looked up at men with those sleepy, clouded eyes, and they had trouble seeing a killer. A crazy woman, yes. The men in the squad all agreed they could smell the crazy on Calliope. A troubled woman and a woman who caused trouble—yes. A killer? Logically, she must be, but logic withered in the face of Calliope's calm recitations, the call-and-answer of 'I take the Fifth,' 'I have nothing to say.'

'I'll make sure you have a pair of light-colored pumps,' Teena promised. And, while she was at it, she would take the liberty of bringing a few other items. There was a Roberto Cavalli that no one had been able to carry, much less afford.

* * *

Cassandra sat on the padded stool in the dressing room, wearing nothing but her bra and underwear. The lighting was stupidly harsh. She reminded herself of Tisha's drawings, only aged thirty years. This had gone too far. She had come here to introduce herself, ask for a meeting, but her nerve had failed and now she felt deceitful. For her earlier books, she had relied on her memory and her journals, maybe a few telephone calls to friends and family. How did someone talk to someone new, especially this sad woman whose thin frame couldn't quite fill her clothes, pretty and well chosen as they were. Where did one begin? 'At the beginning,' her father always said when she was in a panic over a paper for school.

Strange though it seemed now, she had sometimes struggled with her English assignments, at least in the public school system; the Gordon School had been far more open to her nontraditional approaches. In ninth grade, still in public school, Cassandra had been given a failing mark on a paper on Faulkner because she had attempted to write it in the voice of Benjy. The teacher knocked off a point for every misspelled word and sentence fragment. 'I have a hunch,' her father said, 'that your teacher has not, in fact, read *The Sound and the Fury.*' No matter how harsh or kind her teachers' assessments, her father had gone over her papers and evaluated them according to a different standard. He had critiqued

169

her metaphors, drawn red lines through clichés, insisted that she could do better. 'Too neat, too proper,' he said. 'I didn't raise you to be a mynah bird, mouthing teachers' banalities back to them.'

She made eye contact with her own image in the triple mirror and practiced her lines silently. *Hi, I'm Cassandra Fallows and I'm researching a book about Calliope Jenkins.* Not exactly correct. *Hi, I'm Cassandra Fallows and I'm writing another memoir, but it's also an investigation into the life of Calliope Jenkins.* God, how did journalists do it? She knew how they approached *her,* via publicists and e-mail, sometimes at public events. She found the latter a little gauche. But if that tactic was gauche, then sandbagging someone at her job was lower still. Cassandra had felt flush with success, digging up Teena's address and going to her home, but days had gone by without a reply. Luckily, a neighbor— not the suspicious old man, but a harried young mother unloading groceries—had let the location of Teena's employment slip, along with the fact that no one ever called her Sistina. The nickname, Teena, had set Cassandra up to expect a tackier and younger person, which she realized now was silly. Twenty years had passed. Teena had to be in her forties at least and she looked to be well into her fifties.

She pulled on the rose-colored dress that the unsuspecting Teena had chosen for her. The former detective knew her clothes: The dress, unprepossessing on the hanger, was remarkable on the body and the color made her skin glow. She had eschewed the high heels—she had a horror of putting her feet in shoes that other women had worn—so she raised up on tiptoe, hands on her

170

hips, surveying herself. Where on earth would she wear it?

*   *   *

At the cash register, even as she paid for the dress and allowed Teena to hand-sell her a lightweight spring coat to complement it, more than doubling the bill, Cassandra still could not figure out how to say her piece. She clung to the fleeting hope that her credit card might prove to be an icebreaker—other clerks, in other stores, and not just bookstores, had made the connection on occasion. But while Teena's glance seemed to snag on it, she didn't say anything, only walked around the counter and handed her the hanging bag, a bit of Nordstrom protocol that had always amused Cassandra.

'I wasn't actually planning to shop today,' she said.

'Sometimes, that's when you find the best things.' Said with a smile, but also finality. The sale had been made; she was done with her. Although Teena was probably one of the ones who followed up with handwritten notes.

'No, I mean—I came here to meet *you.*'

Teena's face froze. No, no, no—Cassandra heard her father's voice, castigating. *That's weak, Cassandra, inaccurate.* Teena's face clouded over. But that wasn't it, either. Her expression changed subtly—a new mask, which established that the previous face had been a mask as well. Teena Murphy probably had masks upon masks upon masks.

'Why would anyone want to meet me?'

171

'I'm writing about Calliope Jenkins—'

Teena Murphy threw up her hands, almost as if warding off a blow. 'I'm afraid I can't help you.'

'Why don't you take my business card?'

Teena accepted the card, dropped it, then had trouble retrieving it from the carpet. Was something wrong with her hand?

'It's not a book *about* Calliope Jenkins. But I knew her, when we were children, and I think it's interesting, the way our paths diverged—'

'What was she like?'

Asked in an anguished rush, the words seeming to escape Teena's throat in spite of herself. The question caught Cassandra off guard. But then— shouldn't that be the central question? What had Calliope Jenkins been like as a child, as an adult? Did the child predict the adult and her life in any way? Cassandra should be prepared to answer this question. It was nothing less than the spine of her book.

She was even less prepared when Teena said, 'Buy another five thousand dollars' worth of clothing, and I'll talk to you on my break.'

Chapter Sixteen

Gloria was rolling the dice on her Eagle Scout, going for the psych evaluation in advance of the petition to move the case to juvenile court. She had mapped out the strategy with her client and his guardian. It was a little awkward, the guardian being the dead father's brother. He could barely stand to be in the same room as the boy. A well-to-do engineer, he had decided that standing by his nephew was the best way to maintain appearances. But he couldn't conceal his anger toward the boy, much less his fear.

He sat with Gloria now, waiting in the hallway of the county courthouse while the boy met with psychiatrists.

'He has to be crazy, right?' the uncle asked Gloria.

'I think it will be determined that he needs long-term psychiatric help,' Gloria said, knowing she wasn't really answering the uncle's question. 'We don't *need* that finding to have him tried as a juvenile, but it could help.'

'What if he comes out with a clean bill of health?'

He won't, Gloria wanted to say. *He killed his parents and his twin sisters, for no discernible reason, and he's been lying about it ever since, although not particularly well.* Instead, she said, 'It won't prevent me from petitioning the court to have him tried as a juvenile. But he's sixteen, at the upper edge of the age limit, and if he's considered sane, such as it were, that will be tougher.'

'But if he's tried as a juvenile, they have to let him out—'

'At twenty-one,' Gloria said.

'So he gets five years. That's a little more than a year per homicide.'

'Even in the adult system, a first-time offender might draw concurrent rather than subsequent sentences.'

'But not five years.'

'You'd be surprised. I mean, no, I can't imagine a judge would sentence him to five years, but I

173

wouldn't be shocked if he served less than ten.'

'He would be only twenty-six,' the uncle said. 'Still a young man.'

'A young man who had served ten years in the Maryland prison system. If you believe in fresh starts, that's not the best way to get him one. Look, this isn't a gimmick or the exploitation of a loophole. He's entitled to be tried as a juvenile. He's under eighteen. A decade or so ago, that would have been the assumption, the only option. Have you read the emerging science on the adolescent brain? They shouldn't be driving cars, if you ask me. I know this is terrifying, but if your nephew did what he is accused of doing—and he has not confessed, please keep that in mind—it was not a decision born of sound reasoning, whatever they say in there.' She jerked her head toward the closed door.

'But as a citizen,' the uncle pressed, 'would you want him on the street at twenty-one?'

'I'm his lawyer. I want the best outcome for him. The state takes care of the other citizens. It's a pretty good system, if you ask me.'

The uncle, looking vaguely nauseous, excused himself. Gloria was glad for the distraction of Harold Lenhardt, even if she knew he was on the other side, rooting for her to lose this round. She liked Lenhardt. Everybody did. Even some of the people he locked up ended up liking him.

'Smart strategy,' he said by way of greeting.

'Have you ever considered,' she said, 'that it might be better for the family if this isn't dragged out in court?'

'Let me guess. He's working on these tales of amazing abuse, Mommy and Daddy doing horrible things to their kiddies. He killed them to make it stop, then killed his sisters because they could never be made whole again. Meant to kill himself, but found that it's actually hard to get a shotgun in your mouth. I say "working on" because it's all bullshit, but I'm betting that's where he goes next, after he finally lets go of the intruder story.'

Gloria had known that no decent murder police would be fooled by her client, and Lenhardt was considerably better than decent. She shrugged, giving nothing away. She hoped.

'Hey, did some writer call you?' Lenhardt asked.

'From the *Beacon-Light*? Of course.'

'No, not about this. That old case, whatchamacallit. She tracked me down, trying to get a lead on Teena. I figured she must want to talk to you as well.'

So Cassandra Fallows was trying to find Teena Murphy. Not that Teena would talk, but it was interesting. Teena, Reg, Gloria—could she find Calliope?

'Oh, *her.* She's been leaving messages. I've been ignoring them.'

'Gloria Bustamante, avoiding publicity. I guess they're ice-skating in hell right now.'

Gloria smiled. She loved being misunderstood. Let people think she was a publicity hound, let them think she was a not-so-closeted gay woman, let them think she was a drunk. She would rather have a million misimpressions stand than have anyone know who she really was.

'I ran into Teena. She looked like shit.'

Gloria barely remembered the detective's face.

'She didn't seem interested. In this lady or her book. But you know, Teena would dearly love to

175

be vindicated.'

'Wouldn't anyone?'

'Ain't it the truth. Like your little Eagle Scout who's in there now, talking to the psychiatrists. He thinks he was right. His logic might not be our logic, but he has some sort of reason for what he did. The question is, does that make him crazy? Or just plain evil?'

'Pretty big philosophical questions for a Tuesday, Lenhardt.'

'Yeah. Is evil insanity? Or a really unpleasant version of sanity? Like, there's a part of me that thinks, a kid who did what he did—and the fact that we couldn't break him down into confessing only convinces me that he did do it—he has to be crazy. But maybe not according to the law, you know?'

'You been paying attention to that case in New York?' Gloria kept her voice as bland as possible. 'The one where they're going to release the guy who *didn't* kill his parents when he was a teenager but got worked over by some really zealous homicide detectives who wrung a half-assed confession out of him? He served twenty years.'

Lenhardt waved his hand, refusing the change of subject. 'At least when I sit in a room with a kid like that, I've got somebody nearby with a gun. I don't know how you do it.'

Gloria did, but it wasn't any of Lenhardt's business. It was easier, in some ways, to work with defendants like this, where she was sure of what had happened. Much easier than trafficking in the kind of ambiguity that Calliope Jenkins had presented. Everyone was so sure that she had killed her baby. Actually, Gloria was, too. But she

176

had believed that telling the truth might be better for Callie, whereas everyone else was adamant that she stick with the constitutional strategy. For a long time, Gloria hadn't understood why. When she did—when she did, she left the firm. Should Gloria break down, talk to this writer after all? But, no, she had nothing to say. She had suspicions, suppositions, but in the end, she had walked right up to the door and refused to open it, chosen another door, and walked out.

'Do you think Teena still blames Calliope Jenkins for everything that went wrong with her life?'

'She has to blame someone,' Lenhardt said. On this topic, his injured colleague, he dropped the glibness. 'That case, it's like a curse, isn't it? Like something you'd see in an old movie or that episode where the Brady Bunch goes to Hawaii. First Teena, then the social worker—'

'I'd have committed suicide, too, if that happened on my watch.'

'Officially, an accident,' Lenhardt corrected. 'Ran her car into a tree.'

'Freud said there are no accidents.'

'Bobby Freud? Good police, but he never worked traffic investigation that I know of.'

Gloria had to laugh. She knew better than anyone that life was full of accidents.

The doors to the hearing room opened and Gloria's client walked out, all smiles until he saw her. He adjusted his face into a more serious, thoughtful grimace, probably on the assumption that was what she wanted. On the assumption that she *cared* how he presented himself, which was wrong. He might be evil, whatever evil was. She

177

really wasn't sure. She honestly didn't care.

Chapter Seventeen

Her clothing quota met, Cassandra ended up taking Teena to a nearby sushi place, a recommendation from another customer who overheard Cassandra say that she preferred protein at her midday meal. Teena, despite her long tenure at the mall and a residence a few miles south, didn't seem to have any idea where someone might eat in the area. Now that they were at the restaurant—Sans Sushi/Thai One On; Cassandra couldn't help thinking how her father would wince at *that*—it was apparent that Teena was one of those odd people who didn't care about food. However, she seemed almost too interested in the glass of white wine that had been set before her. Not that she was drinking rapidly, quite the opposite. She conspicuously ignored it, taking tiny sips, then staring away. Yet she stole glances at the glass when she thought Cassandra wasn't looking and also studied Cassandra's little cup of chilled sake.

Although she had bought Teena's compliance, Cassandra did not feel she had permission to plunge right in, ask the questions she wanted to ask. The whole setup felt vaguely unethical. Was this checkbook journalism? Was she obligated to write about how she procured the interview? She had learned, in her second memoir, to keep her relatively cushioned lifestyle off the page, not to invite the reader's envy. Would the context make

Teena look shrewd or greedy? And would it be unfair to describe the preoccupation with the wineglass and all that suggested?

'I don't usually drink at lunch,' Teena said out of the blue, as if reading her thoughts, but perhaps she was merely following Cassandra's eyes as they tracked hers.

'Hey, I'm having sake, which is more potent than wine. I often have a drink with lunch. Americans can be too abstemious.'

'I don't know that word,' Teena said, the kind of frank admission that was rare in Cassandra's circles. No one among her New York friends ever admitted ignorance. Most of her New York friends were men, however. Challenged on the word, she wasn't sure she could define it.

'Overly concerned with being good, virtuous,' she said, knowing she was probably wrong.

'That's one thing I've never been accused of. I do like to drink. But I'm not an alcoholic. There's a test you can take. I found it online. I drink alone, but then, I live alone. And I can't remember the last time I had a drink at lunch, and I wouldn't have risked this one if it weren't the end of my shift. As it is, I'll make sure I don't drive until at least an hour after I've finished that. At my size, I could blow the legal limit without being close to drunk. I *never* get drunk, but the blood doesn't always agree with the brain.'

Poor thing. All those rules—didn't she know the score-keeping marked her more completely than her habits, whatever they might be? Had she struggled with alcohol before she left police work? Cassandra decided it was time to prod Teena toward the topic they had agreed to discuss.

'I thought ex-detectives ended up doing consulting, security and the like. Or private investigation. It never occurred to me that I would find you in Nordstrom's designer collections.'

'How long have you been looking for me?' There was a flattered wistfulness to her voice, as if she couldn't help teasing out the story of Cassandra's pursuit.

'A week or so? I found your name in the newspaper stories, the ones from back around the time . . . it happened. The archive on the local database only goes to 1991, but when I dropped your name into it, I found a small item. Something about an accident, a settlement.'

'I was injured on the job, but it wasn't exactly officer-of-the-year stuff. I was lucky to get anything. There are a lot of legal limits in those situations, according to the FOP counsel. In fact, it's kind of like *Let's Make a Deal.* They offered me the box—coverage of all related health issues for life, full pension although I was way short of my twenty—but I went for the curtain. And it looked like I was going to get the goat until the car manufacturer kicked in. I got luckier than I had a right to be. My colleagues thought I was greedy, trying to get money for an accident that everyone believes was my fault.'

'Was it?'

'*No.* I dropped my weapon while trying to subdue a suspect, she kicked it under the car, I reached in to get it, the parking brake popped. I'm lucky I even have the use of the hand, but those surgeons at Union Memorial are good. That's where you want to go for hands in Baltimore.'

Hard not to look at the hand under discussion,

180

but it appeared normal enough, although Cassandra remembered the moment back in the store, how difficult it had been for Teena to pluck Cassandra's business card from the carpet.

'It was curious to me—the article about your settlement didn't reference Calliope Jenkins.'

'Why is that curious?' Bristling, on alert.

'Well, it was a big deal, right? Like with me, no matter what I do—if I, say, saved a child from drowning—the writer will feel obligated to mention that I wrote *My Father's Daughter.*'

'Interesting.'

'Yes, I've written two more books since then and—'

'No, I mean it's interesting, the example you used, saving a child from drowning. I guess you think I failed to save a child.'

'No, no, no—'

'Because I *didn't*. What I failed to do is to get a sociopath to admit she killed her child. There's a difference. Calliope Jenkins's son is dead, was dead, long before my department got involved. That falls on others—Department of Social Services, the hospital personnel who sent a baby home with a crack-addicted mother who had already had one child taken away from her. Did you find *their* names?'

'Well, the one who died in the car accident. And there was a social worker who had to testify before a state legislative committee about why Calliope didn't get the mandated follow-up visits—'

'A supervisor, a boss, covering her ass and her employees' asses. They were almost as bad as Calliope, sitting there and invoking her constitutional rights, like she was Gandhi or

181

Martin fucking Luther King.'

'Not to play devil's advocate, but Calliope didn't receive that much attention, didn't become the symbol of anything. One thing that interests me is that her story played out about the same time as Elizabeth Morgan's. Remember her?'

Teena shook her head. She was emotional, angry, but trying to calm down.

'Anyway, Morgan was white, educated, and accused her ex of abusing their daughter. She remained in jail rather than reveal her whereabouts. I knew all about Elizabeth Morgan but never heard about Calliope Jenkins until last month. I think that's part of what I'm writing here.'

'What are you writing, exactly?' Said with a squint, and Cassandra thought she might be catching a glimpse of the detective that Teena had once been.

'At this point, it's easier to say what it won't be. It's not true crime, not exactly. It's not just about Calliope. Still, I think there's a story there, about where we started out and ended up. Not just us, but the other girls in our group. One of them is married to the lawyer who defended Calliope—'

'Reg Barr, that pussy hound. I feel sorry for whoever married him. He landed the boss's daughter, right? I heard that was the only way he kept his job.'

Cassandra flushed, hurried on. 'Yes, Donna Howard, also in our class. And he was the younger brother of yet another girl in our group, Tisha. Then there was a fourth girl who's apparently become a very proper church lady after a wild youth. I think our stories add up to something much larger than the parts.'

'Did you know Calliope well? Because I'd love any insight you have into her. I sat in rooms with her for hours on end. I was young, pretty raw, but I was *good* at what I did, and I couldn't break her. Was she that strong willed as a kid?'

Cassandra didn't know the answer, which was the stumbling block, the enormous hole at the heart of the project. She had written about her father, and however skewed her vision of him might have been, he was an open book to her. Ditto her two husbands, no matter how they might have chafed at her versions of them. But Calliope was an enigma, a quiet girl she had largely ignored. She had to report Calliope's life not only after Dickey Hill Elementary but during Dickey Hill Elementary. And for that, she needed Calliope.

'She was . . . kind of self-contained. Do you know where she is?'

'Not in Maryland, I know that much. I—look, this is illegal, you can't repeat this or write this—I used the credit department one time to try and track her down, using her old address. I think—I keep thinking that one day, I'll get a phone call or open the paper, and she'll be dead. And I'll be happy. At least, I think I'll be happy. But I might be angry, too, because she's the only one who knows.'

'Knows what?'

Teena looked at Cassandra as if she were an idiot. 'Where she hid her baby's body, what she did to him. It's not really that hard to hide a body. You'd be surprised at the dead people who never get found. And regardless what people think, it's not that hard to try someone for homicide without a body. Look, I don't know how much you know

183

about murder police, but the fact is, the obvious answer is the obvious answer. A kid disappears. His mother, a disturbed woman with a history of mistreating her children, won't say anything. She killed him. I want her to say that out loud, just once. On her deathbed, in a letter. I want—' She gestured limply with her right hand, the damaged one.

'What?'

'I don't know, actually. That's the problem. Calliope Jenkins isn't a person. She's a black hole, and I don't mean that in the nasty way it sounds. She sucks people in, you get inside her, and there's nothing there. She's dead inside, and she manages to kill anyone who comes near her, one way or the other. One kid abandoned to the system. One kid dead. The social worker who screwed up. And, okay, *me*. For seven years, Calliope drank up the attention like it was water or air. She loved it, she fucking loved it. She thrived. The rest of us fell apart.'

Teena had not eaten any of the teriyaki she had ordered. Now she pushed it around her plate while she slowly sipped her way to the bottom of her wineglass.

'What do you think happened?'

'Shaken baby, something like that, when she was high.'

'The record on whether she was an addict is in dispute. A user, yes, but not necessarily an addict.'

'If she wasn't an addict, she was insane.'

'Drugs, insanity—either one would make a charge of first-degree homicide unlikely, right?'

'Yeah. *Yes.*' Teena was shifting back and forth between her old cop persona and her present-day

184

role as a proper Nordstrom sales associate.

'And seven years—that's probably as much time as she would have served for manslaughter, or whatever the lesser charge was? So she did the time, after all, perhaps more time than she might have.'

Teena lifted her eyes to Cassandra's, then lowered them, fixing her gaze once again on the sake, then reaching for the bottle, turning it around in her hand.

'Hatsumago,' she said. 'Is it wine?'

'Actually, sake is a kind of beer.'

'I don't drink beer, never have. Now, see, that's another reason I know I don't have a drinking problem. There's a six-pack of Sierra Nevada in my fridge, been there almost a year. I bought it for a cookout, then decided I didn't want to go. But I would never drink it, even if there wasn't any other alcohol in the house.' A wry smile. 'But then—there always seems to be some kind of alcohol in my house.'

Cassandra felt herself warming to Teena Murphy, something she hadn't expected. Her father had schooled her to be open-minded in most things, but he also had instilled an undeniable class snobbery. And he had been particularly disdainful of police officers. She remembered him sneering at the television during the '68 Democratic Convention in Chicago, his rage almost out of proportion to the events, appalling as they were. He was not the kind of man who would settle for a word like *pig*, not when he could say *cochon* and then make a joke about Circe. Of course, it was around the end of his marriage; he had left Cassandra's mother by then.

185

Cassandra knew firsthand now that divorce made people almost crazy with rage. In fact, she believed that the person who left was often angrier than the person who stayed behind.

'As I said, she did seven years. Isn't that a kind of justice?'

'Justice,' Teena repeated, musing over the word. 'I confess, I was never much interested in justice. Maybe that shocks you, but that's not really a police's job. The state's attorney's office screwed up lots of solid cases we sent them; juries voted to acquit because they didn't like cops. I couldn't control justice. I lived for results. I was the third female homicide detective in that department. I told them if they put me on Calliope Jenkins, I would get her to crack. She cracked me. The day I got injured? The woman had eyes the same color as Jenkins's. That's the last thing I remember. I looked into those eyes and the next thing I knew, a car was rolling over my arm as I reached for my gun. You don't know, you can't know, how many times I sat there, staring at her. Calliope, I mean. We had staring contests. And every time, I was the one who broke. She could hold a person's gaze forever, all the time, saying the same things. *I take the Fifth. I have nothing to say.* Even her own lawyers thought she was a freak, especially Barr. You ask me, he was scared of her.'

'Scared of her?'

'He always seemed nervous when we went over to the jail to talk to her. But she didn't mind talking. That is, not talking. She was in jail; she could have passed word back that she wasn't going to talk, her lawyer could have blocked us. Don't you see? She *liked* it. She liked being in that room

186

with me, liked fucking with me. She loved it. She was—I don't know, showing off.'

'Showing off? For you? For her lawyer?' Cassandra could understand the temptation to show off for Reg.

'I know, I know. I sound crazy. But you asked. I was pretty when this started.' Teena looked startled by the train of her own thoughts. 'Yeah, I was. Cute as a button. Had a big career ahead of me, a one hundred percent clearance rate. *Everybody* talked to me in the box. I didn't see why Calliope Jenkins would be any different. But she was.'

Teena balled up her napkin and threw it on her untouched plate. 'I don't know that I have anything I can contribute to your book. But I sure look forward to reading it.'

Chapter Eighteen

Nothing really surprised Calliope anymore. She wouldn't claim to be psychic, someone who could see the future. Far from it. She simply had learned to expect the worst, all the time, and life seldom disappointed on this score. Every trip to the mailbox, every ring of the phone, made her uneasy. No news was good news. Right now, she was clutching a bag of groceries to her chest and staring at the caller ID screen on her phone, trying to decide which was worse, taking the call or listening to the message on the voice mail later. *Suck it up,* she told herself. Get it over with.

'Callie!' Reg Barr, his baritone as warm and

187

sweet and full of shit as ever. Thank God they hadn't invented a phone that could transport smell. The man was a cologne addict. Callie had gotten to the point where she claimed she was allergic, and he still wouldn't stop wearing that shit. Aramis, Paco Rabanne, whatever. He probably wore something grander now, something not only expensive but hard to find, picked out by his pretty little wife. He probably still stank to high heaven.

'What's up, Reggie?'

'Just checking in. You know.'

'Why, Reggie?' She loved using the nickname he had shortened, knowing he despised it. She would call him Candy if she dared, but it was tricky, knowing how far to push Reggie Barr.

'C'mon, girl. You know I always want what's best for you.'

Man lied natural as breathing. Although—scary thought—he probably believed most of the crap he said. He thought he had done right by her, he really did. God, he was dumb. Not book dumb. He knew what he was doing in a courtroom, when it came down to it. Outside of a courtroom, he was what her mother would call pig-ignorant. Slick, with charm that ran a mile wide and an inch deep.

'Everything's good,' she offered, semisincere. Nothing was bad. That is, there was no new bad, just the old bad, which she had lived with for so long she barely noticed it. That was a kind of good, right?

'Anything going on?'

Shit, had someone seen her back in Baltimore? But, no, Reggie would have gone straight for that if he had the goods on her.

'Not much. I did like you suggested, got a volunteer job so I wouldn't just be sitting around. I work at the Nearly New shop over to my church.'

'Get first crack at the good stuff, huh?'

She wanted to correct him, tell him that she wouldn't abuse her position that way and that the Nearly New in Bridgeville wasn't exactly awash in Gucci, anyway. But he was making conversation, not thinking about what he said. He was probably doing three other things as he spoke to her—checking e-mail, reading stuff on his desk, motioning to a secretary to bring him a cold drink. It had been a long time since Callie Jenkins had been deemed worthy of Reggie Barr's undivided attention.

'What do you want, Reggie?'

'Not a thing,' he said. 'Got some paperwork coming up. Same ol' same ol'. Okay?'

'I always do what I'm s'pose to do,' she reminded him.

'You're a good girl,' he said, and her heart broke a little because she remembered those words in a different context and knew she would never hear them again. Could never be that again. *A good girl. Such a good girl. My good, beautiful girl.*

'If you're ever in doubt, you call me.' A pause. 'You will call me, won't you, Calliope? Don't let someone sweet-talk you into doing something that wouldn't be in your best interest. Anyone else tries to talk to you, you just give it a pass, right?'

She knew she should just reassure him, let him hear what he needed to hear. She wouldn't make trouble for her mother. He had to know that. But it was hard not fucking with Reggie Barr just a little.

189

'I don't know, Reggie. I'm not sure I've ever done what was in *my* best interest.'

But she had made this mistake before, treating him like a boy, someone even more on the outskirts of things than she was, yearning just as hard after things they weren't supposed to have. Yet Candy—no, Reggie, no, Reg—he had ended up on the inside of things, whatever the opposite of outskirts were, so far in he could barely see out anymore, and he never missed a chance to assert himself on this score. He wasn't like her, and he wouldn't let her suggest that he was.

'Look, Callie, I'm serious. If need be, I'll drive over there and go through all of this with you. The statute of limitations—'

'I know,' she said wearily. '*I know.*'

'Well, there's knowing and there's knowing.'

'Agreed.'

'Keep in mind, everything was for you.'

She choked back a laugh, faked it into a cough.

'Oh, you can feel sorry for yourself, play the martyr in your mind. But don't forget this one little thing, something I know, even if you were careful never to tell me.'

She waited, let him have his moment.

'You did it, Callie. I know you did it. I don't know it in a way that would force me, as an officer of the court, to do anything about it. But you're not fooling me.'

'I got nothing more to say to you,' she said, and hung up. It was only then that she noticed she had been clasping a bag of frozen peas to her midsection the entire time, leaving the front of her shirt drenched and icy, her fingers stiff and immobile with cold.

190

Sirens

The week before my tenth birthday party, my father suddenly became fixated on the idea that I must have a special cake. I had been trying to persuade my parents that this was an important birthday—two digits!—but hadn't realized I was having any effect until my father decided that the cake was, in fact, a big deal.

'What kind of cake do you envision, Cassandra?'

'Yellow cake,' I said. 'Chocolate's not right for birthday cakes.'

'No, I mean, what is the theme?'

'The party has a mermaid theme,' I said, 'so it should be a mermaid.'

'Sirens,' he said, 'Lorelei.'

This worried me. 'No, just regular mermaids, Daddy. Not the sirens. They were bad. Nice mermaids, like Hans Christian Andersen.'

'She had a bum life, you know that, right? When she gave up her tail for legs, every step was like walking on glass splinters, and the prince didn't marry her.'

'That's not the way it is in my storybook.'

'They sanitize the books, dumpling. All the stories. Trust me. But, okay, sweet, happy mermaids, frolicking on a sea of icing. It will be yours. I'll place the order tomorrow.' The next night, he came home unusually animated, full of stories about the wonderful cake and how breathtaking it would be. 'The people there, they listened to me,' he said. 'They didn't thrust a book at me, say, 'This is what we can do.' They've never

191

done a mermaid cake, but they're going to create one for Cassandra.'

'I don't know why you couldn't go to Bauhof's, down in Woodlawn,' my mother said. But my father said this new bakery was much better. On Saturday, the day of my party, he made a great production of it: 'I am Poseidon, gone to capture the mermaid and bring her back to do the princess's bidding.'

'She's a happy mermaid,' I called after him. 'She's not going to be a slave or walk on splinters.'

'She shall do whatever you desire,' he promised.

Almost four hours later, as my mother's carefully planned party began to wind down, my father still had not arrived home. When the first parents began showing up, my mother put out the ice cream, explaining the situation in a low, tight voice. We ate the ice cream, not wanting it to melt. Fatima complained loudly about not having her cake and ice cream together. 'It's the whole point of birthday parties,' she said, and some of the other girls agreed. 'You get everything. The cake and the ice cream and the ice cream is all three flavors, pink and brown and white.'

'Strawberry, chocolate, and vanilla,' I corrected, embarrassed by my father's absence, aggrieved that Fatima would complain. My mother had always taken a dim view of Fatima's manners. Perhaps she had a point.

'*You're* vanilla,' Fatima retorted. 'And that's the one everyone likes least.'

'We should sing and figure out a way to have candles, even if there isn't cake,' said Tisha, our peacemaker. They did, with me blowing out the candles in an old pair of candelabras festooned with grapes, one of my parents' wedding gifts. Meant for romantic dinners, they hadn't seen much use in recent years. They were matte gray with tarnish, but my mother said there wasn't time to shine them. I blew out the candles—but there were only four, not the ten I had earned—and made a wish. I wished for a cake, with mermaids. I was angry and humiliated.

It did not occur to me to be anxious, although I later learned that my mother spent that afternoon racked with fear for my father, that there had already been reports of small outbursts of violence. It was my birthday and I was ten, and all I knew was that I didn't have a cake. It was a catastrophe of the highest order.

My mother was loading the dishwasher when the telephone rang. Fatima, her mother late as always, was assessing my gifts, creating a hierarchy. ('Books!' she said with a snort. 'Who wants books?') Callie, who was going to Fatima's for a sleepover because her mother was working, perched on a kitchen stool, mute as ever, drumming her legs to some tuneless song she was humming. I don't remember my mother's end of the conversation, which didn't strike me as particularly noteworthy—a lot of monosyllables, no hint of high emotion. When she hung up, she was like an animal who had started to cross a road, only to be confused by oncoming traffic. She darted toward the front door, returned to the kitchen. She got her purse, put it down. She trotted around the dining room table a few times. She bit her fist.

'Your father,' she said at last. 'He's been . . . hurt, he's in the hospital. But they said I shouldn't go tonight, because—well, it doesn't matter. Besides, we have to wait for Fatima's mother.'

'She's late a lot,' Fatima said complacently, continuing her inventory of the gifts.

'A car accident?' I asked, not being able to imagine anything else.

'He was hit by . . . something. He was driving and he got out of the car, I guess. I don't know. They think he's going to be okay. But we can't go to him, not tonight.'

'Was the cake in the car?' I couldn't help it. The issue of the cake was huge in my mind.

My mother cocked her head, studying me. Then, with extraordinary calm and purpose, she walked across the kitchen and slapped me hard, twice. Fatima's eyes were huge, and I'm surprised she had the presence of mind not to catcall, as she might have at school. Callie didn't even seem to notice.

LOW COUNTRIES

March 14–21

Chapter Nineteen

Cassandra looked at the page, astonished. There was Callie, waiting for her in her own book. Sitting on one of those wooden stools in her mother's kitchen, swinging her legs, and humming. Cassandra had forgotten even mentioning Callie, but then, it *was* a fleeting reference. Callie was a name, paper-thin, a bystander, without any of the vividness that Cassandra had tried to bring to her portraits of Tisha, Fatima, and Donna. Was that Callie's fault or hers?

Cassandra seldom reread her own work, but she had been dipping in and out of *My Father's Daughter* because Tisha's criticism continued to rankle days after their lunch. Had Cassandra been unkind, unfair? Had she gotten things wrong? She honestly could not understand Tisha's reaction. Here, in the birthday section alone, was yet another reference to Tisha as a leader and a peacemaker, the one who smoothed everything over.

At any rate, she was glad now that she had reread the book, not only because she had found Callie, waiting quietly for her in her own pages, but because it reminded her of that private bond between Fatima and Callie. Perhaps they had stayed in touch? Tisha had mentioned Fatima was *churchified* now, no longer in contact with the others. Good—then they couldn't prejudice Fatima against speaking with her. But how to find her? Cassandra picked up the Moleskine notebook in which she had, per her usual habits, been keeping notes, which she later transcribed to her computer. 'Fatima/Spelman.' She had jotted that down from memory, after Tisha left her in the restaurant. It was a start.

* * *

Cassandra entered the church the way frail old women lower themselves into a pool—slowly, cautiously, self-aware. It wasn't because she was white, although she was the only white face here. Cassandra felt uncomfortable in any church. She had not been in a place of worship for years, not since her twenties, the era of first marriages in her crowd. The older marriages, the second and third marriages, had tended to be in restaurants or city halls or outdoor venues. Cassandra herself had never been married in a church. Her first wedding had been a giddy event in a field in upstate New York, neither parent in attendance. Her mother said she wouldn't come if her father and Annie were there, and then her father reneged, as he often did. The second time, Cassandra and her husband had gone to city hall, then thrown a small party that evening, thinking to delight their friends with the announcement, yet it had cast a pall over the gathering. Ah well, most of the guests probably knew that her new husband, all but billed as her savior at the end of *My Father's Daughter,* was already actively unfaithful.

But then, she herself had cheated as well, two nights before, and the man was among their guests. That very night, as readers of her second book knew, he had insisted on accompanying her to buy more champagne, then pulled her into an alley where they kissed passionately. No, the surprise wasn't that the marriage broke up but that it managed to last almost three years. Luckily, her lover was a lawyer, and he had persuaded her to get a prenup, not that he was around when the marriage finally crashed under the weight of so much infidelity—mainly her husband's, her little fliers aside—that she felt almost wistful for the days of almost fucking someone else on her wedding night.

That was ten years ago, on the eve of her fortieth birthday. Cassandra had learned her lesson. She was good now. Apart from the married lover. But she was going to end that soon, and then she would be truly good.

Like Fatima, who was a member of this church, a fact that Cassandra had sussed out with surprising ease via Spelman's impressive alumnae association. Cassandra had found that contact on Spelman's home page, where she was briefly distracted by the information on the college's white dress tradition. (The 'don'ts', in particular, held her attention, along with the prim guidelines for proper undergarments.) True, the college had no intention of giving away the whole score— address, phone—but it did provide Fatima's married name when Cassandra explained they were childhood friends.

A quick search through the *Beacon-Light*'s newspaper archives had kicked up Fatima's new surname in connection with a piece about this church, a famous one apparently, old and venerated. But the congregation had grown so huge that the church was moving to a new 'superchurch' in the suburbs, a plan that had excited quite a lot of coverage. Fatima was quoted as wondering how anyone could object to the Lord's presence, even if it did mean more traffic. For now, there were two Sunday services, one at eight and one at eleven, to handle the overflow crowds. If she were truly prudent, Cassandra knew, she should attend the first, to be on the safe side, and then return for the second one if Fatima didn't show.

But she couldn't believe that Fatima the party girl had changed to the extent that she would attend an 8 A.M. service. Cassandra chose to arrive fifteen minutes before the later one, taking a seat in the back. However, the church was vast, with a balcony for overflow seating; she wasn't sure she would be able to spot anyone here. True, Tisha had been instantly recognizable, but Cassandra hadn't been trying to pick her out of a crowd. It also seemed rude to peer too intently at the women around her, as it only called more attention to the outsider in their midst. Also—but there she was.

Bigger. Okay, *enormous,* a ship of a woman, steaming down the center aisle like an ocean liner. Yet that confident energy convinced Cassandra it was her old classmate; Fatima may have weighed more than two hundred pounds, but she clearly thought she looked good. She did. She wore a fuchsia suit and a matching hat, the kind of hat that few women could carry, with a curling feather *and* netting. The hat matched her bag, her bag matched her shoes. If it weren't for the setting— and Tisha's warning—Cassandra would have assumed this vivid peacock of a woman was the same fun-loving borderline bad girl she had known years ago.

Fatima, she thought, her mind wandering as soon as the service began, had been one of those girls mothers such as Lenore didn't want their daughters to befriend. Loud, a little tacky. Of course, what it all came down to was the preternatural sexuality, evident to grown-ups when Fatima wasn't even ten years old. She had been the first to get her period, in sixth grade, announcing this fact with great flair to the girls in their set— and not minding in the least when the boys overheard. By then, she already had a head start in the breast department, one of those girls who sprouted overnight, developing so quickly that even she seemed surprised anew, every day, by these massive things on her chest. Fatima started dating in fifth grade. By the time Cassandra was reunited with her old friends in ninth grade, there were rumors that she wasn't a virgin. But Cassandra had always believed the gossip was generated by the more racist girls in the class, those pinch-faced Catholic school refugees who didn't get Fatima or understand why Cassandra was friends with her.

Now here was Fatima at midlife, in church, with a husband in tow and what must be their three sons, all teenagers. Should Cassandra even try to speak to her here? In front of her family? Suddenly, the whole adventure seemed inappropriate. Perhaps she could follow them from the church, take down their license plate, even tail them. No, that was sillier still.

As her mind raced, she was going through the motions of an earnest congregant, rising and sitting and singing as instructed. Eventually, the service broke down her defenses, forced her to relax, listen to the actual words being said. Cassandra began to see, dimly, the appeal of it all. Not this particular God, who seemed a little harsh to her, but the enforced time-out, the necessity of stopping and taking stock once a week. Besides, the music was sublime. She wished she could lose herself in it as those around her did—heads bobbing dreamily, arms rising with sinuous languor—but she would have looked ridiculous.

The service over, her mind still wracked with indecision, Cassandra was waiting at her pew to file out when Fatima seemed to catch sight of her. She examined Cassandra intently, it seemed, before her gaze moved on. Had she recognized her? Outside, as the crowd milled along the sidewalks, enjoying the relative mildness of the first weekend of March, Fatima approached her.

'Are you—?'

'Cassandra Fallows, Fatima. We went to school together.'

The name didn't seem to register.

'Back at Dickey Hill?' Cassandra persisted. 'With Tisha Barr and Donna Howard? Remember, we all started in third grade together, when it first opened—'

'I remember *them,* but that was a long time ago.' Said stiffly, a little grudgingly. Had Fatima jettisoned her entire past when she reinvented herself as a churchwoman? Was that required? Couldn't this God, Baptist though he might be, forgive a girl for enjoying the effect that her precocious breasts had on the boys around her? Because wasn't that what it was all about, even the inept blow jobs she had allegedly given? Fatima's only sin was being the first of her crowd to discover the thrill of finding out that she was desired, wanted. It was a forgivable offense at any age.

'You came to my house.' Almost pleading now, and not just because she needed Fatima's help for the book. She couldn't bear to be forgotten by this girl who loomed so large in *her* memories. 'The place near the school, at the end of Hillhouse Road, the dead-end road?'

'Oh, *Cassandra*. The rich girl.'

She laughed, relieved and defensive. 'I wasn't rich. In fact, after my father left, my mother and I had a tough time of it. Don't you remember how you made fun of my lunches, how I once ate peanut butter every day straight for a month?'

'There was a swimming pool—'

'Never filled.'

'Still—you weren't *poor*. I didn't even think of my mother and me as poor, and we had a lot less than you. No one in that school was poor.'

'Not even Calliope?'

The name seemed to spark something in Fatima—a tiny, almost imperceptible flinch. Yet all she said was, 'People didn't generally think of themselves as poor back then. Not where we lived. Our neighborhood was proof that you *weren't* poor. The poor people lived where we used to live.'

'But Callie didn't live up northwest, near you. She was one of the girls from over Edmondson Avenue way. Right? Isn't that where you first knew her?'

'Look—what do you want?'

That was the Fatima that Cassandra

remembered—blunt, to the point, yet still charming somehow. Fatima told you when she was mad at you, made fun of your lunch and your clothes. But she never stayed mad, and she didn't mean to hurt anyone.

'I'm writing a book. About all of us.'

'What kind of book?'

'A memoir, something like my other books—' Cassandra could tell from Fatima's expression that, unlike Tisha, she had no idea that Cassandra was a writer. 'About how we were then and how we are now.'

'Who would want to read such a thing?'

Cassandra could see no polite way to point out that thousands of people would like to read what she wrote. *As long as it was a memoir, not a novel.* She was inured to the reality that most people didn't read, that the majority of people she met couldn't even fake familiarity with her name or work. But how had Fatima, who appeared in both books, mentioned by name, managed to miss this? Hadn't someone, in the last ten years or so, asked, 'Hey, are you the Fatima in that book?'

Cassandra said, 'Well, I'm going to write about all of us, but I'm going to use Callie's story—'

Again, there was that flinch, a slight flaring of the nostrils, a tic left over from childhood.

'The thing that happened to her?' Fatima asked.

'Yes, and—'

'I wouldn't have anything to say about that. I really don't have anything to say about *any* of that. You leave me out of it.' A demand, not a question. 'That was a long time ago. I can't be associated with such things.'

She turned, and the crowd parted for her.

Cassandra didn't even consider trying to follow. She stood, conspicuous and yet ignored, her mind caught by Fatima's question: 'The thing that happened to her?' The phrasing seemed odd, suited to an accident or an act of God, not the presumed murder of a child, seven years of martyrlike silence, and now, for all intents and purposes, a successful disappearing act. Nothing had just happened to Calliope. And even if one took that view, how could it hurt Fatima?

Chapter Twenty

Donna Howard-Barr had that uncanny knack for getting others to do her bidding, all the while making it seem that it was she who was bestowing the favor. Today, for example, she had summoned Tisha to her home near downtown Baltimore, indifferent to the havoc wreaked on Tisha's day or the way it would put her smack in the middle of rush hour when she headed home. The ostensible purpose was to lend Tisha the Howard silver for Easter. Never mind that Tisha hadn't expressed any interest in Donna's family silver or that she had agreed to have the dinner for the second year in a row when the tradition was to switch off. Again, Donna had made that seem like something she was doing for Tisha's sake. 'You must be eager to entertain,' she had said, 'given how beautiful your dining room looks with the new wallpaper and dining room set.'

No, the offer to lend the silver was a summons. Donna needed to talk to her sister-in-law, but she

205

could never say things *plain*. Tisha, who almost always spoke her mind, found this tendency baffling but also enviable, because it worked for Donna, produced the desired results. Donna's serene expectation that things would go her way was a self-fulfilling prophecy. Reg was a hardheaded bull of a man, quick to argue with anyone about anything, but he was the first to cave in to Donna, and not because her father had been his boss for so many years. Not that Tisha, now cruising the streets of Bolton Hill for a parking spot, could criticize her brother when she was almost as spineless around Donna.

Grant Donna this: She had a way of making an occasion of the most basic encounter. Out in Columbia, if Tisha had gone to a friend's house to pick up something, she would have been sure to find the place in cheerful chaos. A kid's project on the dining room table, washing machine chugging away, shoes piled by the door, Mom in sweats or yoga pants, a cell phone interrupting every few minutes as they tried to catch up with one another. Donna's home was hushed and perfect, not unlike the lady of the house. The only visible signs of a child's presence were Aubrey's perfect little pink rain hat, hanging on the massive hall tree, and matching rubber boots, placed neatly on the rush mat beside it.

The dining room table had been set for late-afternoon tea. If it had been anyone else, Tisha would have snorted at the affectation. But Donna—makeup perfect, hair perfect, dressed in smart slacks and a blouse for what appeared to be a fairly ordinary day at home—had always been able to carry this kind of show. For all her quiet

206

modesty, she had an unwavering belief in herself. She was a Howard, the last of the Howards, given that her uncle Julius had never had children. Tisha, who had taken her husband's name, had been a little miffed at Donna's adamancy about being known as Howard-Barr, how quickly she corrected anyone who tried to shorten Aubrey's name to her father's alone. But if Tisha had been the last of the Barrs, she might have felt the same way.

'How many for Easter dinner this year?' Donna asked, pouring tea, passing a plate of homemade cookies. Well, she had time to bake. Even now that Aubrey was in second grade—at a private school, a luxury denied Donna because of her uncle's political ambitions—Donna still employed a full-time babysitter who took the girl to school and fetched her at day's end. A full-time babysitter who did housework during those school hours. With that setup, Tisha would bake cookies, too, maybe find a cure for cancer.

'The four of us, the three of you. Your parents, Reg's, and mine. Do your uncle Julius and aunt Gladys have a place to go?'

'I'll check with him.'

Uncle Julius was always the wild card, falling in and out of favor with his brother with a regularity that baffled Tisha. Julius Howard had always been dogged by vague rumors of bad behavior, especially back in the early eighties, when he withdrew abruptly from the election for city council president that had appeared to be his to win. But the Howards, whatever intrafamily quarrels they might have, always presented a united front to the world, whether it was Julius

Howard's derailment on his way to being Maryland's first black U.S. senator or Donna's first marriage.

'Do you have your menu planned?'

Tisha laughed. 'Donna, it's five days away.'

'Yes, only five days away.' But Donna laughed, too. She had a sense of humor about herself, to an extent, which is the most anyone ever has. She could mock her own ruthless sense of organization, her need for just-so perfection. If Donna were having the dinner this year, the menu would be planned, and she would have multiple lists on her so-called smart phone. Tisha, chained to her cell because of the kids, had resisted the new gadgets, declaiming, 'Smart phones lead to stupid people.' Personally, she didn't see that one could really improve on a list made on paper, items crossed off one by one. The very making of the list helped to cement it in one's mind.

'I suppose you'll serve your ham again,' Donna said.

'I think I would have an insurrection on my hands if I didn't.' Tisha did a ham braised in Coca-Cola, a recipe that had come down through her father's family, originally from Georgia.

'Oh, I know. Everyone loves it. But since you're doing the dinner two years in a row'—again, no acknowledgment that this was being done at Donna's behest—'I thought you might want to experiment. I found the most intriguing recipe for a tangerine-glazed ham—'

'Uh-huh, I'll stick with the basics. Coca-Cola ham, mashed potatoes. You want to try your hand at something new, feel free. But, you know, if the Easter ham ain't broken, don't glaze it with

208

tangerines.'

Donna let it go, let her win. Which meant she had larger fish to fry than the menu.

'Reg tells me that you had lunch with Cassandra Fallows, our former classmate.'

So that was it. Donna hated to ask for gossip out-and-out, but she loved dishing it.

'Against my better instincts. I couldn't help thinking she might really want to catch up, but it was all research for another book. Bad enough to show up in the first two unawares. I'm not going to *volunteer* for that treatment.'

'She wasn't unkind to you,' Donna said. 'Or me. If anything, she was almost too laudatory.'

'But that was what bothered me. She built us up—not so she could tear us down, but to heighten everything. That girl, she could make a five-act tragedy out of spilling chocolate ice cream on a new dress and never even stop to think that there's this thing called detergent. You know me, I can't stand made-up drama. The world provides enough.'

'I was thinking of calling her, asking her over.'

'Donna.'

'You know the old saying. Keep your friends close, keep your enemies closer.'

That caught Tisha short. As exasperated as she was with Cassandra Fallows, she didn't think of her as an enemy. And Donna had always made it a point of pride not to engage with the portrait of her presented in Cassandra's books.

'I grant you, she's a fool, and her books are maddening, but still—'

'What she's writing now—it can't help reflecting on Reg. And the firm of Howard and Howard.'

209

Howard, Howard and Barr, Tisha amended in her head.

'After all, she's not going to get Calliope to talk, even if she could find her, and from what I hear, no one knows where she is, not even Reg. So how's she going to fill in all that space? What if she attacks the legal strategy, suggests that the defense was all about showcasing the firm's innovation but not done with Calliope's best interests in mind?'

'Would she? Did she say something to Reg—?'

'No, but she's been trying to get to Gloria Bustamante, the first lawyer. What if Gloria sees a chance to burnish her image at Reg's expense? You know what a publicity whore she is.'

Actually, Tisha didn't. Donna often forgot that she moved in a world that, while all of fifteen miles away, was quite different from Tisha's. People in Donna and Reg's circles might gossip about Baltimore's lawyers—who did what, who said what. Where Tisha lived, the hot topics were high school redistricting and the bad-tempered basketball coach.

'And,' Donna said, 'she cornered Fatima at her church just two days ago. At her *church,* out of the blue.'

'Fatima called you?' Tisha felt wistful. People grew apart all the time. She and Donna might have drifted away from each other if not for the familial connection. Besides, the Fatima she missed didn't exist anymore; she had been subsumed by the new holier-than-thou version who didn't want any reminders of the girl she had once been. Still, Tisha would have been thrilled to hear her voice on the phone, for any reason.

'Fatima called Reg, asked what was up.'

210

'Reg? Why would she call Reg?'

Donna shrugged. 'The home number is unlisted. He's easy to find. Cassandra did the same thing, after a fashion. Found Reg, then found you.'

Tisha looked at the place setting in front of her. The Howard china, like the Howard silver, was only three generations old, not quite the grand heirlooms that Donna made them out to be. Her mother, Irene Thomas Howard, had come from a well-to-do family, and these had been her mother's. They had been passed down to Donna upon her first marriage, and they weren't to Tisha's taste. The plates had a cluster of peonies in the center with a thick red-and-gold rim; the silver was similarly ornate. She had a hunch that Donna didn't really care for them, either, which was why she was so generous about lending the pieces out.

'What do you think it would accomplish, Donna, talking to Cassandra?'

'Whether she realizes it or not, I think Cassandra is acting out of spite. The reason I never minded the first book as much as you did is that the story was at least balanced. She failed us and we failed her. I don't care if the latter never happened—at least she placed it in a framework where we were reasonable, acting on our own wounded feelings. But writing about Callie's defense could have real repercussions, not just hurt feelings.'

'So if you befriend her, she won't write that book?'

'It's one option. Not the only one. But the easiest one, for all of us.'

'And if it doesn't work?'

The front door opened, Aubrey arriving home with her babysitter. The well-trained little girl

211

hung up her coat before entering the dining room, hugged her mother and her aunt, then waited to be invited to share the cookies with them, taking the three that her mother prescribed. She clearly wouldn't dream of wheedling for more, nor did she try to invade the adult conversation, not until Tisha asked her about her day. She spoke of school, Grace and St Peter, with great enthusiasm. Funny, neither Donna nor Reg had been an outstanding student. Was it vanity on Tisha's part to see something of herself in her niece's hungry mind, her interest in art *and* science? It wouldn't be long before people would be telling the girl to choose, that one of these interests had to dominate and crowd out the other. Tisha, who had bought the propaganda and chosen art over science, had been delighted when her book club had introduced her to the work of Andrea Barrett, with her stories of biologists and history. Now that was *real* writing. Why couldn't Cassandra, who clearly had talent, direct her mind toward similarly ambitious work, instead of mining these wispy little childhood slights?

She helped Donna clear the table and wash the dishes by hand, Donna protesting all the while that Tisha should get on the road. Sure enough, she hit the tangle of rush hour on I-95 and cursed her own good manners. It was only then, stalled on the highway, whirling the radio dial in search of a traffic update, that she remembered how hard Donna's face looked when asked what she would do if Cassandra didn't prove malleable. Tisha almost felt sorry for their onetime friend. She herself would never want to inspire that look of stony composure. Donna, like most people used to

212

getting their way, was formidable when denied.

Chapter Twenty-One

'I hear you're having dinner with your father again,' Lennie said.

Cassandra, who had been folding laundry as she spoke to her mother, almost dropped the portable phone cradled between neck and shoulder. Her parents had not, to her knowledge, initiated contact with each other for years. On those occasions where they had been forced to share the same space—usually events centering on Cassandra—they managed to be polite, nothing more. Things between them had been more strained since Annie's death, as if all that frosty goodwill had been for Annie's benefit.

'Y-y-y-yes,' Cassandra said, starting to lose her grip on the phone, then dropping the T-shirt in her hands in order to grab the receiver before it fell to the floor. She wanted to point out to her mother that she really did need to discuss the format of her father's interview at the Gordon School. Besides, her mother was free to call *her,* to ask and even issue invitations. But Cassandra didn't raise either point because she knew how Lennie would reply. Reminded about the Gordon School event, she would say something self-deprecating, self-pitying. ('Funny, I was the one who taught there all those years, yet it's your father onstage. . . . I can't imagine spending fifty dollars to watch that. . . . Oh, no, I wouldn't dream of you buying a ticket for me. I do know the story, after all.') As for the idea that she could ask for anything, from anyone, even her daughter—Lennie refused to believe that. Cassandra had dated a man once who had a dog so well trained that he could leave him in the room with a steak on the table, and the dog would only stare at it sorrowfully. That was Lennie all over, but she had taught herself this trick.

'He called me to get your local phone number,' Lennie said. 'He wrote it down on a piece of paper and lost it.'

'I'd love to have lunch or dinner with you. If you're free.'

'Thursday lunch?' her mother offered.

Cassandra understood why her mother had picked that particular time slot. She was having dinner with her father Wednesday night; Lennie wanted the advantage of going second, the opportunity to criticize her ex-husband slyly, much as she had every other Sunday night when Cassandra returned from another weekend in his care. Those weekends had, in fact, been rather dreary, but Cassandra had refused to betray her father's inadequacies, such as the meals at Pappy's Pizza. (A novelty at first, but not when one went every other weekend.) Or the endless hours of television they watched together, to the accompaniment of her father's muttering. Like every child who had yearned for unfettered access to something and then gotten it, Cassandra had quickly learned how tedious a glut was. When her father took her to see *A Clockwork Orange*—she was all of thirteen—she had understood instantly how Alex's treatment worked, having been through the same thing. Oh, technically, she could have walked away from the television at any time, picked up a book. Eventually, she did, but she had wandered through her own teenage wasteland first.

'I have plans Thursday,' she said apologetically. 'Donna Howard and I are having lunch.' *Howard-Barr*, she reminded herself. *Married to Reg Barr, who is much too attractive for his own good. For my own good. And, incidentally, Donna Howard-Barr is the only person who seems to want to talk to you, who actually called you, so don't fuck it up.*

'She was always my favorite,' her mother said. 'Such beautiful manners.'

Not to mention rich and well connected, Cassandra thought. But she felt she shouldn't be too critical of her mother on this score. She, too, had an awed regard for Donna, who moved with balletic grace, careful to avoid colliding with anyone or anything. Cassandra, a great bumper into things, forever bruising her hips and elbows on tables and countertops, wished she had that kind of delicate control, but it would have meant slowing down. Funny, of all the old classmates, she would have put Donna as the least likely to help her. She had been reserved and reticent as a girl, not inclined to confide in anyone. Then again, given her family, Donna was sophisticated, a little more worldly. She understood that Cassandra was going to write something; Donna might as well participate, get her side in.

'What about lunch on Wednesday?' Cassandra offered.

'Two meals out in one day?' Her mother found this scandalous. 'No, no, you couldn't possibly.'

You couldn't possibly, I do it all the time.

'You come here. I'll make shrimp salad. I'll get

those cookies you like, from Bauhof's, which is called Louise's now, but I think they use the same recipes.'

Cassandra's sweet tooth had abated in recent years, and it was now salt that she craved. She could sit inside a bakery and not be tempted beyond a nibble, while a bag of tortilla chips undid her. Yet even as she resented her mother's belief that she was still a little girl who liked pink-and-white refrigerator cookies, she was touched by it, too, and happy to sustain the illusion. She would go to Dickeyville, eat her mother's gloppy shrimp salad, scarf up whatever cookies were served, and if this undercut her appetite later that evening, when her father was taking her to one of Baltimore's best restaurants—ah well, that was probably the point.

*   *   *

'This Chef has a French place, too,' her father said, inspecting the dining room at Charleston, 'and I prefer that, in some ways. But the acoustics are hell. Shall we split a bottle of wine?'

Cassandra eyed her father's martini glass, with only a swallow left. He had been in the bar, waiting for her, when she arrived five minutes ahead of their reservation. Was he on his first drink or his second?

'Do you really think—'

'Cassandra, I know my capacity, my limits.'

She let this pass. But Cedric Fallows's life had been shaped by his ignorance of his capacity, his limits, as they were about to discuss. And although it wasn't suitable for the audience at the Gordon

School, Cassandra had a question she had never dared to ask her father before, and she hoped to slip it in tonight, amid these rich courses and sips of whatever wine he wanted. Her apartment was two blocks away. He could sleep on the pullout sofa if it came to that.

'Red or white?'

'White wine,' her father said, 'is insipid.'

His old prejudice seemed a shame, given the rich variety of Low Country seafood on the menu, but Cassandra recalibrated her taste buds, began checking out the plates listed under VIANDES. There was foie gras in the appetizer course, but she preferred that accompanied by Sauterne, although she wouldn't dream of mentioning this to her father. Wine—all alcohol, in fact—was supposed to be his bailiwick. Some fathers remained forever in charge of the yard or the cars. Her father ruled the liquor cabinet.

Cassandra had been interviewed far more than she had served as an interrogator, but she was developing her own elliptical style these days, inspired in part by Joan Didion's comment about how she let shyness work for her, so that subjects rushed to fill her awkward silences. Cassandra could never fake shyness, especially with her father. But she could lead him, as if down a series of switchbacks, to the topic she really wanted to discuss. They began easily enough, over light green salads, talking about the problems posed by her father's story. He was a white man who had collided with a seminal event that affected African-Americans far more profoundly in the end. Was his story meaningful in any larger way, or was it just a heightened love story?

'You mean, is it *War and Peace* or *Anna Karenina*?' her father said. 'A little bit of both. In the end, I simply was in the wrong place at the wrong time.'

'The fact that you were white—isn't that part of the reason you were beaten so badly? Sort of like what's-his-name, in the L.A. riots all those years later, the man who was pulled from his truck.'

'I suppose,' her father said. 'But Annie was attacked first. Don't ever lose that part of the thread. Other people were attacked, even killed. And they tended to be black.'

She tried to get him to sketch the scene, but her father had always been stubborn about the facts surrounding the beating itself, insisting he didn't remember anything after the first blow. He could describe Annie, how he had watched in horror as she got knocked down, then rose up again, as crowds began running down the street toward a drugstore that was being looted. The contemporaneous accounts of looting were, as Cassandra knew from researching her first book, borderline racist, portraying all the rioters as craven opportunists, intent on stealing, burning buildings to destroy the credit records that recounted who owed what. But her stepmother had introduced Cassandra to women who could explain what it was like, that confused afternoon, how they believed they were on the verge of an apocalypse. What began as a desperate quest for food and medicine and baby formula spiraled out of control. It was Judgment Day. 'It didn't,' Annie said dryly, 'bring out the best in anyone.'

At the same time, Annie had always insisted she had no plan, that she was coming home from work

218

when the riot erupted around her and she was knocked down, men tearing at her clothes, prompting Cedric Fallows's ill-considered bit of gallantry. Would he have gotten out of his car if the woman he had seen had been less beautiful? Probably not, Cassandra knew, although she could never quite bear to put those words on paper. She granted her father his love-at-first-sight version, but she was not required to point out that this love was sparked by Annie's gorgeous shape, her beguiling face whose only flaw was the gap between her front teeth. Her father adored that gap.

'Cassandra, I'm not sure you realize how badly injured I was,' her father said now. 'I didn't suffer actual brain damage—thank God, I cannot imagine what my life would have been like if my mind had been impaired—but it was *healthier* for me to forget, and my brain complied.'

'Wouldn't it have been healthier still if there had been more talk of post-traumatic stress disorder then? It's my observation that your conscious mind may have granted you a respite, but your subconscious is a land mine. You jump at small noises, for example, like a door opening unexpectedly.'

'I jumped at small noises back when I could hear them,' her father said. 'Now, I think, a gun could go off and I wouldn't flinch.'

She backed away then, not wanting to push him too hard. And, to be truthful, not wanting to delve into her father's decline, because it also implied her own. Instead, they discussed her father's view of the riots, which was admirably benign, all things considered. But then, he had absorbed Annie's version of things. Her world had rejected him almost as thoroughly as his had rejected her, isolating the couple. It was a good thing that their love had held up, Cassandra often thought, because they really didn't have anyone else. Her father's colleagues, polite liberals, did not judge him, but they did not invite his new wife to their homes, and they could be thoughtlessly condescending when he brought her to events at the university. Annie wasn't a stupid woman, just not a bookish one. With her husband's encouragement, she had earned a nursing degree. But that mattered little to his friends.

As for Annie's family—when she married Cedric Fallows, she was dead to them.

And so the meal went, Cassandra pressing, then retreating, circling around and around, getting ready for the right moment to hit her target. She found it over the cheese course, her father mellow with port.

'I still miss cigarettes,' he said.

Cassandra was amazed. 'You quit almost forty years ago.'

'Yes, I did, and I've never strayed, not once. But after a meal like this—I would love a cigarette.'

Strayed was all she needed.

'Daddy—when you met Annie, you were an experienced, well, adulterer. You had several lovers before her.'

'Affairs, not lovers. I never loved them.'

'Okay, several *affairs*.' There had always been moments when this semantic distinction rankled, and this was one of them. 'I guess what I'm trying to say is that you were experienced at cheating. But when you began the affair with Annie, after you got out of the hospital, you didn't try to hide it. You flaunted it, made Mother acknowledge it, all but forced her to kick you out. Why did you do that?'

'Cassandra, I think you know.'

'No, I don't. That's why I'm asking.'

'Then what do you think? You know something of adultery—much as that pains me to say. I would never tell you what to write, and your second book is quite well done, but I won't pretend that I wouldn't be happier if that document never existed.'

'Are we having a teaching moment? Are you using the Socratic method to get me to explain your life to you?'

'I think you have a theory, and you want to know if it's right. So go ahead, tell me, Cassandra. Why, after a history of furtive behavior, did I enter so flagrantly into the affair with Annie, refusing to conceal what I was doing?'

'I think it's because you had always lied—to Mother, to those other women. To be an adulterer is to be a liar. The only way you could make Annie special was to never tell a single lie to her—or even about her.'

He sipped his port.

'This is not,' her father said, 'going to be part of our onstage discussion?' He did her the courtesy of pretending it was a question.

'No, but—'

'Then let's leave it here, with a meaningful silence, where I neither affirm nor contradict your sense of me.'

She let him drive home, then instantly regretted it, thinking of those dark final miles to

221

Broadmeade. She left a message on his machine, demanding that he check in, pacing well into the night when he didn't.

He called about ten the next morning, ostensibly to ask if she remembered the name of the wine he had selected and whether she thought Wegman's might carry the goat cheese. But Cassandra understood that the call, the timing of it, was to remind her that concern was a parent's prerogative, not a child's. She was not his caretaker. Yet.

Chapter Twenty-Two

The Barrs lived in a block very much like Cassandra's own back in Boerum Hill. In fact, the old town houses here—they were too stately to be called rowhouses—were even nicer and the neighborhood had more green, or would, when the trees budded later this spring. Her parents had lived in an apartment here briefly, in the first year of their marriage. 'Across the street from F. Scott Fitzgerald,' her father had always said, and it was years before Cassandra realized that Fitzgerald was not an actual neighbor but a literary ghost that her father liked having nearby.

She wondered at the Barrs' choice of the neighborhood, the house, if it were a statement of sorts. Donna's parents had lived not even a mile from Cassandra's childhood home, but it had seemed like a different world, a modern-for-the-era split-level backing up to the wooded hills on the other side of the Gwynns Falls. Everything in the Howards' house was new and shiny. She may have jumbled two parties in her memory, as Tisha claimed, but she definitely retained vivid impressions of the sixth-grade 'graduation' party held there. And, yes, they had called it a graduation party. Lately, there was earnest hand-wringing over the excessive celebration of minor milestones, which amused Cassandra. Not only had her sixth-grade class staged a graduation, she had marched in a cap and gown when she finished kindergarten. There was nothing new about this.

But the party at the Howard house had eclipsed the school celebration. She remembered the dress she wore, a very short—really, too short—patterned dress, a Christmas gift. Cassandra had grown two inches in five months, reaching what would turn out to be her adult height of five-four, and the hemline was barely decent. The boys teased her about it. Teased her about her dress and her hair, which she hadn't washed in three days in anticipation of the party because her hair was more manageable when it was dirty. Instead, she had sprayed some bizarre aerosol product on it—Psssssst. God knows what was in that concoction of pressurized chemicals. She would have done just as well shaking talcum powder over her head. There was a little powder visible on her dress and the boys had claimed she had dandruff, brushing at her shoulders in imitation of a popular commercial. She had wanted to think the boys teased her because they liked her. But even then, she didn't have much capacity for self-delusion. The boys in her class, black and white alike, didn't see her as a girly-girl, while they clearly thought Donna and Tisha deserved that kind of attention.

223

She could swear little Candy Barr had been there, doing his dance, but maybe that had been at Tisha's birthday party two months earlier.

And Callie? Would Callie have been there? Having stumbled on this forgotten girl in her own pages, Cassandra kept wracking her memory, hoping to discover Callie lurking in some other overlooked corner. It was a big party, everyone must have been invited. But that didn't mean everyone was there.

'Cassandra,' Donna said, opening the door to her. She had aged well, almost as well as Tisha. Donna's delicate prettiness was more susceptible to the years; it was the 'interesting' girls who improved. But her voice was the same, sweet and low, forcing one to lean in close to catch each word.

'You look the same,' Cassandra said.

'You don't,' she said, inspecting the outfit revealed as Cassandra shrugged out of her trench coat. 'Are those slacks Armani?'

Cassandra nodded, pleased. The pants had gone a long way toward meeting Teena's quota, as had the cashmere turtleneck that Teena had picked out, in a mossy green color that Cassandra never would have chosen. But she was also pleased that Donna recognized the designer. She felt as if they were on some new plane, more equal than they had been in school. Back then, she had stroked the blond wood case of the Howard color television cabinet, wondering at the glory of such a thing. Now she and Donna lived in similar houses, wore similar clothes.

'The hair, though,' Donna said. 'I think I might have known you from the back, just from the hair.'

The hair. With those two words, Donna effortlessly reestablished the old order. Cassandra might have been her peer now, financially, but Donna wasn't ready to offer her equal stature across the board.

She decided to make a joke of it. 'Sixth grade was hard, but I don't think I had turned gray yet.'

'No, that's true,' Donna said, leading her into the formal living room, which tended heavily toward chintz—good taste, if a little safe. Not Cassandra's taste. 'Your face has grown into that mane. Sometimes it was hard to see you under all that hair.'

I was hiding, Cassandra wanted to say. *I needed that curtain of hair to make it through the day, sometimes, after my father left.* She had worn it so far forward that it almost covered her face, and the boys called her Cousin It.

'Well, it's quite a transformation,' Donna said. 'I feel so boring next to you. Staying in Baltimore, marrying a boy I've known all my life. When Reg told me about running into you, I couldn't help being intrigued by your new project. A book about us and where we ended up. No one will want to read my chapters, though! What did Tolstoy say? All happy families are alike?'

'I always thought,' Cassandra said, consciously taking on her old role, the provocateur, the contrarian, 'that was utter bullshit. Happiness doesn't come in one flavor any more than ice cream does.'

Donna rewarded her with a laugh, her old shy, difficult-to-coax laugh, a key weapon in Donna's arsenal. 'You're right. There's a world of difference between chocolate and vanilla, but if

225

vanilla makes you happy, so be it.'

Was Donna implying Cassandra was vanilla? But, no, Donna was not one to stab and poke that way. Cassandra was the one who had used language to bully, tease, assert.

'It occurs to me just now,' she said, lying smoothly, her father's daughter, 'that you may be one of the most important figures in what I'm doing, the one person connected to everyone.'

Donna frowned prettily. Donna had always been able to do even ugly things prettily.

'Oh no,' she said. 'Tisha was the personality around which we all revolved.'

'Yes, back in school.' She may have imagined it, but Cassandra would swear that Donna looked disappointed at her ready agreement, had hoped for more of an argument. 'But you married Reg, who worked for your father, and he worked on Callie's defense. I can't help wondering—did you ask your father's firm to take on Callie? Or was it a coincidence?'

'I suppose the *coincidence* was that my father was simply one of the most successful lawyers in the city.' Donna's manner was a little stiff. Was it really that wounding to be reminded that Tisha had been the spark plug of their group? 'It was my understanding that the ACLU brought him into the case. I was . . . away, when it started. I was in Knoxville for much of the eighties. There was a—I was—I was married, before. And not one of those starter marriages. It lasted seven years and the ending was . . . quite bitter.'

'Hey, I had two of those,' Cassandra said, and this admission seemed to relax Donna.

'It's awful, isn't it? Divorce. I'd never go through

226

it again.'

That pussy hound Reg Barr. Teena Murphy had tossed that off almost parenthetically, as if everyone knew and no one cared. It was of more interest to Cassandra than she wanted to admit. She knew the compromises involved in being married to a man who would not stop sleeping with other women, no matter how discreetly. But she couldn't imagine Donna putting up with it. Perhaps Teena was referring to premarriage Reg.

'Was it strange,' Cassandra said, 'dating a man—marrying a man—that you could remember as a little boy?'

'It was. In fact, I felt a little embarrassed at first, as if two years were some horrible gap. Plus, he was working for my father. But he pursued me, was determined to have me, and I have to say, I was flattered. Reg was quite the ladies' man, he had his pick of women. I could never see why he settled on dull old me.'

Cassandra knew she was expected to contradict this premise as well—protest that Donna was never dull, merely quiet, a personality in her own right. Instead, she found herself saying, 'Well, you were the boss's daughter and he did end up making partner.'

Her tone was light, but apparently not light enough.

'He made partner *before* we were engaged. And it grieved him so, the gossip about how it was because of me. Reg earned that partnership, earned the right to take over when my father retired. You know, it's only nepotism when you can't back it up. Reg could have gone out on his own, been a star wherever he worked. It was in my

227

father's best interest—in the firm's best interest—to keep him in the fold.'

'Did he ever speak of Callie to you, when he was representing her?'

'Of course not. Attorney-client privilege.'

'Did he ask you about her, try to glean information about her as a child? After all, you and Tisha had known her, a little. If I were her lawyer, I'd have been keen to talk to her childhood friends.'

'That's not law, that's psychology,' Donna said. 'Of use in a presentencing, but it had no relevance to Callie's case. Besides, if you think about it—what did we really know about Callie? No one ever went to her house, only Fatima knew her people. And she was so quiet. Never volunteered in class and when the teachers made her participate, she looked as if she were on the verge of passing out. Do you remember Callie ever saying anything?'

'I remember her singing. And laughing. But, no, she wasn't a big talker.'

'Except to Fatima. She whispered, sometimes, to Fatima, and then Fatima took Callie's comments for hers. Half the funny things that Fatima said? Callie whispered them or wrote them in the margins of her notebook.'

Notebooks. Cassandra had a Proustian moment, remembering those notebooks. There were not many variations, then—or perhaps her mother had simply not allowed variations. Everyone had a denim cloth–covered binder with loose-leaf paper. Neatness counted, and neatness was not Cassandra's strong suit. Donna, though—Donna's notebooks had been exquisite year-round. She never used those sticky little reinforcements to

228

mend the broken holes, because her holes never broke. She never doodled on the outside, although she covertly filled her pages with drawings. And when they had to make covers for the school-issued textbooks, hers were folded and fitted with the precision of origami, while Cassandra's managed the trick of being simultaneously lumpy and shredded.

'Yes, she and Fatima did have a special bond. But Fatima doesn't want to talk to me.'

'Really? Well, she's reinvented herself, you know how that goes.' Was Donna suggesting that Cassandra had engineered a similar reinvention or only that she understood how such things were done? 'She doesn't speak to me, either, and she wouldn't even have that Spelman degree she's so proud of if it weren't for my uncle Julius. He wrote her recommendation. Fatima didn't begin to have the grades.'

'That was nice of him.'

'She volunteered in his office, the summer after we graduated. Remember how special we thought we were, because we were the class of '76?'

'It wasn't such a big deal at the Gordon School,' Cassandra said. Could Donna really have forgotten that she did not graduate with her? Had she not read Cassandra's book? 'We thought of ourselves as hippies, and it was uncool to be patriotic.'

Donna shook her head. 'I don't know, Cassandra. I don't see how these little things add up to a book. We knew a girl. She was accused of a horrible crime—which she almost certainly committed, even if she never confessed. So what?'

'I admit I don't know where I'm going with this.

229

But given all the connections, how can I not talk to you and the others who knew her?'

'And Reg. You want to talk to Reg.' It sounded like a challenge.

'Tisha said he wouldn't talk to me.'

'Tisha forgets that she's not the boss of Reg anymore. I am.' Donna allowed herself a wink, but Cassandra realized she was deadly earnest.

'What about the first lawyer on the case, who also worked for your father? Can you get her to talk to me?'

'Oh, Gloria.' Donna made a face. 'She's drunk half the time, anyway. And, you know, she left the firm, went out on her own, abandoned Callie. Reg was the one who saw it through to the end.'

'So he's the one I have to talk to.'

'If you feel you must,' Donna said on a sigh. 'I'll ask him to make time for you, as a favor to me. But all it's going to do is establish that this is a dead end. It's such a . . . small, sad story. Do people really want to read these things?'

'In my experience? Yes.'

Donna smiled. '*In your experience*—that's a funny phrase if you think about it. What else does anyone have? What else do we know but what we've experienced?'

Her voice was benign, musing, and the questions were perfectly fair. But Cassandra couldn't help feeling she had been put in her place somehow. She asked about the painting over the mantel—a Horace Pippin, not that Cassandra knew who he was, but the piece's quality was undeniable—and the rest of their visit passed easily, filled with reminiscences that matched up, more or less. Unlike Tisha, Donna had no quarrels with what

Cassandra had written and was unabashed in her admiration for the rewards she had reaped. It was, in fact, quite pleasant.

*   *   *

Eighteen hours later, Cassandra was in bed with Donna's husband, more surprised than anyone. She was definitely more surprised than Reg, who, from the moment she opened her door to him, treated the meeting as a ruse for them to be alone. In fact, he was so sure of his interpretation that he was puzzled by her hesitance, treated it as a coy act, and, as he broke her down, she began to believe it might have been. By the time she reassembled the timeline in her head, reminded herself that her interest in Calliope had started long before she had encountered Reg—he was inside her and she was beyond caring.

She gripped his shoulders as if at risk of falling from a great height, as if she were far above the world, Leda in the beak of a swan Zeus. *Would she put on his knowledge with his power?* How did the rest of it go? The only other line she could remember was *And Agamemnon dead,* and she had forgotten who Agamemnon was. Then she felt guilty, thinking of a black man as a swan, an animal. Yet she was really thinking of him as Zeus, was she not? A god to her mortal? But that, too, struck her as wrong, freighted, too similar to her father's way of justifying Annie's arrival in his life by comparing her to Aphrodite. Then it came to her—Agamemnon was the warrior who took Cassandra as his trophy after sacking Troy, and the two were later murdered. Leda, pressed to the

231

swan's breast, catches a glimpse of the future, but Cassandra was the one who had the true gift of prophecy.

'So this is the one place where you're quiet,' Reg said afterward, just, when they were still entwined. 'Me, too. It's funny, isn't it, how big talkers like us go quiet in bed?'

Cassandra nodded.

Sick Bay

My father was in the hospital for three weeks. I wasn't allowed to visit him, according to the hospital rules, but my mother was reluctant to leave me home alone, so I would sit in the waiting room with my homework. Then, having ventured that far into the city, crossing streets that just days ago had been torn by rioting, my mother felt we deserved some kind of treat, especially on Fridays. We would head farther out Eastern Avenue, to Highlandtown and Haussner's, a Baltimore institution. A German restaurant, it had filled every inch of wall space with nineteenth-century art. The sheer volume of paintings, their random and haphazard placement, made me assume they were tacky, on a par with paint-by-numbers pictures or black velvet portraiture. In fact, my father had treated Haussner's as an object lesson in aesthetics, sneering at the paintings and encouraging me to sneer, too. But when I returned to the restaurant as an adult, I learned that the paintings are considered very fine examples of nineteenth-century art.

My mother, however, did not lecture me about the décor. She chose the restaurant because it was a good compromise for an adult and child, a place where she could get a cocktail and, say, veal or liver, while I had a Shirley Temple and potato pancakes. We ate in silence and I became aware of how much conversation my father provided, how he guided and ruled our dinner table discussions. The quiet wasn't awkward, not in the restaurant, which had a happy cacophony. But it was strained and worrisome at home.

At the end of the second week, in the lull after we placed our order, my mother suddenly said, 'You never ask any questions about your father.'

'You said he was going to be okay.' A panicky thought struck me. 'He is, isn't he? You *said*.'

'He's going to be fine. They were worried at first. He was beaten very badly and—well, they couldn't be sure—the brain and all—but he's going to be fine. He may need more time to recover physically, but he'll be fine.'

'Why did they beat him?'

My mother held up her drink, something called a lime rickey, and studied it in the light.

'Things that happen in a riot, they don't make sense. People get out of control and the energy just feeds itself. If your father had stayed in the car—but he didn't stay in the car.'

'Why?'

'He saw someone being . . . hurt, and he went to help her. It was very brave, actually. Foolish, but brave.'

Neither my mother nor I had met Annie at that point. But the next week, my father's final one in the hospital, a woman approached me in the waiting room. If you had asked me at the time, I would have said she looked like Diahann Carroll or Diana Ross. By which I would have meant, *She's a beautiful black woman and those are the beautiful black women I know.* In fact, Annie was beautiful in a way that was new in 1968. Her skin was dark, about as dark as skin gets, her nose broad, her lips full.

But while her face spoke to a standard of beauty that was just coming into its own, her body was a throwback to the 1950s, almost cartoonishly curvy in its proportions, with a tiny waist, generous hips, and, frankly, the largest natural breasts I had ever seen on a woman. As I had already started wondering what my own breasts might look like when they arrived—Fatima had recently purchased a training bra, and all the girls in our class were thinking about their breasts-to-be—I couldn't help staring. Could something like *those* sprout on my chest? My own mother's bosom (and that's the word I would have used at the time, although with much giggling) was modest. This was an era where our chests chose us; we did not choose our chests. One's developing body was a random, freakish event, a card dealt facedown that you got to turn over somewhere around twelve or thirteen.

I was so entranced by this stranger's bosom that it took me a moment to realize that she was speaking to me.

'You must be Ric's daughter,' she said. 'I can see the resemblance.'

This took several seconds to sort out. My father was a man. Girls didn't resemble men. Besides, it was an article of faith in my family that I looked like myself, no one else.

The woman knelt down, putting her face level with mine. 'I'm Annie. I was with your father . . .'

'Are you the woman who was being beaten?'

Her face flickered with pain. Later, I would piece things together, understand that my mother had been euphemistically inexact in describing the attack on Annie. But my ten-year-old brain could not have processed the reality of rape.

'Beaten? Well . . . almost, I guess. But it was nothing compared to what happened to your father. I feel awful about that.'

'You didn't do it.' A ten-year-old's insistence on fairness coming to the fore. Children, blamed for things they haven't done, are naturally judicious.

'No, I didn't. I guess you're here with your mama?'

'Yes. She's in my father's room, two oh eight. You can go in because you're a grown-up.'

'You come every day? That must get boring.'

'I get my homework done. We usually come earlier, and there's a treat after, snowballs on weekdays, a restaurant on Fridays. Or'—I lowered my voice as if my father, down the corridor, might hear of this perfidy—'we eat off TV trays and we pretend we're on a flight to Europe and the TV is the movie.'

'That sounds nice.' Annie's face and her voice didn't match up. I could tell she thought it was queer or that I was too old for such a childish game.

'Did you come here to thank my dad? Because he saved you?'

'Well, I am concerned about him. But people in the hospital shouldn't have too many visitors. They get tired.'

'He's better. He's getting out Friday.'

'Still—I'll let him have this time with your mama.'

My mother came out then. I blurted in a self-important rush, 'This is Annie, the woman Daddy saved. She came to thank him.'

My mother regarded the woman's chest, much as I had. 'How nice,' she said. 'You should go in now, while he's awake. He's still sleeping a lot.'

'Annie Waters,' the woman said, holding out her hand to shake. 'It's nice to meet you.'

'Visiting hours will be over soon,' my mother said. 'I wouldn't want you to miss your chance.'

My mother's voice was ultra-polite, the way she always was with strangers. Annie headed down the corridor and we left, driving home through neighborhoods that terrified and fascinated me. The curfew was past, the days were expanding toward their summer length, but my mother was still nervous. She didn't relax until the final mile of our journey, when we entered the leafy lane that took us through the park and into Dickeyville.

'Do they hurt, when they come?' I asked my mother.

'What?'

'Bosoms.'

'Oh—no, what gave you that idea?'

'Teeth hurt, when you're a baby.'

'Well, teeth have to break through the gum. Your breasts just . . . grow.'

It was hard for me to see the difference, except that teeth were hard.

'How do they know when to start?'

'They get signals from your body when you start being a teenager.'

'Adolescence,' I said sagely. It was a big word, one used to describe almost everything that teenagers did. It was, apparently, quite terrible.

*   *   *

Absentmindedly, my mother started to turn up our street, forgetting to continue on to the pharmacy for the promised snowball. I hated having to remind her of her promise—to this day, I hate having to ask for things already promised me—but my mouth was aching for that sweet syrup.

'Mama, the pharmacy?'

'You sure it won't spoil your dinner?'

'I'm sure.'

Back home, she asked me if I wanted to play airplane, but I remembered the look on Annie's face and said I'd rather not. We never played it again, in fact. Two days later, my father came home. Two months later, he called my mother and said he was moving out. He had fallen in love with Annie Waters. *She is my destiny,* my father said. *Fate put her in my path for a reason.* My mother cried, said he was a liar, that he had always been a liar. 'No,' he said. 'I was a liar, but I'm telling the truth now. I was meant to be with this woman.'

I know exactly what was said because I listened in on the extension. In love, my father was as full of clichés as anyone, but there was no comfort in pointing that out. I put the phone back, neglecting to disguise the button's click, but my mother either didn't notice or didn't care.

HOW TO COOK EVERYTHING

MARCH 24–27

Chapter Twenty-Three

Cassandra always thought of Baltimore Penn Station as an endearingly tiny place, the kind of train station found in a Lionel train set or what locals called a Christmas garden. High-ceilinged, with old-fashioned wooden benches and only four gates in regular use, it had one of everything else—one newsstand, one coffee shop, one bar, one set of restrooms, one shoeshine stand. Paradoxically, it was the more recent additions that looked run-down and tired—the electric tote board for the Amtrak trains, which never seemed to have the right information; the illuminated signs above the ticket windows, which tended to be on the fritz. It was a remarkably pleasant waiting room, even at seven on a late winter's morning, the weak, watery light forgiving, the commuters mellow for a Monday. Most people were headed south, toward Washington, with only a handful walking down to the tracks when Cassandra's Acela Express was called, and although the northbound train was crowded, it wasn't full, and it was easy to snag a seat in the Quiet Car. Cassandra, used to New York's Penn Station, couldn't get over how *gentle* the whole experience felt.

Gentle made her think of Reg, although it could be argued that he was anything but. Then again, everything was making her think of Reg—the rowhouses sliding by the train, so sad and ramshackle from the rear; the triptych of water crossings, each expanse slightly larger, culminating in the wide views along the Susquehanna in Havre de Grace; the Wilmington skyline. The newspaper in her hand, the laptop she had opened but ignored. Her head was full of Reg, yet she had spent no more than five hours with him since their first evening together.

She didn't want to go to New York, but the trip had been planned, entered on too many people's calendars—her editor's, her agent's, and, last and now least, her lover's. She would have to break up with him tonight. Oh, she had juggled lovers before and she wasn't foolish enough to think that this . . . *thing* with Reg had any potential. Or was she, in fact, exactly that foolish? All she knew was that she had no interest in faking her way through an evening with Bernard. They had been moving toward an ending anyway, and here it was. Reg had not precipitated this. Her response to Reg simply established how very *over* she and Bernard were. It wouldn't be that awful, she reasoned. She would do it in the restaurant, cold-hearted as that might seem. If she let him come back to her house, he would wheedle for one last night, and she wanted to avoid that at any cost. She would do it early, before they ordered entrées. That way he could storm out, if he wanted. Or he could stay, and they would have a companionable, civilized end to what had been a pleasant affair, nothing more. If anything, it should have been a summer fling, the kind of thing that ended when his wife came back from their house on the Cape.

The lunch with her editor actually loomed much larger in her mind than the dinner with Bernard. Should Cassandra tell Ellen about sleeping with Reg? It was a . . . complication that would have to be addressed at some point, an undeniable conflict of interest. If she had stayed with her old editor, Belle, whom she considered a friend, she would have been eager to sort this out with her, personally and professionally. Ellen, her new editor—the truth was, Ellen intimidated Cassandra.

The train pulled into Philadelphia, the midway point. She might as well open her laptop and review what she had accomplished on the book. She was done before Metro Park.

*   *   *

'No pages?' Ellen asked, her bright eyes darting around the restaurant. 'You haven't started writing yet?'

'It's hard to start writing until I know a little more,' Cassandra said. 'Remember, I haven't lived this book, and it's not a product of pure imagination. I'm still poking around, trying to find Callie Jenkins. It's surprisingly difficult.'

'But you finally got to her lawyer, right?'

Oh yes. 'He agreed to meet with me but says he has no idea where she is. And, you know, increasingly I feel it's not so much about the legal battle but about this cipher of a girl. It's almost as if I'm writing the memoir that Callie can't write for herself.'

Ellen frowned, buttering a piece of bread that she would never eat. She seldom ate anything, not in Cassandra's presence, and she almost thrummed with a hummingbird-like energy. Yet she was the one who always insisted on lunch, taking Cassandra to the restaurant of the moment,

243

whatever it might be, then fidgeting in her seat as if she couldn't believe she had to spend ninety minutes talking to just one person, ignoring the e-mails arriving on her BlackBerry, away from the phones, not that she ever picked up her own phone.

The dynamic had been different, of course, when Ellen was courting Cassandra. Seducing her, to be blunt. She had started by whispering in Cassandra's agent's ear: Cassandra's publishing company had never really understood her. *My Father's Daughter* was a word-of-mouth fluke, a child that had thrived despite almost criminal neglect. True, they had published *The Eternal Wife* very well, but a publisher would have to be stunningly incompetent to undermine Cassandra Fallows's second memoir. They didn't love her, they didn't appreciate her. Ellen did, Ellen would.

Her next move was to take Cassandra to lunch, eschewing the obvious places in favor of a low-key restaurant in Cassandra's neighborhood. Yes, back then, Ellen had come to her. 'Why start gossip if we don't need to?' Ellen had said of that first meeting in Brooklyn. They had a lovely three-hour lunch, complete with a bottle of wine, although Cassandra later reflected that she drank most of it; Ellen's glass never seemed to need refilling, although she consumed gallons of water. Ellen's praise for Cassandra's work was headier than the wine, however. She spoke about discovering Cassandra's first book when she was a senior in college, how much it had meant to her. She was bowled over—her exact turn of phrase—by the raw honesty about sex in the second memoir. She would be happy to publish anything that Cassandra wrote, anything. 'I would publish your grocery lists,' she said. 'I bet they're poetry. I don't believe you can write a bad sentence.'

As it happened, it was only a week later that Cassandra's editor, Belle, sent a sorrowful e-mail about Cassandra's proposed novel, then a scant thirty pages and a semicompleted outline. *It gives me no pleasure to say this,* Belle wrote, *but the writing lacks something. I wish I could tell you exactly what it was. The best I can do is say that your fiction seems tentative, as if you do not believe in the power of your own imagination, the authority of your voice. In these pages, you haven't committed to the story and you seem to be papering over that fact by trying to divert us with these tangential bits of research—the history of the hospital, for example, the 'open my records' movement among adoptees and their biological parents. Those digressions worked in your nonfiction, but here it feels like padding. We probably should talk.*

She should have taken Belle up on that invitation. But the e-mail stung—not because it was unfair, but because it hit, with uncanny precision, the nexus of Cassandra's own fears and insecurities about the work. Meanwhile there was Ellen, willing to pay more money than Cassandra had ever dreamed, for anything that she wrote. *Anything.* And Ellen cooed over the proposal, pronounced it brilliant, said it seemed to her a remarkable idea, a vehicle for true fusion. And when the early reviews, in essence, echoed all of Belle's fears, Ellen stood by Cassandra. 'They aren't reviewing the book,' she said. 'They're reviewing your contract. It's not unlike what happened when Martin Amis published *The*

Information, and all the press was about his agent and his teeth and his marriage.'

Cassandra did the math: Ellen would have been in high school at the time Amis published that book. How could she know such ancient publishing history? But Ellen was a freak, the type of young girl who set her sights on being an editor when she was eleven or so, who liked to tell people that she used her bat mitzvah money to subscribe to *Publishers Weekly* and *Kirkus.* Before she was twenty-seven, she made a name for herself with her uncanny knack for picking up debut novels for bargain prices and building them up beyond anyone's expectations. Perhaps that was the problem. Both she and Cassandra had strayed from their usual paths when they joined forces. Ellen had paid a lot of money; Cassandra had tried to write fiction. Ellen couldn't take the money back, but she could nudge Cassandra to return to her more lucrative niche.

'I do think you have to answer the question,' Ellen said now, frowning at her bread and breaking it into pieces. 'Did she or didn't she?'

'Only her hairdresser knows for sure,' Cassandra said. Ellen's blank expression reminded her of their age difference; she clearly didn't have any memory of that old Clairol ad. Okay, no more jokes. 'It's tricky—after all, her lawyer can't comment publicly—but I think she must have. In fact, I'm beginning to think that's why the first lawyer left the case so abruptly. She learned something—or Callie told her something—that compromised the defense, ethically. Which must be why she won't talk to me.'

'I'm not asking for a true-crime book,' Ellen

246

said. 'That's too down-market, not at all your audience. But there has to be a journey. Even if you can't say explicitly what you think, the reader has to know. You have to somehow persuade readers to feel empathy for someone generally regarded as a monster. And it's got to go beyond the "Oh my, she was crazy!" vibe of that Texas case, the woman who drowned her kids. There's nowhere to go with plain crazy.'

Cassandra spread taramasalata on a breadstick. Ellen's advice, crass as it might sound, wasn't off base. She still wasn't sure what she would end up doing about the inconvenient fact that she had slept with one of the principals. If she was lucky—and, in fact, she usually was—she and Reg would sate themselves quickly, no one would ever know about the affair, and they could both go on with clear consciences. But wouldn't it be fun if she could surprise Reg with her enterprise and ingenuity as an investigator? What if she ended up telling Reg things about this case that he never knew, never suspected. He didn't even know where Callie was. Teena, too, had failed to find her. What if Cassandra could succeed? Only where to start? She thought of Fatima outside the church, anxious, even fearful. *That thing that happened to her?* What had happened to Callie? What did Fatima know?

'Do you want dessert?' Ellen asked in a bright, cheerful way that somehow managed to indicate that she hoped the answer was no.

'I wouldn't mind coffee,' Cassandra said, feeling a little contrary. 'And I always like to peruse the dessert list, dangerous as it is to women of a certain age.'

'You look phenomenal,' Ellen said. 'You've always been fit, with that nice skin, but there's something . . . extra. Kind of glowy.'

'Microdermabrasion,' Cassandra said, blushing.

Chapter Twenty-Four

Teena wished that Cassandra had asked her to do something more difficult, although she wasn't sure what that might be. Still, it was too easy, pulling up the home address of this woman, Fatima, from the billing department. Teena even had the perfect cover story: She wanted to write her a note to thank her for a recent purchase, a tack that Teena did use, as did several Nordstrom sales associates. Cassandra most certainly would have gotten a note if Teena hadn't essentially extorted her.

Once she pulled the account, she couldn't help noticing that Fatima, who had a store card, sometimes paid only the minimum balance and every now and then missed a payment. Never more than one, and never more than once or twice a year. Her buying seemed to follow a binge-like cycle; the account would lie fallow for months, then she would come in and drop a thousand, give or take. She also spent a lot of her money at the basement level, the Rack. Quantity over quality, then.

Teena mentioned that observation to Cassandra, keen to offer something extra. A mere address itself was a puny gift, even if that was all Cassandra had requested.

'Hmmm,' Cassandra said. 'That would fit with

the girl I knew. And the woman I saw. When you buy clothes that memorable, you need more of them.'

Her voice was muffled and a little subdued, but Teena chalked that up to the cell line, buzzy and unsteady from the train. Most people didn't think twice about cell phones these days, but the thought of speaking on one from a train, a train returning from New York, was glamorous to Teena. She wondered what Cassandra's apartment looked like, what filled her days back in New York. It was hard to hold on to the idea that Cassandra was only another Baltimore girl, not that different from her. More educated, sure, but Cassandra's professor father had probably earned less money than Teena's dad, who had his own heating and cooling business.

Teena didn't remember the old neighborhood over by the racetrack; they had moved the year she was born. But they had gone back, from time to time, so her parents could impress upon their children how far they had come. They would drive around Park Heights on a Sunday afternoon, then head up to the Suburban House for what her father called, with no malice, good old-fashioned Jew food. Teena, a picky eater, made do with a bunless hot dog, shocked at the things her father ate with such obvious enjoyment. Gravlax. Kreplach. Borscht. Even the names sounded threatening, like creatures in a science fiction film. But she liked the drive, the tour of what they had left behind. Her brothers remembered where the bike shop was and—this shared in hushed voices— the pet shop, where a neighborhood girl had been murdered. The crime had taken years to solve and turned on the kind of obscure detail now omnipresent in television shows: Sand found on the girl's body was determined to be from some exotic, faraway locale, not indigenous to the United States. That sand had led detectives to the pet store and a clerk who had snapped one day merely from encountering a privileged, pampered girl.

It would be a stretch to say that this story made Teena decide to become *a police,* as she would learn to say. Certainly, such details figured hardly at all in her life as a cop. There hadn't been much Caribbean sand or many criminal masterminds in her career. Perps were stupid. The job wasn't about matching wits but matching wills, and the detective had the advantage of being able to shift tactics, tone, even facts. The detectives also had the privilege of movement—the freedom to stand, to pace, to leave the room. Yet Teena seldom availed herself of it. She sat. She sat until her ass, which lacked for padding, went numb, then continued to sit some more. It was in her stillness and her silences that she broke people down. Men, especially, treated her like a blind date they had to appease, make conversation with.

Then she met Callie, who could challenge her on every front. Quieter, stiller. It was eerie how long that woman could go without speaking, how immobile she became. She made Teena think of some impossible plot, from *Batman* or maybe *The Wild Wild West,* where the hero slowed his pulse until it was almost nil and people took him for dead. Callie Jenkins's eyes were dead, but her squared shoulders and straight spine indicated *something* was inside her, holding her together.

God? But if God kept Callie strong, that suggested Callie felt righteous, which meant—what, exactly? Under what scenario did a woman kill her baby and come to believe she was justified? Insanity, of course. But Callie submitted to psych test after psych test and always came back sane. Or sane enough to hang, as Lenhardt liked to say.

What new tools did cops have now, what could they do? Teena recognized that the television depictions were bullshit, but things must have come pretty far since her day, when she entered data on those green-gray monitors with the pulsing cursor. Now a home computer could do things undreamed of when she first started working homicide. But it couldn't find Callie Jenkins. She had tried. Of course, with a call or two, someone downtown would help her. Maybe not in the city homicide squad, where McLarney was the only survivor from her time. But Lenhardt, out in the county, he could help and would, without a single question.

But Teena never asked anyone for anything, ever. That was another thing that fascinated her about Cassandra, the ease with which she requested favors from people. Sure, she said 'please' and 'thank you', she had manners. Still, she had a way of asking that indicated she expected people to do her bidding. Where does that kind of confidence come from? Money, fame? No, Teena had known plenty of losers who were the same way. Some people were comfortable with building up favors. Teena had kept her balance sheet clean, neither asking nor giving. And when she ran into trouble, there had been no one there for her.

The Acela home was delayed, one of those mysterious malfunctions where the train slowed to what felt like five miles per hour for long stretches. They were inching through New Jersey south of Trenton, having just passed the put-upon slogan along the bridge: TRENTON MAKES/THE WORLD TAKES. Cassandra said good-bye to Teena and returned to the Quiet Car from the vestibule where she had made the call, happy to be alone with her thoughts. She was pleased, of course, and grateful to Teena for her assistance. But she had cottonmouth and a headache. Not exactly a hangover, although she had drunk quite a bit the night before. Too much.

The breakup with Bernard had been far more troublesome than she had imagined. He had *cried*. In public. At her favorite restaurant, a place she went to at least twice a month when she was home.

'Bernard, this isn't love,' she had said as softly as possible. The tables were very close together here, a storefront that used to be a pharmacy and had kept some of the old-fashioned fittings.

'It is for me,' he said. 'I was ready to—'

She wouldn't even let him say what he had been prepared to do.

'I'm wrapped up in my work. I don't have time for a lover.' This did not seem to console him. 'Besides, it's wrong. You're married. I can't do this anymore.' *Because I've moved on to sleeping with an old friend's husband who's integral to the book I'm trying to write. Nothing wrong there!*

Bernard had settled down and even ended up enjoying the meal. The restaurant was that good; its food transcended heartache. By dessert, he was

252

in such good spirits that he began enumerating all the reasons that Cassandra was right about the breakup, which was really an excuse to list all the things he disliked about Cassandra. She was a little full of herself, did she know that? Not an out-and-out narcissist, but self-centered. She thought everything was about her. They had dated only six months and had few interactions with others, but on those rare occasions they did, she was already correcting his version of stories.

'You're always saying, "No, no, you're telling it wrong." As if there's one right way, and it's your way.' He went on to say that she was passionate in bed but a little cold elsewhere, too good at taking care of herself. Self-contained in a way that wasn't attractive, yet bossy and needy, too.

The only part she had bothered to contradict was the bit about storytelling. 'You're an investment banker,' she had said. 'If I attempted to do what you do—or even explain what you do—you'd almost certainly correct me. I'm a storyteller. It's what I do. I can't bear it when a story isn't told right.'

'Jesus, Cassandra, everyone tells stories.'

'Yes,' she said. 'But I do it better than most.'

'On the page,' he said. 'Where you write and rewrite and rewrite. But that doesn't mean you're some great raconteur, you know. You're not . . . Homer.'

'Well, I'm not blind,' she said.

They had both laughed at that, which had soothed his feelings, let him assume she agreed with his other points. She didn't, but she had to let it go. She had to allow him to sit there, counting up all the ways in which he didn't like her. It was the price of breaking up with a man. God, how many breakups had there been like this? When did it ever end? At thirty, she had assumed *that* was all over. By *that* she meant the ups, downs, stomach-twisting ways of infatuation and love. Then at forty, she thought she must be off the hook, that her second marriage, while a little passionless, was a mark of her newfound, hard-won maturity. Instead, it was only proof that she was still capable of marrying the wrong person. Then Bernard, in fact, had seemed evidence enough that she had finally entered the phase of cool, composed, not-losing-one's-self love. But it hadn't been love at all.

Reg was *that* all over again. *Candy.* How she longed to call him that, to remind him how far back they went, but some instinct warned her that Reg would not welcome his nickname. Still, she loved that they were familiar with each other's previous selves, even if they never alluded to that fact. She had known the silly, laughing, dancing pest. He remembered the frowsy-haired girl. They admired the new outer shells, so smooth and shiny, but recognized them as the façades they were.

The train, designed to go one hundred miles per hour, chugged lazily toward Baltimore, stuck on a track that could never handle its full speed. Cassandra didn't mind. Nothing was waiting for her in Baltimore tonight. She and Reg had plans to meet tomorrow afternoon, in her apartment. *Reg will be proud of me when I find Callie without his help. I'll have to be careful of his feelings, not flaunt it in such a way that it makes him feel inadequate. But the more I leave him out of it—well, the more I can leave him out of everything.*

He had a child and a wife he adored, according

254

to no less an authority than his own sister. His reputation was such that even Teena knew he ran around. This was the kind of affair immortalized in popular song. Too hot not to cool down, et cetera, et cetera. *Epic poetry does it better,* her father would contradict, displeased whenever anyone claimed pop culture could have a power that art did not. But this was one area where she had to disagree with her father. Poetry—hushed and proper—had nothing on music when it came to expressing these kinds of feelings. Stupid songs competed in her head, the songs of her early teenage years, gooey with feeling. If she had a blue denim notebook, she would have doodled his initials on it and entwined them with hers. It was going to end badly. It had to end badly. She told herself she didn't care.

Chapter Twenty-Five

Everyone knew Baltimore was small; it was almost banal to make the observation now. But it was a fitful, unpredictable smallness. Gloria could go years, literally, without seeing someone and then the person suddenly seemed to be everywhere.

That was the case with Reg Barr, the whole Barr-Howard clan. Reg truly had receded from her thoughts over the years. Now he was practically omnipresent. There was the writer's query, then Reg's own call. A new billboard advertising his legal services had gone up on North Avenue, visible from Gloria's daily drive into the city. Gloria chose a new route. She opened the newspaper, only to find herself staring at Reg's wife—the boss's daughter, as Gloria still thought of her—opposite the comics, cooperating with a particularly vapid feature, 'Five Things I Have to Have Right Now'. Gloria would have assumed Donna Howard-Barr was above such things, but she was apparently willing to pimp herself out to draw attention to a fund-raising event for the Alpha Kappa Alpha scholarship fund.

Donna's five 'urgent' needs fascinated Gloria. A high-end gas grill, sustainable patio furniture in Brazilian cherry, a pair of Christian Louboutin shoes, the new translation of *War and Peace,* a Gee's Bend quilt. Gloria couldn't help Googling the last item, which turned out to be a specific kind of quilt from Alabama. Not to her taste, but undeniably striking. Overall, the portrait Donna presented was quite deliberate. *I'm homey, I care about the environment, I'm girly, I'm intellectually engaged, I have exquisite taste.* But then, Donna had always been a canny custodian of her own image. Gloria bet that Donna would have those items, too, before spring ended. Donna Howard-Barr was not one to put off her urgent needs. Except, perhaps, that copy of *War and Peace.*

And here was Reg yet again, this time in the courthouse elevator on a gray Wednesday morning, holding the hand of an exquisite little girl. Gloria almost didn't get on, but there were too many people around and she wouldn't want anyone to think that she was avoiding Reg, because that could be interpreted as a weakness. Not because anyone remembered or even knew their history, but because Gloria believed she was always being scrutinized for chinks in her armor.

'Take Your Daughter to Work Day?' Gloria

256

asked.

'That's April,' the girl said with a child's literal-minded need to provide accurate information. 'Besides, it's children now, not just daughters. It's spring break.'

'The babysitter is ill and Donna has some big luncheon today,' Reg said. 'My sister's coming down to pick her up later this morning.' Then, as an afterthought, 'This is Ms Bustamante, honey. She and Daddy used to work together. Gloria, this is my daughter, Aubrey Barr.'

'Aubrey Howard Barr,' the girl said. 'My mother's last name is my middle name.'

Aubrey. Gloria was trying to remember if she had known that Reg and Donna had a daughter. She must have, but seeing the child produced an almost visceral reaction. *You son of a bitch,* she thought, knowing she was being unfair, even irrational. A daughter, about eight or so. Pretty, of course. Reg and Donna couldn't have anything but a pretty child. Poised, like her mother, but with the spark of Reg's personality. A daddy's girl, her hand tucked in his, dressed in a contemporary version of fifties finery—wool coat, hat, pink tights, and postmodern Mary Janes, the toes almost whimsically bulbous. What was it like for a womanizer such as Reg to have a daughter? Gloria thought it rather neat, the perfect O. Henry ending for a man whose conquests were working their way down, chronologically, according to the rumors she had heard. In a year or two, he would be sleeping with his friends' daughters. The actual daughters, toothsome interns, although probably not at his own firm. Reg had some boundaries. How horrible it must be for a man like Reg to have a daughter.

257

He would be almost sixty when she made her way into the world, his power fading. He would watch impotently from the sidelines, his knowledge of men a grim prophecy from which he could never protect his daughter.

Good.

'Don't you look like the Cheesy Cat,' he said. Gloria wasn't aware that she was smiling.

'Cheshire Cat,' his daughter corrected primly. She was quite a stickler for accuracy, little Aubrey Howard Barr. Only in this case, her father hadn't misspoken.

Gloria got off at the next floor, although it wasn't hers. She had forgotten the private joke of Cheesy Cat. What had been its origins? Something to do with the horrible vending machines in the old Howard & Howard headquarters, the off-brand snacks they downed late at night. They called them Cheesy Cat Chips because they tasted more like pet food than something humans were supposed to eat. Gloria was the one who always had change or crisp dollars—this was back in the day when vending machines were finicky about the bills they took—while Reg or Colton Jensen, another associate, volunteered to make the run down three floors. The chips turned their fingers orange, and they had to keep a roll of paper towels nearby, lest they leave orange thumbprints on documents. 'The curse of the Cheesy Cat,' they would joke.

They had a lot of jokes. Reg and Col had performed their own version of 'You Can Call Me Al', changing the lyrics to reflect the endlessly mundane things they were asked to do. *You can get me coffee. You can do my photocopying*. There was an apple-shaped partner who was forever hitching his pants up over nonexistent hips, punctuating his fatuous pronouncements and incessant instructions. One night, Reg had taken to imitating him, while Col—Jesus, Col, dead from AIDS almost seventeen years now, one of the early casualties—shook a bag of chips behind him. They had laughed until they had collapsed in tears. 'You see, Gloria'—pants hitch, the sound of rattling chips—'the rule of habeas corpus dictates'—pants hitch, rattling chips—'that the law may not be an ass, but the lawyer most certainly is.'

Perhaps one had to be there. Gloria had been there, and she could no longer remember why it was funny, just that it was. They were ambitious, they were giddy, they were never going to be like the people for whom they worked. And then, one day, they were exactly like them. How did that happen?

People understood mourning a lost love. If she'd had romantic feelings toward Reg, even if it were one-sided, people would sympathize with the kick she felt when reminded of their former closeness. But the intimacy lost with a friend—that could be just as intense. He had been young then, and if she, in her thirties, couldn't quite claim that, she was his peer in the office hierarchy, his running buddy in a running conversation about the weaknesses and peccadilloes of their bosses. She had thought such conversations were intended to do nothing more than pass the long evenings. 'For amusement purposes only,' as the video poker machines in Baltimore bars said. But it was a lie on the machines and it turned out to be a lie in their relationship as well. Gloria excelled at the law, but Reg understood the culture of law firms in general

259

and Howard & Howard in particular. That made all the difference.

To be fair, he hadn't pushed her out, not at all, but he also hadn't followed her. Reg wasn't the type to jump out a window just because Gloria said the building was on fire. Reg couldn't see the smoke, much less the flames. Besides, she never told him why exactly she quit so abruptly. But he had to suspect it was something dire, something big. She wondered if he had ever figured it out. She wanted to believe Reg wouldn't tolerate it if he knew. One could argue that he was the only winner in this sad game, getting the partnership and the boss's daughter. Ignorance was bliss. Did Reg deserve that bliss?

*   *   *

Tisha was so delighted to have her niece for an afternoon that she didn't bother to call Reg on lying to her about why he needed a babysitter. Not that she was sure what the lie was, only that he was misrepresenting the situation for some reason. Could have been as simple as guilt—Reg and Donna should have been able to roll a little better with life's contingencies, such as their child care being shot straight to hell. Tisha certainly never asked Donna to bail her out when her kids were small. Or it could have been—but she didn't want to think about what else it could have been. She had her suspicions about her brother, but she had never confronted them even in her own mind, much less tried to bring him to task. He loved Donna, she was sure of that. In fact, she often thought he loved her a little too much, tilting over into worship. *Then why did*—but she could not go there. Not about her brother. She knew, she suspected, but when the idea threatened to become too concrete, she all but stuck her fingers in her ears and closed her eyes. *La-la-la-la, I can't hear you.*

Ushered into her brother's office to fetch Aubrey—feeling, as she always did here, terribly suburban, such a *mom,* a kind not usually seen in the overdone offices of Howard, Howard & Barr—she asked only, 'What's up?'

'Not much. Got everything under control.'

'What do you mean by that?'

'Nothing, Tisha. I'm grateful to you for bailing me out, is all.'

'It's a favor you're doing me. Aubrey and I are going to have fun, aren't we, baby?'

The girl beamed. It *was* going to be fun to spend an afternoon with an eight-year-old. Tisha's kids were generally sweet, for teenagers, but her company was not their first choice, not anymore. She tried to remember what eight felt like, from the inside. She had been eight when she met Cassandra, that first day of school back at Dickey Hill. Why had she grabbed that bony white elbow and invited that strange girl to join the threesome of her, Donna, and Fatima? The world knew Cassandra's version, and Tisha was glad for that. She came off better in Cassandra's version. But it wasn't how she remembered it.

Fact was, there was a girl from their old school whom she didn't like and Tisha had to put someone else in that fourth desk, *fast,* or she would have joined them. The first day was like a game of musical chairs; there were enough seats,

261

but not enough good seats, and as the minutes ticked down, a few kids were milling about, looking not only for a place but for a place where they would be welcome. Tisha had wedged Cassandra into their group to avoid—she could call up the face but not the name, see the girl in her blue plaid dress, her processed hair ragged at the ends, a home-done job. Even at eight, Tisha had a big-picture view of things, made lightning-quick decisions with a surprising ruthlessness. *You're in, you're out.* Aubrey, like her mother back then, seemed innocent of such motives and judgments.

Or—again like her mother—perhaps she trusted there would always be someone like Tisha to do her dirty work.

'Can we go to Frank's Diner?' Aubrey whispered in the elevator, glancing anxiously at the ceiling, almost as if she thought Howard, Howard & Barr was keeping watch on her, reporting back to her mother.

'We sure can.'

'And can I have French fries with gravy and a slice of cake?'

'You can have French fries with gravy and a slice of cake and a milk shake.'

'Can I have French fries with gravy and a slice of cake and a milk shake and . . . onion rings?'

'You can have French fries with gravy and a slice of cake and a milk shake and onion rings.'

It was their version of the old memory game Johnny Has a Ball of String in His Pocket. Tisha always let Aubrey win. Although, come to think of it, there was less and less *letting* as of late. Aubrey's memory, required to hold nothing more than eight

262

years of life, was sharp, while Tisha's was increasingly mushy. She felt like an old PC going up against one of those new Macs with the Intel chip. *Everything under control*—why did she want to attach so much meaning to a simple phrase? What was Reg up to?

'You lose,' Aubrey said with a happy squeal of a giggle after their menu had grown to almost a dozen items. 'You forgot the milk shake.'

'It's what brings the boys to the yard,' Tisha muttered.

If her own children had been with her, they would have mocked her for the outdated reference, hooted at her for thinking she could keep up with pop culture and by doing so keep up with them. Tisha did listen occasionally to the music her children favored, if only to monitor the kind of ideas they were absorbing in spite of themselves. But Aubrey, who didn't even understand the double entendre of Kelis's milk shake, put her hand in her aunt's and skipped down Baltimore Street. Had Tisha ever been this happy, at any age? She must have been. The problem was that such simple, ordinary bliss seldom formed memories. It was too smooth and silken to adhere. It was the bad stuff, ragged and uneven, that caught, like all those plastic grocery bags stuck in the trees of Baltimore. It was—Babette, that was her name, Babette, standing in the middle of Mrs Klein's third-grade class, wounded and puzzled by Tisha's snub.

*   *   *

Cassandra was spent. Although she seldom

napped, she found herself drifting off as Reg showered. He would need to stay in there a long time to rid himself of the scent of sex, of her. She wished they could go out now, have an early dinner, but she knew the rules, how things worked. Just on the edge of wakefulness, she relived the last two hours. Thinking about it was almost as good as doing it had been. She understood brain chemistry, recognized that this kind of passion was impossible to sustain, but, boy, was it fun while it lasted. It was strange, how little they talked, but what was there to discuss? They knew each other's pasts and the present wasn't a topic on which either wanted to dwell. She blinked her eyes, broke back into full consciousness, glanced at the clock. Had an hour really passed? The water was off, the apartment quiet. Would he have left without saying good-bye? She put on a robe and walked into the living room, where Reg was at her laptop, wearing only a towel.

'Just checking my e-mail,' he said. 'I hope that's okay.'

'I thought you had a BlackBerry.' He had, in fact, placed it on the nightstand while they were having sex, and it had vibrated intermittently throughout.

'They're great for reading e-mails, but I'm too fumble-fingered if I have to reply more than yes or no. However, it looks as if the office survived without me.'

She straddled him, blocking his view of the computer, rubbing his neck.

'Careful,' he said. 'You'll make me late.'

She could indeed, and it was tempting. But it was enough, for now, to know she had that power. She wouldn't have it for long. That was how these things worked, although this didn't feel like anything she had known before. Still, it was important not to take advantage, not to make trouble for him. And important to show him that she had the self-control to break away as needed. She gave him a long, fluttering kiss, running an index finger along his earlobe—then stopped before it went too far.

'You're right,' she said. 'You have to go.'

'You're wicked,' he said, but she heard nothing but admiration in his voice.

* * *

The Charles Benton building, named for the longtime city and state budget adviser, was an incongruous presence on the stretch of strip clubs known as the Block. Local rumor held that Benton had insisted it be built there in hopes of destroying the Block. The more extreme version claimed his wife had once worked as a dancer at one of the clubs before embracing a life of Christian piety. Gloria, aware of the chronically inaccurate gossip about her life, had trouble putting stock in any of this, but it was interesting, strolling past the famed Two O'clock Club to go look up campaign finance reports.

'You can get those online,' the clerk said. She was young and bored, so young that it hadn't occurred to her that her job might be less boring if she actually welcomed opportunities to do it. That was one of the lessons of youth: It wasn't work that was boring but the lack of it.

'I know,' Gloria said. She didn't, in fact, but she had ventured down here and hated to think of it as

265

a wasted trip. 'But that's only for the more recent reports, right? I'm looking for a report from 1979.'

'Nineteen seventy-nine?' She made the date sound as distant as 1776 or 1492.

'Yes—but also—' Gloria did the math in her head. The city races were in odd years, but the state election calendar ran on an even schedule, with the senate up for reelection every four years. 'Nineteen ninety. And 1998.'

'That might take a while,' the clerk said. 'I might not be able to get it by the end of the day.' She pointed to the clock, which showed it was almost four.

'I'll have someone from my office pick them up tomorrow.' She paused. 'It will be someone from the office of Gloria Bustamante, okay? Picking up the campaign records for Julius Howard. Gloria Bustamante's office, state senator Julius Howard's finance reports, for the senate race, but also for city council president.'

She hit both names hard, hoping the girl was a gossip or that there was someone lurking nearby who would find this interesting. Let another rumor fly out of the Benton Building, she decided. Let them know that she was snooping, not that she had any idea what she might find. The fact of Reg's daughter had hit her hard. She had a hunch— nothing more—that someone else would be even more shocked to see this miniature version of Donna Barr. Excuse her—Donna Howard-Barr.

266

Chapter Twenty-Six

Callie set out her supplies as she did every Thursday morning now. Butter to soften, eggs to reach room temperature. Flour and sugar were always at the ready, in canisters labeled as such. She loved those canisters, which she had purchased from QVC with her first-ever credit card. She loved how it had felt, going into Lowe's when she first moved over to the shore and buying the things she needed as she needed them. Back then, she hadn't envisioned how important flour and sugar would become to her, and she might choose differently if she were outfitting her kitchen today. The porcelain containers were pretty but heavy, and she lived in fear of dropping one of the lids and breaking it. Yes, she could afford to buy a new set, or superglue the broken lid, if such a thing were to come to pass. But she never got over that fear of breaking things. *You clumsy child,* her mother would say to her, as if Callie were cursed, possessed by a demon that made her drop and spill and trip. *You stupid child.* Now her mother's hands shook and she often dribbled food and liquid down her own front, pretending all the while she didn't notice. If Callie said, 'Mama, there's a spot of juice on your robe,' Myra Tippet replied, 'No, there's not.'

Callie hated lying. She knew most people would find that funny, given that it was the general perception of things that she was the biggest liar that ever was, and worse. But she did not believe silence was a lie, on a par with false words. Long before she had taken refuge in silence, she had made this distinction. Her mother had been adamant that Callie never lie, not to her. Callie didn't, but she refused at times to give her mother the evidence she required in order to punish her. *Who ate the peanut butter? Who left the towel on the floor?* Her mother would shake her and shake her and shake her, but Callie wouldn't even cry. As long as she didn't say any words, she wouldn't be a liar.

What should she bake this morning? She had been thinking about one of her more complicated recipes, ginger cookies frosted to look like half moons, but the children liked simpler things. She flipped through a new cookbook, one borrowed from the library, and found a recipe for strawberry cupcakes. Too early for fresh strawberries, but she had frozen, and the recipe said that was okay. Not preferable, but okay. Once, she would have been wracked with doubt over such a choice. The instruction *Season to taste* almost left her in tears. How could she be trusted to make such a momentous decision on her own? How could she leave it to her taste, her mouth, so clearly inferior to everyone else's?

When she first started baking, Callie had watched the various cooking shows on television and treated their words as gospel. Then she had realized that there was a multitude of small disagreements as one traveled from the Church of Martha to the Church of Paula to the Church of That Italian Girl Whose Name She Could Never Quite Get. She began to check out cookbooks at the local library, looking for one authority she could respect, someone with standards yet not overly fussy. No one was right. Again, it was that chiding quality, the smug murmur of the playground all over again. *You can do it that way, but you should do it this way.* She almost found the guide she was looking for in this British woman, but then she saw her on television and decided she was too beautiful and poised. A woman like that could never really understand someone like Callie, what went on in her little neat-as-a-pin kitchen, her messy mind.

Months went by before Callie realized she could, in fact, *buy* a cookbook if she desired. More than one. Other than her time at community college, she had never purchased a book for herself. She drove over to Salisbury, where there was a Barnes and Noble. The selection overwhelmed her and she went outside and sat in her car for a while, fighting the urge to turn around and go home. Once, only once, when she was twelve, she had been inside Donna Howard's house and sneaked upstairs, where she had thrown open the closet doors and looked at the clothes hanging there. How did someone ever choose from such a bountiful array? The bookstore reminded her of that feeling. It had been much easier at the little library, taking what was there. She had never even put a book on hold. Eventually, she persuaded herself to go back inside the bookstore and emerged with not only a cookbook but a coffee drink, which had required almost as much in the way of decision making.

The book she had chosen was fat and bright yellow. *How to Cook Everything,* it promised. No photographs, just simple line drawings, and written in a style that reminded her of her favorite teacher, back in junior high, a biology instructor who explained things in such cheerful, confident tones that Callie didn't stop to think if a task was hard or difficult, or even that biology was a science and she hated science. This book had the same kind of brisk you-can-do-it attitude. She found herself speaking to the author, Mr Bittman—she couldn't imagine using his first name, although they were probably not that far apart in age—as she worked. 'Must I use milk in my omelet, Mr Bittman?' 'Yes, Callie, it does make a difference.' 'What are your thoughts about cake flour, Mr Bittman? Piecrusts?' 'I believe in using all butter in piecrusts.' Although she had a radio and a television in her kitchen, she worked in silence, the better to commune with her teacher.

In the early days, she had tossed out the things she made, feeling wasteful, not sure what else to do with them. She liked baking sweet things, but she didn't have much of a sweet tooth, strange to say. The seven years in jail had taken a toll on her digestive system and she found she could eat only simple things, in small amounts. A piece of fruit or a cup of yogurt at breakfast, soup at lunch, a sandwich at dinner. She learned from Mr Bittman how to expand her menu. She roasted a chicken and marveled at how good it tasted, then stretched it out for days—cold chicken for lunch, chicken salad with homemade mayo. She squeezed a lemon wedge over a piece of fish, broiled, not fried. But she felt she must bake at least once a week, and she had no idea what to do with all that food.

She tried to give her baked goods away, attempted to interest local shops and food pantries, only to run into all sorts of rules and regulations. Eventually, she found a private Christian school down toward Cambridge that allowed her to sell her treats at lunchtime and donate the profits back to the school. Callie had a feeling that even this arrangement was vaguely outlaw, susceptible to being shut down by the health department at any moment. And she wasn't sure that she wanted to get in too deep when it came to the school's beliefs. They struck her as the kind of Christians who were a little short on forgiveness, who would not want to consort with her if they knew about her past. She had even worried, for a moment, that her name registered with the principal, but that was pure paranoia on her part. If her first name hadn't been shortened, all those years ago, it might have been more memorable. But, bless Tisha, she had been Callie since she was nine, and while it wasn't the most ordinary name, it could slip by where Calliope never did. It had been strange, a month back, to hear that version of her name again. She had thought—maybe hoped, to be honest—that something might happen. What, she didn't know. Something, anything, to relieve the sameness of her days, not that different from jail when you got down to it. Dull days, haunted nights.

The cupcakes were almost too easy to make. She paged through the book, the kind filled with stories and gorgeous photographs, more incredible than any fairy tale Callie had known as a child. Fairy tales, with their evil people and inexplicable behavior, made perfect sense to Callie. A cookbook where every food memory seemed to be a happy one—that was something she couldn't

271

quite fathom. Hadn't anyone else ever dropped a fast-food burger and had it snatched from her hand, told she couldn't eat it because it had touched the ground? Didn't anyone else ever spill her sweet tea? She couldn't imagine buying this book. Besides, she had yet to be disappointed by Mr Bittman. He had promised to tell her how to cook everything, and she had yet to find anything she wanted to cook that he couldn't help her with. Callie was big on promises, too. She kept the ones she made, no matter how often others broke their promises to her.

Why hadn't she baked for her boys, either of them? Of course, Donntay didn't live long enough to eat solid food. Why hadn't she been able to keep a spick-and-span house as she did now? Was it simply a matter of being older? Or was it also about having money? Could she have had money before? But she had never asked, and even now, she took it with reluctance. She wasn't a gold digger, and despite what some people thought, her pregnancies had not been an attempt to trap or embarrass anyone. But she had been overwhelmed by motherhood, unprepared. And something more. Once, when Gloria made her talk to a psychiatrist, Callie had tried to describe the feeling, akin to living in an airless tunnel. In the weeks after her boys were born, she couldn't quite breathe and she felt as if her eyelids were closing of their own accord. Not because she was tired, necessarily, although she was exhausted.

Of course, she was brokenhearted, too, but she couldn't tell that part, could she? Oh, she knew what Gloria promised, how she could tell her or the psychiatrist anything and it would be held confidential. Anything, of course, except the circumstances of what really happened that morning, the day that Donntay died.

She packed the cupcakes into the boxes she now kept on hand and drove down to the school, her car fragrant with strawberries. The boys hung back at first, but the girls went crazy for those pink cakes and the boys soon realized it was pink or nothing. She charged fifty cents, which meant thirty-six dollars for the school. The principal said Callie could deduct it all from her taxes if she kept records, but Callie didn't take deductions. With a paid-for house and Delaware's low property taxes, it didn't pay for her to fill out the longer form. Besides, that would have been another lie, claiming she was doing charity when she was really baking to hold on to her own sanity.

Driving home, she thought about the cake that had been served at Donna Howard's end-of-school party. Instead of the usual sheet cake, it had been more like a wedding cake, multiple layers in a hard sheen of frosting, a garden of flowers spilling down its side. Tastewise, it had been disappointing. The flavors were too grown-up for kids, Callie realized now. Could she make such a cake? It wouldn't do, not for the school, but the challenge appealed to her. She had come a long way in the five years since she had been amazed to learn that creaming butter did not, in fact, mean adding cream to butter. She could make a layer cake, but what would it take to create one of those hard-candy icings, more like armor than sugar? She would have to consult Mr Bittman. She imagined him standing next to her, his voice soothing and mellow, reaching in to show her a technique. The

273

librarian had said there were videos, that Mr Bittman had a blog that Callie could read on the library computers. But Callie had her version of the man and she didn't want anything to intrude on that. She would make the cake and take it to her mother's nursing home, where the staff was always grateful for her treats.

With every spin of her hand mixer, with every egg cracked and every cup of flour sifted, she told herself that she was making a lie true.

Chapter Twenty-Seven

Cassandra got lost three times en route to Fatima's house. The street names were vaguely familiar, but any landmarks that might have helped orient her in this northwest suburb were long gone. Following the signs to what she was promised would be the town center, she found herself at a mall. She thought she remembered the mall from a years-ago trip, but it had been newer then, glossier, with high-end stores such as Saks. Now it looked a little seedy and neglected, and Saks must have been a mirage. *Talk about 'no there there'*, Cassandra thought, reprogramming her GPS.

Finally, she found her way to Fatima's neighborhood, one of those developments with basically a single street name, Rosewood, and multiple suffixes: Court, Path, Lane, Circle. The houses were tightly packed around the cul-de-sacs, the front yards sacrificed to make room for huge driveways that fed into three-car garages. It was nice enough, Cassandra supposed, solidly middle-class. Yet, like the mall, it had the feel of a place that had once been a little nicer, and there was an abundance of FOR SALE signs. She sensed she was in a part of town where people had overextended themselves. Fatima's house, in particular, looked stressed. While generally neat and well maintained, there were signs of larger things that required an expert's care—a slight sag in the garage roof, pitting in the stucco exterior. Yet there was a large Lincoln Town Car in the driveway, shiny from a recent wash.

'Cassandra,' Fatima said on a sigh, resigned yet not surprised. 'How did you find me?'

'It wasn't that hard,' she said. No reason to endanger Teena's job. And it wouldn't hurt to let Fatima think Cassandra might know far more about her than her address and credit history. Although those two details, along with her matriculation at Spelman, were all that Cassandra had. That and her memories of the girl she had known.

Where did that girl go? she wondered, taking a seat in Fatima's neat yet gloriously tacky living room, which was dominated by a credenza of glass, mirror, and metal. It held exactly one book—a white leather-bound Bible—and a series of objects that seemed to have no connection to one another. A porcelain doll, a vase in a vaguely Oriental style, a statue of two deer, a basketball trophy, a ceramic basket of pink flowers, and an enormous family photo with almost thirty people crowded in the frame, all wearing T-shirts that proclaimed HOLLINS FAMILY REUNION. The last made her happy for Fatima, the idea that she was part of such a large and loving family. Fatima had been an only child, raised by a single mother. For all her brashness, there had always been a hint of loneliness, too.

But while the woman facing Cassandra still bore a physical resemblance to the girl—albeit much, much, much bigger—the essence of Fatima wasn't there. This was a fearful woman, reticent and nervous. None of these words had applied to the young Fatima. Nor did Cassandra recognize the almost deferential tone in which Fatima began to speak.

'So you're a writer.'

'Yes, I mentioned it to you at church the other day.'

'I don't read much. There's not really time. And Gaston—he's my husband, you saw him there—he didn't really approve of what I did read. Romances and the like. He said they were frivolous and not exactly Christian.' She lowered her voice as if they might be overheard, although the house gave every appearance of being empty. 'I still sneak a Zane every now and then. Do you know her?'

'I know *of* her,' Cassandra said. 'She's very successful.'

'She's from Maryland,' Fatima said, suddenly skeptical, and Cassandra realized that Fatima believed the writing world to be not unlike her megachurch, a huge congregation of people brought together by a single common interest and geography. If Cassandra didn't know Zane, could she really be a writer?

'Well, she's very private, isn't she? The thing I want to talk about is—'

'Callie. I know, you told me at church. I got nothing to tell you, though. I don't keep up with her.'

'But you certainly remember the girl we knew back then. You knew her better than most, in fact. She wasn't part of our crowd, but she was from your old neighborhood, right?'

'We went to School Eighty-eight together.' That was a Baltimore-ism, using the number instead of the name. 'That part of Edmondson Avenue was rough, even then. My mama was glad to get me out of there.'

'Rough?'

Fatima shrugged. 'Rough for the times. Mean kids, lots of fighting. Not the kind of rough you see now, with kids taking guns to school and the like. But harsh enough.'

'And you moved in across the street from the Barrs, Tisha and Reg.' Childish, but Cassandra enjoyed saying his name when she could.

'Yeah.' Fatima managed to get a lot of emotion—doubt? fear?—into that one syllable.

'What was Callie like?'

'You saw. Quiet. All she wanted to do—all she ever wanted to do—was stay out of trouble.'

'I don't recall her ever being in trouble at school.'

'Not at school. At home. Her mama—her mama was strict. Real strict. It was like—' Fatima paused and Cassandra used all her will not to rush in, fill the silence. *Let it go, let it go,* she reminded herself. *If you don't speak, she's more likely to keep talking, building momentum.* 'It was like, if she was stricter, if she held Callie in hand, then somehow people couldn't gossip about *her.* She took to calling herself by her own name, back when almost no one did that, you know?'

'Her own name?'

'You know, Myra Tippet. Only she put a *Mrs* in front of it, even though there was no Mr, which is why she was determined to be proper. "Mrs Myra Tippet does not cotton to coarse behavior, Fatima." That kind of thing.'

'Oh, third person,' Cassandra said, then hated herself for it.

Fatima smiled. 'Same old Cassandra, always with the right answer. Anyway, it didn't matter how much she called herself Mrs, how hard she was on Callie. Everyone knew that Callie didn't have a father, never did. I didn't either, but at least I was legal, you know? Oh sure, I was *barely* legal. My mother was six months gone on her wedding day and my daddy was gone six months after the wedding day. But I had a father's name on my birth certificate, a real one. Callie's daddy? No one ever knew who he was, including Mrs Myra Tippet, even if she did put Jenkins on the birth certificate.'

'I don't get it. Why would she give Cassandra a different surname?'

'I don't know.' Fatima sucked her lower lip, thinking. 'When you lie, you got to make it specific, right? Or maybe there was a Jenkins among her mens, and she hadn't decided yet that she was going to be born-again proper. She was one of those good-time girls who has had her fun, then figures she's going to be so good that no one can doubt her again.'

'Like you?'

'What are you saying?' A flash of the old Fatima here. Challenging, defiant.

'Tisha told me—or was it Donna—that you were'—she searched her memory for the word,

278

which had delighted her. *'Churchified* now, and didn't want to be around people who knew you back in the day.'

'Who said, Tisha or Donna?'

It seemed an odd point on which to fixate. 'I'm not sure. Tisha, I think.'

'Well—' Fatima was clearly angry yet trying to hold herself in check. 'I'm just trying to have a life. I met a good man, married him. We have three sons. Things haven't always been easy for us—he started a business two years ago, a transportation company. Town cars and limos, the kind of things people don't splurge on in these times, although proms are coming, that should help.'

'When was the last time you saw Callie?'

'We went to community college together. And we worked together for a bit.'

'Where?'

'You don't know that part?'

'No.'

She gave her a long, level look. 'You don't want to mess with them,' Fatima said at last.

'Who?'

'It doesn't matter. Trust me. If you don't mess with them, they won't mess with you. And they'll give you a chance, if you need it. They're not unfair. They'll help you, if you need help. Only you got to let this go.'

'But—'

Fatima leaned forward. There was so much of her now, but there was a firmness to all that flesh, a solidity. Cassandra couldn't help wondering what it felt like inside Fatima's body. She carried herself with the same cocky confidence she had as a girl and there was an almost gleeful exhibitionism

279

about the way she dressed. Caught unawares at home this afternoon, she wore a bright, boatneck tunic covered with green, orange, and yellow flowers, with matching green slacks and yellow flats.

Or had she been caught unawares? She hadn't seemed particularly surprised to see Cassandra, not the way she had been at church.

'I'll tell you this much. I *don't* know where Callie is. Wouldn't tell you if I did, but I don't. You have my word on that. We haven't seen each other since we were almost twenty and I went down to Atlanta to go to school.'

'To Spelman.'

'Yes, to Spelman. And Callie could have gone, too. Maybe not there, but somewhere, finished her education, done something with her life. But she was a stubborn girl, as everybody found out soon enough. She had her way of doing things, and I had mines. I'm not saying I was smarter or better, but I'm happy where I am. Callie could have been happy, too, if she wanted. Happy enough, at any rate. Leave her alone. Leave everything alone, Cassandra. This isn't like some test at school where you have to show everyone how smart you are. You really smart, you'll walk away. Sometimes, that's the smart play.'

'Who are you scared of, Fatima? Who is it that I have to avoid?'

'You don't know them,' she said firmly. 'You don't want to know them.'

'I'm writing a book,' Cassandra said. 'I'm going to tell this story.'

'Then you're going to have to make some shit up, like you did when we were in school.' The church-lady veneer was gone now, and the scrapper that Fatima had always been was in full evidence. 'I remember your little A-plus stories, all nice and neat, how the teachers fell over you with praise. I thought they were boring, but I guess I don't know from *lit-a-ra-chure.*'

Cassandra had a sudden, vivid memory of Fatima in ninth grade, *dancing* her short-story assignment. In a low-cut leotard and a batik wraparound skirt, which she removed halfway through the performance, she had acted out a tale of gang warfare and betrayal, much of it ripped off from *West Side Story,* which she defended on the grounds that *West Side Story* had stolen from Shakespeare, so why couldn't she? Cassandra had thought that an excellent point, although she hadn't been impressed by Fatima's story, not on the page. As words on paper, the piece had been utterly pedestrian, but as danced and spoken and even sung by Fatima—breasts bouncing obscenely, hands and feet moving to a beat only she could hear—it had been impressive, if only as a feat of utter unself-consciousness. Cassandra remembered someone shouting out from the back of the room, 'I just want to say that we couldn't do this kind of thing if they let boys attend our school,' and the approving, defiant applause awarded that sentiment. The teacher had given Fatima a C, saying it was all but plagiarized and not in the proper format.

Later, on the MTA bus they took home each day, an unusually chastened Fatima had asked to see Cassandra's short story, a small, closely observed piece about a religious girl whose hypocrisy leads her to a kind of living hell.

Cassandra couldn't remember much about it except for her attempt to write poetically about the sodium-vapor streetlights of the day, the bright melon-colored globes that had been introduced in the mugging-obsessed seventies. In fact, she had probably called them melon-colored globes and used some unfortunate turn of phrase about how they seemed to float in the winter dusk like a recently discovered solar system. Boy, talk about a darling that needed to be killed. But the teacher had liked it—although she did scold Cassandra for her frequent use of incomplete sentences—and placed a check mark next to it.

'So this is an A paper,' Fatima had said, and Cassandra had heard only admiration. Now it occurred to her that Fatima was left wondering how such a little story, with no shootings or star-crossed young lovers, could earn an A, while her virtuoso performance art had been deemed a C. 'Write what you know,' the teacher had urged them, yet hadn't Fatima done that? What if *West Side Story* was as real to her, from her early days in the old neighborhood, as Cassandra's tiny story was to her?

'It was nice seeing you, Fatima,' she said now, meaning it.

'Have a blessed day,' said the stranger who now had control of Fatima's body. She did not get up to see Cassandra out.

Girl Groups

The year we were in sixth grade, Tisha decided to form a girl group. Here was the twelve-year-old mind at work: Diana Ross was tight with the Jackson Five—she was credited with discovering them, although this was public-relations fluff. Still, our thinking went that if Diana Ross had discovered the Jackson Five, then being in a girl group like the Supremes would create some ephemeral bond with the Jackson Five, and they would discover *us*. Tisha, Donna, and Fatima rehearsed during recess, putting together various dance moves to suit the songs they sang. Rocking their arms to denote baby love, flagging down cars as if to stop them in the name of love.

I asked Tisha if I could join the Cliftonettes, named for the street where she and Donna lived.

'There are only three Supremes,' she said quickly.

'I could be the alternate, the understudy,' I suggested. 'If someone gets sick.'

'Can you sing?' Donna put in.

'Sure.' Couldn't everyone? In music class, I sang loudly, with lots of feeling.

'Are you *sure* you can sing?' Fatima pressed.

I was named the alternate, a not particularly meaningful role for a group that never performed anywhere but the playground, but it made me happy. No one said, *But the Supremes are black and you are white.* It was an era of possibility. We were beyond that.

Or so I thought, until the day I cut Jermaine

Jackson's photograph out of *16 Magazine* and Scotch-taped it inside my blue binder.

'You can't like Jermaine,' Fatima said.

'Did someone call him?' Those were the rules, as I understood them, in dividing the spoils of a boy group. Paul, John, George, and Ringo; Davy, Micky, Peter, and Mike. In almost every set, there were two good ones, one or two acceptable ones, and one out-and-out loser. Apparently life wasn't that different from the game Mystery Date, which ran the gamut from dream (white jacket, corsage) to dud (scruffy, unshowered). With the Jackson Five, for example, no one wanted Michael, not because we had any inkling of the problematic person he would one day become—he seemed pretty normal at the time, or as normal as any preternaturally talented boy in a pimp hat on national television—but because he was our age and seemed younger. Still, that left four Jacksons, and while I knew it was piggish of me to pick the best one, I was the one with the subscription to *16,* one of my father's guilt-inspired gifts.

'No, no one *called* him,' Fatima spluttered. 'But you can't—because—well, you can't, you just can't.'

'You can have Jackie,' I said, feeling myself generous. Jackie was the second-best one, in my estimation. I had earmarked him for Tisha, the capo of our little mafia. *The Godfather* was still a few years away, but we instinctively understood tribute.

'You can't have *any* of them,' Fatima said, and Donna nodded. Tisha was taking it all in, careful not to commit herself.

It was our last spring together, although I had

not yet grasped the reality of our impending separation. I would head southwest, to Rock Glen Junior High, and my friends would go north, to Lemmel. This was not determined by lines on a map; Baltimore had open enrollment. Students could go wherever they wished. But there were lines in our heads and, more crucial, lines in our parents' heads. The black families sent their children in one direction, the whites in the other. Something was happening, something for which we had no words. Finally, Tisha spoke in her emphatic yet careful way.

'We're too old to be cutting boys' photos out of magazines,' she said. 'It's time for real boyfriends, not make-believe ones.'

My mind reeled at this. Real boys? I wasn't ready for real boys. That's why I was reading *16*, with its endless safe, sexless boys and the occasional disturbing presence of Jim Morrison. The relationship between my father and Annie—they were living together, although pretending not to, if only because that would be a disadvantage in the divorce proceedings that were dragging on, almost two years since his departure—was so overtly passionate that I chose to ignore the very fact of passion.

Still, if my father could love Annie, why couldn't I love Jermaine? Were my friends saying that my father's relationship was illegitimate in a way that not even my mother dared suggest? That was the bomb that Tisha was trying to defuse. She would have been successful if a boy sitting nearby, an overgrown hoodlum with greasy hair that hung in his eyes, hadn't begun to laugh.

'Hey, Cassandra can't help it. She's a nigger

285

lover just like her father.'

Here's the strange thing, the part that our contemporary, PC-trained minds can't quite absorb: This statement was far less inflammatory in 1970 than it would be today. If a teacher had heard the remark, she would have reprimanded Curtis Bunch, perhaps sent him to the office or kept him after school. But she would have done the same if he had cursed, and he would have been punished far more severely for fighting or bringing a Zippo lighter to school. Curtis Bunch was a budding arsonist, a famously awful boy, alleged to be fond of suffocating cats in the old insulated milk boxes that still stood on porches and front steps in Dickeyville.

Back then, a boy might have fought a boy over this word, but only if it had been used against him. A passing reference to someone else's father, his shameful behavior—well, it was hard to say who should be angry, what should be defended. Annie was not yet my stepmother. My father loved her, but did that make him—what Curtis Bunch said?

Tisha, Fatima, and Donna stared balefully at Curtis Bunch, yet let his remark pass. I wanted to defend my father. Only—I could not defend my father without disavowing my friends. There was a world of things wrong with my father loving Annie—the embarrassment he had caused my mother, the financial havoc he had wreaked on all of us, the squirm-inducing fact that the affair was driven by sex, no matter how often my father spoke of love. But Annie's race was not one of the problems. Right? Right?

'My father's not—' I began, but I could not repeat those words. 'At least my father's not like

286

yours.' I knew nothing about Curtis Bunch's father but figured he must be pretty awful.

'No, my old man lives at my house, with my mother, not with some nigger,' Curtis said.

'He doesn't . . . I'm not—' I began, then saw my friends' faces, closing to me. The bell rang, and we went outside for recess, where we behaved as if nothing had happened. The Cliftonettes did not rehearse that day. Instead, we played foursquare, one of the few games at which I excelled, but I was off that day, ejected almost immediately, even as Tisha and Fatima managed to hold their turns for much of the game. (Donna, so graceful in other things, was not athletic and preferred watching from the sidelines.) Later, it seemed to me that the other girls had ganged up on me, sent the ball toward me with spin and malice, making sure I lost my turn.

Our friendship appeared unchanged, on the surface. I was invited to the big party at Donna's house to celebrate the end of sixth grade. Of course, everyone was invited, but I felt wanted, included, in a way that others weren't. It would be three years before my friends would literally turn their backs on me, finally delivering the punishment I deserved.

NATURAL SELECTION

March 28–29

Chapter Twenty-Eight

Teena's right hand was throbbing when she woke up, a sign that the weather was changing. It had been a warmer-than-usual March, but the winter months could never be mild enough for Teena. Worse, she had rolled on her right hand in her sleep, possibly to keep it warm beneath her body, but that had only helped to freeze it into a semi-claw position. She had to get ready for work virtually one handed, which made blow-drying her hair a bitch. Still, she managed, and her right hand was more or less back in service by the time she got in the car.

The mall was dead. Teena didn't need to read the newspaper to know what was going on with the economy. She saw it every day at work. The managers had kept repeating, like a hopeful mantra, that business would pick up before Easter. Old-fashioned Baltimore clung to the tradition of new outfits and hats on Easter, even its own version of a promenade, although that had the bad habit of turning into a near riot. Easter had come and gone, and things were about as dead as Teena had ever seen. Forget the housing market, the stock market—if you wanted to know how nervous consumers were, drop by Nordstrom's high-end departments.

Bored, she fed Fatima's name into the computer system again. She had taken it almost personally when Cassandra had reported back to her that the interview was a bust, that Fatima not only wouldn't help her find Callie Jenkins but had dropped all these hints about how dangerous it was for Cassandra to look, how she would regret it. Teena didn't buy that for a second. She could recognize a head game, someone trying to dress up ignorance as purpose and intent. She wasn't sure how the computer, having given her Fatima's address already, could do anything new for her, but she didn't have anything else to do and—

Fatima Hollins's Nordstrom card had been paid off, in full. In arrears a week ago, it would have been at a zero balance now, except that someone had come in and charged six hundred dollars' worth of clothes two days after the account was paid off, which happened to be two days before Cassandra visited the woman's house. Fatima had been on this floor, too, not down in the Rack, although over in the plus-size department.

Teena's first impulse was to call Cassandra. But what did she really know? *Slow down,* she told herself. It was an interesting juxtaposition of facts, nothing more at this point. Cassandra goes to visit Fatima and she suddenly has the scratch to pay off her bill, and then some. But her credit showed an ongoing history of boom and bust. Like a lot of people, she got in a little over her head, then she caught up. Nordstrom, almost all department stores, would go bankrupt if people didn't overspend here and there.

No, it wasn't *Cassandra* whom Teena needed to call. She fed another name into the system, one she hadn't really thought about for years. Yes, there was the account, although it was all but dormant, last used for a few purchases around Christmas. This one probably shopped at more exclusive stores now. But Teena remembered

Gloria Bustamante when she was wearing the Montgomery Ward version of dress-for-success suits, with lumpy shoulder pads that looked like little hens hiding in the folds of her jacket. Gloria was older than Teena, but she had been a late starter, green as they come when they first faced off. Teena remembered feeling sorry for her at the time, regarding her as a glorified paperweight, an object placed on Callie to hold her down, keep her still. When Gloria had quit Howard & Howard, Teena had assumed it was because she was opting for a less combative form of law. Yet she had built up quite a good criminal defense practice, which suggested she had more on the ball than Teena had suspected. What might Gloria Bustamante know?

*   *   *

'What if this were real?' Reg asked Cassandra.

Perhaps because they spoke so little—a consequence of spending almost all their time in bed, not wanting to waste the hours they had—the words seemed overly portentous. Cassandra assessed them, considered all the possible meanings, then decided to keep things lighthearted.

'I thought I was real,' she said, taking Reg's hand and smacking it on her hip. 'Doesn't this feel pretty solid?'

He kept his hand there. 'This is different for me. And not just because you're older than the other women I've been with.'

'Thanks,' Cassandra said dryly. 'Good to know.'

'I mean—look, I've always had . . . diversions in

my life. I assumed you understood that when we started.'

'I understood. Does Donna?' Not quite so lighthearted now.

'I don't think Donna cares,' he said. She turned her face to him, amazed, and he backtracked. 'I'm not saying she knows, on a conscious level, but she suspects. Yet I've been considerate. I haven't shamed her. She can live with that.'

Cassandra didn't want to argue with him, not about this topic. But—those words again—she was her father's daughter, and she couldn't let a piece of illogic go by, even if it was in her best interest. 'I was in Baltimore all of a month when I heard you described as a pussy hound. Could Donna really be that sheltered?'

'I don't know. How much did you know about your father?'

'Not much. But I was a child. I'm not asking about your daughter but your wife.'

'I read your book—'

'You did?' She couldn't help it; this was almost as thrilling as the words she believed she had heard, was still trying to decipher. *What if this were real?* Of course the very use of the subjunctive indicated it *wasn't* real; still—

'Well, I listened to it on audio. They should have had you read it. You have a much nicer voice than the woman they used. Anyway, I don't think your mother knew, not really, and your father was all but rubbing her face in what he did.'

'Not at first. But did you get to the section where he starts using her nickname, the one he always despised? It's clear there that she was beginning to suspect his infidelities.'

294

'Clear to you, writing after the fact. Did you ever ask your mother what she knew, when?'

She was irritated now, much as she didn't want to be. Who was Reg to question the authority with which she had written about her life, her family?

'We never spoke . . . on point about these things. It would have been too painful for her. But I showed my mother what I wrote, and she never contradicted it. Nor did my father.'

'Maybe she just preferred your version. Most people would, don't you think? Would prefer not looking like a fool. Maybe you gave your mother a dignity she didn't feel she had in real life.'

Cassandra struggled to a sitting position. 'Are we having a fight?'

'What?'

'I feel as if we're quarreling, and I don't know why.'

'Sorry.' He put an arm around her, kissed her forehead. She felt like she was seventeen, but the kind of seventeen no one ever gets to be. Comfortable in her skin, flush with knowledge. Leda again, in Zeus's beak, but holding on, his equal. 'I should know better than to challenge a Baltimore girl on her own mother. My fault.'

He got up to shower. Even nonadulterers showered after sex, but it still made Cassandra a little sad. She was sadder that she had distracted him from those provocative words: *What if this were real? What if?* But it couldn't be. And if she weren't careful, the memory of this affair was all she would have to take away from her time in Baltimore. She must focus on the book, on Callie. But so far everything had been as frustrating as her trip through Baltimore's suburbs, nothing but cul-de-sacs that kept looping back. She wondered again at Fatima's implicit threat. How could anyone hurt Cassandra? Unlike Fatima, she hadn't buried her past. She had put it on the page for everyone to see. Friends and critics alike sometimes marveled at this, as if it were an act of daring. But Cassandra, who had grown up in a house where everything and nothing was said, felt it was the simplest way to live. Say the worst things about yourself first, and no one can ever hurt you.

Except, perhaps, the man in her shower, a man she was trying desperately to pretend that she didn't love.

*　　　*　　　*

'There's an old woman down in the lobby, saying she has to see you,' the desk attendant had told Gloria, and that's what Gloria saw when she came down. An old woman, well dressed but slightly stooped through the shoulders.

Then she realized she knew this old woman and she was almost ten years younger than Gloria.

'Detective Murphy.'

'Not Detective Murphy anymore. Not Detective Murphy for a very long time, but you know that.'

'I do know.' Gloria looked at Teena's right hand but made no move to shake it, to greet her in any way.

'I think you know a lot.'

'Almost all of it covered by attorney-client privilege. My client was very adamant about that. The things I learned in the process of her defense—I am not allowed to discuss with anyone. And you know that.'

296

'Almost. You said almost.'

Gloria studied Teena's face. Jesus, she had aged badly. It made Gloria almost grateful never to have been pretty, if this was what pretty could become, what age could take away from you. She had felt that way even when she was young, back when she was working with Callie. *Thank God I'm not beautiful because look what this girl's beauty has earned her.* Teena's well-made, tasteful clothes and careful hairstyle only emphasized how time had ravaged her face. Part of it was that she was simply too thin. But there were her hooded eyes, too, which looked as if she never got a good night's sleep. *Why? So you dropped your gun and your patrol car ran over your wrist? You could have found a way to stay on the force if you wanted to.* Hell, Gloria remembered a detective who had lost his right hand and learned to shoot with his left.

But Gloria understood. She had always understood. Teena had claimed permanent disability because she wanted the punishment of exile, yearned for it. Teena Murphy had always been known for her clothes, but the thing she really loved to wear was a hair shirt. How silly of her.

'Are you a private investigator now?'

'Not exactly.'

'So why do you care?'

'I'm working—' Teena switched course. 'I just do.'

'She got to you, didn't she?'

'Who?' The face might have changed, but the steely composure was the same and only slightly less remarkable than it had been when Teena was young. She had been so prepossessed, poised.

297

Hard to remember, but Gloria had envied her.

'That woman, the writer, the one who's been trying to stir things up. Why would you help her? What's in it for you?'

The lobby of Gloria's apartment building was the kind of large, empty space that one would expect in one of Mies van der Rohe's glass palaces, and her words echoed, taking on a strange emphasis. Gloria may have made mistakes, but she had never lost sight of what was in her best interest. Maybe she had a couple of hair shirts in her own wardrobe, after all.

'I don't know,' Teena said at last. 'Probably nothing. What was in it for you?' She took in her surroundings. 'This, I guess. Your own law office. So that's what you traded, for whatever you knew. I thought you were stupid, but you were a lot smarter than I was.'

Everyone assumed I was stupid, Gloria thought. Book smart, but stupid in the ways of the world. I thought I was being rewarded, but they were counting on my stupidity, my passivity. Then, when I finally took some initiative, I almost derailed my life. Those were my choices, cataclysmic failure or success on my own terms. What would you have chosen? What did you choose?

'Do you know how to read a campaign finance report?' she asked Teena.

'What?'

'Upstairs, I have reports from the Friends of Julius Howard committee. Paper reports from the seventies and nineties. The more recent ones are online.'

'Are you saying—'

'I'm saying I have some reports. You may have

298

them. Anyone can have them. They are public documents. I didn't request them until a few days ago.'

'Why? I mean, why did you request them?'

'I honestly don't know.' *Because I ran into an old friend and he's not my friend anymore and I can't bear it. Because I have tried to figure out for fifteen years now what constitutes justice. Because I have won freedom for innocent people and not-so-innocent people to make up for the fact that I could not help the first client entrusted to me. True, she didn't want to be helped, but it was my job to persuade her to help herself, and I couldn't. So I abandoned her, used my knowledge to sweeten my own life.*

'The early ones, they'll be easy. They were on paper,' she said. 'It's only now that things are online that they've gotten so cagey. You get what I'm saying? You'll find things easily enough in the old files, if you look carefully. But it's the new files you need to study. Stay here.'

She did not want Teena to come up to the apartment. If the day came when she was accused of violating any of her promises, if they tried to disbar her, she wanted her doorman to be able to say she spoke to Teena in the open.

*　　　*　　　*

A few minutes later, she came back with the files. The files and an old CD, Paul Simon's *The Rhythm of the Saints*.

'Music to study by?' Teena asked.

'I am particularly fond of track one,' Gloria said. She was. She had bought this album because she

299

loved the previous one, *Graceland,* which reminded her of the evenings she spent with Reg and Colton, imitating their bosses, singing their parody of 'You Can Call Me Al.' She had bought the next album thinking to re-create those evenings of camaraderie, only to be haunted by one song.

'"The Obvious Child,"' Teena read out loud. 'You mean—'

'I've told you what I can. Check that—I haven't told you anything. Remember that. I haven't told you anything.'

'Got it,' Teena said, and Gloria had a flash of the brash, cocky young woman she had met twenty years ago. Teena had thought Gloria beneath her, barely worth bothering with. She might have been right.

'And, Teena?' Her voice caught her as she was leaving, the files tucked under her left arm, the damaged right one hanging by her side. Not quite dead, but clearly affected.

'Yes?'

'If you do find Callie Jenkins, make sure she knows I didn't tell you where she was. The fact is, I don't know, don't want to know. I would have left her alone, but others won't. Tell her it's not my fault and tell her . . .'

She paused so long that Teena finally had to prompt her. 'Yeah?'

'Tell her that Gloria Bustamante hopes she's doing well. And that Reg Barr has a daughter. Make sure you tell her that. Reg and Donna have a daughter.'

Chapter Twenty-Nine

It was almost 1 A.M. and Cassandra's head was throbbing. As a college student, she had been the queen of the all-nighter, stoking herself on strong coffee and NoDoz, writing twenty-page papers in under four hours, cramming an entire semester's worth of work into the dark hours. But that kind of stamina can't be maintained. Her almost fifty-year-old body was, in some ways, more fit than her twenty-year-old one, loaded down as it was with those extra college pounds, exercise not yet a part of her routine. But her mind was flabbier, no doubt about it. It didn't help that the papers strewn around her held no narrative, no organizing principle, no story to follow. They were nothing more than endless lists of payees and amounts, all of which appeared mundanely legitimate.

Teena, who was using Cassandra's laptop more or less one-handed, wasn't faring much better. She had fed Callie Jenkins's name into the online records in every possible variation and come up empty. Cassandra poured herself another glass of wine and Teena actually frowned. She had been drinking Diet Coke since she had arrived here a few hours ago, toting these papers.

'To think I once thought about being a forensic accountant,' she muttered now, glaring at the computer.

'When was that?' Cassandra said, glad for the distraction, although she knew it meant she would end up rereading these pages again.

'After I—*after.* I wanted to find a way to do

something like police work. But accounting's hard. I dropped my first class after three sessions.'

'Did you have to leave the force?'

'The department,' Teena said. 'Not the force.' She smiled at her own semantic pettiness. 'It depends on how you define "have to", I guess. Maybe I could have stayed. But it was a relief for things to be over, in a way.'

'That sounds like a psychologist's point of view. You wanted to leave so you put yourself in jeopardy, suffered an injury from which you couldn't recover.'

'I could have learned to shoot with my left hand,' Teena said. 'Damn, I knew a guy who was blinded when he was shot on the job, and he managed to continue working as an instructor at the academy. Fact is, with therapy, I might have been able to qualify with my right hand again.'

'Why didn't you?'

'I don't know. I felt like such a failure. Time after time, going down to talk to Calliope Jenkins. No confession. No body. No leads. You know in the movies how you see the detective up against some mastermind and there's all this *talk*? I would have killed to have someone who actually spoke to me. With her, it was this endless silence. She was like someone . . . waiting for a bus. She made me feel like a gnat, buzzing in her ear, and she wouldn't even bother to wave me away.'

'Like freeze tag or statues.'

'You played those, too?'

'I guess most Baltimore girls did. And television tag—I can't remember quite how that went, just that we shouted out the names of television shows.'

302

'And Mother, may I? Baby steps, giant steps—what else?'

'Banana steps?' Cassandra, living on a dead-end street with older children, had seldom played those games. She had watched, when she was younger, on summer evenings, but she was never deemed old enough to play. By the time she was, they had moved on. It had been lonely on Hillhouse Road. That was all she had been trying to convey in her novel. How had such a simple idea gone so wrong? Perhaps because she hadn't been willing to state it directly. Or maybe it was too ordinary an epiphany. Weren't all children lonely in some way?

Her bleary eyes rested on a new page. Payee, amount. Payee, amount. God, political campaigns were boring. Catering bills, janitorial services, office supplies. Her eyes backtracked. Janitorial services, paid out to Myra Tippet. *Myra Tippet.* She had been so focused on finding variations on *Callie, Calliope,* and *Jenkins* that she had skipped past this on the first reading. Cassandra wouldn't even have known the name if Fatima hadn't mentioned it yesterday. *She took to calling herself by her own name, back when almost no one did that. . . . Only she put a* Mrs *in front of it, even though there was no Mr.*

She glanced at the top of the page: This was 1990, three years after Callie's arrest. She tracked back to 1988—there it was again. Not every month, but at least once a quarter, and the amounts were odd: $3,017, $2,139, $4,045. They were credible numbers. But, really, how much did a campaign office need in the way of cleaning?

'Was Callie's mother a cleaning woman?' she asked Teena.

303

'Maybe. I remember she worked at Parks Sausages, I think, but it wouldn't be unheard of if she did some part-time maiding off the books.'

'Drop the name Myra Tippet into the online files, see what comes up.'

Even as a one-handed, one-fingered typist, Teena was swift. 'Nothing,' she said.

Cassandra tried to think this through. 'In 1988, Julius Howard's campaign starts making payments to Callie's mother on a regular-irregular basis. But her name disappears once it's online and easier to search.'

'Interesting, I'll grant you. I'm not even sure if she's still alive.' Another round of lightning, staccato typing. 'Nothing comes up in the Social Security database—when people die, you can find their names there—so I have to think she's alive. No idea where she is, though. I think we should go back to the Paul Simon album. Gloria was trying to tell me something.'

' "The Obvious Child," ' Cassandra said. 'Well, it is pretty obvious, right? She's talking about Callie's missing son.'

'Or Reg's daughter. She was awfully particular on that point, that we should tell Callie about Reg's kid.'

'Why would Callie care if Reg has a daughter? He wasn't even her lawyer until five years in. Maybe Gloria Bustamante is trying to divert us from something *she* did.'

The bit about Reg's daughter had rankled in other ways, too, but Cassandra couldn't tell Teena that. Just the reminder that Reg had a daughter bothered her, because it was that fact that doomed their relationship. Cassandra could love a man who left his wife, but she could never love a man who left his daughter. She had set herself up rather neatly, she saw now. But she hadn't known about Reg's daughter, not at first. Not like Annie, who had met Cassandra in the hospital. She hated to be reminded of that one detail, the only blemish she knew on her stepmother's character. *You saw me, saw us. Even if you fell in love with him the day he rescued you, couldn't you have pulled back from your emotions, walked away? Yes, I know he pursued you after leaving the hospital, and I know how persuasive he can be. But couldn't you have resisted, Annie, for my sake? Was it really that big a love?*

'Myra Tippet isn't enough,' Teena said. 'Unless we can find her, but she's not coming up on any search engine I try.'

'Tippet of the iceberg,' Cassandra said, laughing at her own joke in the slightly hysterical fashion of the sleep deprived. 'But there are still janitorial services on the payee lists, right?'

'You would think,' Teena said, returning to the screen. 'Catering company, banquet hall, office supplies, individuals, catering company, office supplies, limo company, banquet hall—'

'Stop.'

'Sorry,' Teena said. 'It's just easier sometimes if I say things out loud.'

'No, I mean, go back. Limo company. What was the name?'

'High Styles Transportation Service.'

But Fatima hadn't told her the name of the company, only that it was struggling.

'Address?'

'Rosewood Path in Owings Mills. Hey—'

'That belongs to Fatima's husband, that's the

305

address you found for me. Can you search just for the limo company?'

'Think so.' The quick clatter of keys. Normally, Cassandra would wince at hearing her laptop hit so hard, but she didn't mind in this situation. 'It only appears three times, going back two years.'

'Fatima told me the company's only been around two years. What do you want to bet, though, that the next report shows the company again and the amount is high enough to cover the Nordstrom bill that Fatima just paid, along with the new things she bought herself?'

'Again, political campaigns do use town cars and limos and the like. It would be hard to prove this wasn't a legitimate use.'

'We're not trying a case in court. We're looking for information that we can use to get people to talk to us. Fatima kept warning me about some shadowy "they". Perhaps she meant Julius Howard. Perhaps the reason that Howard & Howard represented Callie in the first place is connected to Julius. What did the old news stories say? Donna's father agreed to take the case as a favor to the American Civil Liberties Union. But maybe he took it on as a favor to Julius, his brother.'

'And why would he do that?'

'The child. The obvious child.'

'Julius is the father of Callie Jenkins's dead child? But there was a birth father on record, another junkie.'

'I don't know. I do know the coincidences are piling up, that it's simply too much.' Cassandra was groping for another fact about Fatima but one not provided by Fatima. Something about Spelman, how she had gotten there, Fatima's offense at the idea that she was churchified, her angry need to know exactly who had suggested she had changed so radically.

'Teena, let me have the computer. I need to look up something in my notes.'

But in the split second it took for Teena to slide the laptop across the table to her, Cassandra remembered. Tisha was the one who said Fatima was churchified. But Donna was the one who complained that Fatima had cut herself off from the group. 'My uncle Julius wrote her a recommendation. She volunteered in his office in the late seventies.'

The late seventies. That was when Julius Howard ran for city council president—and lost. He never again attempted to run for an office that might have given him greater acclaim but had stayed in his safe senate district. The late seventies—Fatima would have been twenty or twenty-one, a juicy girl. She had been juicy at twelve. Had Callie volunteered, too? *We worked together.* Where, Cassandra had asked, and Fatima had dodged the question.

Cassandra stared blindly at her computer screen, trying to organize her racing thoughts, which included one melancholy undertone: *This is going to cost me Reg.* So be it. She wasn't going to get to keep him, anyway. And then: *But what does this have to do with Reg's daughter; why would Callie care?* She still didn't want to think about that. Besides, what she had now was a conspiracy theory beyond conspiracy theories, all wild conjecture. If it weren't so late, she would call her father, ask his advice. He would help her sort it through. Ah well,

307

they were having breakfast tomorrow. She rubbed her eyes, once, twice, three times. And, as if in a fairy tale, the third time brought forth a genie from the bottle. Not a genie, per se, but a line of text on the computer in front of her, which was still showing the expenditures of Julius Howard's campaign in the last reporting period.

Amuse Catering, Bridgeville, Delaware.

She heard her own young voice in her head, cocksure and patronizing. *'Although you pronounce it wrong, you're named for one of the Muses. I was almost named for one of the Muses, but my father decided to call me Cassandra instead, for the woman who had the gift of prophecy.'* Saw Callie taking this in, smiling slightly, pleased to know her name, mispronounced though it might be, had such a highborn origin. 'Does that mean I'm funny?' Callie had asked. 'Not *amuse*,' Cassandra corrected. 'A. Muse. The Muse of epic poetry.' And she had rattled off the other eight, because she was the kind of little girl who could. It was probably the longest conversation she and Callie ever had, and Cassandra had done almost all the talking.

'Why would a state senator, one from Baltimore, use a Delaware catering company?'

Teena shrugged even as Cassandra used the database's search function. It showed up every quarter. As with Myra Tippet's janitorial services, the amounts were odd enough to be credible, averaging out to $15,000, four times a year. Not a lot. Probably not enough to repay a woman for seven years of her life, but it might seem generous to Callie. And tantalizing to a reporter, if one ever checked these records. But who would research

Julius Howard, dedicated backbencher that he had become? Who could find Callie Jenkins in Amuse Catering, a Limited Liability Company registered in another state?

'This is her,' she told Teena.

'It's a PO box.'

'She'll have a driver's license, living where she does. I bet that's public information. We can get that. Not here, tonight, but we can get it.'

Teena held up her left hand and it took Cassandra a moment to recognize the invitation for a high-five. She slapped her lightly, feeling triumphant. But she also felt sad, contemplating what all this intrepid enterprise was going to cost her. Not only Reg, but any chance of rapprochement with Tisha, much less Fatima or Donna. She realized, in that moment of seeing the possibility recede, how much she had hoped to reconnect with her old friends. She had always understood that Reg was merely hers to borrow, perhaps even a subtle get-even. But she would have liked to have Tisha as a friend again, to have someone in her life who knew the whole of her. Not just the parts she had written down and shaped, but every ragged detail, every playground moment, every tiny triumph, every enormous failure. Even the frowsy hair.

You don't want to mess with them, Fatima had warned. She was genuinely fearful, but she owed and was owned by the Howards in a way that Cassandra never could be. If the friendships had lived—but they hadn't, and that had been *their* decision, the consequence of their inaction. She would find no joy in hurting Donna and her family. But she couldn't help but be exhilarated by the

309

opportunity to find Callie and get her story.

'Even with all this, she still might not talk,' Teena warned. 'After all, you're threatening her livelihood.'

'I can promise her part of the book's profits, if it comes to that, replace the income she's going to lose. But you're right, she might be reluctant to speak. I'd like to go alone, if you don't mind.'

Teena opened her mouth as if to object but ended up nodding. 'Yeah, change it up. Seven years, she never said more than a dozen words to me, the same words over and over. Maybe it will be different with you.'

And maybe it won't, Cassandra realized. *What will I do then? What does it take to make Callie Jenkins talk?*

Chapter Thirty

'What do you think?' her father demanded the next morning.

'Very striking,' Cassandra said, inspecting the restaurant, housed in one of Baltimore's old mill buildings. These reclaimed mills made Cassandra feel old, given that she had grown up less than a mile from the Dickey Mill in its final years, when the trucks still rumbled in and out. Then again, on four hours of sleep, everything made Cassandra feel old.

'Not the décor, the *food.* It's part of the locavore movement, devoted to area foods.'

'All I've had so far is a cup of coffee, and that's not local, surely?'

'It's March,' her father said, defensive of his discovery. 'And they're not a hundred percent local or all we'd be eating would be, I don't know, some kind of roots with eggs, I guess. But, philosophically, they're trying to use as much local food as possible.'

Cassandra usually admired her father's proclivity for novelty, especially now that it was fixated on food. He often surprised her with his knowledge of odd cuisines, many of which weren't even available in the Baltimore area. In fact, she often found herself wondering as he spoke, say, of Malaysian food, if his knowledge was secondhand, gleaned from reading. But then, how else did a classics professor approach anything, except via text? And dining with him was more agreeable than eating with her mother, who chose the same old places and worried about the prices, expressing shock if Cassandra dared to order a starter and an entrée, and never mind the anxiety prompted by the very words *à la carte.*

'I'm sure it will be good,' she said. Her head was pounding from lack of sleep. It had been 2 A.M. by the time Teena had left, although their additional hour of searching had provided no new leads. Still, she couldn't complain about what they had discovered: Myra Tippet, Fatima, Callie Jenkins, all receiving money via Julius Howard's campaign. She hadn't had time to check with a lawyer on the legality of this, not that she cared. The main thing was to persuade Callie, once she tracked her down, that she had something to lose by not confiding in Cassandra.

'Cassandra, are you even listening to me?'

'I'm sorry,' she said automatically. 'Late night.

311

The book took an interesting turn. I think I've found Callie Jenkins.'

'Ah.' Her father waited and she realized that he expected her to fill him in on the latest developments and, as usual, seek his counsel. She suddenly realized she no longer wanted to. For one thing, she couldn't tell him the whole story, the complication of Reg. He would scold her—not for the affair, of course, he wasn't that much of a hypocrite. But the ethics would disturb him. Her father was funny about that. However abominable his personal behavior, he had always been ethical in his professional life. His personal life had cost him dearly at Hopkins, which had been unfair. He was far from the only philanderer on faculty and, unlike some others, he wasn't a serial seducer of students. Besides, whatever his personal failings, he was a terrific teacher, demanding yet fair. He had taught until his seventy-fifth birthday and never phoned it in or gone on autopilot.

In his final year of teaching, Cassandra had sneaked into the back of a lecture hall and listened to her father speak about Homer. 'The wine-dark sea,' he had intoned, 'also known in various translations as the wine-red sea.' He had reviewed the problems of translation, the doubts that some scholars had about Homer's description. He touched lightly on the Fagles translation, which had broken his heart, largely because he could not deem it objectionable in any way. It had been, Cassandra knew, her father's fantasy that he would produce such a work, a seminal translation. But it had been a mere fantasy, and it had been wrecked when someone else achieved what he could only dream of.

Abruptly, he had broken off from his prepared talk and asked, 'How many of you are in the writing sems?' The latter being Hopkins shorthand for the writing seminars, a Masters program of considerable reputation. A few hands went up. 'With all due respect,' he said, 'you will probably never come up with anything that will rival Homer. Even a phrase as deceptively simple as "the wine-dark sea" will prove to be beyond most of you.' Then, in an exceedingly kind tone: 'But it's still worth trying.' Cassandra had realized she was being held to no less a standard, despite the fact that the writing sem students would have killed to reach her level of success. She would never write a line as good as Homer. Was that an unfair standard? Or was her father admirable in his obstinate principles, his refusal to lower the bar even for his daughter?

Now she found herself wondering if she might at least have his admiration for her enterprise, if not for her writing.

'Callie is in Delaware, although I'm not sure where. I have to check to see if I can get the address through the Department of Motor Vehicles or some other source.'

'And what will you say when you confront your Holy Grail? Are you prepared?'

'I think so.' Again, refusing the implicit invitation to share, seek his counsel.

'Real life,' her father said, 'can be disappointingly banal. Suppose she says, "Yes, I killed my child, leave me alone."'

'It would be an answer.'

'Answers are overrated.'

She tried again. 'It would be a beginning.'

313

'Toward what end?'

'I don't know. That's what makes this interesting to me. I've lived my other books before writing them. I knew the endings and I shaped my memories to justify them in a sense. Even with the novel—'

'Not your best work,' her father said. 'You're a good writer, Cassandra, but fiction doesn't suit you.'

She had to swallow hard to keep from crying. How embarrassing, to be fifty and still capable of being moved to tears of shame by a parent. Childish, petulant thoughts warred within her, eager to escape. *My words were good enough to help buy you the apartment at Broadmead. No, fiction was your métier, as an adulterer. I could never come up with better stories than the ones you told Mother.*

Instead, she found herself asking, 'Did Annie feel bad about breaking up our family? That's one answer I wish I could have.'

'What an interesting transition,' her father said. He was many things, but not obtuse. 'I've never liked that term—*breaking, broken*—when it comes to families and relationships. They're not vases. They're dynamic organisms that grow, change, and adapt. Imagine if we applied Darwin's ideas to our relationships and saw them as evolving, changing in order to facilitate our survival.'

'But living organisms—at least vertebrates—have things within them that can be broken.'

'Bones, not hearts. The heart does not break. The heart falters, the heart stops, the heart develops fatty deposits—'

'*There's* a poetic image.'

He laughed and Cassandra joined him. She

314

didn't have the will to push him forward, to demand emotional reparations at this late date. She didn't have the *heart,* as a muscle or as a metaphor. Then again, perhaps she would ask him onstage at the Gordon School, use her five hundred onlookers to demand the answer that had long eluded her.

*   *   *

Cassandra was getting ready to leave for Delaware when her cell rang. She saw her mother's name, thought about not answering, felt guilty for the thought, then picked up just before it went to voice mail.

'About dinner tonight . . . ,' her mother began.

Had she double-scheduled her parents? How could she have made such a mistake?

'Oh, Mom, I was about to call you. Something urgent has come up and I have to cancel.'

'That's all right.' It clearly wasn't.

'It's for the book. I've found Callie, I have an appointment with her.' She hated to lie, but it was easier than admitting that she was driving almost two hours to confront a woman on her doorstep.

'Of course. You probably should have left earlier, but then you had breakfast with your father, right? He just called.'

'Really?'

'He said you looked tired. And a little thin.'

'I was up late, that's all. I doubt I've lost any weight.' Although perhaps she had. Since meeting Reg, she had been buzzing along on that amphetamine-like high, uninterested in food. Then again, her father's choice of restaurant, while interesting in theory, had been challenging in practice. He hadn't been far off about the root vegetables and eggs. The so-called local cheese had been appalling.

'Can we reschedule for tomorrow, Mom?'

'Well, it's a Sunday and I hate going out on Sunday, everywhere is brunch, brunch, brunch, you can't get a BLT. I'm not saying that I want a BLT, that's only an example—'

'Dinner, then.' She hated to interrupt but saw no other choice.

'You eat so late.' Cassandra generally liked to eat dinner at seven or seven thirty, no later than eight.

'Dinner,' she repeated, making it an edict. 'Someplace new. But we can go at six or so.'

'I'm not sure I know any new places—'

'I'll figure it out, Mom, and call you with a plan.'

*   *   *

On a summer Saturday, the drive to Bridgeville would have been choked with beach-bound traffic, but Cassandra made good time, even on the long two-lane stretch of 404, and found herself there in less than two hours. She took the bypass by mistake and had to backtrack, finding herself in the heart of one of those small towns that declared, 'If you lived here, you would be home by now.' Was that a tautology? The houses along the main streets were charming enough, inviting even, and Cassandra wondered if she could live in such a place, then decided immediately that she never could. Everyone would know her business. In fact, she had obtained Callie Jenkins's address not through the Department of Motor Vehicles, but because Teena had asked a cop friend to call an acquaintance here, chat him up, ask if he knew Callie by name or description. 'Oh, yes, the tall black gal,' he had said. 'Keeps to herself, drives a maroon Chevy Beretta, has a mother in a nursing home over to Denton, I think. Lives on Walnut.' All Cassandra had to do was cruise the street and look for the car.

There it was, in a driveway. The house was plain, nothing special, not one of the Victorian charmers on the central road, but a white-vinyl-sided Cape Cod with green shutters. Cassandra circled the block, circled again, and would have gone around a third time if she wasn't worried that she would draw suspicious glances from neighbors. She forced herself to park. Even then, she needed another five minutes before she got out of the car and went to the door.

Her knock didn't bring forth any sound at first and she was almost relieved. Good, she could go home. But then she heard a slow, gentle tread, someone light-footed, not at all in a hurry to see who was calling unannounced on a Saturday afternoon.

'Yes?' the woman said, peering at Cassandra through the storm door.

There are people you can recognize ten, twenty, forty years after childhood. Tisha, Donna, even Fatima fell in that category. They had changed, but they were still recognizably themselves. But Cassandra hadn't seen Callie Jenkins since she was fourteen and she had undergone the kind of metamorphosis that was straight from a fairy tale, 'The Ugly Duckling' to be exact. The newspaper photos of her had not captured her extraordinary beauty, which was worn yet still very much in evidence. She must have been a knockout in her twenties, yet the photographs had been singularly unflattering. The editors had probably always chosen shots of her frowning or grimacing. Or perhaps it was simply that she was so often looking down in those pictures. But given how she appeared now, at fifty, she must have been amazing in her twenties. Tall, lean, yet not without curves. Strong features, huge blue-green eyes. Her hair and clothing, the things that she controlled, were less remarkable. Not that she was unkempt or messy, just that she had expended very little effort on them. She wore green slacks and a black sweater; her straightened hair was pulled back into something that was neither a ponytail nor a chignon.

'Can I help you?' she said, her voice polite and curious, nothing more.

'Callie? I'm Cassandra Fallows, we went to school together.'

Callie took a step back, one arm braced against the door, as if Cassandra might try to break it down.

'I remember,' she said. 'You always were a hand-up-in-the-air girl.'

'What?'

'One of those girls who knew all the answers. What do you want?'

'I'm a writer, I'm working on a book—'

'No.'

'But—'

'I can't talk to you. Just can't. I'm sorry.' She took another step back, started to close the main door.

318

'I know about Amuse Catering.'

That stopped her.

'And your mother.'

'Leave my mother out of this.'

'Fatima, too. Did you know that? She gets money, too, through the campaign, presumably for keeping silent.'

'I am a caterer,' Callie said. 'I make baked goods for a local school.'

'Do you bake enough to pull in sixty thousand a year?'

'Look, call the cops if you want. Call a press conference, tell everybody how smart you are. I still won't talk to you.'

Cassandra didn't want to say the last thing she had to say, in part because she didn't want to find out why it mattered. But she had no choice.

'Reg Barr has a daughter.'

Callie Jenkins narrowed her green eyes, stared Cassandra down. If she had been lying, she would have folded then and there. So this was the woman whom Teena had faced, the one who had defeated her.

'With Donna?'

'Of course with Donna.' She bristled at the implication that Reg was faithless, despite her firsthand knowledge that he was exactly that.

'Donna couldn't have children.'

'I don't know about that. I only know there's a child.'

'When?'

It seemed an odd question. 'About eight years ago. Maybe nine. She's in grade school, I know that much.'

Callie Jenkins hugged herself as if she were

freezing, although the storm door was thick enough to keep the day's chill out. Her head swung back and forth, as if she could negate what she had been told if she were simply adamant enough. *No, no, no. No, no, no. No, no, no.* Tears began streaming down her face, although she seemed unaware of them. Her head continued to shake and then her body almost convulsed. For one panicky moment, Cassandra thought the woman might be on the edge of a seizure.

Then Callie opened her storm door to Cassandra, motioned for her to come inside.

Evolution

There were several oddities about the Baltimore City public schools in the mid-seventies. The first was the district's open enrollment policy, which allowed students to attend any school they desired, although the matter of transportation then fell to the family. Most people chose the neighborhood schools, and given how segregated the city was, this led to de facto segregation in the schools. By the time I started high school in 1972, everyone knew it was only a matter of time before the system was challenged and dismantled. White flight, which had begun even before the '68 riots, stepped up.

To further complicate things, the city used a junior high school system, with high school beginning in the tenth grade. Unless one qualified for the 'A' course, which meant—this must seem odder still to non-Baltimoreans—that one could attend ninth grade at one of the public, same-sex high schools.

This system, too, was rumored to be on the verge of change. In fact, Polytechnic, the all-boy school, would admit its first female student before I graduated. The all-girl school, Western, to this day has not accepted a male student. Allegedly, this is because no boy has ever expressed a desire to attend. It seems suspicious—thirty years, and not a single cheeky boy has come forward, flush with the odds, eager to be the one male in a school of girls. But even in my day, before Poly had enrolled its first female student, my classmates were vehement about keeping Western all-girl. They actually marched on the board of education, protesting coed education in the city's two most prestigious public schools. I didn't join the march, but then, by the time my old friends took up that cause, I had transferred to the Gordon School. I attended Western for only a year before my parents decided I wasn't safe there.

The problem, as ever, was that I couldn't shut up. For eight years, I had been the smartest girl in my class; now I was in the A course, which was filled with similar girls from all over the city. Those who had known me—and I was happily reunited with Tisha, Fatima, and Donna, among others—had no problem letting me occupy the top rung in the classroom. Others appreciated the challenge, reveled in the competition as much as I did.

But my class at Western was full of girls from all over Baltimore, including many from parochial schools. These girls, for the most part, could not keep up in any class that required thinking. They could memorize anything, ace any set of true-false questions, soar when presented with multiple choices. But asked to apply their knowledge, they balked. My particular nemesis was a tall, unhealthy-looking girl, her no-color hair worn in pigtails that managed the trick of being tight and messy at the same time. Martha, poor thing. She harangued the teachers who challenged her, practically begged for her education to be as boring as possible. Asked, for example, to write a poem in a chosen meter, she demanded to know why she had to write a poem, why she couldn't recite one from memory. She had a ferocious memory.

Nothing enraged her more than ninth-grade social studies, where we were taught about Darwin and natural selection. It wasn't true, she railed. She wasn't offended by evolution, per se. The problem was that Martha believed we respond to challenges in our environment within a single generation. Giraffes needed long necks to reach food, and their necks grew. *No, Martha,* the teacher said again and again, *there was a gene that favored the development of long necks and giraffes that didn't have it were weeded out of the gene pool over time.* Martha was not foolhardy enough to call the teacher a liar, but she demanded proof and refused to be satisfied by the answers provided.

We quickly came to hate each other. And it was not enough for me to earn the highest marks, to say the smartest things, to charm the teachers that Martha alienated. I had to run her down as well. I hate remembering this about myself, but I will not dissemble about my young cruelty. I not only mocked her ideas but her hair and her complexion, aflame with acne. My friends encouraged me in this, enjoying the skirmishes between the two of us. We were cheap entertainment for the entitled. Tisha, Donna, and Fatima were among them, coolly regarding our antics from a great height, gods pitting the poor mortals against one another for their own amusement.

For that was the sad and strange reality of ninth grade—the girls from whom I had been separated in seventh and eighth grade were no longer my friends. We were *friendly*—we rode the same public bus home every day and talked easily among ourselves. But a gulf had opened. At the time, I thought it was about boys. By ninth grade, they all had boyfriends, and I didn't. I didn't even have a clue how to get one. After all, it wasn't something written down in a book, and I certainly couldn't ask my father about it. A pity, as he was an expert in what men liked.

He took me to school every day that year, out of his way though it was, and early, too; he didn't need to be on campus until ten o'clock. Still, he drove over every morning from the apartment he and Annie had rented a few miles away. I think my mother made him do this, intending it to be a kind of penance. But the result was that I had twenty, twenty-five minutes alone with my father every morning, and I considered that time precious. If I couldn't tell him about boys, or my yearnings toward them, I could at least tell him everything else. I regaled him with stories about Martha—her narrow-mindedness, her obstinacy, her possible racism.

'This girl, Martha,' he said. 'Is she from one of the parish schools? Saint Bob of the Foundering

323

Flock? Our Lady of Perpetual Motion?'

I snorted. The joke was new to me. 'Something like that. She's from the Northeast Side.'

'Well, you know what that's about.'

I wanted to nod knowingly, in sync with my father. But I also wanted to understand what he meant. Reluctantly, I exposed my ignorance and asked him to explain.

'With all this talk of integration and busing in the air, the parochial school students are terrified that they're going to get caught up in some system-wide change. So they enroll in the A course rather than risk getting sent across town next year. But some of them got in because their teachers wrote them recommendations. It cheapens the entire system.'

To this day, I don't know if my father was speaking factually or if this was his own version of a conspiracy theory. We all have them, don't we? Hard-core beliefs that, when examined, turn out to be nothing more than a set of prejudices strung together. My father had a low opinion of religion and an even lower opinion of Baltimore's white working-class neighborhoods, places where he and Annie literally had to fear for their lives. You'd never catch them, for example, at Haussner's. I forget, at times, how much my father had to pay for his love, how bold and even brave he was in his determination to be with Annie.

My battles against Martha and the contests with her became an odd bright spot in those days. I grew reckless, crueler. I mocked her religion. In English, assigned to write fiction, I turned in a story that was transparently about Martha, a girl who ends up in a small social hell because she has failed to absorb the Bible's teachings about

324

kindness and charity. I read it aloud, never looking her way. It was the second most popular of all the presentations. The class favorite, I have to admit, was Fatima's, an utterly incoherent story about street violence that transcended its crude plotting and Fatima's less than keen writing on the basis of her performance, in which she danced part of the story.

But Martha had her backers, more loyal friends than I had. A few days after the short story incident, we were in gym class. It was spring and we were playing softball and I was lost in brooding, as PE constantly threatened my precious straight-A average. To improve my grade, I often volunteered to do small tasks for extra credit. On this particular day, I agreed to bring in the equipment and was roaming the field, in search of stray balls, when Martha and her friends approached me.

'Another stellar day for you in phys ed,' Martha said. 'You dropped a fly ball, struck out, and dribbled that one little hit down the first-base line, getting on base only because their pitcher overthrew it.'

'Yes, well, I guess if I need to become a great softball player, I'll evolve that way in my lifetime. Isn't that how your belief system sees it? Perhaps that's why your complexion is so pitted—it doesn't need to evolve. But trust me, Martha, natural selection is going to make sure that your genes never get back in the pool.'

I turned my back to continue gathering balls. Martha—I assume it was Martha—kicked me from behind with a force unlike anything I had known. I had been paddled a few times as a child, and there was the awful night my mother slapped me. But I had never been in an actual fight. Martha's kick knocked me off my feet. I curled up like a potato bug, trying to shield myself, and now all three began to kick and hit me and pull my hair. I struggled to my feet, only to be knocked down again. But in that brief moment I was up, I saw Tisha, Donna, and Fatima standing at the far end of the field, watching with mild interest. No, I couldn't see their faces or their expressions—at that distance, they were recognizable to me by their heights and shapes, especially Fatima's—but their posture, the very casualness of their stances, made it clear how little it concerned them. It was all of a piece for them, I realized, no different from what happened in the classroom. There, Martha and I fought with words. Here, it was fists. Cool.

It's three on one, I wanted to yell to them. *It's unfair.* Still, no one came to my aid, until a teacher finally realized what was going on and raced across the field to save me.

Fighting was a serious offense, but Martha and her friends were given detention, with no discussion of suspension or expulsion. And no talk of an apology, either. No one said, in so many words, that I had brought this on myself, but that implicit accusation hung in the air: I deserved the beat-down. Scared to return to Western, I finished up the year with tutors, who came to the house after school for two hours of lessons. When the school year ended in June, my mother announced that her employer, the Gordon School, was willing to give me a scholarship. I never saw Tisha, Donna, or Fatima again.

What happened to us? How did we go from being friends to strangers? Why did they stand at the end of the field and watch three other girls beat me? All I know is that I was no longer one of them; they considered my beat-down fair, retribution for the humiliation I had heaped on Martha all year. Martha and I were like the wrestlers who appeared on channel 45, and while I had been Gorgeous George, it was time for me to be defeated. My father, the classics professor, could have explained it to me. No one gets to be the hero forever, no one escapes her destiny.

AND AGAMEMNON DEAD

March 29–31

Chapter Thirty-One

Cassandra sat in Callie's kitchen, a cup of Lipton tea cooling in front of her. There was a plainness to the surroundings that was novel to Cassandra. She was accustomed to homes such as hers, stage settings of a sort, decorated and arranged to give instant teasing insights into their owners. Callie's house was as sterile as a builder's model. It didn't appear to be an aesthetic, but a lack of one, a complete absence of choices. Things were white— walls, mug, appliances—unless they weren't. The beige linoleum floor, the blue-and-white platter that Callie had insisted on filling with cookies, despite Cassandra's protestations that she wasn't hungry.

'I made these this morning,' she said.

'They're so perfect, so uniform,' Cassandra marveled, breaking off a piece. She wasn't being polite. It was a soft ginger cookie with a crescent of white frosting, dark moons in partial eclipse. 'Are they difficult? It must be a project, dipping them into the icing.'

Callie didn't say anything, not right away. Cassandra was beginning to catch her rhythms, her conversational style, if one could call it that. Callie was like a nervous driver waiting to merge onto a highway. She needed lots of space and time to make her move.

Cassandra glanced around, trying to find anything in the room that was personal or idiosyncratic. There was a wall calendar from a local insurance agent, the month of March illustrated by what Cassandra guessed was an Eastern Shore landscape. Small pencil jottings had been made on some of the squares, but she couldn't read them from where she sat. Her eyes came to rest on a set of white ceramic canisters.

'I keep the tea bags in the coffee bin,' Callie said, following Cassandra's gaze.

'What?'

Callie flinched, but she didn't need quite as long to reenter the conversation this time. 'Those canisters. I ordered them from QVC, from that woman, you know, with the big cloud of silver hair. Sort of like yours.'

Cassandra nodded, although she didn't have a clue what Callie was talking about.

'And, you know, flour and sugar, I put flour and sugar in them. But I don't drink coffee, so I keep my tea bags in the one that says "coffee". Do you think that's okay?'

Cassandra—feeling mocked, toyed with—almost snapped, *I don't care if you keep heroin in there.* Then she realized Callie was in dead earnest. This was a woman so cowed that she required permission to keep tea bags in a canister marked COFFEE. From where Callie sat, across this plain oak table, the world was full of rules that no one would share with her. Perhaps that's why she kept her surroundings plain. She didn't know what was allowed, didn't trust her own choices. Cassandra imagined Callie sitting in front of the television, rehearsing her call to QVC, fearful that she wouldn't know how to do it.

'Fatima told me that your mother, Myra, was very strict with you.'

Callie started to nod, then lifted her chin as if to

take it back. 'She meant well.'

'Does she live with you?'

'In a nursing home, in Denton.'

'At your expense?'

Another aborted nod. Another long silence. Cassandra flashed back to the one real memory she had of Callie as a girl, preserved in her own book: Callie sitting on a high kitchen stool and swinging her legs, utterly unperturbed by the sight of a mother slapping her child.

'I can't keep her there all by myself,' Callie said. 'Couldn't begin to.'

Cassandra started to ask, *Who helps you, then?* But questions, the slightest rise of a voice, with its implicit demands and obligations, didn't work with Callie. Teena had warned that nothing worked with Callie. Yet she had responded to the statement about her mother, acknowledged that she was receiving financial help that she couldn't afford to lose. Perhaps Myra Tippet's nursing home expenses were buried in Julius Howard's campaign finance reports as well.

'You feel obligated to her.'

'She's my mother.'

'Even though she was . . . strict with you.'

'She did her best.'

'Abuse is never—'

'I didn't say *abuse*.' These words came swiftly, only to be followed by another long silence, as if Callie had surprised herself with her own vehemence. How many words did Callie say in a week? Probably not as many as Cassandra used in a day. Sometimes, on long drives, Cassandra put in her earpiece, so people would think she was on a Bluetooth device, and chattered away to keep herself company. Did Callie even think in words, or were her thoughts more imagistic, visual?

Callie cocked her head as if listening, amazed, for the echo of her own sharp words. 'No, I didn't say *abuse*. That's a big word. People said that about me, and it wasn't true. I never abused anyone. I'm not going to say that about someone else.'

Then what—but no, no questions. Maybe no words at all. Cassandra sipped her tea, thinking, trying to be still. Perhaps silence was a kind of language, too; perhaps not talking could be a form of communication. She willed herself to be patient, to block the words fighting to escape. The moment stretched into a minute, then another. She began to wonder if Callie meant to communicate with her telepathically.

'I'm not very good at this,' Callie offered.

Cassandra didn't even nod this time, just blinked and sipped her tea.

'People thought I was strong, all those years. But I'm not much good at telling things. I get mixed up.'

Sip, blink.

'You say Donna has a child. A girl. Does she look like her mother?'

Cassandra all but held her breath, not sure she should answer, worried that her voice would break the spell.

Callie answered her own question: 'I bet she does.' Then she started to cry. In this, she was not silent at all, but loud and raucous. Guttural, animalistic noises seemed to claw their way out of Callie's throat. Her nose ran, her eyes streamed. Cassandra got up and, finding nothing else, brought Callie a paper towel from the dispenser mounted on the wall. Why did the fact of Reg's daughter disturb Callie? That was a question Cassandra had no desire to ask out loud, much less have answered.

'Callie, you don't have to tell me anything.'

'I understand,' she said. 'But you're here, you . . . know things. You're going to tell people what you know. Maybe you have to, because of the law or something. But then what happens? It's not just me. It's my mother, too. I have to take care of her.'

'You have to take care of yourself first, Callie.'

She looked at Cassandra as if the idea were completely foreign to her, then inhaled deeply several times, as if preparing for a physical task, a race or a dive from a high board. Something that required not only energy but courage as well.

*   *   *

Callie took a deep breath. She was thinking about a hill near the school, a hill that had seemed impossibly large when they were children. There had been a beautiful tree at the foot of the hill—a willow, that was what it was called—and the hill was thick with clover, waiting for patient children to find the four-leaf varieties hidden there. Callie had been one of the patient ones. The hill was a block from school property and she couldn't play there after school; she had a bus to catch. But on fair days toward the end of the school year, teachers sometimes led them there as a treat. Once, someone—Fatima, most likely—had started a game in which they raced down the hill by rolling on their sides. Giggling, colliding, they had

335

tumbled down that hill over and over. When Callie arrived home that afternoon, she presented her mother with a bouquet of dandelions, violets, and three four-leaf clovers. Three, and no one else had found even one. Callie's mother had spanked her with a hairbrush for getting grass stains on her school dress.

Now she was back at the top of the hill, keen to roll down, crazy for it. But scared, too, because she had learned the consequences of abandon. There were always consequences. They would put her mother in some horrible place that would make her current nursing home seem like a palace. They would reopen the case against Callie. *No statute of limitations on homicide,* as she had been reminded so many times. *The seven years you did for contempt won't be applied to what you owe the state for that. We can't protect you if you tell.*

Besides, why should she disrupt everything? She was happy, right? Not happy, exactly, but content, as content as she was going to be in this life. What would all this *telling* accomplish? For years, not-telling had been proof of her strength, a testimony to the force of her love, her essence. Now—now it proved that she was a fool. He had played her. So what? Everybody got played.

You'll feel better if you talk, the little detective had told her over and over again. She had tried to convince Callie that she was weighted down by her secrets, tortured by them, that she could free her baby's soul if she would only explain what happened to Donntay. But Callie had understood that her secret kept her grounded, that it became the evidence of a love that the world otherwise denied. Even now, she still believed she had been

336

loved, was loved. No matter how badly he had behaved, he truly loved her. It was all she had, the treasure of her life, and if she opened her mouth, she wouldn't have that anymore.

She wiped her eyes, blew her nose, went to the refrigerator and got ice to tame her swollen lids, wrapped her hands around the now cold mug of tea. Was the tea cold, or was it that her hands were chilled from the ice? She sipped the tea and still couldn't tell. The extremes of life—hot, cold, high, low—had been lost to her long ago.

'I guess the first thing I want to say is that I don't think I killed my boy, Donntay. But nobody was going to believe that because my first child was taken away from me, right?'

She saw Cassandra's hand snake into her leather bag, remove a small recorder, and hold it up quizzically, seeking permission. She shook her head.

'Listen,' she said. *'Listen.'*

To her amazement, Cassandra returned the tape recorder to her bag. Someone would do as she said? She had never had that power over anyone. Except him, in the very beginning, and in the beginning, she hadn't wanted to tell him to do anything, except to keep doing what he was doing. Keep calling her, keep loving her, keep telling her how special she was. Funny how that worked, how you had the power when you didn't need it, then couldn't get it back when you were desperate for it.

'When I was in community college, Fatima told me I should come and work on Julius Howard's campaign for city council president. She said he was going to be the state's first black U.S. senator

337

and it was worth being a part of, even if there was no pay. She was right. It was the best thing that ever happened to me. I fell in love.'

'With Julius Howard,' Cassandra said, and Callie wanted to laugh at how sure she was, how smart Cassandra Fallows still thought she was. She was still a hand-in-the-air girl, after all. Only she was wrong this time. Perhaps that had been his intention all along. Anyone would make that assumption, Callie saw now. She was almost proud of him, in spite of herself. He always was smart. That's why she had been flattered when he dropped Fatima and chose her, because he was *smart*. Fatima said it wasn't love, that he didn't work that way, that you had to take what you could get from him and move on. But she knew it was love with them and she wouldn't take anything. Oh, he left her alone for a while, but he always came back. Until she got pregnant.

'Not with Julius. With Andre. Donna's father. We had an affair that lasted almost two years. And then I got pregnant, and he broke up with me, and I went a little crazy. I think that's where it starts. I guess that's where it begins.'

She couldn't help enjoying the look on Cassandra's face. Back in school, Cassandra's arm was always shooting up straight and tall, quivering like the tails on those dogs that hunt. Not that Callie had ever seen such a dog outside a cartoon, not as a child. Living here on the shore these past—oh, God, was it really thirteen years?—she saw both pointers and retrievers in the late fall, flushing birds from the marshes, happy and eager to be of assistance to their owners. *Why?* she always wanted to ask. *What's in it for you? A pat, a*

338

kind word, a treat, but you never get to keep the duck. There are others who will love you, who will give you the same deal, food and shelter, and require nothing more than your devotion.

But she understood because she had sold her own life as cheaply. She had dropped her babies at the feet of the man she loved, exchanging their lives for a pat on the head, a scratch behind the ears, a few murmured promises of love.

Chapter Thirty-Two

Cassandra was so full of tea by the time she left Bridgeville that she needed two bathroom breaks before crossing the bay. The second time, at a McDonald's on Highway 50, she realized that, other than a few bites of cookie, she had not eaten since that unsatisfying breakfast with her father. She ordered a Quarter Pounder with cheese, à la carte, which the counter girl found disturbing, trying to cajole her into a Value Meal. 'There's no value,' said Cassandra, 'in paying for things you don't want.' It was the kind of thing her father often said. The Quarter Pounder, however, was disturbingly good, Proustian good. She remembered being seventeen, walking that razor-thin line between slut and popular girl. The key had been confining sex to boyfriends, but a relationship could last as little as a month and still be legitimate. But then Cassandra had fallen hard for one boy, Chris. He hadn't been particularly popular or outstanding, although such reputations meant much less in a place like the Gordon

339

School. In a graduating class of sixty, there was room for more nuanced personalities, less of an emphasis on cliques. Chris had been allowed to be Chris—a Dungeons and Dragons freak, a pothead, a musician, a cross-country runner.

Brainy and sardonic, he was a good match for her. Then he broke things off, without explanation, without even an official good-bye. Without any words at all, in fact. Worse, he didn't start going with someone else. It was one thing to be dropped in favor of another girl, harsh as that was. For someone to dump you and choose solitude meant you must be really boring.

Cassandra had started eating to console herself, consuming Quarter Pounders in great quantities. Although boys usually brought her home from school by then, her father still drove her every morning. She had stopped confiding in him, however. The September of her senior year, after her summer of conciliatory eating, her father intoned one morning, 'Quarter Pounders. Aka four ounces. You've added, what, the equivalent of forty, sixty of those to your frame?' She had gone on a diet and, in essence, been on one ever since. Dieting was a kind of martial law in her life— never suspended, sometimes relaxed, frequently tested. She wondered if Callie ever thought about what she ate. Over the course of their long, halting conversation, she hadn't managed to finish her tea and didn't even nibble at her exquisite cookies.

Cassandra pulled out her Moleskine notebook and began writing from memory. Callie's story was simple almost to the point of banality. She had an affair with Andre Howard, became pregnant. He broke up with her, she broke down. About six

340

months after her child was born, she was reported for neglect and the baby was taken from her and put up for adoption. She had drifted through the next few years, self-destructive and aimless, incapable of holding a job, indifferent to returning to school, although that was the one thing that Andre Howard offered her. The state senate had a scholarship program with virtually no oversight, Callie had explained. That, along with Julius Howard's recommendation, had been Fatima's ticket to Spelman. Callie didn't want to admit that her relationship with Andre Howard was anything like Fatima's, and she refused his help, holding out for love. Other men liked her, she liked using them, and when she was with a man, she took up his habits, good or bad. She was smoking crack—on the pipe, as she put it—when she gave birth to Donntay, which put her back under the supervision of social services. She insisted she wasn't a fiend, as she called it, just a casual user. Once Donntay's father left, in the final month of her pregnancy, she barely smoked at all.

Then she woke up one morning and Donntay was dead. She hadn't done a thing, had never laid a finger on him, but who would believe her? A sometime crack smoker, a party girl, one baby already taken from her. Hysterical, she had called Andre Howard. She had called him off and on over the years, and he was invariably kind. He swore he loved her, wanted to be with her, but there was always a reason he couldn't be. His brother's political ambitions. His wife's sadness over Donna living far away. He even cited Donna's inability to have children. He couldn't abandon his wife and start a new life with Callie if his wife didn't have the consolation of grandbabies. That's what he told Callie when she sat in jail, and upon her release. He had to stay with his wife because she was never going to have grandchildren.

Yet he had concealed her second child's body, protected her from prosecution, at great risk to himself. This, to Callie, proved he loved her.

God, what a sad, deluded story. Who would believe it? Cassandra wasn't sure that *she* believed it. Oh, that wouldn't keep her from writing it. Let the competing versions of the truth fight it out on the page. Only—this story could not be confined to the page. Callie was alleging that Andre Howard, one of Baltimore's most venerated citizens, had conspired with her to hide her child's body, preventing a proper inquiry into his death. That wasn't the sort of thing that would go unchallenged, starting with Cassandra's publisher's lawyers, then moving into the criminal courts, where a new inquiry would be inevitable. Andre Howard would probably deny everything and what would she have then? The word of an admitted crackhead versus that of a man famous for propriety and good deeds.

She had more than Callie's words, however, even if Fatima refused to corroborate the details. There were the campaign finance records, the obvious payoffs. Could those be explained away so easily?

Her sandwich demolished, Cassandra ate the pickle that had slipped from the burger and nibbled that, although she didn't really like pickles. She had called Teena within minutes of beginning the drive home, thinking she would be excited by the news. But Teena had been angry, dismissive.

'What, she's claiming sudden death syndrome?

That's brilliant, especially with no body. Did she wait all these years to spring that shit because it's uncheckable now?'

'Why would she lie?'

'Sheesh, Cassandra, because that's what people do. They lie. Especially when they're still vulnerable to being charged with murder. She's had twenty years to come up with this story. Frankly, I think she could have done better.'

'What about Andre Howard? If he believed that her baby wasn't a homicide victim, couldn't he at least say that he didn't conceal a murder? I guess he would be guilty of obstruction of justice, but nothing more—'

'I don't believe her on that score, either. The guy had an affair with her, fathered her first child—okay, he's a sleaze and he wouldn't want that found out. But would he become a coconspirator in a murder on that basis? I don't think so.'

'Still—' It was a good point, but Cassandra knew there was a counterargument to be made. She was simply too overloaded to find it.

'The first baby is enough to explain the blackmail,' Teena insisted.

'But the payments don't start until after Donntay dies.'

'As far as we know. They might have funneled money to her directly, then started using the campaign after she became a murder suspect, which made her more problematic. Look, she got into trouble and she reached out to a powerful man she could force to help her, because she had something on him. He came up with a legal strategy that allowed her to avoid being charged. But the idea of Andre Howard arranging the

343

disappearance of the baby's body? No one will ever believe that. I think she's claiming his involvement now because she's terrified of losing his financial support. He'll find a new way to get money to her, and then she'll deny everything she told you. Did you get this on tape?'

'No, she asked me not to record her.'

'Aw, Jesus, Cassandra. You've got *nothing*.'

'I'm not building a court case, Teena. I'm a writer. All I need is a story, and I have it.'

'Until she recants,' Teena said. 'She's using you.'

Who was using whom was highly problematic in this situation. Cassandra had the answer she had been instructed to find. It was not, Cassandra admitted to herself in McDonald's, a particularly satisfying one, but then, most answers fail to satisfy. Presented with a mystery, the human mind snakes out in a thousand directions; it is the *possibility* of an answer that seems thrilling. But when the puzzle is solved, tension dissipates. That is the nature of questions. Even on a quiz show, the real excitement comes in the moment *before* the answer, the agony of waiting to discover if the contestant is right or wrong. Cassandra had her book, if she wanted it, an ending toward which to write. It was more of a straightforward true-crime story than she had anticipated, albeit one filled with contrasts and symmetries. Callie, the poor child of an abusive single mother, finding a father and a lover in Andre Howard. Donna, the prized princess of one of Baltimore's most prominent families. She considered for the first time how close the two names were, Donna and Donntay. It was almost as if Callie were trying to establish some sort of connection to the Howards.

Cassandra would simply take herself out of it, write a straightforward narrative about the Howards and this quiet girl who had gone off like a bomb in their lives.

Except—Cassandra couldn't take herself out of the story because she had slept with Callie's lawyer, who happened to be the Howard son-in-law. What was she going to do about that?

She found herself fixating on an image of herself at the microfiche machines in the library, her first glimpse of Reg. She had a flash of Reg in bed, but she tried to put that out of her mind. '"The Obvious Child,"' Gloria Bustamante had said. Well, hinted, suggested. She was as cagey as her client had been naïve. Cassandra had assumed the child was Donntay, then Aubrey, whose mere existence had unlocked Callie's long-held silence. But what if the obvious child was the first one? The child taken from Callie permanently based on an anonymous tip about her mental state. The child Cassandra said Andre had fathered. Cassandra saw herself at the microfiche, the days of 1988 literally flashing by her, the machine's movement and smell making her faintly queasy. A stray fact had boomeranged out, striking her as odd but not vital, then skipped away before she could grasp it.

Then she knew. She understood what Gloria had figured out, what Callie could not bear to admit to herself. Andre Howard had made a mistake, but it was not a unique one, far from it. He could have weathered the fact of an illegitimate child. It was Andre Howard's way of handling his mistake that would have earned him public contempt.

Cassandra ordered a diet soda for the road,

prompting a lecture from the counter girl on how she should have gotten the Value Meal after all. Everyone loves to say *I told you so*. Back behind the wheel of her car, she dialed a number that she knew better than to call on a weekend. But it was business, of a sort, and undeniably urgent.

Chapter Thirty-Three

Reg had asked almost no questions when he returned Cassandra's call about a possible meeting, saying only that he would see her at his home on Sunday afternoon. She had assumed that the choice of location was to underline the professional aspect of the encounter. He probably thought that an empty law office would be an invitation to trouble.

It had never occurred to Cassandra that Donna would be present.

'Reg wanted me here,' Donna said, composed and lovely, still in her churchgoing clothes. Even Donna, proper as she was, wouldn't sit around in a green knit suit on a Sunday afternoon. 'Given that your book touches on my life, too.'

'Your life?' Cassandra echoed.

'As a child. Wasn't that part of the plan? To write about several of us as we were when we were young, and how we are now?'

'It was one idea,' Cassandra admitted. 'It's taken a turn, though—'

'Of course, I guess you get to be the most successful one,' Donna said. She was good at managing the trick of talking over another person without appearing rude or impatient. 'That's what makes it interesting to you, right? Tisha is a nice suburban mama, Fatima has had this amazing transformation from good-time girl to church lady, and I'm mainly known as someone's daughter and someone's wife. But you're our little star.'

Her voice was good-natured, her face smooth. Cassandra might well have been imagining the crackle to the tone, like the very thin crust of frost that snaps beneath one's feet after the first true cold night of the year. She glanced quickly at Reg, trying to read him, but he kept his back to her as he fed kindling into a fire, which seemed de trop on a March afternoon. In fact, Cassandra suddenly felt extremely warm and almost wished it was a hot flash. Perimenopause would be preferable to this creeping sense of shame and humiliation. Had Reg told Donna about their affair? She should have broken off things with him definitively before she visited Callie. She never should have started in the first place.

But for all her discipline in other aspects of her life, she had never been very good at denying herself the men she wanted.

'Donna, I'm not sure you should be here,' she said.

'Please,' Donna said, throwing up her hands as if Cassandra had told a mildly amusing joke. 'Reg and I have no secrets.'

Again, Cassandra wished she could see Reg's face, but he seemed intent on avoiding eye contact. Had any fire ever required so much tending and poking?

'I found Callie Jenkins this weekend.'

'In Bridgeville, yes,' Donna said.

'You know where she is? Reg told me he had no idea.'

Donna nodded. 'He did tell that one tiny lie. I'm sorry about that, but it's not to anyone's benefit, not even Callie's—*especially* Callie's—to dig this up. You've heard how no good deed goes unpunished? My father tried to help Callie and she spreads these ridiculous lies about him. It makes no sense, but people are used to the truth not making sense. That's the key to your business, right?'

'My business?'

'The things you write. Truth is stranger than fiction. Which sets people up to believe a story like Callie's, preposterous as it is. It was easier to give her free legal help and pay her rather than allow her to humiliate him with her outlandish lies.'

Cassandra had learned something helpful from Callie; a person didn't have to speak right away, rush into a silence. She sorted through Donna's words and, eventually, put her finger on the flaw.

'What about Fatima, Donna? What sort of outlandish stories does she tell, why does she get paid? Or is it simply that Fatima, who also was a volunteer for the campaign, might be able to corroborate the affair? And, as I understand it, detail her own sexual relationship with your father.'

'Fatima's husband runs a limousine service. Campaigns use transportation services all the time. I'm sure Fatima would be happy to explain that to you.'

'But it's not against the law to lie to me. Will she be willing to say the same things to a grand jury?'

'Oh, I don't see a grand jury caring about this,'

348

Donna said. 'Besides, as you just said—no one risks anything by lying to you, so why do you assume Callie was telling the truth?'

Reg had finally turned away from the fireplace, but he seemed happy to let his wife run the conversation. His face was a study. Cassandra couldn't tell if he was angry or upset. Or betrayed. *You lied to me,* Cassandra wanted to say. *You told me you didn't know where she was.* Then again, they were both adulterers and lying is the cornerstone of adultery. Hard to be offended on that score. She had a sudden image of Reg, wrapped in a towel, sitting at her laptop. She remembered Fatima's resigned greeting at her doorstep, the very lack of surprise. Reg could have used the spotlight function to scour her computer for certain names, check on her progress. Was that the only reason he had slept with her?

'Perhaps,' she appealed to Reg, 'this should be a private conversation?'

'Agreed,' Donna said with a sympathetic nod.

Yet it was Reg who left the room.

'You'll have to forgive him,' Donna said. Cassandra really understood, for the first time, the phrase about butter not melting in someone's mouth, how cool a mouth had to be for this to be possible. 'It's been a lot to process. He knew my family was helping Callie. He didn't know it was essentially blackmail, although he had his suspicions. Uncle Julius has always had his . . . proclivities.'

'Uncle Julius's proclivities, but not your father's?'

Donna looked a little lost. She was strong, but she wasn't used to fighting her own battles, out in the open. Donna operated in a world where unpleasant things remained implicit. Where, for example, a husband learned not to ask too many questions about the client he represented at his boss's request.

'This is not about my father,' Donna said. 'That's all you need to know. And he should not be humiliated because some aging crack whore suddenly wants more money.'

'Callie didn't ask for money. She risked the money she has by talking to me.'

'She's playing you.'

Teena had said the same thing. But Teena had been crushed, disappointed that Callie hadn't made a true confession.

'Let me tell you what I've figured out on my own. Callie had an affair with your father. She had a baby. He broke up with her about a month before the boy's birth and she was angry, angry enough to put your father's name on the birth certificate. Granted, birth certificates aren't truly public, but it was a problematic document, something she could hold over his head forever. She could have demanded support, and a court would have ordered genetic testing.'

'Yet she didn't. What does that tell you?'

Cassandra had thought that part through. 'That she was in love with him and believed he would leave your mother for her, eventually. That's how he controlled her. But she was depressed, hysterical. Her behavior was increasingly erratic. It must have been worrisome for the upstanding Andre Howard—the good Howard brother—to have such a loose cannon. It was absolutely providential when the boy was taken and put up

350

for adoption.'

'A godsend for the boy. Otherwise, he might have ended up dead, like his brother.'

'We're talking about *your* brother, Donna. Think about this. Your half brother—Aubrey's uncle—and he's lost to you. Unless he signed up for one of those registries they started offering adopted children and their biological parents in the eighties. About the time that Donntay, the second son, died.'

'Are you going back to writing fiction, Cassandra? Maybe it will work out better for you this time.'

The insult carried some sting, but it was clumsy by Donna's standards.

'I think your father was the anonymous tipster who reported Callie for neglect. Even if he wasn't, he seized that opportunity to convince Callie to put the boy up for adoption. Her parental rights were terminated less than six months after the initial report. That doesn't happen unless a parent relinquishes custody. The most inept public defender on the planet wouldn't have allowed that to happen. But Callie agreed to release her own son.'

'Oh, this is new,' Donna said. 'She's adding to the story now.'

'No, she didn't volunteer this. She's ashamed that she surrendered him so willingly. But when I called her last night, she admitted that your father persuaded her that she should let the boy be adopted.'

'The story just gets more and more fantastic, doesn't it?'

'I think it gets more logical. It explains why your

father would agree to help Callie when her second child died. Yes, *their* child had essentially been disappeared; the birth certificate was now a confidential document that no one would ever be allowed to see, not even their son. But Callie was still out there, and she was increasingly unpredictable. She was using drugs, and she was depressed again, just as she was after the birth of her first child. Which indicates that her mental state might have been postpartum, not that her defense attorneys seemed to care or notice. He needed something to hold over her, and a homicide charge worked nicely. Never mind that the circumstances, as Callie described them, would have allowed for a defense that her child died of sudden infant death syndrome, that an autopsy might have proved that her child wasn't abused. If she's telling the truth, an autopsy would have been in her best interest—but not in your father's. He trained her in silence, in secrets, and she never questioned him. But Gloria did. Gloria started poking around. Is that why she left and was replaced by Reg?'

'Did Gloria tell you that? Because she would be disbarred—'

'Gloria Bustamante won't even take my phone calls.' It was true, as far as it went. Gloria was probably on safe ground, giving them public records and the CD, but why make life complicated for her? Cassandra wasn't even sure if Gloria knew why the fact of Aubrey would unlock Callie's secrets.

'Callie Jenkins was an unfit mother. Her first child was taken from her—'

'For neglect, not abuse. Callie says she never

352

raised a hand to either child, and I believe her. Because she knew what it was to be hit, and she wouldn't do that to her own children.'

'*Please*. We all know that abused children are more likely to be violent. Besides, her second son was a crack baby, which is why she was assigned a social worker in the first place. She probably shook him to death when he wouldn't stop crying.'

'Crack babies were a media myth.'

'All babies cry. We'll never know what happened, will we?'

'Because your father took that baby away, made sure that Donntay's body wouldn't be found. Who benefited from Callie sitting in jail seven years, saying nothing? Primarily your father.'

Donna tapped her foot as if merely impatient with the conversation, the time she was wasting on a Sunday afternoon.

'Look, what do you want from us?'

'Nothing. I'm here as a courtesy. I am going to write about this, but given the nature of what's happened, there will probably be legal consequences even before my book comes out.'

Donna swatted at the air as if trying to catch a tiny bug in her palm. 'There won't be any legal consequences. Oh, sure, the state's attorney may be pressured into looking into the case if you can persuade anyone to print this outlandish nonsense. But it's going to come down to my father's word against Callie's. Who do you think will be believed?'

'That's not my concern. I'll write what I know, and people can decide for themselves what the truth is.'

Donna clearly found it odd that anyone—

Cassandra, readers, strangers—would not understand immediately that a Howard was so much more valuable than other people.

'Maybe I wasn't clear,' she said. 'What do you need to drop this?'

'You can't buy me out of my book contract, Donna. Even if I didn't have a contract I would feel obligated to tell someone what I knew. If I don't, I become an accessory. I'll be talking to the state's attorney this week.'

'Do you want Reg?' She might have been offering tea or coffee.

'What?'

'For keeps? It could be arranged. You have to admit—you are going to have some problems with credibility if you insist on writing this. The scorned woman and all.'

What if this were real? Cassandra had thought Reg was asking what would happen if their affair became something serious, long lasting. Now she had to wonder if he had inadvertently tipped her to the charade it was, a situation meant to distract and, yes, discredit her.

'Did you tell your husband to sleep with me?'

Donna sighed as if being tested by a slow salesclerk. 'I told him to help you with your project, thinking that would help us keep tabs on you. I didn't order him to fuck you and rather hoped he wouldn't. But I know my husband. I know all about him, despite what people think. And you—well, you've related your promiscuous tendencies in great detail for millions of readers. You can't keep your legs together on a bet, which is a bit unseemly at our age, Cassandra. Even Fatima grew out of that.'

'Perhaps with your father's help.'

'Look, I don't care what happened between you and Reg. My husband loves me.'

'Do you love him?'

Like a skilled politician, Donna didn't bother with questions she didn't want to answer. 'You could have a nice life together. Not here in Baltimore—he'd be untouchable, professionally, after humiliating me in such a fashion, leaving me for this neurotic white woman who can't shut up about herself. But someone would buy out his interest in the firm and he would be rich, even after giving me my share.'

Cassandra felt almost as outraged on Reg's behalf as she did for herself, reduced to this loathsome caricature in a few deft words. *This neurotic white woman who can't shut up about herself.* But then Donna, Fatima, even Tisha would argue that she had done the same to them, nailed them to the page with a few lines of blithe description. Donna's version of Reg as a man who would do anything she told him was even more unflattering.

'Secrets are like floodwater, Donna,' Cassandra said. 'They're eventually going to find a place to breach. You can't control Callie anymore. You can't embarrass me. I've always told the truth about myself, unattractive as it may be.'

'Are you sure?'

'Of course I'm sure.' She couldn't help flushing. She had several things she preferred to keep secret. Not so much the affair with Reg—she was resigned to that becoming public if she took on the Howards. But there was Bernard, and Bernard's wife.

355

Donna walked over to an antique secretary, a fussy overwrought piece, the kind of item that decorators called 'important,' a euphemism for *hideous.* A truly confident woman, someone secure in matters of taste, would never have allowed it to be foisted on her. Donna removed a manila folder from one of the desk's cubbyholes and brought it to Cassandra.

'What—' It was a police report, no more than two pages. A police report dated April 6, 1968.

'Read it out loud if you like.'

Cassandra chose to read it to herself: *Police received a call to the 1800 block of Druid Hill Avenue for a report of an assault. Patrols found a number one male beating a naked number two male while a number one female tried to intercede. The assailant, Manfred Watson, told police he had found the victim, Cedric Fallows, in bed with his girlfriend. The victim fled the couple's apartment*—'This is bullshit.'

'Your book was bullshit. Check a timeline, Cassandra. Next month marks the fortieth anniversary; there's no shortage of information available. There were a few incidents early in the weekend, but not in that neighborhood. The real violence started late that afternoon. Your father sneaked out to have sex with his girlfriend and got his ass kicked by her common-law husband. He used the riots as a cover.'

Stunned as she was, Cassandra couldn't help realizing that these bare, utilitarian sentences threaded a tiny needle. Her father's insistence on the errand, her mother's thin-lipped tension. The cake—Annie worked at Silber's bakery. She had probably made Cassandra's mermaid cake. He

356

might have met her two months before, buying that hideous Washington's Birthday cake for her mother. Here was the reason her usually articulate father had never been able to convey the assault with any real sense of drama, why Annie had been awkward and diffident when Cassandra met her in the hospital. Only—it was not her father who had spread the story. Cassandra was the one who had carried it into the world. He was simply too proud to call it back.

'My family's privacy for your family's privacy,' Donna said. 'Not that your family really has any privacy left, but you know what I mean. Your version can stand, uncontested. But not if you start talking about Callie.'

Cassandra's mind raced, overwhelmed. She wanted to argue that there were significant differences between their fathers. Yes, Cedric Fallows had lied, but it was a lie meant only for his wife and daughter, not the world. Andre Howard had lived a much larger lie, indifferent to the people he hurt as long as he could maintain his reputation. Her father's story was only part of her first book, which at least had the merit of being utterly sincere. Yet, wasn't Cassandra, too, taking advantage of Callie in a sense?

'It's not always a shameful thing, keeping secrets,' Donna said. 'And it's not hurtful, not in this case. Callie Jenkins killed her son, and she spent seven years in jail. Your father told a lie. My father succumbed to blackmail.'

Cassandra found her voice again. 'People who allow themselves to be blackmailed usually have something to hide.'

'Cassandra, everyone has something to hide.'

She was not being facile or glib, Cassandra realized. Donna was on intimate terms with secrets, and not only her father's. *What happened in your first marriage?* Cassandra wanted to ask. *Why is it such an untouchable subject, even for Reg? Is it the reason you can't have children? Can you really be that cavalier about Reg's cheating? Doesn't it get exhausting, being you, keeping track of all the things you're not supposed to talk about, maintaining this perfect façade?*

She said, 'I'll get back to you, Donna. Obviously, this is not my decision alone. But this much I can tell you—I'm passing on the offer of your husband.'

She left Bolton Hill and drove across town, seeing and not seeing the familiar streets, absently cataloguing the few landmarks that had survived her childhood. The zebra-striped house; the shady avenue through Leakin Park, where the trees were starting to bud; the long-vanquished Windsor Hills Pharmacy, overtaken by the adjacent gas station and a minimart. Gravel crunched beneath her tires, summoning her back to the world. Her mother, drawn by the sound of a car, came out of the garage, wiping her hands on a rag.

'Cassandra,' she said. 'I thought we had agreed to meet at the restaurant. Besides, you're hours early.'

'More like forty years late.'

Chapter Thirty-Four

Lenore was stripping a small end table in the unheated garage. 'Excuse me if I keep working but it's almost too cool to be doing this, and I don't dare use a space heater, so I have to keep going.'

'I don't recognize that table,' Cassandra said, trying to find a dust-free spot on which to sit, or at least lean.

'I trash-picked it,' her mother said with evident pride. 'There's still a lot of dumping in the park. Hard to tell if the wood on this piece is good enough to stand on its own, but I can always paint it.'

The solvent smell was familiar, if not exactly soothing. As a child, Cassandra had been embarrassed by her mother's thrift—trash-picking, shopping at the Purple Heart and garage sales. Once Cassandra began making good money, she had reveled in buying what she wanted when she wanted it, refusing to clip coupons or wait for sales. And she adamantly refused to learn how to repair anything. She recalled her mother's first project, in which Lenore had decided to install a shower fixture in the old bathroom adjacent to Cassandra's room. It had required three trips to the hardware store over the course of a rainy Saturday and the result had been a Rube Goldberg contraption, with multiple—well, Cassandra didn't know to this day what those pieces of hardware were called. The new fixture had extended out almost six inches and she was forever bruising herself on it. But Lenore improved.

Today, she could install a garbage disposal, put up molding, lay a new floor—using adhesive tiles, but still, she could do it. She could even handle projects requiring wiring. But she was in her seventies, her hands losing strength and dexterity. What would her mother do, who would she be, when she could no longer fix things?

'I know,' Cassandra said. 'About Daddy and Annie.'

Lenore didn't even look up from her work. 'Did he tell you, then? He has been worrying about it.'

'How—' *The phone calls.* That's why her parents had been talking to each other. Cedric hadn't been needling Lenore about Cassandra's visits with him. He had been confiding in his ex-wife, the only living person who knew his true story. 'Did you know always? From the beginning?'

'Not from the *very* beginning,' Lenore said, starting on the table's legs, sighing a little. 'I always forget how hard legs are, relative to the top. I say I'm going to do the legs first, save the easy part for last, then I forget. It's so much more rewarding, stripping a flat surface.'

Cassandra was not going to let the matter drop. 'When, then?'

'Not long after he left for good. I had my suspicions before, of course. His insistence on getting out of the house the day of your birthday party, then seeing Annie at the hospital. But she was such a different type for him, after all those bony faculty wives. I tried to tell myself he couldn't possibly love her. I'd think, *She doesn't even read the* New York Review of Books!'

Cassandra couldn't help laughing and Lenore joined in, once she realized that Cassandra's amusement was not at her expense. Her mother's objections mirrored her own long-standing confusion over her father's choices.

'Did you ever see the police report?' Part of her hoped that her mother would say, *Police report? There was no police report.* What did it matter? Her mother had all but confirmed the report was accurate.

'I had a copy at some point, thinking it might give me leverage, financially. But you can't get blood from a stone, as your father liked to say, and there simply wasn't that much money.'

'But why did you let me believe his . . . version of things? Why would you let him get away with lying to me, when—when—'

Lenore didn't need Cassandra to finish the question. It had probably been uppermost in her mind for years.

'When I could have swayed you to *my* side? Well, even when I hated your father—and I hated him for a long time, Cassandra—I didn't want you to hate him. Your father had bestowed quite a legacy of issues on you. But also—also—'

Lenore's eyes began to tear and she had no hands with which to wipe them, given the heavy rubber gloves, the fingertips coated with paint thinner. She tried to press her eye to her shoulder, a futile gesture that almost made Cassandra cry. 'You were always a daddy's girl, Cassandra. I could have made him look bad in your eyes, but that was never what I wanted. I only wanted you to think that I was interesting, too.'

'I do,' she said. 'I think you're extraordinary.'

And just because she had never said it aloud didn't mean it wasn't true. Her mother *was* extraordinary. Cassandra thought back to the opening of her first book, the story of how she had found speech. How quickly Cassandra had skimmed over her mother's role in that beloved anecdote, the unnerving choice she had made when she pointed the family car down the icy slope of Northern Parkway. What was it like to be home alone with a small child—a silent one at that— while one's husband moved in a world of ideas and clever talk? Was her mother really that different from Callie, depressed and overwhelmed, yearning for a man she could never have? Cedric had courted her and wooed her, recited Poe's 'Lenore' to her—then moved on. Long before he met Annie, he had, in essence, abandoned Cassandra's mother. Yet she had refused to use her knowledge to turn Cassandra against him.

Lenore shook her head, refusing the compliment. 'No, I was silly and embarrassing, the one you tolerated. That wouldn't have changed if I let you find out your father was lying to you. I didn't want your *relative* admiration. I wanted the real thing.'

'I never thought you silly.' She had, though. 'And I was only embarrassed when I was a teenager. Every teenager is embarrassed by her mother.'

'Perhaps *silly* isn't the right word. Boring, I guess. *My Father's Daughter.* The title alone makes it clear. It was as if you hatched from an egg, as if that elephant, you know, had brought you to life.'

Her father would have invoked Zeus and Leda, Cassandra knew, but she liked the fact that her mother chose Dr Seuss. 'Horton?'

'Yes, Horton, that was the one. As if the elephant hatched the egg while I was off

362

gallivanting.'

Lenore recovered herself, more or less, and returned to her work. Her shoulders twitched a little, as if she was still holding back some strong emotions, but she was otherwise composed.

'I came here first, the moment I learned,' Cassandra said. 'You should know, there's . . . someone threatening to make this public, but I can keep that from happening. It's your decision.'

'More your father's, I would think. Go talk to him.'

'I will. But his counsel will be steeped in self-interest. He made his choices. You didn't. What should I do, Mom?'

She realized it might well be the first time in years that she had sought her mother's advice out of something more than politeness.

'Are you asking if I'll be humiliated if that old story comes out? A little, I suppose, but nothing compared to what your father will experience. At the same time, I think he'll feel relieved. He's been dreading this thing at the Gordon School.'

'Shit.' Cassandra had quite forgotten the fund-raiser. Whatever she decided to do, she couldn't go forward with that farce. But if she canceled, she would have to offer a plausible explanation, perhaps even cover whatever money the school had already spent in preparation. Secrets are like floodwaters, she had warned Donna. But that was before she knew she had her own secret to protect.

'Why didn't Daddy say anything before the book came out?'

'It was too late. It's not like you came to us first and said what you were going to do. It was already done and sold. Of course, we didn't imagine that so many people would read it—'

'Of course.' Funny how galling that still was, being reminded that her own parents had not expected her to be successful.

'Even if we had, he never would have made you pull it back. *You* believed every word, after all. You took your father's story and made it something lovely. And it was true, in the important ways.'

'How can you say that?'

'He and Annie did love each other. He risked his life for her. Her boyfriend went after her first, and your father defended her. To him, it didn't matter if he met her in the middle of a riot or buying that stupid Washington's Birthday cake at Silber's bakery. It was love at first sight, a transforming event. He liked seeing that in print. Besides—he was proud of you, honey.'

'Proud when the book began selling, you mean.'

'No, proud that you finished a book. He couldn't get over that. In fact, that was the first time we spoke in years. He read that early copy you gave us—'

'The galleys.' She remembered that plain little book, bound in a matte blue cover, with great affection. The day she had taken her advance copy out of the Federal Express envelope, life had been all sheer possibility. In many ways, life had exceeded the dreams and hopes she had that day. So why wasn't she happier?

'Right, and he called me, probably for the first time since you left high school, and said, "Can you believe this daughter of ours?" Oh, he was downright obnoxious, going all over town about what a good writer you were.'

'Really?'

364

'Really. I was the one who said—what about the, um, fact that it's not exactly true? And he said, "She wrote it so beautifully that she made it true."'

Too little, too late. 'That's the advantage of being duped,' Cassandra said. 'One is nothing if not sincere.'

Indifferent to the dust and dirt, Cassandra slumped on an old kitchen stool, a relic from her mother's Swedish phase, possibly the very stool on which Callie had sat forty years ago. It was quiet on Hillhouse Road on a Sunday afternoon, quiet enough to hear her mother's steel wool moving up and down the table leg, the wind in the trees, the thrum of traffic on Forest Park Avenue below. She looked at the table. The grain was mottled, cheap pine most likely. Her mother would end up painting it. Her trash-picked find would cost her dozens of hours, and in the end, she would have a table that she could have purchased for fifty or sixty dollars at any midprice furniture store. But she worked with what she had. Everyone did.

'What are you going to do, Cassandra?'

'I'm not sure, Mom. There are financial implications, legal implications. At the very least, I owe a book, and if I don't deliver it, or something in its place, I have to return a rather large amount of money.'

'Do you have it?'

'Maybe. My financial situation is complicated by the fact that I have memoirs out there posing as nonfiction, when the very spine of the story is false. If they recall it, pulp it—well, I'll lose a big chunk of income that I thought I could count on for years.'

Her mother looked stricken at this. Scandal she could weather, but financial problems still unnerved her.

'It will be okay,' Cassandra assured her. 'Somehow. I could sidestep the whole problem by writing a book about you. *My Mother's Daughter.* I'll set the record straight and make you the hero.'

She was joking. At least, she was pretty sure she was joking.

'No thank *you,*' Lenore said. 'Besides, you'll be fifty next week, Cassandra. Whatever you are, whatever you write, you're your own person by now. Or should be.'

HAPPY WANDERERS

September 5–6

Chapter Thirty-Five

No one had ever seen a party like the 'graduation' celebration that the Howards threw for our passage from elementary school to junior high. It was a melancholy night for me, filled with reminders that I would be going to a different school from the others. The color theme, for example, was maroon and gold, the colors for William Lemmel Junior High, and the elaborate cake held the legend HERE WE COME, SCHOOL #79. *I didn't even know the colors for Rock Glen, although I had already attended an orientation where we were taught the school song, to the tune of 'The Happy Wanderer'.*

> *We stand to sing our song today*
> *Its words will be our rule*
> *To grow and learn*
> *To work and play*
> *Our name is Rock Glen School*

'Dag, Cassandra,' Fatima said when I sang it for her. 'You sure do sing loud.'

I also had been given a copy of the school's dress code, a mysterious document that seemed more concerned with potential weapons than propriety. The banned items included clogs (then bulbous, wooden affairs from Sweden), picks with metal teeth, and belts worn unbuckled. The latter was presumably forbidden because an unbuckled belt could be whipped out and used to administer a beating. I wish I could say that the list was an alarmist, reactionary document, but it proved eminently sensible. Rock

369

Glen was a tough school, although those of us in the 'enriched' track usually moved in a rarefied bubble, at a safe remove from the rougher element. The year after I left, there was an actual riot. Lemmel was tougher still, yet this was not mentioned, not at the graduation party.

The Howards' house was a marvel, modern for the time, built in such a way that the front revealed little about its true scale and tasteful luxury. No, the Howards' material wealth was evident only from the back, where the house had been positioned to take full advantage of the lot, on a wooded hill high above the Gwynns Falls. The rear of the house was almost entirely glass, the better to take in that view. Earlier that year, a girl had run down that hill, building up so much momentum that she had plunged into the stream, swollen by recent rains, and ended up drowning. Donna said her family wasn't home at the time, or her father surely would have run down the hill and saved the girl. There was a pool with a flagstone terrace. There was a pool at my house, too, but we couldn't afford to fill it even before my father left, much less repair the cracks and return it to functionality. We danced around the Howards' pool, but no one went swimming, not that night.

The party was winding down when Tisha's little brother burst in, probably sent to summon Tisha for her ride home. Reginald Barr was known as Candy, the kind of nickname that Tisha never would have allowed anyone to bestow on her. Another child, one with a lesser personality, might have been ruined by such a nickname, but Candy embraced it, developing a signature dance that he performed whenever possible, singing an Astors song by the same name. 'Gee whiz,' he sang, spinning in circles as Tisha

370

rolled her eyes, disturbed that her baby brother had crashed the party. But he was singing to Donna, our hostess. I don't remember the lyrics exactly; it was a typical love song, full of sweet lips and blue eyes. But when he got to the part where he declared that the girl would one day marry him, Candy Barr dropped to one knee on that flagstone terrace and held out his hands to Donna, who had covered her face to smother her laughter, soft as it was. Candy didn't mind that Donna was laughing at him, as long as she was laughing. Donna's laugh was a rare thing; we all competed for it.

*　　　*　　　*

'The thing is, he wasn't there,' said Tisha, who had marked the spot with a Post-it in a copy of the hardcover edition of *My Father's Daughter,* now a collector's item twice over—a first edition of a bestseller that had been extensively revised. 'Not at the graduation party. That happened at my birthday party, a month earlier.'

'Well, thanks for setting the record straight on that crucial matter,' Cassandra said. 'Unfortunately, I've already sent in the new epilogue and the book is in copyediting.'

They were in the same suburban restaurant where they had lunched six months earlier, but it was Tisha who had suggested this meeting. She also had chosen a later time, happy hour—'But on the late side, after the teachers clear out'—and was indulging in a glass of wine. Still, Cassandra couldn't help being wary. Tisha was Reg's sister, Donna's oldest friend. She had to have an agenda.

'I'm not showing it to you to prove what you got

371

wrong,' Tisha said. 'It's about what you got *right*. Can't you see? Even then, Reg was crazy for Donna. He wasn't just fooling when he did that dance. He'd do anything for her.'

'I'm well aware of that.'

'He loves her, Cassandra. He loves her more than she'll ever love him, and that's tragic. You may not have understood what you saw, yet you captured the way he put her on a pedestal.'

'Hmmmm.' Tisha's overture, while well intentioned, was cold comfort. What was the point of glimpsing the little things in hindsight? It didn't change the fact that she had been wrong about so many big things.

The more disturbing development was how little anyone cared about setting the record straight. With her father's blessing—as Lenore predicted, he was relieved to let go of his secret—Cassandra had gone to her original editor, Belle, and explained that the heart of *My Father's Daughter* was essentially false. Cassandra had expected the existing copies to be recalled and pulped, but Belle had proposed a new edition with a lengthy epilogue, which would allow Cassandra to clarify the record but also reflect on how she had changed since the book was written.

'It's still a beautiful little book, and so heartfelt,' Belle had said. 'I think it would be more valuable to let it stand on its own, then give readers the context to understand all this new information. After all, that's how you experienced the story, so it's not ersatz or false. This was true when you wrote it. Now it's a different kind of true.'

And as Cassandra worked—interviewing her mother and father, but also steeping herself in the

372

historical record of the time in order to provide a more accurate overview of the riots—she realized that the bulk of her story was unchanged. What were those hurtful words that others had thrown at her? *Martin Luther King was assassinated and ruined my birthday party, boo-hoo-hoo.* Stripped of its fake portent, its never-was link to a seminal event, *My Father's Daughter* turned out to be a genuinely sad story, one about a girl who needed the mythology of a huge historic moment to rationalize a parent's pedestrian betrayal.

The epilogue did not reveal how she had learned the truth; she wrote only that someone had furnished her a copy of the police report. And while her old publicist—another happy reunion—had stoked the media with a few tantalizing details, she had shrewdly kept back the biggest revelation. The orders for the new book promised to be robust and Belle had even floated the idea of an updated version of *The Eternal Wife.* Cassandra was far from the financial ruin she had envisioned when she sold her place in Brooklyn and used part of the equity to make a sizable donation to the Gordon School. She had thought her profits on New York real estate would mean she could buy a waterfront penthouse in Baltimore, especially in this soft market, but between the donation and her decision to return the advance on what was to have been the Callie book, she had just enough to buy a condominium with a view of another condominium.

But she hadn't moved back to Baltimore because it was cheaper. She wanted to be close to her parents, especially her mother, who would eventually have to give up the house on Hillhouse

Road, probably sooner than she thought. A few weeks ago, Cassandra had stopped by unannounced and discovered her mother weeping in the middle of the afternoon. Lenore confessed that she had trouble mustering the necessary strength to open the elbow joint on her powder room sink. Cassandra had taken the wrench in hand and, with much coaching, done it for her.

'You like being back?' Tisha asked now.

'I miss New York. But the fact is, I live within walking distance of several good restaurants, a drugstore, a gym, and a Whole Foods, and that pretty much covers my needs. Plus, I can be at either parent's home within thirty minutes. How are your folks?'

'Still in the same house, still healthy enough to live on their own.' Tisha rapped the bar with her knuckles, although it wasn't actually wood. 'We'll see how long that lasts. I'm grateful that Reg has the money to help them out, when that day comes. I'm not ashamed to say that. I've got two college tuitions.'

'You know, I thought about living in Bolton Hill. It reminded me of my neighborhood back in Brooklyn. But . . .'

'But you were worried about running into Reg and Donna.'

'Maybe. I don't know. It's strange, how little fallout there was. Don't you think?'

Tisha shrugged. 'It was a long time ago, Cassandra. What did you expect to happen?'

'I don't know. *Something.*'

When it came to Callie Jenkins, it turned out that Donna was the one with the true gift of prophecy. Callie had—with Cassandra's advice and money—found a criminal attorney. The lawyer had set up an appointment with the state's attorney, where Callie recounted everything she had told Cassandra. The state's attorney thanked Callie for her 'confession' and said it had been determined that it was counterproductive to prosecute her for her child's death. She had spent seven years in jail, after all. Sudden infant death syndrome was not implausible and with no body to autopsy, a jury would be put in the position of deciding how credible Callie was. City juries were notoriously lenient; it would take only one skeptical citizen to deadlock the process.

In short: The state's attorney didn't believe a word of it but didn't want to waste resources on a trial.

And what of Andre Howard, the money passed through his brother's campaign? That information would be forwarded to federal authorities, Cassandra was told, but Julius Howard would bear the brunt of the investigation. Cassandra had pointed out to Callie that she could go to the newspapers, which would be happy for the information about the Howards. Or Callie could write her own book. Cassandra offered to set her up with a literary agent, ghostwrite the book if need be, for no fee.

Callie wanted none of it. 'I'm not much for telling,' she said. And that was that. Even with her income cut off, she didn't want to leverage her power over the Howards. Her only concern was for her mother, but Myra Tippet's nursing home accepted Medicaid, and given Myra's complete lack of assets, it was no problem to get her qualified. Once the issue of her mother's care was established, Callie was content. She would find a job, she told Cassandra. She didn't need much. The house and car were paid for. The people at the school where she volunteered thought they could find her work.

'But if you sold a book,' Cassandra had said, 'you might not have to worry about money at all. You could go to culinary school—tuitions there are as high as any private college—really do something with your baking. You could—'

Callie had cut her off. 'I'm not much for telling,' she repeated. At the time, it had felt like a reproach. But Callie Jenkins, Cassandra had come to realize, would never prescribe how anyone should live. *You have your way, I have mine,* she was telling Cassandra. Neither way is right, neither way is wrong. There was mild consolation in the fact that the Howards had to live with the possibility that Callie might change her mind, but it was mild indeed. Besides, Andre Howard knew better than anyone how skilled Callie was at keeping quiet. Perhaps he had chosen her, all those years ago, for that quality. But perhaps he really had loved her. Both things could be true.

And now that *My Father's Daughter* was done, Cassandra wasn't sure if she had anything more to tell. Maybe she would try fiction again. Why not? She had been writing fiction all along.

'Are you working on anything?' Tisha asked. Could she follow Cassandra's thoughts? But she was probably just being polite.

'I'm going to take a year off, teach in the Hopkins writing sems, clear my head, make a community for myself. I don't really know anyone in Baltimore except my parents. It would be nice if we could see each other sometimes, keep in touch.'

'That would be ... complicated,' Tisha said. 'Donna wouldn't like it, and Reg doesn't like anything that Donna doesn't like.'

'Do they have to know?'

'They'd end up knowing. Baltimore is small that way.'

Cassandra smiled. 'You make it sound almost as if it would be an affair. But I'm discreet. I have experience in those things.'

Tisha covered her ears. 'I really don't want to think about that, okay?' But she was smiling, too.

Cassandra looked at her old book, the page marked by a magenta Post-it. Tisha had bought this new, many years ago. Tisha had remembered her, despite what she said. 'I probably should have asked you about what I got wrong, from your perspective, in my memoir. And it's true, I've sent the revisions in and I can't make wholesale changes. But I will have opportunities to make small fixes. So if there's something that really bothers you—'

'I don't care about the party,' Tisha said. 'It's not that important.'

'But what about the fight?'

'The fight?'

'That day in ninth grade, when that girl, Martha, attacked me on the softball field. You and Donna and Fatima just watched. I mean, you were standing off in the distance, but you didn't do ... anything. I had the impression that anecdote bothered you most of all.'

Tisha caught the bartender's eyes, signaled that she wanted another glass of wine, ordered one for

Cassandra, too.

'Well?' Cassandra pressed.

'Okay, since you asked. First of all—did you ever know Donna to get into a fight with *anyone*?'

'Not with her fists,' Cassandra admitted. 'But then, neither did I, in part because you and Fatima had my back in elementary school. You did know it was me on the ground, didn't you?'

'Yeah, I knew it was you. Even in your gym suit. And it was three on one, which was pretty cowardly. But you know what else we saw, from where we stood?'

Cassandra shook her head.

'Four white girls. If we had run over there, the teachers who came to break up the fight would have assumed that it was the black girls against the white ones and we started it. Cassandra, those three cracker girls could have been beating the shit out of a nun and I wouldn't have gone over there. That's just how it was.'

'But we were friends.'

'We were,' Tisha agreed. 'When we were younger. We grew apart when we went to different junior high schools. It was that simple. And then, when you never came back to Western after freshman year—well, until I read your book, I didn't know what had happened.'

'Really?' This had never occurred to Cassandra, that there was any mystery to her side of the story. But then, she had the advantage of her own perspective. For thirty-five years, she and Tisha had been separated by nothing more than fifty yards or so. Standing on the same softball field, on the same day, seeing the same thing, yet not. Okay, they grew apart. But couldn't they grow back

378

together?

'Are you sure,' she said, 'that we can't see each other from time to time? Or at least talk on the phone? I like talking to you. You know me, Tisha, in a way new people in my life never will. And you're honest in a way that almost no one is.'

The restaurant around them was busy and hectic, but Cassandra didn't register any of the sounds. She was looking at Tisha, watching her think, her eyebrows drawn down tightly, her lips compressed.

'Oh, hell,' Tisha said at last, tipping her glass toward her for a toast. 'We can get together like this, from time to time. It's not like Reg and Donna would be caught dead in the suburbs.'

Chapter Thirty-Six

Callie drove across the bridge—in broad daylight, on a Saturday afternoon, well after the weekend traffic had thinned. Now that she was free to go where she wanted, no longer bound by restrictions, said or unsaid, she had discovered she felt no urgency to return to Baltimore.

But, although she wasn't much for telling, she did have some things to say, one thing to say. Might as well say it now and be done with it. With gas almost four dollars a gallon, she sure wasn't going to waste a trip. She had a job now, down at the school, sort of an all-around helper position for not much more than minimum wage and no benefits. Money was tight, even with her house and car covered. But the people at the school were the kind of folks who would step in and help a person out if she ran into big trouble, sickness or catastrophe. They had turned out to be the kind of Christians who were pretty forgiving after all. She would make it work somehow.

The house on Clifton Road looked different and she wondered if she was mistaken. Then she realized that she had never visited here during such bright daylight hours, that she had sneaked her peeks at dawn or sunset. Even the graduation party had begun late in the afternoon, the light already fading. The house didn't look quite as put-together in this hot September light. She realized it was probably about the same age as her, more or less.

She parked her car directly in front—'Bold as you please,' as her mother might have said—and walked up the sidewalk and rang the doorbell as if she had a right. A woman answered, Mrs Howard. She took one look at Callie and called out, 'Andre, it's for you.'

'What do you want?' he asked Callie.

You, she almost said.

Looking into his face, closer to him than she had been for twenty years, she saw the man she remembered, not the old man that he was now. It was almost as if he had kept those promises and they had had a life together after all, and they had grown old together, so she didn't notice how he had changed. She did not see an old man. She saw the man she loved.

Him, he probably saw a middle-aged lady where a sweet young woman once stood.

'I wanted you to know that I signed up for that registry. So if our son signs up, too—'

'We have no son,' he said. 'I don't care what lies

you put on a birth certificate.'

'So if our son,' she repeated, firm yet respectful, 'should sign up, I will meet with him and tell him why he was put up for adoption. If he wants an explanation, he's entitled to it.'

'That poor boy was entitled to a life. Would that you had done the same for your other son.'

That hurt, but she wouldn't give him the satisfaction of knowing he still had the power to wound her. She pitied him in a way. She had been his heart's desire and he had denied himself because the price, by his estimation, was too high. He would have been happy with her, whether he admitted it or not. And whatever she was, she was not unhappy. Not happy, exactly, but not unhappy. She at least had the consolation of knowing she had given herself wholly to a cause, to her love for him. If the cause had turned out to be less than worthy—well, so be it, that didn't tarnish her commitment to it.

'I forgive you,' she said. 'I can't promise he'll do the same, but I'll try to help him. If I ever meet him.'

'Forgive me for what?'

She patted his cheek, a gesture more like a daughter's than a lover's. 'It's okay that you weren't strong. I was. I was strong for you.'

For all the words she had practiced, all the things she had imagined saying, these were not among them. Yet she realized she was right. She was strong, he wasn't. It had been weak of him to pursue her, weaker still for him to try to erase the evidence that she had been in his life. She had heard that men often felt humble watching what women went through in childbirth. What had

Andre felt, as she sat in jail, knowing it was all for the love of him, that she could bear what she had borne all for the promise of his love.

'Stay away from us,' he said. 'I'll get a restraining order if need be. And don't even think about spreading those lies. There are laws against slander, against libel—'

'It's okay,' she assured him. 'I'm done.' She was. You had to forgive in order to be forgiven. If she ever did meet her son—their son—she hoped he would grant her the same generosity. Callie had forgiven not only Andre but her mother. Her mother meant well. She wasn't responsible for that restless, rootless anger, for her fear. Cassandra had tried to argue with Callie, said she shouldn't make excuses for what Cassandra called abuse. She wasn't. Accepting people for who they were was the furthest thing from making excuses.

She drove east, the sun still high, paying the toll to cross the bridge that she might never cross again. Unless her son, now almost thirty, did in fact find her. Cassandra had said, 'Let's stay in touch,' and seemed sincere, but when had they ever been in touch, what was there to 'stay'? She was grateful that Cassandra had found her—freed her, really—but Cassandra simply talked too much for Callie. Even Callie's mother, chattering away in the nursing home, didn't put so many words in the world. Cassandra would probably start nagging her about a book again. Callie had no use for that.

Besides, how could she tell her story when she wasn't sure that she trusted it? On bad days, she wondered—had she shook Donntay? Maybe fed him something she shouldn't have? Put him down wrong and smothered him? She didn't think any of

382

those things were true, but these ideas came to her on her bad days, taunted her, messed with her head. If there had been a new trial, if they had put her on the stand, she would have had to admit she couldn't really remember what happened, only that she believed what she believed, what she needed to believe: She woke up one morning and her son was dead. Once she told that much, she would have to tell the next part, how her only thought was, *Now I can call Andre.* That was the one thing she couldn't forget, the memory she never questioned. She had looked at her little boy's body, so still and stiff, and her heart had jumped with the thrill of knowing that she had an excuse to call Andre. He always took her calls in times of trouble, and she got in the habit of cultivating trouble. Bad men, bad decisions. That wasn't natural, and it wouldn't sit well with others, but it was true. It was the one thing she knew about that morning with absolute certainty. The split second after she registered the fact that her son was dead, she had thought, *Now I can call Andre.* Back then, any thought could lead to him, any moment. A bird is singing. *Andre.* The toast is burning. *Andre.* I have a paper cut. *Andre.* The baby is crying. *Andre, Andre, Andre.*

She took the long way, going around town on the bypass to the Food Lion to buy butter. Peaches were still in season and she had a cobbler recipe she wanted to try, but Mr Bittman was quite firm in his opinion that piecrusts should be all butter, no lard or shortening. She admired such firm opinions, the certainty that other people brought to things in their lives. She just was never going to be one of them. She doubled back to Bridgeville,

coming up Main Street. IF YOU LIVED HERE, the
sign promised, YOU'D BE HOME BY NOW.
   She was.

Author's Note

As is often the case in my novels, there is a real-life Baltimore crime that forms the spine of this novel. Jackie Bouknight had a son, Maurice, who disappeared while she was being monitored (not very well) by the Baltimore City Department of Social Services. Asked to produce him, she refused and spent more than seven years in jail on a charge of contempt. To this day, it has never been learned what happened to Maurice Bouknight. And that is all I know of the original case, although a friend had a glancing courthouse encounter with Jackie Bouknight that got me thinking about her. This is wholly a work of fiction, about made-up people who happen to inhabit real places.

The Enoch Pratt Central Library's collection of newspapers on microfiche helped jog my memory about the decades in which I actually grew up. The University of Baltimore's amazing online archive about the '68 riots was essential. And the regulars at the Memory Project proved to be good sleuths, tracking down primary sources that established how Martin Luther King Jr.'s assassination was announced on national television.

I've played with Baltimore's architecture, a novelist's prerogative. There were not five houses on Hillhouse Road in the 1960s and '70s; the Fallows's house is an invention, although I gave it the never-filled swimming pool of a house I remember there. I played similar tricks with Teena Murphy's home, the Howards' house, and Bridgeville, Delaware. However, there is a lovely wine bar on Route 108 in Columbia, the Iron Bridge, and I am told by reliable sources that teachers do like to go there. As do I.

Thanks to the individuals who rally round every year for this insanity: Carrie Feron, Vicky Bijur, Joan Jacobson, David Simon. This year, Lizzie Skurnick and Lisa Respers also pitched in.

This book is dedicated to the memory of a man who once burned a manuscript on impulse. I always thought that story was apocryphal, but he confirmed it for me a few years ago. And I have to admit, I understand the impulse now in a way I didn't at the time. Still, I wish he hadn't burned it. Asked about the incident, he said, 'Who wants to read another fucking tender moment about a white-trash redneck kid discovering Joyce? Or, better yet, Raymond Chandler.' If you had written it, Jim, I would have wanted to read it.

Laura Lippman
November 2008